Dear Reader,

Welcome to the seventh title in the series of *Great Lakes Romances®*, historical fiction full of love and adventure set in bygone days on North America's vast inland waters.

Like the other books in this series, *Rosalie of Grand Traverse Bay* relays the excitement and thrills of a tale skillfully told, but contains no explicit sex, offensive language, or gratuitous violence.

We invite you to tell us what you would like most to read about in *Great Lakes Romances®*. For your convenience, we have included a survey form at the back of the book. Please fill it out and send it to us.

At the back, you will also find descriptions of other romances in this series, and a biography in the *Bigwater Classics*tm series, stories that will sweep you away to an era of gentility and enchantment, and places of unparalleled beauty and wonder!

Thank you for being a part of *Great Lakes Romances®*.

Sincerely,
The Publishers

P.S. Author Donna Winters loves to hear from her readers. You can write her at P.O. Box 177, Caledonia, MI 49316.

To Kerri,

Rosalie
of
Grand Traverse Bay

Of north & south!

Donna Winters

Donna Winters

Great Lakes Romances®

Bigwater Publishing
Caledonia, Michigan

ACKNOWLEDGEMENTS

I would like to thank the following for their contributions to this fictional endeavor:

First and foremost, my Lord and Savior, Jesus Christ, the source of my inspiration. He answers my prayers and makes all things possible!

And on the human level:

JoAnn Grote, who supplied historical facts and descriptions of North Carolina settings

Roselyn Smith, who proposed a two-sentence story idea for the premise of this book

Jacqueline Clay, who persevered despite numerous setbacks to complete the cover art

Shirley and Jeannie Soest, who spent several hours sharing their knowledge of horses

Lola Sage, who took me on a long and lovely ride in her horse-drawn wagon

Shirley and Bob Slocum, who treated me to a Sunday afternoon sleigh ride on a crisp January day in 1995

Rachel Balke, who read my manuscript with unbridled enthusiasm

And Sue Englund, who provided new graphics and friendship in equal measure

To JoAnn
who sent me North Carolina by mail

and to Roselyn
who suggested the story in the first place

CHAPTER

1

Traverse City, Michigan
July 2, 1900

The odor of coal smoke tinged the air as eighteen-year-old Rosalie Foxe slipped into a window seat aboard the half-full Grand Rapids and Indiana train bound for Detroit. She ignored the stares at her crippled right shoulder and arm as she used her left hand to set her valise on the empty seat beside her and take out the little volume of poems by John Henry Boner of her native North Carolina. Laying aside the embroidered bookmark, she started to read.

But she couldn't concentrate. The nightmarish accusation leveled against her earlier that morning repeated again and again in her mind. Desperate to block it out, she closed her eyes and envisioned herself in her daddy's carriage entering the long driveway at Tanglewood, the beloved home she'd left a month ago.

The old, familiar oaks, poplars, and magnolias stretched their boughs in welcome, shading her from the blistering heat of summer in the Piedmont. Passing stables and horse pastures, she wondered whether Vanda Mae, her horse-crazy sixteen-year-old sister, was out riding in the woods. She wondered, too, whether her sister's cherished mare, Tassie, had produced the foal that had enticed her to remain in the oppressive heat rather than seeking the cooler realm of the mountain resort at Blowing Rock as their mother had.

Rosalie's daydream continued, carrying her past barns and servants' quarters to the circle in front of an eighteen-room manor house that stood on a rise like a rectangular brick fortress guarding the meadow below. How relieved she was to hurry inside and up the sweeping staircase to the spacious bedroom that had always granted her shelter from the cruelties of the world.

The thud of a passenger car window dropping shut jolted her back to reality. She was not in North Carolina, but in northern Michigan on a sojourn that had been a graduation gift from a cherished aunt and uncle she had seldom seen in her growing-up years. Again, the contempt-ible words that had cast slurs on her trustworthiness and sent her packing for Tanglewood echoed in her mind. She bowed her head in a silent, urgent prayer. *Lord, right now I'm feeling like the small end of nothing whittled down to a fine point. Please carry me back to Tanglewood just as quickly as—*

Her petition was interrupted by Kenton McCune, the thirty-one-year-old attorney friend of her Aunt Lottie and Uncle Benjamin. He put her valise on the floor and sat on the aisle seat beside her, his neatly trimmed mustache and goatee accentuating the grim line of his mouth.

"Miss Foxe, I am disappointed in you. I didn't think you'd leave Traverse City at a time like this."

His clipped speech contrasted so sharply with the easygoing drawl of North Carolinians that it still grated on her ears despite the fact that she'd spoken with him a dozen times or more. Her gaze moved from his meticulously creased pants to his pin tucked white shirt to his hazel-come-grey eyes. She spoke unhurriedly.

"You think I stole the mortgage money from Uncle Benjamin and Aunt Lottie, don't you now?"

Kenton leaned close catching the essence of her peach blossom toilet water. "*Did* you?"

The question and his nearness augmented her discomfort. "You'd have to be crazy as a betsy bug to think I'd do that. I made the payment on the candy store Friday morning, just like they asked me to."

"You're sure?"

Rosalie glared at him, then raised her book between them in an effort to ignore his question, the scent of his sandalwood soap that reminded her so much of her daddy, and the peculiar effect this Michigander was having on her nerves.

Kenton lowered the book with one finger—the nail-less one he'd smashed in a baseball game awhile back. But he'd hit a home run in that game and in her mind she could still see him dashing around the bases.

He continued. "Running away makes you look guilty. Tell me again you didn't take the money."

Rosalie sighed heavily. "I did *not* take it, Mr. McCune. Now, are you satisfied?"

"No. Not until you get off this train. You're the only

person who can help me keep Gowen from foreclosing on Ben and Lottie." He paused, his expression more solemn. "Besides, your aunt and uncle will be deeply hurt to think you've abandoned them."

Rosalie snapped her book shut forgetting to replace the bookmark still on her lap. "You may be a smooth-talking Yankee lawyer from Harvard, Mr. McCune, but that butters no cornbread with me at-all. I mean, do you really think you can convince me to stay?"

Kenton picked up the bookmark and read it aloud. "'Do unto others as you would have others do unto you.' Did you make this?" He jiggled it in front of her. "Or did you steal it?"

Rosalie snatched it from him. "Of course I made it! I try to live by its motto, too."

"Then live by it now! See this thing through. You can't run from your troubles, Miss Foxe."

She looked away.

He drew a deep breath. "The city is about to fill up with guests for the Independence Day celebration. Ben and Lottie need your help at the store now, more than ever. Besides, you promised to attend the Carnival Ball with me tomorrow night."

Placing the bookmark inside the front cover, Rosalie focused on him. "My mind is made up. I'm going home to Vanda Mae and Daddy. I miss them something fierce. I miss Shani's grits and red-eye gravy. *Most* of all, I miss Willy Jo Winthrop." She named her neighbor and best friend, the twenty-two-year-old next door.

"But—"

"I know you only invited me to the ball to please Aunt Lottie. I never wanted to go in the first place. The sooner I

4

get away from here, the better." The instant the words came out, she regretted speaking falsely—about her desire to go to the ball at least. Only a distinguished few had been invited and she had counted it a privilege not to be relegated to the gallery like the rest of the public.

Kenton glared at her. She was fidgeting with the satin bow at her neck, the one with the crimped tails she always wore. It was unlike any he'd seen before he'd met Rosalie—unique, like the young woman who wore it. For an instant he wanted to grab hold of that ribbon and lead her off the train, but he put his frustration into words instead.

"Go home to Tanglewood, then. I'll give Ben and Lottie your good byes." He made his way toward the exit at the back of the car.

Rosalie turned to watch him go, her stomach churning. Deep inside, she knew he was right. She couldn't outrun trouble.

He disappeared from view just as the conductor shouted, "Last call! All aboard!"

As the train rumbled out of the station, Kenton paused beside his carriage and talked to his grey gelding like he always did when trying to sort out his options. "She's gone, Judge. What do you make of that?"

The animal snorted and bobbed his head.

"All right, so you're glad. I know she hurt your feelings, the way she carried on about your color when she first came to town." He took hold of the horse's bridle and patted his nose. "Trouble is, I don't know what I'm going to tell Ben and Lottie."

He was about to climb into his carriage when he spotted Rosalie a few feet away looking as forlorn as faded forget-me-nots. He wanted to scold her for the worry she'd caused but thought better of it.

Reluctantly, she approached him. "You can tell Aunt Lottie and Uncle Benjamin that your only witness has postponed her return to North Carolina and is walking home from the station."

She seemed so vulnerable standing beside his rig, her valise hanging from her left hand, her right arm clutched tight against her side. He took her bag. "I'll drive you home. You can tell them yourself."

Her brown eyes flashed. ".You know very well I'll never ride behind that grey gelding of yours—or anyone else's!"

He sighed. "I thought maybe this time would be different."

"I changed my mind about leaving, but I haven't changed my mind about grey horses."

He set her bag in the carriage. "I'd think you could trust Judge by now. You've known him long enough."

"A lifetime wouldn't be enough. I'm still paying for the last time I trusted a grey horse—a gelding like Judge—six years ago." She rubbed her right shoulder remembering the day she'd fallen from Hurricane never to ride a horse of *any* color again, and never to ride in a vehicle drawn by a grey one.

"You can't tell a horse by its color, Miss Foxe." He paused, struggling to suppress his frustration. "I'm sorry you fell off your gelding, but there's no logic in avoiding grey horses for the rest of your life."

She laughed. "I know that, Mr. McCune. I never claimed to be logical. I allow my emotions to be my guide, and right now they're telling me to take a nice, leisurely walk beside this fresh water bay you Michigan Yanks are so fond of while I think about the fine mess I'm in."

As Kenton McCune drove toward Ben and Lottie Marshall's candy shop, he took mental account of his day. Despite continuing sunshine, it now seemed clouded with trouble over a certain North Carolina miss, and the problems of his dear friends. Foul weather had moved in with the phone call he'd received from the middle-aged bachelor brother and spinster sister less than an hour earlier telling him about Cutler Gowen's visit, his threat to foreclose at the end of the month, and the discovery that as a result, Rosalie had departed for home with one small bag, leaving a note to forward her trunks. Ben, with no rig of his own and the knowledge that Rosalie planned to leave on the eleven fifteen train, had placed the urgent call and asked Kenton to intervene.

Aside from preventing the young miss's escape, Kenton was deeply troubled over Gowen's eagerness to evict the Marshalls from their property. The entrepreneur had arrived in town months ago, taken over the mortgage on the Marshalls' Front Street shop from its previous owner—as a favor to the Newtons who needed cash, so he said—then proceeded to purchase a parcel a few blocks west of it and erect his American Candy Company factory. Although the Marshalls made the bulk of their profits on fudge, avoiding direct competition with the hard candies that Gowen produced and sold wholesale, his threat to close them down now seemed to suggest ulterior motives from the very start.

Coming to a halt in front of the Marshalls' confectionery, Kenton picked up Rosalie's valise and headed inside. The warm day seemed even hotter in the store where Lot-

7

tie, whose round form stretched the limits of her white dress and apron, stood behind the glass case weighing roasted nuts for a customer. Ben was cooling a batch of vanilla fudge—Kenton's favorite—on the marble table in the center of the store, perspiration trickling down his plump cheeks to dampen his white collarless shirt. Both paused in their duties the moment they saw him.

Lottie was the first to speak, fussing with the neck strap of her apron as she focused a worried look on the bag he carried. "Is that valise all you found of Rosalie?"

Ben spoke before Kenton could answer. "She's gone back to Tanglewood. I knew it." He tossed down his spatula, embedding it in the mound of fudge.

Kenton shook his head. "She's still in Traverse City. I tried to drive her home, but you know how she is about Judge."

Finished with her customer, Lottie turned to Kenton. "Right skittish. I'd forgotten about that when Ben rang you up."

Ben peeled off his wire glasses and mopped the sweat from his forehead and nose. "I suppose she insisted on walking home."

Kenton nodded. "I'll set her bag in the back."

Ben put on his glasses and stuffed his handkerchief into the pocket of his baggy white pants. "While you're here, you might want to take a look at that notice from Mr. Gowen. It's on the back table."

Kenton had set the bag beneath the table in the back room and was reading through the eviction notice when Ben joined him.

Closing the door to the shop, the confectioner spoke in confident tones. "I'm sure Rosalie made the payment like I asked her to."

"You're absolutely certain?"

"I had a long talk with her after Cutler Gowen came by." He tapped the eviction notice. "She remembered some things about her trip to his office that I think you'll find very intriguing." With a sudden change of topic, Ben asked, "Did I tell you Erik and Bridget Olson were here from Omena last week to pick up a load of fudge for The Clovers?"

Kenton shook his head, unwilling to discuss mutual friends just now. "Ben, about your niece."

He scowled. "Patience, Kenton. This is all part of the same recipe." A smile began to emerge. "The Olsons inquired about you and said to give you their regards. If they aren't the happiest-looking newlywed pair I ever did see . . . " The smile faded and once again, Ben seemed all business. "The payment they gave me for the fudge will be of particular interest to you."

When Ben had finished sharing his information about the Olson money and other details Rosalie had described about her trip to Cutler Gowen's office, Kenton asked to see the mortgage agreement. Within minutes he had verified the requirement for only thirty days' notice of eviction upon failure to make a payment, and the complete lack of a grace period within which to bring the loan up to date.

Deciding on a course of action, Kenton told Ben, "I can see this won't wait until your niece is done with her walk. I'm going to find her."

"With that grey gelding of yours?"

Kenton shrugged, heading out the door with the knowledge that Miss Foxe's fear of his horse was a minor inconvenience compared with the trouble over the Marshalls' mortgage.

Driving immediately to the Germaine Brothers livery, Kenton parked his own rig and rented a buggy hitched to a chestnut mare, then spent his lunch hour in search of Rosalie. He found her not near the bay, but in Hannah Park on Sixth Street across from Mr. Hannah's Queen Ann mansion. She was sitting on a bench feeding the ducks near the Boardman River. Kenton sat down beside her.

"I've just had a talk with your uncle. I understand you paid his mortgage with a twenty-dollar gold piece."

She didn't answer right away, but continued tossing scraps of stale bread to the ducks, speaking to them by name. Her attention still on the hungry fowl, she said, "That double eagle had a nick in it."

"On the edge near the word 'God.' Your uncle mentioned that."

She tossed out the last of her bread and turned to Kenton. "'In God We Trust.' Seems ironic, putting it on gold and silver coins. I mean, if we really trust in God, why do we rely so much on money?"

"Would you recognize it again if you saw it?"

"Do you believe in God, Mr. McCune?"

"That's not the question right now. The question is—"

"Of course I'd recognize it if I saw it. I've hardly thought of anything else since Mr. Gowen marched into the candy shop this morning."

"Then we must go to Mr. Gowen's factory right now and straighten this thing out." Kenton started to get up, but Rosalie's next words stopped him.

"It won't do us a lick of good. That Hackbardt woman who works as Mr. Gowen's secretary stole that coin and has no intention of letting anyone catch her."

Kenton considered the accusation, and the fact that he'd recommended Clarissa Hackbardt as secretary to Cutler Gowen last month, despite knowing she'd caused problems for the Olsons before their marriage. The young Wisconsin woman had convinced him that her days as a schemer and conniver were all in the past, and that she would make an excellent assistant to the entrepreneur. Kenton couldn't assume Clarissa's guilt with no evidence, especially since, to his knowledge, she had no past history of mishandling money.

"Do *you* believe in God, Miss Foxe?"

The firm set to Rosalie's chin softened. "Of course I believe in God, but I doubt very much that will have any effect at all on circumstances involving the likes of Miss Hackbardt."

"'Judge not, lest ye be judged,' Miss Foxe. Let's pay a call on Miss Hackbardt and allow her to answer for herself."

On the ride to Cutler Gowen's factory, Rosalie answered Kenton's questions about her previous visit there to make the mortgage payment, reiterating the details she had shared with her Uncle Benjamin earlier, such as the fact that Cutler Gowen's secretary had marked the payment down in a ledger book, and that she had offered no receipt. When they arrived at their destination, she preceded Kenton through the door.

The Hackbardt woman was sitting behind her large oak desk at the rear of the small reception area, her hair coiffed perfectly in a Gibson Girl pouf, her white blouse spotless and without a wrinkle. She looked just as she had when Rosalie had brought the mortgage payment, and like before, the heavy scent of rose perfume hung in the air.

11

Clarissa greeted them cordially. "Mr. McCune, Miss . . . "

Rosalie introduced herself. "I'm Miss Foxe, the niece of Benjamin and Lottie Marshall. I came here Friday morning to make the mortgage payment on their store." Recollections of the woman staring openly at her crippled arm as she was now doing, came flooding back.

Clarissa rose, offering a smile Rosalie found ungenuine. "Forgive me. I have a *terrible* memory."

Rosalie ignored the smile. "I suppose then, you haven't any memory at-all of my coming here."

In imitation of Rosalie's southern drawl, Clarissa said, "None at-all, Miss . . . Foxe, was it?"

Rosalie was about to accuse the woman of outright deceit when Kenton spoke up. "Miss Hackbardt, Miss Foxe assures me that you marked the payment down in a ledger. If you'll check your book, I'm confident we can resolve this problem."

"Certainly, Mr. McCune. I should have thought of that." Clarissa stepped up to a bookcase lined with leather-bound volumes and extracted a burgundy one with the year '1900' imprinted in gold on the spine. Opening to the page with the most recent entries, she searched the listings, then turned the book around and set it in front of Kenton. "I'm sorry. I find no record of payment on the Marshalls' mortgage for the current month."

Rosalie couldn't keep the sarcasm from her voice. "Why am I not at-all surprised?"

Clarissa flashed her a wicked smile which turned suddenly sweet when Kenton had finished his study of the page and addressed her again. "I'd like to speak with Mr. Gowen."

"He's with a—"

Kenton cut her off. "We'll wait."

Clarissa closed the ledger. "But you have no appointment."

Kenton leaned forward. "My business will take but a minute. We're not leaving until I speak with him."

She indicated the empty chairs. "Suit yourselves." She sat down to her typewriter, filling the office with the slow rhythm of its tap . . . tap . . . tap.

Rosalie fidgeted with her lace gloves, occasionally exchanging glances with Kenton, who was checking the gold cufflinks in his French cuffs at least once every minute. She was thinking that her own single-handed proficiency on the typewriter could surpass Clarissa's two-finger method by several words per minute when the door to Cutler Gowen's office opened and the entrepreneur—his dark, wavy hair plastered against his head with a heavily scented pomade—emerged with his client.

While Clarissa saw the broad-shouldered, auburn-haired visitor out, Kenton rose to address Gowen.

The other man spoke first. "McCune, I was certain you'd show up here before this day was out, and you haven't disappointed me."

"About the Marshalls' eviction notice."

Rosalie stepped face to face with Gowen. "You had no right, Mr. Gowen. No right at-all to tell my Uncle Benjamin and Aunt Lottie to leave their store when they've made every payment on time."

"Now, now, Miss Foxe." Gowen spoke in soothing, golden tones. "I can certainly understand your distress, since the money for the payment was evidently entrusted to you."

"And I entrusted it to your secretary! It was a double eagle with—"

Kenton cut her off. "Miss Foxe, enough said."

Gowen clucked his tongue. "Lies always catch up with their perpetrator, Miss Foxe."

Rosalie drew a sharp breath to respond, but Kenton intervened. "Mr. Gowen, you maintain that the Marshalls' mortgage is in arrears." He pulled the eviction notice from his pocket and laid a shiny new double eagle on top of it. "Let me make the payment now. What difference can one day make?"

"All the difference, McCune."

Rosalie strode to Clarissa's desk and began opening drawers. Frustrated with the limited use of her right hand, she made her left hand work faster, searching the contents, tossing papers, pen nibs, seals, and rubber stamps in a heap on the blotter.

Gowen didn't flinch. "Theatrics won't convince anyone of your innocence, Miss Foxe. I suspect you kept the twenty dollars for a hat or some other fancy goods at Hamilton and Milliken."

Rosalie was about to argue when Clarissa came through the door. "Miss Foxe! Just what do you think you're doing?" She stormed across the room.

Gowen caught her by the arm. "Let her be, Miss Hackbardt. You and I both know she's looking for something that's not there."

Having searched the last drawer, Rosalie slammed it shut, turning to Gowen. "I reckon that coin's a lost ball in high weeds now, but I had to look, anyway."

Kenton took Rosalie by the elbow. "We're finished here, Miss Foxe. Let's be on our way."

Gowen preceded them to the door, holding it open graciously. "Excellent idea, McCune. And Miss Foxe, you might as well tell your aunt and uncle to start packing. At the end of the month they'll be moving elsewhere."

Rosalie paused on the threshold to give him a sharp look. "You know what I think, Mr. Gowen? I think you're slicker than a bucket of boiled okra, but you'd better watch out. One day, you'll be sipping sorrow with a teaspoon."

As the door closed behind them, Rosalie heard Clarissa's sing-songy voice mimicking her final words in an exaggerated drawl. A knot formed in her throat. When she thought of her aunt and uncle being put out of their home and business by the likes of Clarissa Hackbardt and Cutler Gowen, she was provoked to the point of tears.

Outside the door, Kenton paused, taking her by the shoulders. Immediately, she shrugged off his hands and looked down, unable to bear anyone but Willy Jo Winthrop touching her imperfect arm.

Kenton lifted her chin, forcing her to meet his gaze. "Don't put me off, Miss Foxe. I meant no offense."

Her throat constricted tighter still, making it impossible to speak.

He continued. "I'm not about to let Gowen get away with this. If it wouldn't inconvenience you, I'd like to make an inquiry at the bank before we leave. Maybe the double eagle with the nick in it will turn up, and someone might remember Miss Hackbardt or Mr. Gowen making the deposit."

Rosalie nodded, a spark of hope brightening her glum mood as she rode the two blocks to the bank. She had accompanied her aunt and uncle here many times during the past month to make deposits from the candy shop. Her father's draft from People's National Bank in Winston-Salem had been deposited here, too, for her to draw on to cover her expenses during her northern sojourn. She was thankful that Mr. Johnson, the president of the First National Bank, was a cheerful sort. He greeted her by name as she crossed the marble floor to reach his desk, then spoke to Kenton.

"How can I be of service on this bright, sunshiny day?" He waited until his guests had been seated, then sat again in the chair behind his desk.

Kenton explained. "Our request is a rather odd one, but important . . . "

Mr. Johnson fussed with his bow tie as he listened, then he asked a clerk to gather together all the double eagles on the premises. But when Rosalie and Kenton inspected them, none had a nick near the word "God."

Mr. Johnson accompanied them to the door. "I'm sorry to think the Marshalls might lose their shop. The hard candy from that new factory in town has its appeal, but it certainly can't compare to the fudge and other sweets the Marshalls put out." He paused at the door. "I know that for a fact, and not because I bought any of Gowen's goods. He was in here the other day handing out horehounds and lemon drops."

Rosalie spoke up. "I'll tell you what I think, Mr. Johnson. I think Mr. Gowen is eager to take over Uncle Benjamin and Aunt Lottie's shop so he can put his own goods in there."

Kenton pressed his hand against Rosalie's back. "Miss Foxe, we'd best be on our way."

Rosalie stalled. "Mr. McCune, do you mean to imply you think I'm wrong?"

16

Kenton smiled. "Quite the opposite. I think you're right, and I think we'd best keep looking for that coin." To Mr. Johnson, he said, "You'll keep your eye out for it, won't you?"

Mr. Johnson nodded. "I'll be in touch the moment it comes through."

On the way to the rig, Kenton told Rosalie, "I can think of a couple of places where that coin might be. One of them is relatively easy to investigate. The other is next to impossible."

Rosalie stepped into the carriage. "I'd give a small fortune to take a look through Miss Hackbardt's personal possessions right now."

Kenton settled beside her and set the buggy on a southward path along Cass Street. "I can't promise you'll get the chance to go through Clarissa's things for yourself, but I know a couple of ladies who can be persuaded to investigate for us, and they won't charge one penny." He continued straight until making a left turn onto Washington Street.

"Mr. McCune, if you don't mind my asking, exactly where are you taking me?"

"Are you any good at euchre, Miss Foxe?"

"My Aunt Ophelia says a deck of cards is the devil's prayer book," Rosalie informed him, adding with a laugh, "but I'm better at euchre than I am at hearts."

He chuckled. "Then I suggest you keep that a secret from the Doyle sisters."

"Are you saying a few hands of euchre will give us the access we desire?"

"You're a very bright young woman, Miss Foxe."

"Bright enough to know when to lose."

"You took the words right out of my mouth."

Kenton pulled up in front of a sign that read, "Doyle Sisters Rooming House." The modest home had been freshly painted sea green with fuchsia and violet trim. Despite the colorful exterior, Rosalie found the interior pale, with ivory lace at the windows and a dusty rose pattern on the parlor sofa and chairs. True to Kenton's prediction, the cards were brought out and a game of euchre was required before Miss Ava and Miss Eda would permit discussion of the real reason for his visit. The steeple clock on the mantel had struck a quarter past four by the time he had explained about the missing double eagle and the consequences to the Marshalls.

Kenton spoke cautiously. "So you can see why we're wondering if . . . there's any possibility you would consider looking in Clarissa's room for the coin."

Miss Ava blinked rapidly. "I would never consider going through Miss Hackbardt's personal belongings. Would you, Eda?"

Miss Eda touched her lace handkerchief to each of her temples. "Of course not, sister."

Miss Ava blinked some more. "You do understand, don't you, Mr. McCune? Why, if word got out that we were so nosy as to go through our boarders' things, not a soul would come to stay with—."

Miss Eda interrupted. "But sister, have you forgotten? We were planning to give Miss Hackbardt's room a thorough cleaning this very afternoon."

Miss Ava thought a moment. "Eda, your memory is a constant source of amazement to me. We'd best fetch the carpet sweeper and dust rags this very minute, and I think we should ask Mr. McCune and Miss Foxe to come upstairs and supervise, lest we miss any dirt or cobwebs."

Rosalie and Kenton followed the sisters up the stairs to a bedroom at the rear of the house. A jewelry box on the dresser immediately aroused Rosalie's curiosity, piqued further when Miss Ava dusted its cover, but showed no inclination to look inside.

Meanwhile, Eda had started on the secretary. After dusting its shelves of books and bric-a-brac, she tried to open the slant top but found it locked. Touching her finger to the empty keyhole, she said, "Sister, I don't suppose we have an extra key to this desk, have we? I'd be remiss in my duties if I didn't straighten up inside for Miss Hackbardt."

Miss Ava sighed. "I fear not."

Unable to restrain herself, Rosalie took a hat pin from a cushion on the dresser. "I'll take a stab at that lock, Miss Eda." Using her left hand, she unlocked the desk within seconds.

Kenton was amazed. "How did you do that so quickly?"

Miss Eda's eyes grew wide. "Yes, how *did* you do that? You're awfully clever for one with . . . who . . . "

Rosalie made light of the reference to her lameness. "I've picked much tougher locks than that single-handed, so to speak. I learned it from Gaspar, Daddy's hired man. He was an escape artist with a circus side show before Daddy hired him to take care of his horses."

Kenton chuckled. "I never would have guessed that answer."

Eda said, "Nor would I." Turning her attention to the desk, she began tidying it up, searching every pigeonhole thoroughly. She had removed a crystal paperweight and appeared to be on the brink of a question when Miss Ava held up a pair of white lace gloves she had found in a dresser drawer.

"Eda, look. Aren't these the brand new gloves you were missing last week?" She handed them to her sister.

Eda offered the paperweight in exchange. "And we were looking high and low for this a few days ago. We turned the place upside down in search of it—all except for this room. Remember?"

Ava's eyes sparkled as she cradled the piece of etched crystal in her hands. "Mother's Steuben paperweight. I'd given up hope of ever seeing it again."

Eda said, "You even asked Miss Hackbardt if she'd seen it, and she denied any knowledge of its whereabouts."

Following a moment's thought, Ava said, "Eda, you and I are going to have to do a much more thorough cleaning than we had planned."

"Sister, do you mean what I think you mean?"

Ava nodded. To Rosalie, she said, "Would you be so good as to take mother's paperweight downstairs and set it on the center table in the parlor? And Mr. McCune, would you please fetch Miss Hackbardt's trunk from the attic? We must start packing her things immediately. She'll soon be home from Mr. Gowen's office."

When Kenton had fetched the trunk, Rosalie helped the Doyles fill it with Clarissa's belongings. They emptied the desk and dresser drawers, and had packed up all but the jewelry case when Eda went to set it in the trunk.

Ava stopped her sister. "I think we'd best look inside this." Setting it on the dresser again, she tried the clasp, but it was locked. She offered Rosalie a hat pin. "Do you mind?"

In less time than Rosalie had needed to open the desk, she had released the clasp and begun to lift the lid. A music box started up, sending the tinkling strains of *After the Ball is Over* into the room. With Kenton, Eda, and Ava looking on, Rosalie opened the top wide.

She had been so certain she'd find the double eagle, but there was no sign of money in the velvet lined tray, only some cheap paste lapel pins and a mother-of-pearl cameo.

Ava blinked rapidly. "I don't see anything of ours in there, do you, Eda?"

She touched her handkerchief to each temple. "No, sister."

The music box wound down as Rosalie started to close the lid. Kenton stopped her, his hand covering hers.

"It looks like there's another compartment beneath the tray."

A warmth flowed through Rosalie. Was it Kenton's touch, or her anticipation of what they might find?

He began lifting the tray from the box. At that exact moment, the front door opened and Clarissa's voice floated up the staircase. "Miss Ava? Miss Eda? Anybody home?"

CHAPTER

2

North Carolina
the same day

The chestnut mare groaned. Vanda Mae, still dressed in the riding breeches and shirt she'd put on the day before, roused from the bed of straw where she'd been dozing, brushed a loose strand of dark hair from her eyes, and knelt at the horse's side.

"Easy, Springer. Easy, now. I'm right here."

The mare lifted her head a trifle, snorted, and lay it down again to resume the quiet moaning she had kept up for the past several hours. Now, in the bright afternoon light streaming through the stable window, Vanda Mae could see that a yellow tinge had developed in the area around Springer's eye.

The young girl wrapped her arms about the animal's neck and pressed her cheek against it. The smell of her breath was so bad, it fouled the sweet scent of the fresh straw bedding that had been brought into the stable that morning, causing Vanda Mae to pull away. She stroked the small, diamond-shaped patch of white on Springer's face.

"I know you're mighty bad off right now, girl, but you'll get over this. You've got to!"

The animal whined.

Anguished thoughts filled Vanda Mae with regret.

Somehow, the gate had come open and Springer had gotten out of her pasture a couple of days ago. Though she hadn't strayed far, she'd eaten the dirt that was blocking her innards, killing her. If only . . .

At the other end of the stable, Vanda Mae could hear the boot heels of Gaspar, who looked after the two dozen or so horses at Tanglewood. Moments later the short, slender man entered Springer's stall. At the touch of his hand on Vanda Mae's shoulder, she turned to him, searching his deeply tanned face as he knelt beside her and examined her horse. When he spoke, the dark eyes that met her gaze were shrouded with concern.

"*El aciete,* the oil, is not working. We must end Springer's suffering." He started to rise.

She grabbed his hand, rising with him. "Not yet, Gaspar. She just needs more time. Give her until tomorrow. *Please!*"

Taking her firmly by the wrist, he released her hold. "*Lo siento,* I am sorry, there is no other way. Even Dr. Whitehead has said so. I get my rifle." He strode off.

Tears sprang to Vanda Mae's eyes. She dropped down beside Springer, hugging her tightly. "I love you, girl!" Her throat too tight to say more, she could only think of all she'd miss with the horse's demise.

Never again would the elegant mare prance across the meadow as if to say "Look at me!" when Vanda Mae was perched atop the fence watching her. Nor would the animal come galloping past Vanda Mae in "catch me if you can" playfulness when she appeared with halter and lead, only to stop a hundred feet away from her to wait patiently. And no more would Springer nuzzled her neck, nibble at her hair, and whinny in her ear as if to say, "I love you."

23

You've been my best friend for so many years, I don't know what I'll do without you! came the heartbreaking thought.

Springer grunted, her complaint so weak, Vanda Mae knew Gaspar and the veterinarian were right. They shouldn't let the suffering continue.

The hired hand came toward her now. At the sight of his rifle, Vanda Mae bolted down the center aisle of the stable past Tassie, who was confined until the birth of her foal. Grabbing a halter from the tack room, she ran toward the horse pasture. Hurricane and Firelight—the stallion who had sired Tassie's foal—were standing in the shade of an elm a hundred yards away.

Vanda Mae started to climb over the board fence. She had reached the top when the crack of Gaspar's rifle shattered the stillness, sending a sharp stab of nausea deep into her. Scrambling off the fence, she ran toward Hurricane, slipped the halter over his head and climbed on.

"Go, boy!" she whispered into the animal's ear as she nudged him with her heels.

He trotted toward the gate at the far side of the meadow where she quickly dismounted and let him out onto the two-rut drive. When she mounted the grey gelding again, he seemed to read her emotions, moving from trot to canter despite the warm weather.

Though Vanda Mae's heart was at a gallop, she dared not ask Hurricane to move faster in the heat. Passing a barn, more stables, a field of corn and another of alfalfa, she followed the road into the woods that covered much of her father's four hundred acres. Two minutes later, with the clearing at the end of the drive in sight, she began to slow down. Should she turn toward the Winthrops', or toward the town of Clemmons?

Heading toward the Winthrops', the grey gelding soon cantered past the drive to their barn, then into more woods. The odor of manure grew thick in the air. Rounding a curve, Vanda Mae spotted a wagon on the road a couple hundred yards ahead. Though she didn't recognize the horses, she knew the driver with broad shoulders and red hair was Willy Jo.

She cautioned her horse. "Easy, boy. Take it down. We don't want to spook Willy Jo's team." Hurricane had slowed to a trot when several pops from a shotgun sounded close by.

Hurricane bolted. Nearly coming unseated, Vanda Mae clung tight to his mane. "Whoa, Hurricane! Whoa!" she cried.

Bound on his own course, Hurricane galloped on, passing too close to Willy Jo's wagon. Behind her, Vanda Mae heard the pounding of hooves, the rattling of the harnesses, and the panic in Willy Jo's voice.

"Danny! Dolly! Whoa, now! Whoa!"

Vanda Mae knew they were bearing down on her. She pulled hard to the right. "Whoa, Hurricane! Whoa!"

Heeding her plea this time, he slowed down and moved off the road beside a cornfield.

Willy Jo's wagon barreled past in a cloud of dust. Veering off the road, they made a wide circle through the corn to change directions. Taking to the road once more, they charged past Vanda Mae.

She turned and followed as they veered sharply onto the drive to their barn. But the corner was too tight.

Tipping up on two wheels, the wagon started to over- turn leaving a trail of manure behind. Willy Jo jumped free just before the buckboard crashed onto its side and separated from the team.

Still yoked together, the horses ran blind, barely missing a huge magnolia tree and the fence around a pasture. Moments later they came to a halt beside a row of tulip poplars.

Willy Jo started toward the wagon.

Vanda Mae urged Hurricane on, catching up with him before he reached it.

"Willy Jo, I'm sorry!"

He turned to her, his blue eyes flashing. "Vannie-Mae Foxe, this is a fine fix you got me in!"

"You should have had better control of your team!"

"Horsefiddles! They were okay, till you came along!"

"Hurricane spooked. I tried to get him to slow down but—"

Willy Jo ran a hand through his hair. "I've a mind to *shoot* that horse!"

Vanda Mae jumped down. "Don't you ever say such a thing!"

"He's nothing but trouble! First for your sister, now for you—*and* me. You ought to make him into a bucket of plaster and a pot of glue!" Willy Jo turned and strode off.

Unable to control her rage, Vanda Mae ran up behind him and shoved him, landing him smack in the spilt manure.

"Don't you *ever* threaten to shoot Hurricane again!" she warned, hand on hip, finger wagging.

He scrambled to his feet. Dung dropped in clumps from his overalls. His face turned the color of the clay on which Vanda Mae was standing. "You little—I'll get you for this!"

"Catch me if you can!" she taunted, starting to climb onto Hurricane.

He grabbed her by the elbow, preventing her from mounting. Somehow her feet tangled with his and she fell on her backside—right into a patch of manure.

Willy Jo offered a hand, his words as contrite as the look on his face. "Fiddles. I didn't mean for that to happen, Vannie-Mae. Truly."

Taking a fistful of the slimy manure, Vanda Mae slapped it against Willy Jo's palm, gripping tightly and pulling herself to her feet. "You're forgiven, Willy Jo. Maybe."

She released her grip and wiped her hand against the front of her breeches. Taking hold of Hurricane's halter, she turned toward home, knowing she couldn't mount him with the manure all over her behind. It would put a stain on his pale grey coat that would be almost impossible to wash off.

Her steps slowed, vividly remembering the blast of Gaspar's rifle. A sense of dread settled in her stomach at the thought of returning to Tanglewood. She glanced over her shoulder. Willy Jo was inspecting his wagon, contemplating the problem of turning it upright. She went to him.

"Let me help you with that, Willy Jo."

The look he gave her sent the same message as his words. "Go home, Vannie-Mae. I don't need your kind of help. You're the one who got me into this fix."

"It's only right you let me make amends."

Willy Jo walked away from her, pausing at the rear of the wagon to inspect the axle. She followed, unwilling to be dismissed so easily.

A moment later he faced her, his nose wrinkling. "You

stink."

"You stink worse."

"No point taking a bath till I get myself out of this mess."

"It will take you all afternoon to shovel that load back onto the wagon. I'll help."

"This is no job for a girl."

"I've been cleaning stables since I was old enough to fetch a manure basket. This is no different."

Willy Jo grabbed the rim of the left rear wheel and levered his weight against it. The wagon creaked but hardly budged. Moving to the front, he took the remnant of a snapped tug in his hand, then dropped the frayed leather strap in disgust. "I'll have to get new tugs from the tack room." He started in the direction of the barn. Vanda Mae followed, leading Hurricane.

A long silence ensued, a silence during which Vanda Mae pondered the mess she'd gotten Willy Jo into. Perhaps she shouldn't have stayed in the hot, steamy Piedmont to witness the birth of Tassie's first foal. Perhaps she should have gone with her mother to the cooler mountain resort of Blowing Rock where she and Rosalie had spent many summers. At least then she wouldn't have gotten Willy Jo into this stinking mess. And she wouldn't have been home to witness Springer's demise. She silently prayed that these calamities weren't an omen of things to come, that Tassie would have an easy birthing. And that it would be soon.

Willy Jo glanced at Vanda Mae. He'd seen her a time or two from a distance since he'd come home from agricultural college for the summer, but he hadn't gotten close enough to notice the changes in her till now. Her manure-stained riding breeches and oversized shirt couldn't mask the fact that she was growing into womanhood. And though he didn't want to admit it, her oval face and dark hair were a trifle prettier than Rosalie's had been at sixteen.

He saw, too, that Vanda Mae had turned melancholy and quiet. He wondered if she was lonely, staying in the Piedmont when her good friend—his own younger brother, Bobby Dan—had gone to Blowing Rock along with both their mothers. They had almost reached the barn when he voiced his thoughts.

"You look sadder than a hog in a bathtub, Vannie-Mae. I guess you're sorry you didn't go to Blowing Rock after all."

The young girl's shoulders drooped. He touched her arm. "You're not fixing to cry, are you? Your daddy would take you there if you asked."

Vanda Mae turned away burying her face against Hurricane's neck in an attempt to check her tears. Drying her cheek on her shirt sleeve, she faced Willy Jo, her throat clogging with emotion. "I don't care about Blowing Rock. I . . ."

"What, Vannie-Mae?"

She drew a tight breath. "Springer's dead! She had colic real bad and Gaspar had to shoot her!" Tears began streaming down her face.

Unsure how to console her, Willy Jo put his arm lightly about her shoulder. "Horsefiddles. I'm sorry. I didn't know."

Vanda Mae hung her head. When she faced him again, her words tumbled out unbridled. "Springer was my best friend. She knew me better than anybody. I don't know what I'm going to do without her!"

Willy Jo resisted the urge to tighten his arm about her while he searched for a comforting reply. "You've still got Tassie, and Firelight, and . . . " He couldn't count a horse as skittish as Hurricane among her assets.

"It's not the same," Vanda Mae mumbled, trying once again to dry her face on her shirt sleeve. "I've never been so fond of a horse as I was of Springer."

Willy Jo pulled his handkerchief from his back pocket and handed it to her. "I know what you mean."

She pushed his arm off her shoulder. "No, you don't! Not a few minutes ago you were ready to *shoot* a horse!"

"That was just my temper talking! I'd never hurt a horse." He patted Hurricane's shoulder, then glanced at the stable. "I've got work to do. Daddy was expecting me in the lower pasture with that manure long ago, and here I am in a bad fix."

Still reluctant to head home, Vanda Mae followed him toward the stable, hitched Hurricane to the fence post outside, then wandered in and down the center aisle. Beyond the stalls of the roans that were Mr. Winthrop's driving horses was a box containing a horse she'd never seen before—a dark chestnut mare that didn't look like the hacks to which she was accustomed.

She spoke as she stroked its thick mane. "Who are you? You're a right pretty one, aren't you?" She couldn't help noticing the unusual blaze on the animal's face—a narrow streak of white that flared distinctively on the right side, and the sprinkle of white hairs at her brow line.

Willy Jo came out of the tack room, new tugs looped over his shoulder. "That's April, my new Morgan. I bought her last week. Mama doesn't know it yet, but she's going to enter 'Best Lady Rider' for the first time in twenty years at the Forsyth County Fair this fall, and she's going to win on April!"

"Not a chance!" Vanda Mae challenged. "Now that they've redrawn the county line to include Tanglewood, I'll be entering your fair, and you know Springer—" she stopped herself short. Swallowing hard, she turned to April again, her words a mere whisper. "You just might win at that, girl. You just might."

"April has a lot to learn, but she's already showing great promise as a jumper. Horsefiddles! She'll be taking a four-foot rail in no time!"

The horse began nibbling on Willy Jo's hair. He laughed. "You want to be brushed, don't you girl?"

April nickered.

"All right, but only for a minute."

He set down the tugs, entered the box stall and began stroking her with a soft brush. As Vanda Mae watched, she noticed another distinguishing feature about the mare—that she had three white socks. Only the left rear leg was completely chestnut.

Not five minutes had lapsed when Willy Jo's daddy marched into the stable, his flaming red sideburns accenting the cross look on his face.

"Willy Jo!"

He tossed the brush aside and hurried out of the stall, picking up the tugs.

"Is this what they teach you about farmin' at agricultural college? How to shirk your chores to brush that fancy ridin' horse of yours?"

Willy Jo's face reddened. "No, sir."

"I told you I wanted to spread manure on the lower pasture this afternoon. Now, I find the wagon upset, manure all over the drive, and the new team nibblin' on the tulip poplars. What've you got to say for yourself?"

Vanda Mae spoke up. "It's my fault, Mr. Winthrop. Hurricane—"

His angry gaze remained locked on Willy Jo. "I declare, when you come back from school, it's as if you've forgot what it means to work."

"I'm sorry about the manure, Daddy. I'll—"

"Ya graduated agricultural college, bought a fancy horse, and it seems to me you've spent nearly all your time fussin' over her. I've a mind to sell her just so's I can get a good day's labor out of ya!"

Willy Jo's response was firm, but respectful. "I only ride her evenings when my chores are done, sir."

Jabe Winthrop seemed unconvinced. Taking the tugs from Willy Jo, he said, "Fetch a couple of pitch forks and get Lincoln to help ya." He referred to his farm hand. "I want that load of manure in the lower pasture in an hour." Pulling a bent card from his pocket, he added, "And I'm callin' this Danvers fellow we met at the auction and tellin' him this Morgan mare is for sale."

"But, Daddy, she belongs to me!"

"Not till you've paid back the money ya borrowed from me to buy her!" He strode away.

Vanda Mae went after him. "Mr. Winthrop, sir, don't trouble yourself calling that fellow. My daddy will buy April for me. How much do you want?"

He turned to her, a set look on his face, and named a figure. "That's what was paid for her plus ten percent. Pay before tomorrow or I'll sell to Danvers."

"I'll have the money to you, Mr. Winthrop. I promise!"

Without a word, he tramped out of the stable.

32

Vanda Mae turned to Willy Jo. "I'm sorry—"

The flush on his face deepened. "Go home, Vannie-Mae, and take April with you! Her blanket, bridle, and saddle are hanging in the tack room." He stepped past her.

Vanda Mae followed him. "I can't take April. She's not paid for."

Willy Jo paused to face her. "Horsefiddles! Your daddy's got to see what he's buying. You can save him the trip over here." He nudged her in the direction of the tack room. When she hesitated, he said, "Better for you to have her than some fool who'll ruin her with a severe bit and a heavy hand. I saw how Danvers treats horses at that auction, and I'd never let him near April. Now take her and git!"

As he walked out the door, she said, "I'll make it up to you, Willy Jo! I promise!"

Dark clouds were beginning to gather by the time Vanda Mae had ridden home to the stable where Springer had lain ill. She cross-tied the new horse in the center aisle while she removed her saddle and bridle.

Springer's stall was empty now. Gaspar had evidently gone about the business of disposing of her remains, so Vanda Mae thoroughly cleaned and disinfected the loose box and led April to her new quarters. Filling the manger with corn and the rack with hay, she headed for Tassie's box on the way out to check on the mother-in-waiting.

Even from a distance the sight of her almost made Vanda Mae cry. Tassie's coloring was nearly identical to her sister, Springer—chestnut with a white diamond on her forehead. Could she ever look at the mare and not be reminded of the horse she'd lost? As she approached the foaling box, she tried to console herself with the knowledge that at least she still had Springer's sister, and after two unsuccessful attempts at breeding, would soon have her foal to help chase away today's sorrow.

Drawing nearer, she noticed the mare was dripping with sweat and her stall showed evidence of intestinal complaint. These symptoms, along with the way she shifted from one side of her box to the other reminded Vanda Mae of Springer when she had first taken ill. Unschooled in the natural workings of her own animal's body—as any Southern miss of status was expected to be—Vanda Mae felt panic rise within.

She patted Tassie's neck. "Easy, girl, easy now. I'll get you some oil." She started toward the tack room as fast as her feet could carry her, running headlong into Gaspar and nearly falling into an empty manger.

He caught her by the shoulders to set her right. "Slow down, little one! What's the hurry?"

"Tassie's sick—just like Springer was! We have to give her oil!"

"Not so fast. Let Gaspar see."

When she returned with him to Tassie's stall, the horse was more skittish than before. Just as Gaspar was about to enter her box, she let loose a huge stream of fluid from her hind quarters.

Vanda Mae knew from the blood-tinged color it wasn't urine. Her heart raced. "Gaspar, help her! Don't let her die!"

Cautiously, he entered the box. Inspecting Tassie's underside and the discharge, he exited the stall and focused on Vanda Mae. "Tassie's not sick." A smile spread on his ruddy, narrow face. "She's ready to have her baby!"

Vanda Mae wanted to laugh and cry at the same time.

Then a new worry took over. "We must help her! What do we do?"

Gaspar took off his straw hat and wiped his damp forehead on his sleeve. "We can do nothing but wait, little one. Tassie knows what to do."

Vanda Mae watched as Tassie lay down and began to strain, stood up again, then repeated the process. The horse's actions seemed exacerbated by the rumble of an approaching storm. Gaspar spoke soothingly in Spanish but Tassie showed no sign of calming down.

Vanda Mae's apprehension increased. She paced across the center aisle and back. "Tassie's in trouble, Gaspar, I just know it!"

He regarded her sternly. "*Señorita*, do not fuss!"

"But she's—"

"You are upsetting her! If you cannot watch calmly then go to the house and I will fetch you when she is finished."

"Go to the house? Never!" Vanda Mae retorted, instantly ashamed of herself. "Forgive me, Gaspar. I'm jumpy as a hay bug from all that's happened today." Silently, she prayed, *Lord, please keep me quiet. And please help Tassie deliver her foal! Thank you!*

Tassie continued to get up and down, straining harder and harder. Rain began beating down on the stable roof. When several minutes had passed and the mare was laying on her side, a shiny membrane began to appear below her tail.

Gaspar put his fingers to his lips, then took Vanda Mae by the hand and opened the door of the box. In a low tone, he said, "Do you see the sack and the front feet inside?"

Vanda Mae nodded. One foot was positioned ahead of

the other.

Gaspar continued. "This is good. Tassie will have a normal birth."

No sooner had he spoken than a clap of thunder boomed overhead. The mare strained violently, expelling more of the membrane. The nose, head, and chest of the foal came into view.

Gaspar knelt down a safe distance from Tassie inviting Vanda Mae to do the same. "Watch closely," he told her. "The foal will break the sack and start to breathe."

Minutes later, when the storm had quieted, it happened just as he said. Then Tassie became more violent than ever. Vanda Mae clutched Gaspar's arm with one hand and pressed the other over her mouth to keep from crying out.

With her baby half born, Tassie took a short rest. Then giving a fierce effort, she pushed forth the foal's hips and hind quarters, except for the rear legs.

With the mare again at rest, Gaspar led Vanda Mae out of the box and closed the door. "We must let Tassie be. If she gets too quickly to her feet, her little one could die."

Awed by what she had already seen, Vanda Mae continued to watch in silence. The thunderstorm over, sunshine began peeking through the window. A few moments later the foal's hind feet appeared. Soon after that, Tassie rose. The cord attaching her to her baby broke, then she settled down beside her little one.

Vanda Mae was so touched by the sight of mama and baby nose to nose getting their first real look at one another, she couldn't have spoken a word even if she'd wanted to. Instantly, she fell in love with the tiny horse who also bore the colorings of her kin—a tiny diamond-shaped patch of white on her chestnut forehead. The prospect of caring for it and watching it grow so dominated her thoughts, she was hardly aware of the dinner bell ringing in the distance. Glancing at Gaspar, she saw that he was smiling as proudly as if he were the new arrival's daddy even though he'd witnessed many such births in his years at Tanglewood, and with the circus horses before that.

He told her, "This is the most important moment in the little one's life, when it learns who its mama is."

Tassie undertook a thorough washing of her foal from the white marking on its face to legs so spindly they seemed almost ugly. When she reached the newborn's hind quarters, Vanda Mae realized that the newcomer was a female. "I have the perfect name for Tassie's foal," she announced. "Jewel, for the diamond on her forehead."

"Jewel," Gaspar repeated with approval.

When the filly tried unsuccessfully to gain her feet, Vanda Mae said, "I hope she'll be a jumper in a few years. Until then at least I have—" She caught herself short. "Gracious! In all the excitement about Tassie, I forgot to tell you about April!" She was about to lead him to the opposite end of the stable when the dark-skinned maid—once nanny for her and Rosalie—appeared at the door, her hands set on her wide hips.

"Miss Vanda! Mr. Gaspar! I done rung the dinner bell long ago!" she announced.

"Don't scold, Shani," Vanda Mae begged. "We've been watching the most amazing miracle take place." She beckoned the woman to Tassie's stall.

Shani caught her breath when she saw Tassie and Jewel. "My, my, my. Ain't they a pretty sight? Now I know why nobody come to dinner."

"Do you think you could possibly bring it to us?"

Vanda Mae pleaded. "Jewel hasn't yet made it to her feet, and I'd hate to miss seeing her take her mother's milk for the very first time."

Shani thought a moment, then a smile appeared. "Miss Vanda, you're the spoiled rottenest child this side of the Atlantic Ocean. But I suppose I can bring you and Mr. Gaspar each a plate of dinner."

She'd turned to leave when Vanda Mae remembered April. "Shani, wait! I've got something I want you and Gaspar to see." She led them to April's stall. "Isn't she beautiful? And she's all mine."

Gaspar's brow wrinkled. "Is she not the new Morgan of the Winthrops?"

"*Was*," Vanda Mae informed him, adding proudly, "now April's all mine." To Shani, she said, "Did Daddy tell you what time he'll be home tonight? We need to take the payment for April to Mr. Winthrop."

"Your daddy done caught the train to Durham this mornin', child. Said to remind you he won't be back till tomorrow night."

Vanda Mae inhaled sharply. "Tomorrow night? But . . ."

Gaspar spoke up. "Surely, payment can wait until then."

Vanda Mae made no reply, Jabe Winthrop's angry words ringing in her head. *Pay before tomorrow or I'll sell her to Danvers.*

CHAPTER

3

Michigan

Rosalie stared in disbelief at the three gold coins in the bottom of Clarissa Hackbardt's jewelry box. None of them was a double eagle.

Kenton shut the box while Ava and Eda answered Clarissa's call from the front hallway in turn.

"Come upstairs, Miss Hackbardt!"

"We have a surprise for you!"

Ava set the jewelry case in the trunk and closed the lid. "Mr. McCune, would you be so kind as to fasten the straps, please?"

Kenton immediately obliged. He was still tightening the last buckle when Clarissa reached the door to her room, her face a puzzle. "Mr. McCune, what are you doing with my trunk?"

Before he could answer, Ava said, "Miss Hackbardt, I trust you have friends you can stay with tonight."

Eda spoke next. "If not, the Park Place has nice rooms, so I've been told."

Rosalie couldn't help smiling. "It's just as well you're moving out, Miss Hackbardt. I'll be in need of a place, should Mr. Gowen put me and my kin out on the street. Your room should suit just fine, if need be."

Clarissa put her hands on her hips. "So that's what this is all about. A twenty-dollar gold piece that doesn't even exist."

Ava's eyelashes fluttered. "This is about my mother's paperweight."

Eda dabbed her temple with her handkerchief. "And my brand new lace gloves."

Clarissa sighed. "I only borrowed them. If you wanted them back, all you had to do was ask."

Ava said, "I *did* ask. Just last week. You told me you hadn't seen the paperweight."

Clarissa was about to argue when Eda spoke again. "We can't countenance behavior such as yours from our guests. You owe us fifty cents for room and board this week, due now." She put out her hand.

Clarissa reached in her pocket and handed Miss Eda a half dollar.

Kenton hoisted her trunk to his shoulder. "I'll carry this downstairs for you, Miss Hackbardt. You'd best ring up Germaine Brothers to have it transferred."

The dinner hour was fast approaching, and when Clarissa finished using the telephone, Rosalie rang up Ben and Lottie to let them know she'd be late for the evening meal. Seven o'clock had come and gone by the time Clarissa and her trunk departed.

The Doyle sisters saw Kenton and Rosalie to the door, Miss Ava blinking furiously as she spoke. "Miss Foxe, you're welcome to take up quarters in Miss Hackbardt's old room. We'd enjoy your company."

Eda said, "We could get up a game of cutthroat euchre every afternoon."

Rosalie smiled. "Thank you, ladies, for the offer, but

I'm of a mind to prove to Mr. Gowen that I made that mortgage payment before he can put me and my aunt and uncle out on the street."

As Kenton drove Rosalie home, she began to recall their earlier conversation. "On the way to the Doyles', you said there were two likely places the coin might be found. We've eliminated one possibility. What's the other one?"

"Where would *you* look next?"

Rosalie thought a moment. "I'd look through Cutler Gowen's office."

Kenton smiled. "The more time you spend with me, the more your mind works like mine. Just look at how far you've come since this morning!"

Rosalie chuckled. "All the way from the train depot. That's at least two blocks from here, isn't it?"

Kenton laughed. "At least."

When the lighthearted moment had passed, Rosalie said, "About Mr. Gowen's office. I don't suppose there's any way at-all I could get in there for a look-see, is there?"

Kenton scratched his goatee.

"Can you get the police to search it?"

Still thoughtful, Kenton stated, "We have only your word that you made the payment. No proof, not even a receipt."

Rosalie sighed. "I sure got my tail in a crack this time. I wish I were back home. My uncle's the sheriff of Forsyth County. He'd get things straightened out real quick."

Alarmed, Kenton asked, "You aren't thinking of running off again, are you?"

Rosalie shook her head, still mulling over her quandary as Kenton pulled the rig to a halt in front of Marshalls' shop. He started to get out, but Rosalie stopped him, her

41

hand on his arm. "Mr. McCune, I just thought of something. I wonder if the cleaning lady at Mr. Gowen's office has seen anything at-all that could help us?"

Taking her hand in his, Kenton said, "There's little chance of that, but I suppose it wouldn't hurt to ask. Mrs. Potter—Constance Potter—cleans the office there and at several other buildings around town, mine included. Now let me see you to the door." He started to let go of her hand, but without aforethought, she held tight.

"I'm going to ring up Mrs. Potter tonight and inquire. Time's a-wasting, Mr. McCune. I've got to try *something!*"

He looked down at the hand clutching his, noticing to his surprise that he rather liked Rosalie clinging to him.

In that same instant, Rosalie realized to her embarrassment that she was still holding Kenton fast. She tried to let go, but it was he who prolonged the contact this time, firmly squeezing her fingers.

He spoke in a calm, but compelling tone. "Promise me you won't run home to North Carolina just yet, and that you'll stay clear of Gowen's office."

Rosalie nodded, instantly regretful that she had agreed to the second half of the promise.

"And one more thing. You *are* still going to the ball with me, aren't you?"

She smiled. "I have no reason at-all not to."

"Good. Now let me help you down."

When he walked her to the door, Lottie called to him from the upstairs window. "Thanks for bringing Rosalie home, Mr. McCune. Will you stay to supper? I've kept the hash and eggs hot, and there's plenty for the two of you."

Kenton could envision a serving of Lottie's corned beef

hash with the egg nestled in it, the bright yellow yolk staring up from its white jacket. Hunger pangs urged him to accept, but he'd been away from his office most of the day, and pressing legal matters overruled. "I can't stay tonight, Lottie. Thanks, anyway." To Rosalie, he said, "I'll see you soon. Now you'd better go upstairs and tell your aunt and uncle what's happened today."

Rosalie had little appetite for the hash and eggs her aunt served up, but she managed a forkful at a time amidst a description of her visit to Gowen's office and her encounter with the Hackbardt woman. Recalling Gowen's parting words, she set down her fork and focused on her uncle.

"Mr. Gowen had a message for you. He said you might as well start packing. At the end of the month you'll be moving elsewhere."

The furrow in her uncle's brow lingered only a moment. "That's presumptuous. And preposterous."

Lottie nodded. "Mr. McCune will prevail on our behalf. In fact, I'm confident he'll settle the whole matter before week's end."

Rosalie pressed her case. "But to do that, he'll have to locate the coin I gave Miss Hackbardt. Considering what we've been through today, that's about as likely as a sow standing up on her hind legs and doing a ballet." She described their investigations concerning Clarissa.

When she had finished her explanation and her supper, her uncle said, "That coin can't have gone far. I have faith that regardless of the way things seem right now, Mr. McCune will find it soon and everything will work out."

Lottie said, "I can't believe the Lord would allow us to be put out on the street. Not when we've been perfectly regular in our payments and honest in all our dealings."

Rosalie bit back the argument on her tongue. "I pray you're right."

Determined to keep looking for the coin despite her aunt's and her uncle's complacency, she began to formulate a plan for action as she helped them with the supper dishes. When the last of the pots and pans had been put away, Ben retired to the sitting room to take up his reading. With her aunt still fussing in the kitchen, she looked up the telephone number for Mrs. Constance Potter, then picked up the phone and asked the operator to make the connection.

While she waited for the cleaning woman to come on the line, Lottie asked in a half-whisper, "Who are you ringing up?"

Rosalie whispered, "I'll tell you in a minute."

Then the scratchy voice of an elderly woman grated over the wire. "Hello?"

"Mrs. Potter?"

"Who's this?"

"Rosalie Foxe. I'm an acquaintance of Mr. McCune's. He said maybe you could help me."

"Rosalie who? Foxe? You sound like one of those Dixie belles that comes up here to get out of the heat."

Rosalie spoke as quickly as she could in an attempt to overcome her southern drawl. "I'm from North Carolina and I'm visiting my aunt and uncle, Benjamin and Lottie Marshall. They own the—"

"I know, I know. The confectionery. What are you ringing me up for, anyway? I can't take on any more cleaning jobs just now."

"That's not why I rang you up. Mr. McCune said you might be able to help me. I understand you do the cleaning

44

in Mr. Gowen's office at the American Candy Company."

"That's right."

"Well, I'm looking for a coin that was misplaced there—"

"Well I didn't steal it! You've got your nerve, ringing me up and accusing me of such a thing!" She slammed down the phone.

Rosalie immediately asked the operator to ring Mrs. Potter again. The moment she answered, Rosalie said, "I know you didn't steal anything, Mrs. Potter! Now please don't hang up! My aunt and uncle will lose their store if I don't find that coin!"

Mrs. Potter drew a deep breath. "You'd better explain yourself, girl, and quick, because right now you sound like you're in need of a vacation at the asylum."

Rosalie told her about the payment made with a coin marred by a nick and Gowen's claim of nonpayment and his threat to foreclose on the candy shop. The look of disapproval on her aunt's face couldn't diminish the effect of Mrs. Potter's reaction.

"Why, that rascal, Gowen! You don't mean to let him get away with this, do you?"

"No, ma'am! But I can't do anything at-all now, unless I have your help." Rosalie told of her unsuccessful search for the coin at the bank, and in the Hackbardt woman's desk, jewelry case, and room.

Rosalie continued. "Mrs. Potter, I'm wondering if you'll let me help you when you clean Mr. Gowen's office next time. With two of us looking, maybe we'll find what I'm after."

A pause followed, then the woman replied, "I work alone. Can't have you getting underfoot. Besides, I start at five tomorrow morning—too early for anyone but the birds. I'll let you know if I find that coin, though."

"I can be there at five!" Rosalie insisted. "I help my aunt and uncle make their candy at that hour every morning. I'll work with you tomorrow instead. I don't expect to be paid!"

Patiently, Rosalie listened to Mrs. Potter's labored breathing in one ear and her aunt's whispered protests in the other. She covered the mouthpiece so the cleaning woman wouldn't hear Lottie, and waited for a reply.

With resignation, Mrs. Potter finally said, "I guess it's all right. I've got to warn you, though, Gowen keeps everything locked—his desk, file cabinets, and closet. This will likely be a waste of your time."

"I'll take that chance!" Rosalie said hastily.

"Then meet me at the back door of the factory at five sharp." She hung up.

Rosalie hadn't even finished placing the receiver on its hook when Lottie began her protest. "You can't go to work with Mrs. Potter. What would your folks say, you taking up work as a common cleaning woman?" Without waiting for a reply, she called her brother. "Ben, come in here and talk some sense into this niece of ours!" She fingered the neck strap of her apron while she waited, starting in again as soon as he reached the door. "Rosalie intends to hire herself out—"

"I heard," he said impatiently, placing a marker in the book he'd been reading.

"Tell her she can't go!"

"For the love of fudge, Lottie, I don't know why you're so upset. Rosalie's a full-grown young woman now. If she wants to go clean Gowen's office at five in the morning, I

46

don't see why we should stop her."

Rosalie smiled. "Thank you, Uncle Benjamin. I knew you'd understand."

Lottie scowled at her brother. "We can't let her go out alone at that hour. It's not even light out!"

"I'll walk her down to the factory. Now, if you don't mind, I'm going back to my story."

Lottie focused on Rosalie. "Does Kenton know you plan to do this?"

Rosalie felt a pang of guilt, remembering her promise to stay clear of Gowen's office, but a larger issue was at stake. "He's the one who told me about Mrs. Potter in the first place. Now don't you fret. Nothing at-all will go wrong."

Lottie continued to fuss with her apron strap. "There must be a better way."

"I can't think of one. Good night, Aunt Lottie."

Rosalie retired to her small sleeping chamber off the storage room at the rear of the first floor, her thoughts fixed on events to come as she drifted off to sleep. When she arose and dressed in the early morning hours, she slipped the set of lock picks Gaspar had given her years ago into her apron pocket, and gathered a bucketful of cleaning supplies from the back room. At breakfast, served at half-past four, barely a word was exchanged.

The sun had just peeked over the horizon, sending muted orange streaks low across the bay, when she set out with her uncle for the American Candy Company. Kerchief covering her hair, she walked briskly along Front Street. A warm, gentle breeze caused her apron to flutter, and despite pressing thoughts of her mission, she couldn't miss the enticing aroma of fresh bread when she passed the bakery, or the quiet tinkling of bottles as the milk man made his rounds.

Pausing at the rear door of the factory, Ben set down the bucket he'd carried for her and waited with her for Mrs. Potter. Moments later, a wide-hipped woman waddled toward them through the alley, her shoulders dipping alternately with each step.

Ben put the bucket in Rosalie's hand. "There's Mrs. Potter. I'll see you later." He set off for the confectionery leaving Rosalie to introduce herself.

"Good morning, Mrs. Potter. I'm Rosalie Foxe."

"Hmph," came the reply. Using one of the keys tied to the end of her apron string, she opened the back door and led the way through a series of halls. In the light of Gowen's office, she first noticed Rosalie's crippled right arm, staring at it for a moment, then ignoring it.

With very little discussion, she directed a thorough cleaning of books and book shelves, rugs and mats, pictures and light fixtures. Rosalie was dying to peek inside Gowen's locked desk, file cabinets, and closet. She fingered the set of lock picks in her apron pocket and toyed with the idea of opening a desk drawer while Mrs. Potter waxed the floor in the reception area, but decided against it.

Two hours had passed when the woman gathered rags and feather duster, lemon oil and paste wax into her bucket. "Sorry we didn't find your coin, Miss Foxe. But I warned you last night, Mr. Gowen keeps things locked pretty tight. Now, I've got to get on to the bank and do some cleaning there."

Outside the back door, Rosalie spoke while Mrs. Potter locked up. "Thank you for allowing me to help. Sorry we got nothing more than what the bear grabbed at."

The woman's mouth quirked into a smile. "Don't take

no offense, but you get more accomplished with that one good hand of yours than most womenfolk who've got two. You can work with me anytime you want!"

Rosalie smiled. "Thank you, Mrs. Potter. I consider that a real compliment." She stepped off with the woman, accompanying her until she disappeared inside the bank.

Doing an about face, Rosalie returned to the back door of the candy factory. She checked to see that no one else was in the alley, then took out the lock picks and easily regained access to the building. The door to Gowen's office opened with equal ease. Immediately, she went to the closet. One pick at a time, she tested the lock, but to no avail. She started through her entire set of picks again, jiggling each one to release the lock. Gowen's clock began to chime.

She reminded herself that in less than an hour, Gowen would arrive at his office. With renewed determination she began testing each pick a third time.

Over and again, she thought she was disengaging the lock. Time and again, the door failed to open. She was about to give up when the image of Gaspar came to mind and she heard him say, *Never, never, never give up!* She tried again, more carefully, taking her time, and the door opened!

Ignoring the papers and ledger stacked on a shelf on the right, she set her hand and her mind to opening two locked drawers built inside the cubicle. Picking the lock on the upper one first, she pulled it out only to discover a stack of greenbacks. She shut it and focused on the lower drawer. She was sliding it open when she heard the unmistakable voices of Gowen and Clarissa Hackbardt as they came into the reception room!

CHAPTER

4

North Carolina

The sun had been up for three hours when Vanda Mae gave in to exhaustion and lay down on a mound of straw near Tassie's foaling box. The instant her eyes closed, scenes passed through her mind of Jewel refusing to nurse, then becoming sicker and weaker with septicemia as the night wore on. How thankful she was that the veterinarian had responded to Gaspar's midnight telephone plea.

Silently, she prayed, *Dear Lord, bless Doc Whitehead for coming out in the middle of the night with the medicine. And thank you that he was able to persuade Jewel to nurse. Now please make Tassie's foal well and strong!*

Within seconds, Vanda Mae fell fast asleep. She was unsure how long she'd slept when loud voices at the other end of the stable woke her. Getting to her feet, she saw Mr. Winthrop arguing with Gaspar outside April's stall while another man—a stranger wearing a tall white hat with a wide black band—inspected the mare. She caught Jabe Winthrop's heated words as she hurried toward him.

"Don't you tell me the girl wants the Morgan!" He jabbed the air with his driving whip. "If she did, she'd have paid for the horse last night!"

"Please believe. Miss Foxe want this animal ver' much. Last night she—"

Vanda Mae cut in. "I was up all night with a very sick foal, Mr. Winthrop. I'm sorry I didn't deliver the money to you. I meant to call and tell you Daddy will bring it when he gets home from Durham tonight."

The stranger in April's stall spoke up. "Mr. Winthrop, I'd like to saddle up your Morgan and see how she rides."

Jabe turned to Gaspar. "Ya heard Mr. Danvers. Fetch her saddle."

Gaspar backed away. "Respectfully, sir, I do no work for you." He pivoted and walked out of the stable.

Jabe grumbled, then addressed Vanda Mae. "Ya took April. Now go and get her bridle and saddle like a good little girl."

She smiled. "It's hanging in the tack room, sir." She hurried after Gaspar who was headed for the rig Danvers had parked outside the stable. The hired hand was looking closely at the black gelding hitched to the buggy when Vanda Mae caught up with him. "What is it, Gaspar?"

He didn't reply. Instead, he spoke softly to the horse, peeling back its lips to inspect its mouth. Then he walked around to the right side. There, he pointed to a fresh mark on the horse's hind quarters. "Just as I thought. Danvers makes much use of his whip. And this horse's mouth is scarred."

He continued his inspection until Danvers came out of the stable atop the Morgan, immediately digging his heels into her flanks. Jabe Winthrop stood just outside the door watching the man put the animal through her paces, making frequent use of his riding crop as he switched her lead from one side to the other.

51

Vanda Mae strode up to Willy Jo's father. "*Please* don't sell to that man," she pleaded. "He'll be too hard on April."

Winthrop's gaze remained on the horse and rider. "A tap on the hind quarters now and then can't hurt the animal, Vanda Mae."

Gaspar spoke up. "The Morgan needs gentling, not whipping."

Jabe smiled cynically. "That's a matter of opinion."

Vanda Mae continued to watch as Danvers cut this way and that across the meadow, using his riding crop against the Morgan with every change of direction. She was itching to argue further with Willy Jo's father about his decision to sell to such a man. Just when she thought she would lose the battle with her tongue, Willy Jo came tearing into the pasture atop one of his father's roans, heading straight for Danvers. Though she was too far away to hear their conversation, it was evident from Willy Jo's gesticulations that the exchange was heated. Moments later, they rode up to the stable and dismounted, hitching their horses to the fence rail.

Willy Jo marched up to his father, Danvers close behind. "Why didn't you tell me you were coming here to sell April out from under Vannie-Mae?"

"Couldn't see the point in gettin' ya riled. How'd ya find out?"

"Linc—" Willy Jo interrupted himself. "Doesn't matter. I came to stop you from selling to this man."

Despite the ruddiness flooding his cheeks, Jabe remained calm. "It's not your decision to make, son."

Willy Jo pressed further. "What do you know about him except that he came to the auction, bid up the price on the horse we wanted, then handed you a card with a number to call in case you changed your mind about April?"

Jabe replied in a taut, low voice. "What I know is this man wants the horse, he's got the money, and I'm gonna take it!"

Danvers spoke up. "I'm glad reason prevails. I'm ready to deal." He pulled a roll of currency from his pocket and began peeling off bills.

Willy Jo stopped him with an upward cut of his hand. "Put your money away, Mr. Danvers. They ought to make it illegal for the likes of you to own a horse!"

Danvers seemed unruffled. "Ain't—hasn't your daddy ever warned you not to make accusations against a stranger, young Winthrop?"

"You're no stranger to Doc Whitehead. I won't repeat in front of Vannie-Mae what *he* said about some horses you sold down in Davidson County!"

Impatiently, Jabe turned on his son. "When did you talk to Doc Whitehead?"

"I rang him up not half an hour ago after Lincoln told me that lame sow was looking worse."

When his father waved off the problem, Danvers spoke again. "With all due respect, young Winthrop, I ain't— haven't ever met this Whitehead fella, or solicited his services. His accusations against me are false."

Vanda Mae didn't believe Danvers for a second, and was about to say so when Jabe spoke instead.

"Doc Whitehead is mistaken!"

Gaspar spoke up, words tumbling off his tongue. "Mr. Winthrop, sir, the good doctor makes no mistake, of this I am certain. If he says that Mr. Danvers is unkind to horses, then—"

Jabe turned on him. "You stay out of this, ya circus riffraff!" To Danvers, he said, "If ya want the horse, she's yours."

Willy Jo grew adamant. "I bought April and I won't let Danvers have her!"

"You'll do as I say unless ya can pay off the loan I gave ya!"

Despite his father's words, Willy Jo led April toward the stable.

Jabe pursued. "Just where do ya think you're goin'?"

Willy Jo paused. "This is April's new home. You'll have your money as soon as Mr. Foxe returns from Durham."

Jabe shook his finger at Willy Jo. "If April stays here, then *you* do, too. Ya can pick up your belongin's tonight when ya bring me my money. And ya'd better start lookin' for a job on somebody else's farm 'cause you're off my payroll for good!" He strode away.

A minute later, Danvers and Jabe Winthrop drove off taking the roan Willy Jo had arrived on with them.

The disturbed look on Willy Jo's face tore at Vanda Mae. She searched for words of comfort. "It will all work out, Willy Jo. By tonight you'll have your loan paid off and your daddy will want you home again."

He shook his head thoughtfully. "Fiddles, Vannie-Mae. Daddy and I, we've been having our differences for quite some time. He meant what he said about moving out."

Ever hopeful, she said, "I'm going to pray God will soften his heart and change his mind."

CHAPTER

5

Michigan

Heart pounding, Rosalie shut the drawer in Gowen's closet. She had lost all track of time, too involved in her task to heed the quarter-hour chimes of the clock. It was too late now to prevent him from finding her in his office. Grabbing a dust rag from her bucket, she set to work polishing his already immaculate desk, smiling when he came through the door.

"Good morning, Mr. Gowen! You're looking bright as a peacock's crest this morning!"

Despite her compliment, his expression grew dark and menacing. "You! What are you doing in my office?"

Clarissa entered the room, a look of pure revulsion in her eyes. "I'll tell you. She's been snooping! She's probably already searched every nook and cranny of your office!"

Rosalie drew herself up, squaring her shoulders as best she could. "I'm merely assisting Mrs. Potter with her cleaning, Miss Hackbardt. But I'm quite finished now." She dropped her rag into her bucket, picked it up, and headed for the door.

Gowen caught hold of her right arm. "Not so fast!"

His touch was repulsive. She twisted away, banging him on the shin with her bucket.

He cried out, letting go of her arm to grab his leg.

She hurried out the office door.

"Come back here!" he demanded, following her into the reception area, catching hold of her bad shoulder. "You won't get away with this!" His thumb penetrated deeper as he spoke. "You'd better stay clear of this office from now on, or I'll see to it your aunt and uncle never work in this town again!"

Rosalie wanted to cry out from the pain of his cruel grip. Instead, she issued a warning. "You haven't seen the last of me yet, Mr. Gowen!"

Jerking free, she hurried down the hall and out the door. All the way to the confectionery she dreaded having to tell her aunt and uncle that she'd come away empty-handed. To her amazement, neither of them asked the outcome of her search, but proceeded about their tasks as if the day had begun like any other. She put the entire cleaning escapade behind her as she helped her aunt with customers and her uncle with fudge-making—until an hour later when Kenton McCune came marching through the door and straight up to her.

"You broke your promise!" he accused, barely in control of his temper.

Two customers finishing their purchase turned to stare at them.

Rosalie stood mute knowing color was invading her cheeks.

Lottie ushered the customers toward the door. "Thank

you very much. Your patronage is appreciated!" Shutting the door, she hung up the "Closed" sign, pulled the shade, and turned to Kenton. "What promise are you talking about, Mr. McCune?"

Rosalie answered for him. "I went to Mr. Gowen's office after I gave Mr. McCune my word I'd stay away."

Kenton glowered at her. "That's right. And do you realize what you've done? You've made it ten times harder for me to solve the mortgage problem!"

"But I only wanted to—"

"It makes little difference what you *wanted* to do. What you *did* was make Gowen angry, retractable, and more determined than ever to put your aunt and uncle out of this shop at month's end!"

Ben spoke up. "Easy, Kenton. Anger won't solve the problem."

Kenton fumed under his breath.

Ben set down his fudge spatula and came to face him. "Rosalie was only trying to help. I'm not condoning her actions, but her heart was in the right place. Berating her will only make things worse."

Lottie went behind the display case, gathered some vanilla caramels into a box, and offered them to the lawyer. "Eat up, Mr. McCune. You've got to restore your old, sweet self before the ball tonight."

Kenton looked as if he might choke.

Rosalie came to his rescue. "No offense, Aunt Lottie, but you're not a fairy godmother, and Mr. McCune and I are a far piece from being Cinderella and the prince. I think we'd best cancel our plans for the ball."

Lottie scowled. "You're right. I'm *not* a fairy god-mother, but I won't hear of your canceling! For days now, your uncle and I have been planning to buy tickets for the Opera House gallery so we can watch the two of you at the Carnival Queen's reception and dance."

Ben spoke up. "That's right! This is the first time in years I've consented to staying out past nine o'clock!"

Lottie added, "We're even skipping supper so we can cook the candy for tomorrow. Goodness knows we won't feel like doing it at the crack of dawn." She paused, her gaze moving expectantly from Rosalie to Kenton. When silence reigned, she sighed deeply, heading to the door to remove the "Closed" sign.

Evidently guilt-ridden, Kenton took two tickets from his pocket and offered them to Ben. "Why don't you take your sister to the ball tonight?"

He laughed, then wiped perspiration from his brow with his handkerchief. "If you think I'm sweating now, it's nothing to what would happen if I had to dance at a ball."

Lottie joined them. "You just put those tickets back in your pocket, Mr. McCune. It's a shame they should go to waste, but I suppose there's nothing more to be done."

Customers entered the shop and Lottie started to wait on them while Ben went about slicing the latest batch of fudge.

Appearing contrite, Kenton approached Rosalie. "May I please speak with you outside for a moment?"

She nodded and led the way to the front sidewalk where he paused to face her.

"Miss Foxe, it's been said that the firmest friendships have been formed in mutual adversity."

She regarded him skeptically. "It's also been said that new friends, like one's best coat and patent leather boots, are only intended for holiday wear. At other times, they are neither serviceable nor at-all comfortable."

Kenton looked thoughtful. "Since this is a holiday, do you suppose you could find it in your heart to forgive my anger and accept my friendship—and my invitation—for the ball this evening?"

Following a pensive moment, she said, "I can on one condition—that you'll forgive me for breaking my word and going to Mr. Gowen's office when I promised I wouldn't. I was wrong."

He grinned. "It may be true that friendships are formed in mutual adversity, but they often owe longevity to mutual forgiveness. I'll come by for you at half past nine."

He'd turned to go when Rosalie thought of a better idea. "Mr. McCune! Wait!"

He spun back around, his look uncertain.

"Mr. McCune, why don't you come at half past eight? Then we can watch the Carnival Queen's parade from Aunt Lottie and Uncle Benjamin's front window."

A smile tilted his mustache. "I'll look forward to it!"

Heavy traffic in the confectionery made the day pass quickly for Rosalie. Guests were arriving in the city by the boatload and trainload for the Independence Day events, and it seemed they all needed to feed a sweet tooth. Work left her little time for private thought, but when she was alone in her room to prepare for the ball, she dropped to her knees beside her cot and folded her hands in prayer. "Dear Heavenly Father, I've sinned and need your forgiveness. I shouldn't have made a promise I meant to break, nor said things I didn't mean. Please help me to be more honest in the future. In Jesus' name, Amen." She started to rise, then added "And Lord, please let Uncle Benjamin, Aunt

Lottie, Mr. McCune and me have an enjoyable evening."

She quickly gathered up her robe and headed upstairs to bathe, then returned to her room to don a fancy dress for the ball—one of creamy white satin. The bodice was accented by a lacy overlay that formed a high collar, then draped over her shoulders and dipped to a vee in front where it ended in a point at her wide belt. The skirt had a modest train consisting of eight rows of ruffles, and she felt positively regal when wearing it. A fine white cord beneath the train allowed her to lift it for dancing, and by looping it over her right wrist, she could partially hide the fact that she didn't have full use of her arm.

From her travel jewelry case she took the locket her aunt and uncle had sent her upon graduation from Salem Academy this past spring—a piece that had belonged to her maternal grandmother who had lived her entire life in Michigan and had died when Rosalie was a small child. As she admired the charm of the old gold against the lacy bodice of her dress, she realized it held more meaning now that she'd spent some time in her grandmother's home state.

She had found her gloves and put the finishing touches on her hair when she heard a knock and went to let Kenton in. As she opened the door, the din of the happy street crowd and strains of a the band warming up for the start of the parade at the Opera House began to drift in. But she barely noticed them for the handsome figure standing before her.

Kenton looked well in everything from a baseball uniform to a morning suit, but she hadn't seen any man do such justice to a tailcoat and tie. He was holding a long-stemmed pink rose and hesitated a moment before offering it to her.

Kenton had anticipated the pleasing sight that would greet him when he saw Rosalie, but his expectations fell far short of the vision of loveliness being revealed to him now. He required a moment's thought to find the right words to accompany the rose.

"Miss Foxe, thou art fairer than the evening air clad in the beauty of a thousand stars. Forgive me for borrowing from Marlowe."

She gave a nervous laugh. "There's nothing at-all to forgive, Mr. McCune. I thank you for your borrowed words, and for this lovely blossom." When she had inhaled its sweet essence, she touched him lightly on the arm. "Come inside. From the sounds of things, the parade will be passing by any minute."

He willingly followed her upstairs to the apartment. In the sitting room, Ben had already arranged chairs by the windows overlooking Front Street, and Lottie had prepared a tray of small sandwiches and lemonade which she brought around as soon as Kenton and Rosalie were seated.

The street below, normally calm and dark on any other night, had been transformed by colored lights, redfire, Japanese lanterns, and hordes of masked onlookers. The carnival atmosphere was heightened by the firing of Roman candles and sky rockets, and the approach of the first contingent of the parade, a band dressed in Rube costumes striking forth the patriotic strains of John Philip Sousa. Kenton relished the look of enjoyment on Rosalie's face as the notes of *Stars and Stripes Forever* sailed out, and her pure delight when cake walkers in funny, fetching costumes and a throng of bicycles bedecked in red, white, and blue streamers made an appearance.

The centerpiece of the procession followed--the queen's carriage decked out in colored flowers, its harness trimmed in white as it carried the carnival queen and her two ladies in waiting who had been chosen from many pretty contenders during several days of voting. Kenton watched them closely, a tad proud that his own horse, Judge, had been chosen from several offered to pull the carriage. He was thinking how regal his plumed gelding looked, prancing down the street, when Rosalie took notice.

"You'd think they could have found a *white* horse for the queen's carriage."

Determined not to take offense, Kenton carefully explained. "Queen Edna had her choice of several horses, white ones included. She picked Judge."

Rosalie's face warmed with embarrassment. Unwilling to utter another troublesome word on the topic of Kenton's horse, she sipped her lemonade and let the subject drop.

When the last unit in the parade, a military band, had passed by, Kenton said, "I think it's time we all stroll down to the Opera House and wait for the queen."

Lottie waved him off. "You two go on. Ben and I will be along as soon as I finish here." She picked up the refreshment tray and headed for the kitchen.

Such a crowd was pressing around the entrance to the Opera House when Rosalie arrived with Kenton that she was glad she wasn't given to claustrophobia. As had been announced in the newspaper, the queen and her court made a brief appearance there when the parade broke up, then they were driven to the Park Place Hotel for a rest while their guests were being admitted to the main floor and galleries of the Opera House.

Rosalie had also read in the paper that the queen expected all guests to remove their masks upon completion of the parade, and as some were complying with her wish, Kenton pointed out an exception.

"I see Mr. Gowen and his Miss Hackbardt are still in black masks." He held the Opera House door for Rosalie as she paused to glance over her shoulder.

"How can you be certain it's them?"

"You'll see," he said confidently. "Now let's go inside."

When Rosalie stepped into the main hall, she was amazed at how little it resembled a theater. Chairs had been removed and a hardwood dance floor laid down. In addition, a throne had been set on the stage and draped with rich tapestries of silk in the national colors.

A fourteen piece orchestra had been tucked into the pit below the stage and was playing overtures while the galleries filled with townsfolk. She spotted Benjamin and Lottie in the front row and from the way they waved to her, she could tell they were already enjoying themselves.

When the strains of *America* issued forth, the queen made her entrance to the hall. A hush fell over the crowd when she was led across the floor by two dignitaries.

As Queen Edna passed Rosalie, she couldn't help but admire the royal gown. The sleeves and yoke of the bodice were encrusted with silver spangles and pearls while the rest of the dress, with its pleated front and skirt, was fashioned of cream peau de soie. Over it, the queen was wearing a mantle of royal purple velvet with a cream satin lining and ermine trim. It was fastened with a fancy silver clasp that glimmered as brightly as the gilt crown atop her head.

Behind her were two little blond pages—a boy and a

girl—holding her train. In their burgundy tights, velvet jackets, and caps, the children stole Rosalie's heart.

She nudged Kenton. "Have you ever seen anything so adorable?"

As murmurs of affection echoed around them, Kenton said, "From the sounds of it, most of us haven't."

The children were followed by the ladies in waiting, both wearing pink crepe de chene and silk. As they took their seats on either side of Queen Edna's throne, Rosalie became aware that the couple still wearing black masks were now standing almost in front of her and Kenton, and they were indeed Miss Hackbardt and Mr. Gowen.

She tried to put them out of her mind as the prime minister of the evening, Mr. Thomas Bates, presented the queen.

"Ladies and gentlemen, her royal highness, Queen Edna!"

Enthusiastic applause, cheers, and whistles filled the air. After the queen took a gracious bow, the hall grew quiet again and Mr. Bates expressed words of welcome, concluding a few minutes later.

"The queen would like to extend her greetings to each of her honored guests in person, and will now leave the stage to move among you."

As the guests on the ballroom floor began parting to make room for the queen and her court, Rosalie found herself in even closer proximity to Clarissa and Mr. Gowen than before.

Kenton noticed, too. Taking Rosalie's hand in his, he whispered, "Let's find another place to stand."

Before they could ease away, Rosalie was accidentally pushed into Clarissa, causing the other woman's right shoe to come off.

Rosalie was instantly contrite. "I'm so sorry, Miss Hackbardt."

Clarissa snatched up her slipper. "You should watch where you're stepping!"

At the moment Clarissa slipped her foot into the satin shoe, Rosalie saw that a coin had been fastened inside the heel—a *gold* coin.

"Let me see that!" she demanded.

Clarissa scowled at her, then turned away.

Rosalie caught her by the arm. "You've hidden my double eagle inside your shoe!"

Clarissa wrenched free. "You're mad as a hatter, Miss Foxe, now leave me alone!"

Nearby guests began to whisper and stare.

Rosalie turned to Kenton. "She's got a gold coin in her right shoe. I saw it!"

Gowen pulled a candy from his pocket and offered it to Rosalie with a smile. "Have one of my butterscotch drops, Miss Foxe. It's guaranteed to chase away your delusions and put you in good humor."

Rosalie put palm out. "No offense, Mr. Gowen, but the day I eat one of your candies is the day—"

Kenton finished for her. "It's the day you find the coin you gave in payment for your aunt and uncle's store, isn't it, Miss Foxe?"

Cutler Gowen pulled off his mask, his smile vanishing. "Mr. McCune, Miss Foxe, your accusations about Miss Hackbardt and some twenty-dollar gold piece are getting tiresome." To Kenton, he said, "If your lady friend can't behave more civilly, take her home before she ruins the evening for the rest of us."

"I have a better idea." Kenton focused on Clarissa. "Why not simply take off your right shoe so we can all see whether or not you have Miss Foxe's double eagle?"

Before Clarissa could answer, Queen Edna approached Kenton accompanied by her entourage. "Mr. McCune, I'm so pleased you're here! I've been wanting to thank you in person for loaning your horse for the parade."

While Kenton's attention was on Queen Edna, Rosalie saw that Clarissa and Gowen were slipping away. Releasing her hand from Kenton's, she started to follow, but several couples blocked her way. By the time she emerged from the throng, Clarissa and Gowen had disappeared. She hurried down the stairs and out onto the Front Street walk. They were but a few yards ahead of her. Half running, she caught up with Clarissa and stepped hard on her right heel.

"Ouch!" the woman cried, her slipper flying off.

Gowen started after it but Rosalie scooped it up before he could get a hand on it.

Clarissa hopped on her left foot, clutching her right heel with her gloved hand as she focused angrily on Rosalie. "Give me back my shoe!"

"Not until I see the coin!"

"I said, give me back my shoe!"

Unmindful of Clarissa's plea, Rosalie loosened the coin from the gum that was holding it in place and raised it to the light of the street lamp.

It was only a ten-dollar gold piece.

"I . . . I'm sorry," she said, warmth flooding her face as she handed the coin and the shoe to Clarissa.

Again, Gowen offered Rosalie a piece of candy. "You really ought to eat this butterscotch drop. It's guaranteed to turn a sour moment sweet." He pressed it into her empty hand and wrapped her fingers about it.

Still stunned with disappointment, Rosalie mumbled, "I . . . uh . . . excuse me." She backed away discreetly.

Having put on her shoe, Clarissa linked her arm with Gowen's. As the couple departed, Rosalie could tell Gowen was quietly lecturing Clarissa but she couldn't make out the words. Desperate to know what was being said, she tucked the hard candy into her pocket and followed in the shadows of the buildings. Only some of his words were audible.

". . . shoe is no place to keep your money . . . let me put it . . . "

As Gowen was speaking, Clarissa paused, looking over her shoulder.

Rosalie shrank back into the recessed doorway of Votruba's Harness Shop, distinctly hearing her say, "I think someone's following us."

Gowen clearly replied, "I don't see anyone. Come along, dear. We have our own private celebration to tend to. Tomorrow, the American Candy Company will be the talk of the town."

When their footsteps had receded, Rosalie peeked around the harness shop window, wondering what Gowen had meant. She was trying to decide whether to follow them or return to the ball when her uncle's voice startled her.

"There you are, niece! We've been looking for you!"

She turned to face him.

Lottie was standing beside her brother. "You worried us half to death, Rosalie!"

"I'm sorry, Aunt Lottie. I didn't mean to. I have something to tell you!" Rosalie linked her arms with theirs, words of explanation rolling off her tongue as they headed back toward the Opera House.

Moments later, Kenton found them and Rosalie repeated what she had told her relatives. She was finishing as the four of them reached the second floor of the hall. "I just wish I knew what Mr. Gowen meant when he said the American Candy Company will be the talk of the town tomorrow."

Lilting strains of a Strauss waltz began to fill the air and Kenton offered Rosalie a smile. "I think we should forget about Mr. Gowen and enjoy the evening."

Lottie said, "By all means. I'm still waiting to see the two of you waltz."

Ben nudged Kenton toward the dance floor. "Go on, or I'll never hear the end of it."

He offered Rosalie his arm, and as she walked out onto the ballroom floor, she was determined to follow his advice—and his lead.

The limitations of her right shoulder and arm that had caused moments of awkwardness with dance partners in the past proved no obstacle to Kenton who simply placed both hands at her waist and stepped off in time to the music. He whisked her about the room as if they'd been dancing together for years. When he released his hold to twirl her around, he did so with such strength and elegance it was impossible for her to misstep. Other couples watched in awe, moving back to give them free reign of the dance floor. Even the queen and her court, who had moved to a settee in the corner of the dance floor to receive guests, had paused in their royal duties to look on in wonderment.

In Kenton's arms, time melted as swiftly as a spoonful of sugar in sassafras tea. When the last note of the last waltz had faded away, he walked her home behind Ben and Lottie who had stayed to watch every minute of the ball.

Ben paused at the bottom of the apartment stairs to consult his watch. "This is either the longest, or the shortest night I've ever known."

A firecracker sounded about a block away, prompting Lottie to comment. "It's the shortest—or will be if that noise keeps up. Good night Kenton. Good night, Rosalie."

She kissed her aunt and uncle on the cheek. "See you in the morning—*later* this morning, I mean."

When they had gone, she turned to Kenton. Even in the wan light of the street lamp he was more handsome than when he'd come to fetch her, for now they had shared a congenial evening and the effect was visible in his tender gaze, and in the smile beneath his mustache. But while her conscious thought was of this charming fellow with the glib tongue, a tiny corner of her mind wondered what new problems would surface for her aunt and uncle and their business on the morrow.

Kenton took both of Rosalie's hands in his, realizing he no longer regarded her as the North Carolina miss he'd escorted to the ball as a favor to friends. Now that he'd traveled a mile of circles around the dance floor with her, he saw before him a beautiful young lady who refused to let her physical limitations keep her from enjoying life—or from trying to resolve the difficulties concerning her relatives. As he lifted her hands to his lips and brushed kisses against them, he silently thanked the Lord that she hadn't departed on the southbound train, praying that together they would soon solve the Marshalls' problem.

The low roll of distant thunder interrupted his thoughts turning them to yet a different consideration. He released her hands. "I hope rain won't spoil the celebration tomorrow."

Free of his touch, Rosalie regretted that the evening had come to an end, then suffered a twinge of guilt remembering her affection for Willy Jo. Putting old friendships out of her mind for the moment, she said, "You'll come and watch the parade with us if it's not canceled, won't you?"

A raindrop kissed her cheek. Kenton resisted the urge to do the same. "I'll come by tomorrow afternoon, rain or shine. Good night!"

Rosalie watched him disappear in the faint yellow haze of the street lights, then closed and bolted the door against the increasing rumble of the approaching storm. In her room, she took her time putting away her formal gown, pausing to remove from her pocket the candy Gowen had given her. On a whim she popped the butterscotch drop into her mouth despite Kenton's prediction that she would not eat an American Candy Company candy until the day she had found the coin she had given in payment for the mortgage. Begrudgingly, she had to admit the butterscotch drop was as tasty as any of the hard candies her aunt and uncle produced.

As it melted on her tongue her thoughts shifted to the most pleasurable portion of the evening—the hours after midnight. Gowen seemed to be justified in claiming his candy could turn a sour moment sweet.

By the time she had donned her nightgown, brushed out her hair, and washed her face, thunder was cracking so loudly she knew she wouldn't be able to sleep. Taking from her trunk a pen, stationery, and a book for a lap desk, she propped herself against her pillows and started to pen a letter to her sister. With artful skill, she created lovely word pictures of Traverse City, made no mention of the problems regarding the mortgage, and included only a brief reference to Kenton McCune.

. . . Aunt Lottie, Uncle Benjamin, a lawyer friend of theirs, and I attended an Independence Day Ball this evening . . .

Long accustomed to the fact that Willy Jo wasn't the letter-writing kind and that communication between them was completely reliant on messages passed along by other family members, she included a note to him at the end.

P.S. Sometime when you're out riding, you might travel in the direction of the Winthrops and deliver my greetings to Willy Jo. Please tell him all is well with me here in the North Country and that I have thought of him often.

She resisted the urge to add *up until the last couple of days.*

With the worst of the storm over and the clock reading half past three in the morning, she set her letter, pen, and book aside and crawled between the sheets. Her sleep was intermittent, disturbed by further storms.

Rain continued throughout the morning causing cancellation of the bicycle races and Caledonian games that had been scheduled to start at nine, and all but eliminating customer traffic in the store. At noon the dark clouds began to clear, the sun peeked through, and word was passed along the street that the parade scheduled for one o'clock would begin on time.

Rosalie was puzzled when business didn't improve with the weather and the increasing number of visitors mingling on the walks. And she was perplexed when Kenton breezed through the door at a quarter past twelve with a scowl on his face. He was dressed in his baseball uniform

71

and she wondered if his game had been canceled due to a flooded field. He wasted no time in revealing a different reason for his frown.

"Ben, Lottie, Miss Foxe, have you taken a look down Front Street since the weather cleared?" Met with silence and shrugs, he gravely advised, "You'd better come out here."

Rosalie shadowed him to the front walk, her aunt and uncle close behind. Along the street, vendors had set up stands to hawk red lemonade, popcorn, roasted nuts, waffles, and fresh fruit, but these were not the object of his concern. Following the point of his finger, she discovered a cart about a block away gaily decorated with a red, white, and blue awning and skirt. Around it were gathered dozens of visitors. A huge sign explained the reason for its popularity.

American Candy Co.
Free sweets!

Rosalie was beside herself. "So *that's* why hardly anybody is coming into the store."

Ben shook his finger in the direction of the candy cart. "Gowen can't do that!"

Kenton said, "He can, and he is."

Lottie fussed with the neck strap of her apron. "We've got to do something!"

Ben grumbled. "What? Give away our fudge?"

Rosalie's mind was in a whirl. "Yes! We could give away little samples along with certificates enticing customers to come in and buy a pound of fudge and get a second pound free."

Ben shook his head. "I won't make a penny that way!"

Lottie reasoned, "Maybe not, but at least we'd be able

to cover the cost of supplies. The way it looks now, our fudge will likely go stale before we can sell it all."

Kenton said, "I think your niece has the right idea."

Rosalie grew enthusiastic. "I'll decorate a basket in red, white, and blue streamers and fill it with the fudge cut into bite-size pieces. Aunt Lottie, you write out the certificates. Then, when the crowd gathers to watch the parade, I'll go up and down both sides of the street giving fudge and certificates to all who want them."

Lottie turned to go inside. "I'd better start writing."

Three quarters of an hour later, with Kenton's help, Rosalie had purchased two egg baskets and yards of paper streamers from Wilhelm's Dry Goods. Soon, she had finished decorating and filling one of them with small pieces of vanilla and chocolate fudge—with and without walnuts—and dozens of certificates. Together, they began handing them out while Lottie and Ben prepared the second basket.

Busy as Rosalie was, she paused from time to time to watch the parade. The queen's barouche was one of the early entries, carrying the attractive young woman whose purple robe and gold crown made a pleasing sight. Despite Rosalie's feelings about grey geldings, she silently admitted he looked smart drawing Miss Wilhelm's coach.

Following the royal carriage were two elaborate floats from the Catholic school. The first one carried a number of boys in costumes representing different nations with Uncle Sam in the center. Immediately behind it was another filled with dainty misses in picturesque national dress of many lands.

Not far behind, twelve-foot-high lumber wheels gaily

trimmed with bunting showed what life in Caldwell and Lowdon's lumber woods might be on a holiday. Trailing it was a chariot covered by mirrors and gold paint. It carried the band of the Silver Brothers Show. Their teams of trained dogs and ponies followed, all in line.

Rosalie had turned her back to the procession to hand out more samples when Kenton tapped her shoulder and pointed. "You'd better take a look."

A wave of anger rushed through her when she caught sight of the float to which he referred. A wagon had been dressed with a bunting of patriotic colors and topped with a red and white sign—*AMERICAN CANDY CO. QUEEN*. Beneath it on a throne covered with blue paper flowers sat Clarissa Hackbardt in a white dress and flaming red cloak. A crown of silver topped her head. At her feet were mounds of wrapped candy which she tossed by the handfuls into the crowd.

Children rushed past Rosalie to fetch the treats, knocking the basket out of her hand and pushing her off balance. Kenton caught her about the waist, preventing her from falling, but he couldn't keep the fudge from flying into the dirt and the certificates from scattering across the street, only to land beneath the wheels of Clarissa's float.

The Candy Queen smiled fiendishly at Rosalie's plight.

The act set Rosalie's blood boiling and she clamped her jaw shut to silence the unladylike reprisal on her tongue.

"Never mind her," said Kenton, stooping to gather up the ruined goods. "I'll go and see if the other basket is ready."

Rosalie tried to focus on the parade but angry thoughts prevented her from appreciating the dainty white swan cart of the Traverse City Wagon Works and the examples of their wagons rolling along behind. Even a horseless electric carriage advertising Steinberg's Grand with the legend, *Traverse City and Old Mission R'y*, didn't amuse her, though all around her were laughing.

Kenton returned with the new basket as the automobile rolled by. Together, they were able to pass out most of the fudge and certificates before the parade came to an end.

When the crowd broke up, he said, "I'll come by at half past eight to go with you to the fireworks. I've got to get to the baseball field now."

She bid him good bye and returned to the confectionery, pleased to see that with the parade over, customers were starting to redeem the certificates she and Kenton had given away. In mid-afternoon a young blond girl of about thirteen dressed in a riding helmet, jodhpurs, and boots, came into the store. The sight of her sparked thoughts of Vanda Mae. For a moment, Rosalie wondered how her horse-crazy younger sister was spending Independence Day.

The press of customers quickly brought Rosalie's thoughts back to the job at hand. She helped her aunt behind the candy counter a few minutes longer until a band struck up a concert in the street outside the shop.

Lottie nudged her toward the door. "Go on out there and listen. It's time you took a break." Shoving a penny into her hand, she added, "And treat yourself to some red lemonade. You deserve it!"

Rosalie went willingly, thankful for the break from the close air indoors and the cooling effect of the lemonade. The band—Harrington's Band according to the banner it displayed—was better than most. She thoroughly enjoyed their concert of patriotic tunes. *The Star Spangled Banner,*

America, and *Yankee Doodle* topped their program, but she couldn't believe her ears when the conductor lit into a rousing rendition of *Marching Through Georgia.*

Every fiber of her being tensed. Unmindful of anything but the indignation simmering inside, she stormed into the confectionery.

"I hate this place!"

Lottie turned to her with alarm.

A woman customer swung around to face her, too. "I beg your pardon, young lady?"

Instantly regretful, Rosalie choked out the words, "Nothing . . . nothing at-all."

She ran through the shop to her room at the back. Shutting and bolting herself inside, she leaned against the door.

A wave of homesickness swept over her drowning her in a sea of self-pity. Hearing that Yankee song seemed to bring the troubles of the past few days to a head. Tears began to roll down her cheeks. She buried her face in her apron and slumped to the floor, muttering as she sobbed. "I wish . . . I were back in North Carolina . . . in the mountains. Oh, Mama, how I miss you!"

A knock sounded quietly on her door, then Lottie spoke, her voice laden with concern. "Rosalie, are you all right, dear?"

Her sympathetic tone only made Rosalie cry harder.

Lottie jiggled the door handle. "Let me in, dear."

Rosalie dabbed her eyes and got to her feet, still unable to stop crying and unwilling to obey.

Her aunt knocked again. *"Please* let me in or I'll have to ask Ben to take your door off the hinges."

Drying her cheeks and blowing her nose into her handkerchief, she unlocked the door.

Lottie enfolded her in a soft, warm hug and for a moment Rosalie imagined she was home in Shani's arms. The realization that Shani was hundreds of miles away caused new tears to leak out.

Her aunt released her, drying Rosalie's cheeks with the corner of her own apron. "What's troubling you, child? Surely it can't be as bad as all this."

Rosalie cleared her throat, replying in a shaky voice. "Did you hear . . . that awful song the band played?"

Lottie shook her head. "What would that be, dear?"

Regaining her composure, Rosalie told her, "*Marching Through Georgia*. Imagine them playing such a piece on the Fourth of July!"

"No offense was intended."

Rosalie turned away, pacing to the other end of her small room. Faintly, in the distance, she could hear the strains of *Battle Hymn of the Republic*. She pressed her hands over her ears.

Lottie left her, returning moments later when the song had ended. "Come with me, now. There's something I want you to hear." Taking her by the hand, she led Rosalie through the store and out onto the walk.

The band conductor looked at her and smiled, then turned to his musicians, raised his baton and struck up *Dixie*, following it immediately with a sentimental rendition of *Way Down Upon the Swanee River*.

Rosalie wanted to cry again, but she managed to keep back her tears. When the concert had ended and she returned to the empty store, she pondered the troubles still facing her aunt and uncle over their mortgage. Into her mind flowed one compelling thought.

No matter how much I miss North Carolina, I won't

leave Michigan until I find the coin Clarissa stole!

Nearly three weeks later when Rosalie awoke on a Sunday morning, she couldn't help noticing the soreness in her good shoulder. Setting aside the Joseph Conrad novel she'd been reading when she'd fallen asleep, she rotated her shoulder slowly to loosen the tense muscles, muttering to herself. "That's what I get for carrying a basket full of fudge to the dock three times a day. It's a good thing it's helping some, too. The way Gowen is operating, hardly anybody would bother coming up to the store if I didn't bribe them with certificates for free fudge."

The image of the American Candy Company carts came to mind with their awnings and skirts of red, white, and blue. From the Fourth of July on, she'd seen them every day outside the depot and parked by the dock where hundreds of passengers came off the steamers. She grew angry each time she thought of Gowen stealing customers from her aunt and uncle. In an effort to keep patrons frequenting their store, Rosalie had continued to hand out samples of fudge and certificates for a free pound with each pound purchased from the confectionery.

With the continued competition and the necessity for discounts, income was barely keeping pace with expenses, but as she dressed for breakfast, she said a prayer of thanks that for now, the business was surviving. Later, when she sat down to pancakes and bacon with her Aunt Lottie and Uncle Benjamin, other problems occupied her mind—frustration over her inability to locate the nicked double eagle and anxiety over what would become of her aunt and uncle at month's end.

Curiosity was eating Rosalie up inside over the fragment of conversation she'd overheard between Mr. Gowen and Clarissa Hackbardt. She felt it was leading her to make another visit to Cutler Gowen's office—to search the drawer she'd been unable to investigate; but she hadn't dared brave another early morning venture there after the trouble encountered on the first visit. And no reasonable possibilities had come to mind for further investigation of the young woman Rosalie so disliked. According to the Doyle sisters, Clarissa had taken a room near Cutler Gowen's home on Sixth Street and Rosalie was inclined to believe that the troublesome young woman had rid herself of the coin long ago.

As for Kenton McCune, Rosalie had seen him only on the rides he had provided to and from St. Francis Church on Sundays. At those times he had reported no progress forestalling the foreclosure on the mortgage. When Rosalie had criticized him for not taking a stronger stand with Cutler Gowen, her aunt and uncle had skillfully diverted conversation to another topic. In the privacy of the apartment, they refused to discuss the issue with her, preferring to pretend nothing at all was amiss.

But Rosalie could no longer pretend the problem didn't exist. Swallowing the last of her pancakes, she set down her fork to speak of it now, determined not to be put off.

"Aunt Lottie, Uncle Benjamin, today is the twenty-second of July. Do you realize that in a little more than a week, Mr. Gowen is going to toss us out of here, like bad pennies to a pauper?"

Ben folded his napkin and laid it aside. "How can he? He must know you made the payment. Certainly, the man's got conscience enough to—"

Rosalie interrupted. "Uncle Benjamin, don't you

understand? That man is so low, he could walk under a trundle bed with his top hat on!"

Ben smiled. "I can't believe that, but even if he *is* as bad as you believe, he could suffer a change of heart. The Lord can work miracles, you know." He stacked his plate on Lottie's, carried them to the sink, and began filling the dish pan with water.

Lottie spoke as she slipped napkins back into their rings. "That's right, dear. The Lord will provide."

Rosalie took her dirty plate to the sink. "You two sound just like Mama. She's always saying those things." Picking up the dish rag, she wiped drops of maple syrup from the table, then turned again to her aunt and uncle. "But there's something else she says, too."

Lottie adjusted the neck strap on her apron as she focused on Rosalie.

Ben turned to face her, wiping the dish soap from his hands and pushing up his glasses.

Rosalie continued. "Mama says the Lord helps those who help themselves."

Ben wrapped his arm about her waist. "We know, niece. And we know, too, that the three of us—and Mr. McCune—have done everything humanly possible to solve our problem with Mr. Gowen. Now, it truly *is* in the Lord's hands."

CHAPTER

6

North Carolina

Willy Jo unbuttoned his collar as Fergus Foxe drove the both of them out of Salem and headed home at the end of another hot week at his lumber yard. Despite Vanda Mae's prayers, and his own, three and a half long weeks had passed since he'd seen his daddy or his home—three and a half weeks since Fergus had offered shelter at Tanglewood and a position at Foxe Brothers selling lumber, cement, shingles, and other building supplies.

The lengthy drive to and from work seemed at first an undue burden. Like many others, Willy Jo hadn't understood Fergus Foxe's preference to spend a significant amount of time on the road traveling to and from his country estate each day, rather than staying week nights in the city. Now, after nearly a month in Fergus's employ and in residence at his horse farm, Willy Jo knew the reasons. Evenings at Tanglewood, free of city noise and traffic, were next to heaven after dealing with construction schedules, supply problems, and customer demands. And the winding route home, over hills and through woods, offered a release all its own when taken in a fine buggy drawn by a handsome team, strong and fresh and ready for the challenge.

The long drive also afforded Willy Jo plenty of time to think. Though he longed desperately to return to his father's farm, the instant he considered it, his stomach soured. He didn't miss the arguments, the criticisms, the constant reminders that he couldn't do anything well enough to please his daddy. And he would never apologize for refusing to sell April to Eck Danvers.

Fergus Foxe interrupted his thoughts. "I saw your daddy today."

The words, "Did he ask about me?" slipped out before Willy Jo could stop them.

It seemed like a long time before Fergus Foxe replied. "We had a pleasant conversation about you. I told him what a fine job you've been doing since you came to work for me. Told him if he has need of you on his farm, you're in no way obligated to remain in my employ."

Willy Jo couldn't help wishing that just once he'd heard his own father tell him what a fine job he was doing, but it was a foolish fancy. From the sounds of it, his daddy hadn't even wanted to know how he was!

Fergus continued. "Son, I know you and I come from different customs where our church-going is concerned. But we pray to the same God. He can smooth out the troubles with your daddy."

Willy Jo's warm face grew even hotter. "With all due respect, sir, I've prayed every prayer I could think of since you took me in, but from the sounds of it, nothing's changed where my daddy's concerned."

Fergus laid a hand on his shoulder. "We both need to keep praying."

Privately, Willy Jo wondered what good that would do. Weary of the problem with his father, he turned his thoughts in a different direction. At least some good had come of his troubles. Vanda Mae was enjoying her new horse. Watching her ride April, and mounting the horse himself after dinner each evening to ride across Foxe's four-hundred-acre estate with Vanda Mae and her daddy were two small pleasures he anticipated at the end of the day. A third pleasure was seeing Tassie's baby grow strong. He relished the sight of the mare and filly romping in the pasture. He was anticipating the scene when Fergus Foxe turned up the drive to find Vanda Mae mounted on Hurricane, a saddled April and Firelight at her side. She wasted no time approaching them.

"Daddy, dinner won't be ready for at least an hour. Shani had to go to Winston, to Uncle George and Aunt Ophelia's to see Pearl. She's only just come home." She named her father's brother and his wife, the employers of Shani's oldest daughter who was suffering a difficult pregnancy—the same aunt and uncle with whom Vanda Mae and Rosalie had lived during the school year to attend Salem Academy with their cousin, Lida Jean.

Fergus Foxe scowled. "Pearl didn't have her baby already, did she?"

Vanda Mae shook her head. "False alarm. With dinner so late, I thought the three of us could ride now. By the time we've finished eating, it'll be too dark. Besides, I plan to write to Rosalie after dinner."

Fergus smiled. "You and Willy Jo go ahead. I'm going to take my bath *before* dinner, for a change."

Willy Jo boarded April and when they had returned Firelight to the stable, he headed for his favorite path beside the Yadkin River. Vanda Mae followed him for awhile, then continued on ahead when he dismounted to sit by the water and watch it flow past. She'd been gone only a minute or two when he had the eerie feeling someone was lurking nearby.

"Vannie-Mae?"

He scanned the woods. Finding no sign of her, he hitched April to a tree limb and stretched out on the river bank, leaning back against a tree stump.

He relished these rare moments of solitude. Putting away thoughts of his father, he contemplated the nature of the place—the gentle sway of green rushes and silver reeds, the smell of the muskrats, the low buzz of dragon fly wings as they darted hither and yon. Even the song of the cicadas improved when muted by the wild grape vines and holly along the banks.

He left these thoughts at the unmistakable sound of Vanda Mae riding toward him as she kept up a patter of one-way conversation with Hurricane. He watched her through the trees. How pretty she sat atop the grey gelding. Her long hair was caught to the side in a blue satin ribbon. He was glad she hadn't gone the way of most girls at sixteen, piling her long tresses atop her head, for he like the way they bounced against her shirt with each step of her horse. Her shoulders were square, her back straight and leaning slightly forward from her narrow waist. Only her toes were in the stirrup leaving her heels angled sharply down in the way of a good rider in a hunt seat. He'd told himself his rides with her and her daddy were borne strictly of the pleasure he derived from good horseflesh and his love of the river but he hadn't been completely honest. He valued the friendship he was developing with Vanda Mae, and the growing respect between him and her daddy.

As the young girl came closer, he noticed that her lighthearted horse chat had ended and she wore a contemplative expression. Dismounting, she set her hands on her hips and marched over to where he was resting.

"Willy Jo Winthrop, why don't you just go home and take April with you!"

He sprang to his feet, words of protestation on his tongue, but she continued.

"The only reason you're staying at Tanglewood is because of that horse. Well, you can have her back! I don't want her any—"

"Vannie-Mae Foxe, hush up!"

Her jaw clamped shut.

He wagged his finger. "You don't know a thing about me, or you'd have figured out why I'm still at Tanglewood. But I'll tell you this. It doesn't have much to do with April!"

"It has *everything* to do with April! And your daddy."

"Not quite."

"Why did he insist on selling her? Tell me that!"

Willy Jo sighed. "Because we don't get along. Haven't gotten along in years."

"Then you ought to start."

"It's not that simple."

"Why not? You just walk up to your daddy and say, 'From now on, we ought to get along.'"

He started to chuckle. "You're crazy as a betsy bug!"

"Am not! It makes perfect sense!"

He laughed harder and she joined in.

Moments later, she said, "That's the first time I've heard you laugh since the day you came here to stay. You ought to make a habit of it, Willy Jo. You're much more pleasant to be around when you're in good humor."

"So are you. Now do me a favor. Sit down and be still so I can rest a mite longer. Goodness knows I've put in a hard week at your daddy's business." He stretched out as he had been before she came.

She chose a spot close to the water a few feet away from him. Fidgeting with a grape vine, she began picking leaves and tossing them in the Yadkin.

Willy Jo watched her through slitted eyes. Her mouth was naturally upturned even in thought, and her movements graceful as she flung leaves out into the river. This fascination for the younger Foxe girl caused him shame over his heart's betrayal. If Rosalie were here, would he be distracted by her younger sister?

His ponderings reached no conclusion for they were interrupted by the sound of the dinner bell ringing in the distance—Shani's warning that her meal would be served in a quarter of an hour. He expected Vanda Mae to challenge him to a race back to the stable, but she remained silent as she boarded Hurricane, and instead of trotting, kept her pace to a walk, staying even with him as they crossed the large meadow leading up to the stable.

He sensed something unusual in the way Gaspar was waiting for them outside the stable door. The hired hand knew they enjoyed grooming their own horses after a ride, but he reached for Hurricane's rein, then April's, his dark eyes sparkling.

"Shani wishes you both to go to the house at once. I will take care of your horses tonight."

Vanda Mae climbed down. "Why? I'd like to know—"

Gaspar cut her off. "*Señorita* Foxe, please do as I say. *Pronto!*"

With a shrug of her shoulders she headed for the manor

house. Willy Jo caught up with her, holding open the door to the back room. Much to his surprise, they found themselves face to face with Mrs. Foxe. Mother and daughter eagerly embraced.

"Mama, what are you doing here? I didn't expect to see you till the end of August!"

Standing back, Minnie's focus turned to Willy Jo. "I guess I couldn't wait that long."

At that moment, his mother and younger brother--who'd grown an inch since he'd left for the mountains—entered the room. Before Willy Jo could even greet them, Vanda Mae was in a flurry.

"Bobby Dan! Come outside! You've got to see Tassie's foal!"

When they had left, Willy Jo took his mother's hands in his, aware of her careworn look. "Hello, Mama. This is a surprise."

"I've come to take you home with me and Bobby Dan."

Willy Jo released her hands, lowering his gaze. "I can't go. Not yet."

"Then drive me and Bobby Dan home and at least say hello to your father."

Looking directly into her sad eyes, he said, "I'm sorry. I can't."

She sighed. "That's going to make things mighty awkward come Sunday, Willy Jo."

He waited to hear her explanation, but the opportunity vanished when Fergus Foxe joined them. Looking refreshed from his bath, he put his arm about his wife's waist as he addressed Willy Jo's mother. "Welcome back, Virginia. I understand you-all are going to be here for Sunday dinner." Giving his wife a squeeze, he added, "Do you

87

realize this is the first time in years our two families will be together on Minnie's birthday?"

Feeling trapped, Willy Jo backed away. "I won't be here, sir. It would spoil the party. Now, if you'll excuse me?" He'd taken but one step toward the door when Fergus stopped him.

"Son, these ladies have been fretting about you since the day you left home. They've come back from the mountains strictly on your account. The least you can do is lend them your presence at Sunday dinner."

Willy Jo thought a moment, then swallowed hard. "All right, sir. I'll be here." He silently added, *but it's a recipe for disaster.*

Virginia smiled. "Thank you, son. Now, are you sure you won't drive me and Bobby Dan home?"

When he made no immediate reply, Fergus said, "Gaspar will do it. In fact," he paused to glance out the window, "he's bringing the buggy around this very minute."

With a flick of her hand, Virginia told Willy Jo, "Go and fetch your brother, will you?"

He ducked out the back door. His brother was doing a handstand on the top rail of the fence that enclosed the pasture while Vanda Mae applauded. Willy Jo gave a whistle--the three-note call he and his brother had used from childhood—and they immediately started toward him.

As they drew near, Willy Jo couldn't help feeling a trifle piqued at his brother's continuous showing off—now running ahead of Vanda Mae to do three handsprings in succession, then making an about face to perform three more, landing face to face with her. She laughed at his antics and gave him a shove which sent him into another round of handsprings.

Impatient, Willy Jo whistled once more. His brother said something to Vanda Mae, then headed toward him while she stayed behind.

Bobby Dan's new height was reflected in his assertive attitude toward Willy Jo. "You'd better make your peace with Daddy come Sunday, 'cause I've got no desire to spend the rest of my summer on the farm." He stomped off toward the drive before Willy Jo could reply.

Vanda Mae joined him, her enthusiasm for Bobby Dan obvious. "Did you see your brother's acrobatics? He says he's been practicing day and night!"

She rambled on until they reached the drive where Virginia stood in conversation with Fergus and Minnie beside the carriage.

Willy Jo's mother put her gloved finger to her lips and touched it to his cheek. "See you Sunday, son. I'm counting on you not to let anything spoil Mrs. Foxe's birthday party."

He nodded, helping her into the carriage. Bobby Dan climbed in beside her, sparing Willy Jo neither a word nor a glance. Instead, he pulled a clown face for Vanda Mae who giggled like a child as Gaspar drove away.

CHAPTER

7

Michigan

Sunday morning, a week later, as Rosalie climbed the stairs that led from her bedroom behind the candy shop to the apartment above, she couldn't help feeling low. The candy business was off more than ever. Only two days remained until Cutler Gowen would repossess the building. Worst of all, her aunt and uncle had fallen into almost total silence.

She hoped things would improve before Mr. McCune picked them up for church. Last night he'd rung up to invite all three of them to join him for Sunday dinner after services, promising to take them to a special, undisclosed location. Rosalie prayed her aunt's and her uncle's sour moods wouldn't spoil the affair, even though she herself wanted more than ever to scold their lawyer friend for his inaction regarding Cutler Gowen. But when she had expressed such sentiments to Benjamin and Lottie last evening, they had made her promise she wouldn't mention the subject today.

As she opened the apartment door, a hint of fresh coffee and pancakes hot off the griddle greeted her. Despite the enticing aromas, she paused in the small parlor. Her uncle was finally talking again—more loudly than usual. The anger in his voice caught her by surprise.

"I told you not to send the girl to Gowen's office with the payment in the first place, but you didn't listen. You never listen."

Rosalie knew she should step into the kitchen, but instead she remained frozen in place.

Lottie responded calmly. "I wonder where Kenton is taking us for dinner today."

Ben went on. "We should have let Rosalie go home when she wanted, but you insisted on sending Kenton after her."

Lottie spoke again. "I'm glad of it, too. They got along so beautifully on the evening of the ball, it's a shame they haven't seen one another socially since. I'm glad they'll be together for dinner this afternoon."

Rosalie was about to make her presence known, but her uncle's heated words prevented her.

"Don't you understand? Rosalie's miserable here because of all our troubles—and weary from carrying that candy basket to the dock every day. But *you haven't even noticed!*"

A silent moment lapsed, then Lottie replied evenly, "I have too noticed, just like I'm noticing you, now. And what I'm hearing, Ben, is that after four weeks of telling us it's all in God's hands—after a month of claiming we've done everything possible to solve our problems with Mr. Gowen—you're scared to death we're really going to lose this place."

Rosalie didn't wait for her uncle's reply. Carrying her shoulders as erect as she could, she marched into the kitchen, a smile on her face. "Good morning Aunt Lottie, good morning Uncle Benjamin!" She kissed each of them on the cheek.

91

They bid her good morning, then her uncle started to get up to hold her chair.

She put a staying hand on his shoulder and seated herself. "Uncle Benjamin, it's evident to me that you're about as discouraged as a rice planter up a salt river right now."

He almost smiled.

She went on. "And there's something else I couldn't help noticing, too." She gestured toward the open kitchen window. "The sun's bright as angel's eyes. The sky is blue like the sea of a dream—"

Ben pushed up his glasses. "You've been reading Joseph Conrad—that part about the sea."

Rosalie chuckled. Her uncle had been suggesting she read his favorite author since she'd first arrived in Traverse City and she'd only done so in the past couple of days. "Yes, I've been reading Mr. Conrad's stories. And you know what I think he'd tell you if he were here right now?"

Ben regarded her with interest.

"He'd say a foul wind may be astir, and a tempest may be brewing, but what you've got right now is the calm before the storm, and you might as well enjoy it till it's time to batten down the hatches."

Lottie took a platter of pancakes from the warming oven and passed them to her brother. "The girl's right, Ben. Now let's eat. Mr. McCune will be here before you know it."

When services had ended at St. Francis Church, Kenton helped Rosalie into the front seat of his rig while Ben and Lottie settled in the back. Climbing up beside the North Carolina miss, he drove along Cass toward the bay, regretful that the infrequent conversations between them since the Carnival Ball had been contentious, leaving their rapport tenuous.

He was aware of some tension between the Marshalls, too, but chose to ignore it, pondering instead the pleasant essence of peach blossoms emanating from the young woman beside him. Stealing a glance her way, he saw that the warm breeze was teasing at the ivory lace on her collar, riffling the tails of the pink satin ribbon tied in a bow about her elegant neck. He'd never seen a satin ribbon quite like hers—with the ends fancily crimped and gathered—but then, he'd never met anyone quite like her, either.

Rosalie knew Kenton was looking her way and observed him openly. Despite the strain on their friendship of late, she admitted to herself that he cut a fine figure with his tall silk hat, perfectly trimmed mustache and beard, gray frock coat, and pinstripe pants. He'd been going to some trouble, too, hiring a chestnut mare each Sunday to pull his rig, rather than hitching up his own grey gelding. She couldn't help liking him for it, even if she was still piqued that he was letting Gowen get the best of her aunt and uncle without seeming to lift a hand to help out.

But today, she would follow her own advice and appreciate the calm before the storm, pushing the mortgage problem to the back of her mind to enjoy Kenton's company. Despite the considerable difference in their ages—and opinions—she now realized he was easier to like than she had given him credit for.

As Kenton turned onto Washington Street, he prayed the small smile on Rosalie's face wasn't an indication that she was planning some outrage. She'd proven herself unpredictable so many times, it was impossible to imagine what she might really be thinking. He wanted so badly for his special dinner plans to go smoothly.

He slowed down near the Doyle sisters' home, which prompted Rosalie to ask, "Why didn't you tell us you were taking us to visit Miss Ava and Miss Eda for dinner? It'll be a real pleasure to see those ladies again."

Lottie spoke up from the back seat. "Yes, Kenton, why didn't you tell us? I'd have brought a box of those Jordan almonds the Doyle sisters like so well. Lord knows we've got plenty, business being what it is."

Kenton remained silent until he'd passed the spinster ladies' drive and pulled into the one belonging to the house just beyond. "As you can see, we're not exactly going to the Doyles', although they will be joining us for dinner."

Rosalie asked, "Whose place is this?"

Lottie said, "I don't believe any customers of ours live here. I know all the local folks who come into the shop."

Ben said, "I thought this house was for sale."

Kenton turned to him with a grin. "It was."

Rosalie began to smile. "I think a lawyer must have bought the place—a lawyer with a real fondness for vanilla caramels."

Her aunt leaned forward. "Kenton, is it true? Did *you* buy this house?"

At that moment, the Doyle sisters emerged on the porch and Miss Eda called to them, beckoning with her lace handkerchief. "Welcome to Mr. McCune's new home!"

Miss Ava said, "Come right in! There's just time enough to see the house before dinner."

Ben helped Lottie down while Kenton did the same for Rosalie. As they followed the walk to the porch, she gave the place a good looking-over. Neither modest nor a mansion, it rose three stories high and included a veranda along the front and east sides, a second story balcony containing a hammock, and a pretty little eyebrow window cut into the slope of the slate roof above. Window trim of sienna and bright yellow contrasted nicely with the muted beige-pink tone of the clapboard siding.

Lottie commented. "This place is lovely, Kenton, but I thought you were happy in your old one."

"I was, but I decided it was time for a change, and this house caught my eye." Climbing the steps to the porch where the Doyles were waiting for them, he added, "Besides, I couldn't ask for nicer neighbors."

Ava Doyle greeted them cordially, adding, "Isn't it wonderful Mr. McCune is living next to us now?"

Eda said, "We'll have so many more opportunities to beat—I mean play him in euchre. Maybe we can get up a game after dinner. I've brought my lucky deck—"

Ava interrupted. "Hush sister, and see these folks inside."

Entering through oak double doors, Rosalie left her hat and gloves on the hall tree in the vestibule, then proceeded with the others through a wide hall to a parlor on the left. The front bay window and two side windows allowed ample daylight through Batenburg lace curtains to enhance the mahogany wainscotting and the forest green velvet on the sofa and love seat.

Across one corner of the room stood a spinet piano, and Rosalie couldn't help asking, "Do you play, Mr. McCune?"

Before he could answer, Ava said, "You should hear him. He could be a concert soloist."

Rosalie lifted the piano lid. "Then surely, Mr. McCune, you'll play a tune to put us in the mood for dinner."

Kenton shook his head. "I'd much rather hear—" Stopping himself short, his face grew hot at the realization that he'd almost asked Rosalie to play, forgetting about the limited use of her right hand.

Rosalie sensed his embarrassment. Using her left hand, she quickly played the melody to the words, "While strolling in the park one day, all in the merry month of May." The look of surprise on Kenton's face made her smile. "My sister and I play piano together quite often when we're both at Tanglewood. I'll play with you now, if you like."

Kenton pulled out the piano bench for her and motioned to his other guests. "Gather 'round. There's time for a verse of *A Fountain in the Park* before Mrs. Buckley—my hired woman—serves dinner."

Ada and Eva sang surprisingly good harmony while Ben sang the melody an octave lower and Lottie sang quietly off-key.

When they had finished, a woman in a grey dress, white apron, and mobcap was standing at the parlor door.

"Dinner is ready, sir," she told Kenton.

"Thank you, Mrs. Buckley." He closed the piano lid and turned to Rosalie. I hope you'll play another song with me after dinner."

"Certainly—*after* you show us the rest of your house."

He smiled. "I'm sure that can be arranged."

Rosalie had eaten her fill of Mrs. Buckley's planked trout and freshly picked corn and was savoring the last bite of her peach cobbler when Kenton said, "I'd really like to play another song with you at the piano, Miss Foxe."

"You promised to show us the house first, remember?"

He smiled. "Then let's finish the tour." He rose to hold her chair. The others rose, also.

Then Ava stepped past Kenton. "Mr. McCune, the first thing you must show your friends is the wonderful sleeping chamber you've made for yourself out of the reception room." She led the way to a closed pocket door left of the entry.

Kenton paused, his hand on the door panel, and Rosalie sensed his reluctance to expose his private quarters. She was on the brink of suggesting they skip this room when he slid the door open wide.

Behind it, a heavily carved bed with high posters and a crewel embroidered canopy dominated a room divided by a tapestry dressing screen. On the opposite side of the screen—a scene of a fox chasing a hound—was a corner study made cozy by a leather winged chair, a case full of books, and a table covered with a cluster of photographs.

Ava said, "See? Isn't it stately?"

Rosalie smiled. "Very handsome."

She was about to inquire about the portraits when Kenton slid the door shut, saying, "The rooms I really want you to see are on the second floor. I'll show you."

Upstairs, the decor was much lighter. The Doyle sisters displayed a remarkable talent for pointing out the best features of each of the three bedrooms. One had its own fireplace and bay window and reminded Rosalie very much of her own bedroom at Tanglewood with its sheer Priscilla curtains and soft, pink window seat cushion. The second of the bedrooms was slightly smaller with a lavender canopy on its double bed, while the third sleeping chamber was decorated in browns, russets, and golds pleasing to any man.

Touching Rosalie's elbow, Ava said, "Wait until you see what Mr. McCune has put in at the end of the hall."

Fussing with her lace handkerchief, Eda added, "It's just the cutest thing. I wish we had the same in our place."

As Rosalie followed the ladies toward the back of the house, she was faintly aware of someone ringing the front doorbell and wondered who had come to call. Her silent question was forgotten when she turned the corner to find a small kitchen and eating area complete with a little stove, ice box, sink, and table.

Lottie spoke to Kenton as she gazed about the small, but efficient kitchen. "This floor is set up as an apartment. Are you thinking of renting it out?"

Kenton shifted his weight. He seemed on the verge of answering when Mrs. Buckley came up the stairs calling his name. "Excuse me, please. I'll be right back."

While the Doyle sisters discussed the tidy arrangement of the kitchen with Lottie, Rosalie eased away, aware that her uncle was doing the same.

Despite Mrs. Buckley's hushed tone, Rosalie heard the woman say to Kenton, "Mr. Gowen is here."

Kenton replied, "Tell him we'll be right down."

When Rosalie's gaze met her uncle's, there was no mistaking the pent-up resentment, indignation, and anger waiting to burst forth.

CHAPTER

8

North Carolina

The perspiration on Willy Jo's brow came from more than the summer heat as the buggy carrying his father, brother, and mother pulled to a halt in front of the Foxe home for Sunday dinner. Though he went out with Fergus, Minnie, and Vanda Mae to greet his family, his father made no acknowledgement of his presence until the others headed indoors.

Taking Willy Jo aside, Jabe told him, "I'm only here to please your mother." A reviling look in his eye, he added, "Far as I'm concerned, we've got nothin' to say to one another." He paused to discharge a wad of spit inches from the toe of Willy Jo's polished boot, then turned on his heel and headed for the house.

At the dinner table, Vanda Mae soon grew tired of listening to Willy Jo's younger brother tell how he and his cohorts at Blowing Rock had squandered their time playing practical jokes. They had entered the town office late at night, removed the Independence Day fireworks, and set them off a day early. They had picked the lock on the hotel linen closet, removed all the clean bed linens, and hid them in the stable so the chambermaids couldn't do their work. And they had stolen all the carrots and apples from the locked pantry and fed them to their favorite horses.

In conclusion, Bobby Dan informed her, "I had more fun this year than I've ever had at Blowing Rock, and I have you to thank for it—you and Gaspar—for teaching me how to open locks."

Vanda Mae stiffened. "I'm ashamed of you, Bobby Dan—ashamed that you would put such knowledge to ill purposes! We only showed you how to open locks for the amusement of your friends, not so you'd commit vandalism."

"They were amused, all right!"

Mr. Winthrop laughed. "Boyish pranks, that's all it was, Vanda Mae. Innocent, boyish pranks. If you had a brother, you'd be more understandin'."

She bit back the retort that was on her tongue and stabbed another piece of ham, thankful that her father took conversation in a new direction, extolling the virtues of Willy Jo and his newly acquired skills in the lumber yard business.

Despite Fergus Foxe's compliments, Willy Jo sensed beyond all doubt that his daddy didn't care to hear about his eldest son's virtues. When birthday cake had been served and consumed and the meal finally ended, Willy Jo wanted nothing more than to saddle April for a ride to the river where he could sit all by himself, but Fergus made a different proposal as they were rising from the dinner table.

"Jabe, let's you and me and your boys set a spell in the library. It's the coolest room in the house, it ought to be tolerable."

Jabe pulled a cigar from his pocket. "This and some more lemonade will make it bearable."

Despite the heat in the library, Willy Jo felt frozen out by his father's continued attention to Bobby Dan. A moment of relief came in the form of Vanda Mae when she delivered a pitcher of fresh lemonade. The sympathetic look in her eyes when they exchanged glances assured him that at least one person in the house was understanding of his plight.

A few minutes later, his father blew smoke rings into the air, knocked ashes off his cigar, and said contemplatively, "Bobby Dan, there's somethin' I've been meanin' to discuss with ya, now that you're home from Blowin' Rock. It's time ya took up more responsibilities on the farm—workin' full time from now until school starts up again." To Fergus, he said, "I think he's ready to become a partner in the hog farmin' business, don't you?"

Fergus shrugged. "That's a family matter, Jabe."

Willy Jo felt deeply wounded by the knowledge that his father intended to replace him on the farm—and with the son who truly disdained the farming life!

His younger brother made quick work of his lemonade, set his empty glass on the tray, and moved to the edge of his chair. "If you all will excuse me, I need some fresh air."

Jabe said, "But son, we need to—"

Bobby Dan cut him off. "Later, Daddy." On his way out the door, he sent Willy Jo a piercing look with a message that read, *You'd better settle your differences with Daddy and come home. You know I hate farming!*

He was no sooner gone than Jabe took up conversation again. "Bobby Dan's my clever boy. He's really gonna amount to somethin' one day."

Fergus reiterated his earlier praise. "And Willy Jo has picked up on the building supply business in no time, Jabe. You can be mighty proud of the way he handles himself."

Willy Jo set his glass down so abruptly, he spilled lemonade on the tray. "With all due respect Mr. Foxe, Daddy, I won't sit and listen while the two of you discuss me as if I weren't here!"

Vanda Mae was in the parlor with her mother and Virginia Winthrop discussing the happy news that Shani's daughter had given birth to a healthy baby girl just hours ago when Willy Jo strode past. The way his heels thudded down the hall—despite the cushion of the oriental runner—caused a momentary lull in conversation. Certain Willy Jo was escaping tension in the library by heading out to ride April, and eager to join him, Vanda Mae spoke up.

"Mrs. Winthrop, Mama, it's about time for a Sunday afternoon horseback ride. Care to join me?" Though in cooler weather the three of them had often ridden together—sometimes in the company of her daddy and the Winthrop men—she prayed a little prayer that today, the women would decline.

Her mother answered with a flick of her hand. "You go on, honey. We're not done talking."

Vanda Mae hurried upstairs to change into her riding breeches. She was on her way to the stable, passing the fence where Bobby Dan was practicing hand stands, when he dropped down beside her, full of conversation.

"Vanda Mae, I was talking with a friend of mine yesterday—Porky Steadman. You know him, don't you?"

Without a pause, she continued toward the stable,

Bobby Dan close at hand. "I think his daddy buys lumber from my daddy," she acknowledged with disinterest.

"Well, he and some of the other poor suffering fools who haven't gone away for the summer are getting up a party for Friday night—a trolley party. The Twin City Concert Band is going to be in the second car, and when we get to Hotel Quincy, there'll be some great refreshments. You'll go with me, won't you?"

She stopped to gaze up at the fair haired, blue-eyed fellow who had been her closest childhood friend—the Winthrop she had always considered to be the better-looking, more amusing, more congenial of the two—and came to a startling conclusion. "Bobby Dan, there was a time when I'd have consented in an instant, but I've discovered something about you today. I no longer care to be in your company."

A dark look flashed across his face as she walked away. An instant later he was turning handsprings, halting directly in front of her to pull a clown face so contorted she almost smiled. When she tried to walk around him, he danced back and forth refusing to let her pass, constantly changing his expression until he looked so completely absurd the corners of her mouth drew upward.

His triumphant look matched his words. "I knew I could make you smile! Now say you'll come with me on Friday night."

Smile vanishing, she glared at him. "I'm not happy about you, Bobby Dan. And I'm not going with you. Find someone else."

He followed her into the stable. "What is it with you all of a sudden, Vanda Mae?"

She took Hurricane's halter and lead from the peg in the

tack room and turned to face him. "You've changed, Bobby Dan. You're not the nice person you used to be. Your behavior at Blowing Rock this summer is inexcusable."

When she tried to walk away he trapped her against the wall, placing his hands either side of her head. His look was genuinely contrite. "I'm sorry, Vanda Mae. Truly, I never meant to offend you by what I did. I hope you can find it in your heart to forgive me."

She ducked beneath his arm. "I don't hold grudges, Bobby Dan. I just don't feel a desire for your company."

He matched his stride to hers as she headed for the pasture. "I almost forgot to tell you, Porky Steadman's daddy bought a fancy new thoroughbred—finest horse you ever want to see. She was a winner at Saratoga two years back. If you go with me Friday night, I'll fix it so you get to ride her on Saturday."

She offered a skeptical look. "Don't add fibbing to your list of transgressions, Bobby Dan. There's no way I'm going to believe a winning thoroughbred from Saratoga, New York, wound up in Mr. Steadman's possession and is now his saddle horse."

Bobby Dan raised his hands in protest. "I'm not fibbing! She'd leave your Hurricane in a cloud of dust! Say you'll go to the party, and you'll find out I speak the truth."

She gazed at Hurricane several yards away from her in the pasture, then turned to Bobby Dan. "If Mama and Daddy say it's all right—"

"They'll give permission. My mama's one of the chaperones."

"You'd better not be funning me about Steadman's horse, Bobby Dan, or I won't speak to you for a month!"

"Be ready to leave for Salem at half past six Friday night. We'll drive by to pick you up." He turned one cartwheel, then looked back. "By the way, you'd best not mention the race horse to your folks—not yet, anyhow. Just tell them we're going riding at Steadmans'." He cartwheeled away.

A few minutes later Vanda Mae was astride Hurricane trotting toward the Yadkin. She slowed to a walk as soon as she entered the woods, turning down the path she was certain would lead her to Willy Jo. He was precisely as she'd found him Friday evening, stretched out near a stump while April munched on the leaves of a nearby oak.

Willy Jo gave a start when he heard the clack of a horse's hoof against a rock, then felt relief when he saw it was only Vanda Mae on Hurricane. As on Friday, the uncanny sense of some other presence had been giving him pause. He got up and moved closer to the water, in too ill a humor to welcome conversation.

Vanda Mae couldn't blame Willy Jo for preferring his solitude, but neither could she keep to herself the thoughts that had been crowding her mind since she'd left the house. She slid off Hurricane, looped his rein around a red buckeye sapling and strode right up to the young man.

"Willy Jo, I was wrong the other night, and you were right. It was perfectly ridiculous of me to suggest that you could get along with your daddy."

He simply looked at her. In the silence, a red-winged blackbird began to scold. A mockingbird repeated the sound, then a crow gave an even louder opinion. He chuckled. "Fiddles, Vannie-Mae! Do you realize you've just walked into a perfectly serene piece of the forest and started an argument among the birds?"

She laughed, then plopped down on the stump. "At least I didn't start an argument with you this time."

He half-smiled, then gazed out at the river as if his thoughts were miles away, though she was sure they wandered no farther than the library at Tanglewood.

Her own thoughts remained even closer at hand, focused on the fellow beside her. She was enjoying having an honorary "big brother" at Tanglewood more than she wanted to admit. He was as interested in horses as she and her daddy were, and eager to ride even when her father was too tired. She'd miss Willy Jo if he left, a thought that prompted a question.

"Willy Jo, do you suppose your daddy will ever want you to come home again?"

When he replied, the longing in his voice spoke as eloquently as his words, and the sentiment he shared touched her deeply.

"Vannie-Mae, now that I've been at Tanglewood awhile, I've got a real yen to find myself a new daddy. One like yours."

CHAPTER

9

Michigan

Kenton turned to Rosalie and Ben, apprehension written in the crease between his brows. "Someone is here to see—"

Ben interrupted. "It's Gowen. I heard. I'm going down and have a word with him." He headed for the stairs.

Kenton stopped him, his hand on Ben's shoulder. "Please. Let me handle it."

Ben pulled away. "I've let you handle it up till now and things have only gotten worse. It's my turn."

Lottie emerged from the kitchen alcove, Ava and Eda right behind. "What is it, Ben?"

"Gowen's downstairs."

Ava blinked rapidly. "Mr. Gowen? Here?"

Eda addressed Kenton, her handkerchief aflutter. "I can't believe he'd darken your door."

Kenton tried to explain. "You might be surprised—"

Ben headed toward the stairs. "Gowen's the one in for a surprise. He evidently thinks I'm as soft and sweet as my fudge, and just as easily done away with. It's time he learned different."

Lottie followed her brother. "That's right. It's time he learned us Marshalls can't be pushed around like a batch of warm fudge on a slab of marble."

Ava followed Lottie. "I'd like to bend Mr. Gowen's ear myself."

Eda trailed the others. "I'm with you, sister."

Kenton started after them. "Folks, please. It's not what—"

Rosalie caught Kenton by the elbow. "For weeks we've been waiting for you to solve our problems with Gowen. Now Aunt Lottie and Uncle Benjamin are all but out of business. We deserve our say with that scalawag and there's nothing you can do to stop us!" She hurried past him.

Kenton started after her. "I'm telling you, it's not what you think!"

Rosalie ignored him, following the charge into the parlor.

Gowen rose from the dark green velvet love seat the moment her uncle stepped into the room. "Good afternoon—"

Ben cut him off. "Don't you 'good-afternoon' me, you—"

Lottie interrupted. "deceitful, conniving—."

Ava took up the assault. "—immoral, indecent—"

Eda chimed in. "—unethical, unscrupulous—"

Ava continued. "—venal, vile person. What do you mean, cheating these decent, hardworking folks?"

Eda said, "Yes, what do you mean, Mr. Gowen?"

Rosalie spoke up. "You ought to be ashamed of yourself, Mr. Gowen, *mighty* ashamed, cheating my Aunt Lottie and Uncle Benjamin out of what's rightfully theirs."

Ben's cheeks flushed, his jaws drawn taut as he shook his fist in Gowen's face. "If you think you can just turn me out of my store like lollipops from a mold, you've got another thing coming. I plan to fight till my dying breath for what's mine, the consequences be—"

Gowen cut in. "The consequences might be to your liking, Mr. Marshall. You're practically out of business, anyway. I came to offer a proposal I'm sure will satisfy you and your sister."

Ben pushed up his glasses. "The only thing that will satisfy me is the sight of you ripping up that eviction notice."

Gowen regarded him skeptically. "The *only* thing?"

"The *only* thing!"

"That's a real shame, Mr. Marshall, because I came here with a better idea."

"Don't waste your breath."

"You ought to at least hear me out. Mr. McCune has spent a tremendous amount of time petitioning me on your behalf. Even *he* thought you'd like my proposition."

Ben turned to Kenton. "Is that true?"

Kenton shifted his weight. "Mr. Gowen is determined to foreclose on the property you now occupy, but Ben, as long as the American Candy Company is around, your business there won't ever be what it was. Mr. Gowen has a good offer if you'll only hear him out."

Ben regarded Gowen skeptically.

Indicating the love seat, Gowen said, "Why don't you and your sister sit? We'll talk."

As Ben and Lottie settled on the love seat, Ava nudged Eda toward the sofa. "I want to hear what Mr. Gowen has to say. Don't you, sister?"

Eda dabbed her temples with her handkerchief. "I most certainly do."

Kenton offered Rosalie a chair near Ben and Lottie, then took one beside her, leaving the large chair opposite them for Gowen.

He sat, focusing his dark eyes on Ben. "Mr. Marshall, you're the best confectioner in all of Northern Michigan, American Candy Company *not* excepted. In fact, I'd like very much for you—and your sister—to come to work for me."

Ben smiled cynically. "Work for you? Never!"

Gowen reached for his inside jacket pocket, producing a folded paper. "I'm willing to give you an excellent salary —far above what you were making even when your business was brisk." He offered Ben the document.

Ben hesitated, then opened it for both he and Lottie to read. Seconds later he looked up in surprise. "It says here that in addition to guaranteed employment and generous salaries, you want to buy our fudge recipe for . . . " He pointed to a figure on the page, turning it for Gowen to see. "Is this amount correct?"

Gowen glanced at the number. "That's right. But if you don't think it's fair, I'm willing to—"

Ben was shaking his head. "It's *not* fair—at least not to you. But if you want to pay too much, I won't refuse your money." He turned to Lottie. "Will you?"

She focused on the page, then on Gowen, a speculative look in her eyes. "This is all well and good as far as it goes, but where are we to live once you've put us out of our apartment?"

Rosalie spoke up. "Yes, where *are* we to live, Mr. Gowen? And what about the money Uncle Benjamin and Aunt Lottie have already paid for that building?"

Kenton cleared his throat. "That's been a point of

considerable discussion between Mr. Gowen and me."

Gowen explained. "If you're willing to move into the apartment upstairs here, I'll apply all the equity you have in your candy shop to this house, making you co-owners with Mr. McCune."

Kenton said, "If this place isn't to your liking, Mr. Gowen has agreed to apply the equity to a more suitable property."

Gowen grinned. "I own a choice little house closer to the candy factory."

Ben shook his head vigorously. "This place is fine, don't you think, Lottie?"

She smiled. "It's more than fine. It's perfect!"

Ben turned to Gowen. "The move will be expensive. With business off, we're strapped for cash money."

Lottie added, "And there's all the candy supplies and equipment to sell."

Gowen had ready answers. "I'll buy them at top prices. And I'll provide men and a wagon to move your household goods as soon as you're ready—at no cost to you."

Ben pounded his fist against the arm of the love seat. "You've been planning this for months, probably since the day you took over the mortgage from Mr. Newton, haven't you? Just waiting for the time when you could force us out of the candy shop and move right in. You're nothing but a . . . a . . . "

Gowen put up his hand. "You seem to forget. You defaulted on the mortgage payment."

Ben's face colored deeply. "I did *not!*"

"Then *prove it!*"

Kenton spoke up. "Gentlemen, there's no point in going over old ground. Ben, I'm sorry, but Mr. Gowen's

111

proposals are the best I can do for you."

Lottie touched Ben's arm. "Accept the offer. We'll have good pay, a nice home . . ."

Ava said, "And us for neighbors."

Eda said, "Yes, and a euchre game anytime you want."

When Ben remained silent, Gowen said, "Maybe you need a day to think about it." He started to rise.

Ben put palm out. "No. We'll be ready for your movers come Wednesday morning, and the Monday following, Lottie and I will report to your factory for work."

Gowen nodded. "I'll write a draft to Mr. McCune for your share of this house first thing tomorrow."

Rosalie said, "And be sure to provide Uncle Benjamin with a written statement regarding the transfer of funds. We want no question this time."

Gowen said, "I guarantee there will be no problems, Miss Foxe."

Kenton told her, "I'll personally see that the papers are in order, including a purchase agreement on this place regarding Ben and Lottie's share in it."

While he was seeing Gowen to the door, Miss Ava said, "Mr. Marshall, you won't regret moving to this neighborhood."

Miss Eda said, "We'll be glad to entertain your niece while you and your sister are at the candy factory."

Rosalie quickly reassessed her private vow to remain in Michigan until she had found the coin Clarissa had stolen. "That won't be necessary, Miss Eda. Now that Mr. Gowen has offered fair settlement to Uncle Benjamin and Aunt Lottie, it's time I went home to North Carolina."

Kenton joined them again as she finished speaking. "Miss Foxe, I wonder if you'd consider remaining in

Michigan awhile longer. The fellow who was assisting me at my office has resigned for a better position downstate, and I could use the help of a well-educated young woman such as yourself."

Lottie said, "There's an extra bedroom upstairs here for you to stay in."

Ben nodded. "And far more comfortable than that tiny one you're in behind the shop."

Ava blinked rapidly. "I think you're meant to stay in Traverse City awhile, Miss Foxe."

Eda fussed with her handkerchief. "Maybe Mr. McCune will let you off work early once in a while. It would be nice if we could get in a game or two of euchre before you head south."

Kenton said, "You could start at my office next Monday. That will give you a few days to settle in here. I usually work from nine until six, but you could work whatever hours you wish."

Rosalie was about to accept Kenton's offer when a tiny voice inside prompted her to make a minor change. "Mr. McCune, I'll come to work for you, nine to six, but I'd prefer to start this Thursday morning instead of next Monday. One day is sufficient to move my meager belongings."

Kenton beamed. "Excellent!"

When his smile quickly faded, Rosalie became curious. "Something troubling you, Mr. McCune?"

"Just a minor complication." Smiling again, he said, "I'm really pleased you've agreed to help me."

"I look forward to it," she assured him. To Ben and Lottie, she said, "I'd better write to my folks tonight about the change in our address—*and* in our employment."

113

*　　*　　*

On the following Wednesday afternoon as Rosalie unpacked her trunk in her new bedroom, she couldn't help feeling pleased for her aunt and uncle. They owned a substantial share of this lovely home with papers to prove it, the move from the tiny apartment couldn't have gone smoother, and they would soon be paid better than ever for doing what they loved most—making candy. But certain situations remained a puzzle to her regarding Cutler Gowen's dealings. She decided to ask Kenton about them when he returned from his law office at the end of the day.

At about four-thirty when she was helping her aunt unpack her clothes, Mrs. Buckley called Lottie to the downstairs phone. Rosalie thought nothing of it when her aunt said it was only Kenton checking on dinner plans.

But he arrived home shortly thereafter—almost two hours earlier than Rosalie had expected. And from the front window of her aunt's bedroom, she noticed that instead of driving straight into the carriage house with Judge, he had parked by the curb. A cab drawn by a chestnut Thoroughbred pulled to a halt right behind him. Kenton spoke to the driver, then headed toward the house. When she mentioned the curious situation to her aunt, Lottie nudged her out the bedroom door.

"You'd better go down and see what's on Kenton's mind." She offered a curious smile.

Rosalie hurried downstairs, meeting up with him as he came through the door.

His hazel-come-grey eyes were twinkling. "Miss Foxe, come with me. We're going for an afternoon drive."

He held the door for her but she hesitated. "Hadn't I better tell Aunt Lottie—"

114

"She already knows where I'm taking you. It's just outside of town. Now come." He nudged her elbow. On the way down the front walk, he explained further. "If we're going to ride together to my office every day, I've got to find a horse you trust. I want you to pick one you'd be comfortable with."

Kenton handed her into the cab and instructed the driver to follow him. Ten minutes later he turned at the entrance to a horse farm set back off the road. The front pasture, picturesque with pond and whitewashed fence, held two mares with their foals. Behind it were other pastures holding from three to five horses apiece in a wide range of colors and breeds.

The drive ended at a stable. To the right stood a tall white farmhouse dripping with carpenter's lace. To the left of the stable was a riding ring. A girl of about thirteen was putting a dun-colored mare through her paces. Her fair hair was caught back in a blue ribbon that streamed down her back beneath her riding helmet. Rosalie couldn't help remembering herself at a slightly younger age atop Hurricane, poised and confident in the saddle.

When the young girl caught sight of Kenton, she quickly left the riding ring and hitched her horse to the fence post. Climbing to the top rail, she waved enthusiastically to Kenton, her face beaming.

"Hello, Mr. McCune! Papa's in the stable. I'll fetch him." She jumped down from the fence and hurried off, her progress impeded by a slight limp.

A moment later she emerged alongside a tall blond fellow wearing leather leggings. When he had greeted Kenton with a handshake, the three of them approached the hired rig. Kenton gave Rosalie a hand down, introducing her.

"Miss Foxe, I'd like you to meet some friends of mine, Miss Susan Reddick and her father, Mr. John Reddick, a renowned horse breeder and trainer in these parts."

The young girl looked vaguely familiar but Rosalie couldn't think why. She inferred from Susan's scrutinizing gaze and the looks of admiration sent Kenton's way that the two of them were longtime friends. She offered her hand to the girl and her father in turn. In the slump to Mr. Reddick's shoulders and the lack of conviction in his handshake, she sensed a weariness that no single good night's sleep could cure.

To John, Kenton said, "I'd like you to show Miss Foxe your most trustworthy driving horses—in any color but grey."

John's broad smile spread all the way to his blue eyes, partially erasing the tiredness evident there as well. "Come with me. I've brought in a couple of horses that I think will serve your purpose."

Rosalie made conversation with the Reddick girl as they followed the men to the stable.

"Have you ever been to the confectionery in town? I used to work there, and you look familiar."

Susan thought a moment. "I was there to buy fudge on the Fourth of July. We got a pound free . . . but I don't remember seeing you there. An older woman waited on me."

Rosalie remembered then, Susan had been in the shop shortly before the band had struck up their sidewalk concert—and a bad case of homesickness. Pushing unhappy memories aside, Rosalie quickly changed topics.

"How long have you been riding? I couldn't help but

admire your form."

Susan smiled. "Since I was three. Papa used to set me on the saddle right in front of him!"

Rosalie chuckled. "I have pictures of myself at that age with my daddy on his horse, and others with my mama on her horse as well." She sighed. "An ocean's-worth of water has gone down the Yadkin since then." At Susan's puzzled look, she explained, "The Yadkin is a river in North Carolina where I grew up."

Susan nodded but remained silent.

In an effort to draw her out, Rosalie said, "I haven't been on a horse's back since I fell off and ruined my shoulder. Have you ever fallen off a horse?"

"Have I?" The question was more a statement. "When I was eight I fell off and sprained my wrist. Then two years ago I fell off again and broke my leg real bad. That's why I walk funny."

"Weren't you afraid to ride again?"

Susan nodded vigorously. "After that first fall Papa made me get right on my horse again. I was back to riding before I even had a chance to think. The second time was a lot harder."

Rosalie was about to ask how the young girl had found the courage to ride again when they entered the stable and John drew their attention to a large tan mare with a red mane. "This here's Penny. She's a cross between a Clydesdale and a quarter horse. She's real steady in traffic." Moving to the next stall, he began describing a lighter tan gelding. "And this here's Nick—short for Nickel. He has Belgian and quarter horse in his blood. He's just a little bigger, but every bit as gentle."

Rosalie patted Nick's nose while Kenton entered the

stall with John to give a closer inspection. The process was repeated with Penny, then Kenton focused on Rosalie.

"Which horse should we try?"

Rosalie shrugged.

Susan, who was stroking Penny's withers, told Kenton, "I think you should try Nick."

"Nick, it is. Will you ride with us, Miss Reddick?"

At a nod from her father she grinned broadly. "I'd be glad to."

Within minutes Judge had been taken into the stable and Nick hitched in his place. With Susan sitting on one side of him and Rosalie on the other, Kenton headed down the long drive and turned toward town. At a trot, Rosalie could easily tell that Nick's pace was more relaxed than that of a smaller horse, and in Traverse City traffic, the animal responded steady and sure to Kenton's commands. He asked her opinion as he neared the turn that would take them back toward Reddicks'.

She spoke confidently. "I think we should tell Mr. Reddick that Nick has passed his trial with flying colors." Without a pause, she changed topics. "Now that that's settled, I want Miss Reddick to tell me how she found the courage to ride horses again after she fell off and broke her leg."

"I couldn't have done it without Mr. McCune," Susan said, glancing at Kenton. The look on her face spoke of admiration—and something more. "It took a long time for my leg to mend. Mr. McCune would visit me and bring me my favorite candy."

Kenton smiled. "I've never known anyone so fond of chocolates as this young lady. I used to buy them for her from the Newtons before your aunt and uncle took over the confectionery."

Susan regarded Rosalie with new interest. "Your aunt and uncle own the candy shop?"

"They did until a few days ago. Someone else just took it over."

The young girl's face fell. "Their chocolates were the best. Better than Newtons. I had my fill of those the year I broke my leg, thanks to Mr. McCune!" She giggled.

Kenton turned to Susan. "But after your accident, there weren't enough chocolates in Michigan to entice you to get back on your horse."

"I should say not!"

Her curiosity growing, Rosalie asked, "So what changed your mind?"

Susan replied thoughtfully. "About the time Mr. McCune and Papa—and Mama, too—were trying to get me over my fear of riding, Mama started getting sickly. At first she just seemed tired and she'd sit down to rest a lot, but after awhile she couldn't keep up with her chores.

"Mama said maybe she just needed a visit with her own mother. But Grandma Ivy lives 'way over in Boston and Papa couldn't spare the time or money from the horse farm to take Mama there. Then one day Mr. McCune asked me if there was anything in this world that would get me to ride again. I told him if he could make my mama all better, I'd climb on a horse's back quicker than a scalded cat can jump out a back window."

Rosalie focused on Kenton. "Surely you didn't promise . . . "

Kenton shook his head. "I was in a real dilemma."

Susan continued. "Mr. McCune told me my mama's healing was in the Lord's hands but there was something he

119

could do that might help. He said if I'd start riding again, he'd send me and Mama to Boston to visit Grandma Ivy."

Kenton took up the story. "The next time I visited Susan I pulled two round trip train tickets from my pocket and showed them to her."

Susan smiled. "I'll never forget that, because you tucked them away again as soon as I'd seen them. I thought you were an awful tease!"

"But my plan worked. You asked me to help you saddle up Penny." By way of explanation, he told Rosalie, "Penny is a gentler horse than the one Miss Reddick was riding when she fell. John had sold Susan's horse by then."

Susan said, "My heart was beating pretty fast when Mr. McCune gave me a hand up, but by the time Penny had walked around the pasture I didn't feel so scared. The very next day Mr. McCune and Papa saw me and Mama off at the train station."

"Your mama looked better than she had in quite some time that day. Do you remember?"

Susan nodded. "But the farther we got from home, the weaker she got. I was afraid she wouldn't . . . " Susan lowered her gaze and Rosalie could see that the young girl's eyes were beginning to well up. Moisture prickled her own eyes as well.

Kenton continued. "Unfortunately, Susan's mother never saw Michigan again."

Rosalie said, "I'm so sorry, Miss Reddick."

Susan brushed away a tear and put on a sad smile. "It's okay. Mama lived to see Grandma, and that made her happy." After a moment's silence, she brightened. "So you see, Miss Foxe, I really didn't have enough courage all by myself to get on a horse again. If Mama hadn't taken sick,

I might still be scared of them."

Rosalie pondered the thought. "But you succeeded in putting your fear aside, even if it was for the sake of your mother. You can be proud of yourself for that." Given similar circumstances, Rosalie questioned whether she, herself, would have been equally courageous. She pushed the thought aside as Kenton turned down the drive to the Reddick farm. "We're back and Nick is still performing admirably. It seems you've accomplished what you wanted, Mr. McCune. You've found a horse I can trust."

Kenton only smiled. Pulling to a stop, he helped Rosalie down, then Susan. Her father emerged from the stable to be quickly assured by Kenton that Nick had won approval.

Mr. Reddick issued a friendly warning. "Now McCune, don't wait so long to come visitin' again." To Rosalie, he said, "We've got plenty of trustworthy ridin' horses in all shades of brown. You're welcome to make use of them."

"Thanks for your kind offer, but I'll decline." To Kenton, she said, "We'd best be getting home. Mrs. Buckley will soon have dinner on."

Later, when dinner had ended and she found herself in Kenton's company on the gazebo in the back yard, notions of horses fled from Rosalie's mind and she recalled earlier thoughts about Cutler Gowen. She lowered the book she was holding but not reading, and dared to interrupt his concentration on the newspaper he held.

"Mr. McCune, I was thinking."

He folded the paper and focused on her, his half-smile inviting her to continue. For a moment she was distracted by the way the late afternoon sun enhanced the brown in his hazel and grey eyes, and the blond in his caramel-colored hair. She wondered if she'd be thinking about these things when she went to work with him tomorrow morning.

Kenton couldn't help smiling at the young woman beside him. He'd known even before he'd joined her on the gazebo to read the paper that he was asking to be interrupted, but he'd been drawn to her, anyway. He couldn't help noticing how the breeze ruffled the lace encircling her slim neck, and teased at loose strands of hair the shade of dark maple syrup. She would make a pleasant replacement, indeed, to the fellow who had been clerking for him.

He reached for her book, lifting it enough to see the cover. When his hand brushed hers, a strange and disturbing sensation warmed her within, and she wanted both to pull away and to move closer. Doing neither, she struggled to remember what it was she had wanted to say, but he spoke instead.

"You're reading *Lord Jim*. What do you think of it?"

She forced herself to focus on the question. "I think Uncle Benjamin is right. It's Mr. Conrad's finest work." Remembering now her original question, she continued. "Mr. McCune, speaking of Uncle Benjamin, there are some things I don't understand at-all in regard to his store and the way he's being treated by Mr. Gowen."

Putting thoughts of Rosalie's loveliness aside, Kenton grew serious. "Exactly what do you mean?"

"Not too long ago, he was acting mean enough to bite a snake. Then he comes over here Sunday leaking honey like an overflowing bee tree."

"He *is* a strange fellow—like Scrooge and Santa Clause all rolled into one."

"So why didn't he just make a decent offer to buy the

place outright from the start? Instead, he got into a passel of problems with Miss Hackbardt and that plot of theirs to foreclose on the mortgage. Seems to me, he's spending a dollar to save a dime."

"Perhaps, but there's still plenty of money to be made in the candy business in Traverse City before Labor Day."

Rosalie sighed. "When I think of the way that Hackbardt woman lied to get Mr. Gowen his way, I could just paint her back porch red."

Growing pensive, Kenton continued. "The odd thing is that Mr. Gowen seems to believe Clarissa's story—that the payment was never made. Did you notice how consistent he's been? Every time the subject comes up he claims the double eagle you gave Miss Hackbardt for the July payment never existed."

Rosalie nodded. "Sunday was no exception. It put Uncle Benjamin and Mr. Gowen within a hog's hair of tussling."

"Maybe Miss Hackbardt and the missing coin aren't connected with Mr. Gowen in the way we assume."

Rosalie sighed. "I'd give anything to have a look in *all* of that woman's shoes."

Kenton remained thoughtful. When he spoke again, it was with an air of mystery. "Maybe the real reason for your aunt and uncle's problems lies in Mr. Gowen's past."

"Just what are you getting at, Mr. McCune?"

He leaned closer bringing with him the essence of sandalwood. "I have a feeling about the man. Something just isn't right. I've been making discreet inquiries, trying to find out where he came from and what he was doing before he built his candy factory."

She forced herself to ignore the pleasantly disturbing

effects of Kenton's nearness and focus on the topic at hand. "And what have you learned about the infamous Cutler Gowen?"

Kenton gazed into the warm brown eyes of the woman beside him and his thoughts drifted. At this moment he would far rather learn more about the pretty miss beside him than discuss with her the troublesome Cutler Gowen. He forced himself to remain on track. "It's as if Mr. Gowen never existed until he showed up in Traverse City and announced plans to establish the American Candy Company. When you come to work with me tomorrow, you can help me track down his past—if there is one."

Rosalie nodded, fearing anew that come morning, her concentration on the history of Cutler Gowen would be difficult, at best, with the charming Kenton McCune so near at hand. She started to rise but he stopped her with a hand on her wrist.

"Before you go, there's something I'd like to ask you. I see from the paper that the circus is coming to town Saturday. Since circuses are for kids, and you and I are acquainted with a young lady who would enjoy the show, I was wondering if perhaps the two of us should invite Susan as our guest?" He opened the newspaper and pointed to an advertisement.

COMING!

TO TRAVERSE CITY

SATURDAY, AUGUST 4.

THE HIGHEST CLASS CIRCUS IN THE WORLD

THE GREAT WALLACE SHOWS

Three Rings, Half Mile Race Track, 1,000 Features
100 Phenomenal acts, 25 Clowns, 20 Hurricane Races
4 Trains. 1500 Employees, 6 Bands, 50 Cages, a Drove of
Camels, 15 Open Dens, a Herd of Elephants.

$4000.00 DAILY EXPENSES.

**The Purest, Cleanest, Mightiest, and Most Magnificent
Amusement Institution of the 19th Century.**

The Greatest Performers in the known world are with
the Great Wallace Shows this season, including

THE NELSON FAMILY

Premier Acrobats of the World

THE ANGELOS - AERIALISTS

The 7 Stirks, Bicycle and Skating Experts

THE TEN DELLAMEADS—STATUARY ARTISTS

MLLE. NORDA FRENCH—MYSTERIOUS GLOBE

10 Principal Male and Female Equestrians

THE THREE PETITS, AERIAL BAR EXTRAORDINARY

LEON AND SINGING MULE "TRILBY"

The Sisters Vortex, Triple Revolving Trapeze

OUR STREET PARADE

At 10 am daily is the finest ever put on the streets. A sunburst of
splendor. A Triumph of Art, Money and Good Taste, with Lavish
Luxury of Spectacular Effect, and Greatest Professional Features Con-
ceivable.

Excursions Run on Every Line of Travel. No Gambling Devices Tolerated.

NEVER DIVIDES.   NEVER DISAPPOINTS.

Rosalie smiled as she returned Kenton's newspaper. "Mr. McCune, I'd be delighted to go with you and Susan! I haven't been to a circus since I was a very small child."

"Saturday it is, then! We'll make a day of it starting with the parade at ten o'clock—if that's all right."

"By all means!"

But when Kenton drove Rosalie to Reddicks' the following evening to invite Susan to the circus, he found John far less receptive to the invitation than his daughter.

"A day at the circus is a day wasted," he grumbled, scuffing the gravel in the driveway as if impatient to get back to the stable.

Rosalie was tempted to argue, but bit her tongue.

The utterly crestfallen look on Susan's face made Kenton regret not speaking to John in private first.

She must have had a similar impact on her father, for he softened his stand. "But every kid ought to see the circus at least once. If Mr. McCune and Miss Foxe want to take you, I suppose it's all right. Just remember, you still have Saturday chores to do."

She kissed his cheek impetuously. "Thanks, Papa. I won't forget!"

Kenton said, "Susan, why don't you show Miss Foxe how well you ride around the ring while I talk to your father for a minute?"

The two walked off, Susan bubbling over with horse talk.

Alone with John, Kenton said, "Something's troubling you. Is there anything I can do to help?"

John kicked a small stone into the tall grass by the pasture fence post. "I'll make out." Lifting his gaze to meet

Kenton's, he added, "Didn't mean to come across like vinegar on a hot fudge sundae. Guess I'm more tired than I thought."

"Can't you hire someone to help out?"

Shifting toward the stable, John replied, "I had to let a man go today. Couldn't afford to keep him on. Now, unless there's somethin' else, I've got to get back to work."

Reluctant to leave, Kenton said, "There is one other thing, John." Knowing the man hadn't darkened the door of a church since his wife's funeral over a year ago, he cautiously suggested, "God will help, if you ask."

His friend's jaw grew taut, his cheeks suffusing with color. "I did all my askin' of God when Mary Claire took sick and we all know what come of that." He turned and strode toward the stable.

Later, as Kenton drove through the dusk toward home, Rosalie bubbled over with a description of what she'd seen in the riding ring, concluding, "That young Reddick girl certainly is a testimony to what a person can accomplish with a sufficient dose of determination."

He was secretly pleased to know that, despite his discouraging conversation with John, his daughter had favorably impressed the young woman by his side, just as he had hoped. Their conversation continued on other topics until Washington Street when Kenton brought it back to the Reddicks. Explaining that John was having business difficulties, he said, "I hope you won't think me out of place in asking, but would you please include Mr. Reddick in your prayers tonight? The Lord will know best how to supply his need."

As Kenton turned into his driveway, Rosalie replied, "I'll pray for him. And I'll ask Aunt Lottie and Uncle

Benjamin to pray for him, too."

He brought the carriage to a halt by the side door and helped her down, holding her hand a moment longer than necessary. "Thanks for coming with me tonight, and for your prayers." Standing near, her familiar essence of peach blossom filled his head, enticing him to bend closer and kiss her temple, but she backed away before he could act on the urge.

Pulling free, she said, "I'd best go inside and let the others know we're home." Ducking past the door, she knew her excuse had sounded lame. Surely everyone inside the house full of open windows had heard Kenton drive in. But she'd been desperate for a way to put distance between them and quell the rising tide within her—the longing that would have had her kissing the cheek of this kind, gentle, caring man unless she'd turned away at that very instant.

In addition to her prayers for John Reddick, she would include one for herself, that she wouldn't lose her heart or her head over a man who would be gone from her life by summer's end.

CHAPTER

10

North Carolina

Willy Jo sat down in the library to read after dinner, thankful that Friday had arrived and only one more work day remained in the week. He hadn't even finished the front page of the *Winston-Salem Journal* when he heard Vanda Mae's footsteps and the rustling of petticoats as she entered the room. When he lowered the paper, he was astonished by the vision of pure femininity standing before him—a young lady with her hair piled on her head, a satin bow tied about her high collar, and rows of lace ruffle running down the bodice of her pale lavender dress. Surely, she'd be the prettiest thing ever to step on a trolley at the party in Salem tonight.

She crossed the room to perch on the chair next to his. "Don't tell Bobby Dan, but I'd rather be on a horse at Tanglewood than on that trolley in the city tonight."

"Don't go," he advised, delving into the paper once again.

"I can't beg off now! I promised Bobby Dan! Besides, he gave me his word that I'd get to ride that new thoroughbred at the Steadmans' if I go tonight."

Willy Jo punched the paper into a fold and focused on

her. "You're fixing to take a fall, Vannie-Mae. Steadmans' horse is only green broke. She's not ready for pleasure riding."

Vanda Mae sighed. "How do you know so much about it?"

"Fiddles, she's the talk of Winston!"

"Well, I'm not afraid to ride her!" With more rustling of taffeta, she flitted from the room.

Willy Jo tossed the paper aside and stepped up to the open window, but the warm, humid breeze did nothing to temper his troubled thoughts. Minutes later, when Bobby Dan rang the bell, he wondered if he should have a talk with his younger brother, but decided against it knowing it would only lead to an argument.

Instead, he wandered into the front hall to simply say hello, and was impressed by Bobby Dan's mature image and demeanor. His brother's blond hair was neatly slicked back making him appear older than his seventeen years, and he'd tied a neat striped bow at his collar—using a tie he'd obviously borrowed from Willy Jo's own collection! He followed the young couple out to the drive, wishing he were going along to help his mother keep an eye on things, but he sensed that his presence would be an intrusion.

Nevertheless, when he mounted April a quarter of an hour later for his evening ride by the river, he found himself on the road to Salem instead. When he arrived at Academy Square, he had no trouble recognizing the two trolley cars reserved for the party. The front car was lit all around with colored electric lights. Musicians warming up on their band instruments filled the second car. Hastily hitching April to the post beside his father's rig, he climbed aboard the first car and made his way past the front seats where Vanda Mae, Bobby Dan, Porky Steadman, and their friends were sitting, and settled beside his mother at the back.

To the tune of *Sweet Rosie O'Grady*, the cars rolled up Main Street past Douthit's Fancy Goods, Schaffner's Drug Store, Senseman Company Brooms and Stoves, Vogler and Sons Furniture and Undertaking, Mrs. Stanton's Millinery Store, and past several of the tobacco factories and leaf houses in Winston. All along the way people paused to watch and listen until the trolley came to a stop at the Hotel Quincy for refreshments.

While the others went inside, Willy Jo stayed on the empty trolley. He'd never been much good making polite, party conversation, and the prospect of watching Vanda Mae talking and laughing with Bobby Dan and their young friends didn't hold appeal. He gazed out the trolley window watching the carriages pass by, his mind wandering until he caught a glimpse of a driver wearing a tall white hat with a wide black band. Leaning out the window for a better look, he was certain it was Eck Danvers headed down Main Street toward Salem.

The mere sight of the man angered him, but Willy Jo had to reckon with the fact that Eck Danvers alone had not been the cause of the rift with his daddy. He wanted badly to smooth over the troubles between them, but despite dozens of prayers and weeks of anguishing over the problem since his move to Tanglewood, he still hadn't any idea how a reconciliation could be accomplished.

Such concerns took flight as the young people began to fill the trolley car again, ready for their return ride to Academy Square. Minutes later they arrived back at their starting point. While the others were still saying their good-byes, Willy Jo headed for his father's buggy, planning on lighting the carriage lanterns for the drive home. Suddenly, he realized something was badly amiss. April was no longer tied to the post beside his father's rig!

His heart in his throat, he searched the square, hoping she'd only gotten loose and wandered off to graze, but after a thorough investigation including a score of inquiries, he'd found no sign of her.

His mother, brother, and Vanda Mae were waiting in his father's buggy when he returned. Seeing that Bobby Dan had already lit the lanterns, Willy Jo climbed into the front seat beside his mother to reveal the bad news.

"April's missing."

Vanda Mae's forehead wrinkled. "Where can she be?"

Willy Jo pointed to the hitching post. "I tied her right there, and now she's gone."

His mother said, "Surely she's around here somewhere. Did you—"

"I've asked everyone who parked on this block. No one's seen her."

Bobby Dan said, "I hope this isn't Porky's idea of a joke. It'd be just like him to—"

Willy Jo cut in. "I spoke with Porky. He hasn't seen her." Pulling away from the curb, he said, "I'm going to drive around the school and take another look, but I think we've got a better chance of sneaking dawn past a rooster than we have of finding April."

Darkness had settled over Salem—and in Willy Jo's heart—by the time he'd finished his tour of the Academy neighborhood. The other occupants of the buggy reflected his grim mood. He set off for Tanglewood, deeply disturbed to be leaving without Vanda Mae's Morgan. His thoughts were in a muddle over who would steal her, and why. He'd driven a couple of miles when several blasts from a shotgun rent the air.

The team lurched, throwing his mother against him and all but tossing his brother and Vanda Mae onto the floor.

Before Willy Jo could calm the roans, a lone rider galloped past, whooping, hollering, and firing off more shots.

The team bolted, heading off the road into a meadow.

Willy Jo pulled up hard on the reins. "Whoa, Jenny! Whoa, Jim!"

The pair paid no heed, careening this way and that, nearly upsetting the buggy with every turn.

"Jenny! Jim! Whoa!" he hollered louder, using all his might to pull back.

The team finally rolled to a halt in the middle of the field.

Willy Jo shook his fist in the darkness. "Crazy rider!"

Beside him on the seat, his mother gasped breathlessly. "Scared the life out of me!"

Vanda Mae pointed toward the road. "Look!"

A carriage had pulled off, heading toward them. He recognized Eck Danvers' voice before he could see his face in the pale lamplight.

"Young Winthrop! Didn't expect to see you here."

The surprise in his voice seemed forced, insincere.

"Some mad man with a shotgun just ran us off the road. You see him?"

Danvers shook his head. "Heard shots. Didn't see noth—anything."

Vanda Mae spoke up from the back. "Mr. Danvers, have you seen April, my Morgan? She went missing tonight while we were at a trolley party in Salem."

"Missing, eh?" Again, his bewilderment sounded overdone. "Haven't seen hide nor hair of your Morgan since the day I rode her at your place." Touching the brim of his hat, he said, "Drive careful, now."

When he'd pulled away, Virginia said, "I don't believe I ever met that gentleman, but the name Danvers . . . where do I know that from?"

Reluctant to explain, Willy Jo was relieved when Vanda Mae offered an answer. "He's the one who put Willy Jo and his daddy at odds over my Morgan."

"I see," Virginia said coolly.

Pulling onto the road, Willy Jo couldn't shake the feeling that Danvers knew a lot more than he'd let on, perhaps even the whereabouts of April. But how could Willy Jo ever find out?

When Vanda Mae arrived home and went into the library with Willy Jo to tell her daddy that April was missing, he accepted the news with equanimity as she had expected. But the following morning at the breakfast table, when she said she was going to Steadmans' with Bobby Dan, she wasn't prepared for his reaction.

"You must *promise* you'll stay off that horse from Saratoga."

"I . . . " She glared at Willy Jo.

"No reason to give him the evil eye," her daddy scolded. "Just about every customer who's come to the lumber yard this week has told tales about that filly. Now promise me you'll stay off her, or you'll stay home."

Unwilling to lie, but even more unwilling to stay behind, Vanda Mae mumbled, "I promise."

CHAPTER

11

Michigan

Ready for her outing to the parade and circus Saturday morning, Rosalie headed for the gazebo where Kenton was reading the morning paper. She could hear him chuckling to himself as she sat down on the bench beside him. "I'm pleased to see you've put the frustration of work behind you and are in good spirits this morning." She referred to the dead end they'd come up against in their investigation of Cutler Gowen during the previous two days at Kenton's law office.

He lowered the paper a tad revealing a twinkle of mirth in his eyes, more hazel now than grey. "Listen to this. 'A delightful watermelon party was enjoyed on the shore of the river in front of the residence of Frank Friedrich last evening. One of the watermelons had the misfortune to fall from the basket, and it rolled into the river and was drowned, but the other served the party most pleasantly. A jolly time was enjoyed by all.'"

Rosalie laughed outright. "That takes the whole biscuit! Until this minute, I didn't know a *water*melon could drown."

Kenton folded the paper, his attention on the young miss beside him. Her hair was lit from behind by the morning sun, setting a soft, amber frame about her oval face. He had an urge to take her off to some secluded spot along the bay for a private watermelon party of their own rather than Front Street which would be crowded with circus enthusiasts. He tried to banish the notion before it could take hold, remembering his commitment to Susan who was about to enjoy her very first circus, and the opportunity he would have in the evening to again be with Rosalie in greater privacy. Indicating the cloudless sky above, he struggled to redirected his thoughts to the plans for the morning, but his words sounded contemplative even to his own ears. "Looks like a fine day for a parade. We should go to Reddicks' and fetch our guest."

Rosalie was aware of the tentative tone in Kenton's voice—aware too, that she could easily forego a day at the circus with Susan for a day alone with Kenton. Despite the fact that she'd spent two long days with him at the office, they'd been too busy concentrating on routine legal tasks and the problem of Cutler Gowen for their personal friendship to flourish. They'd been too busy even to smile, and the way Kenton was looking at her now sent a warmth through her that threatened to invade her cheeks. She lowered her gaze and drew a deep breath, then rose offering a playful scolding.

"Come along, Mr. McCune! We'd best get started for the Reddicks'. We've promised Susan a day she'll never forget."

Taking her by the elbow, he escorted her out of the gazebo. "Before we go, there's one thing I need from the house. Wait right here." A minute later he reappeared wearing a red stovepipe hat with a tall white ostrich plume tucked into its wide blue and white striped hat band.

Rosalie eyed him skeptically. "I can't exactly say you're the height of fashion, but you're . . . patriotic."

"I'm sure I look more like a clown than like Uncle Sam, but this *is* a day for clowns. At least you and Susan will always know where I am."

Kenton drove the back streets out of town to avoid the main routes congested with circus traffic. The moment Susan saw Kenton she teased him mercilessly about his hat, then insisted he let her try it on. When it fell down covering her entire face, Rosalie laughed till her sides were sore. Then she tried it on herself, angling it in different directions while Kenton and Susan took their turns laughing.

Placing his novel top hat on his own head again, Kenton drove back to town and parked his carriage at home, away from the crowds in the heart of the city, escorting Rosalie and Susan the few short blocks to the west end of Front Street. Hundreds of people were already starting to congregate in the commercial district and Susan's excitement began to infect Rosalie as the young girl chatted.

"I can hardly wait to see the equestrians! Papa says they ride around the ring standing on the horses' backs, and leap from one horse to another. He says some can even do a backward somersault and land on a different horse!"

Rosalie was about to confirm Susan's expectations when the young girl stopped dead and pointed to the opposite side of the street. "Look at the candy shop!"

Rosalie hadn't been past the store her aunt and uncle had owned since Thursday afternoon when Kenton had driven Nick down Front Street. The prominent white sign she now saw above the door literally made her choke. Kenton read it out loud.

137

"'Clarissa's Confections.'" The bold crimson proclamation was accompanied by slightly smaller blue lettering beneath. "'American Candy Company.' If that doesn't take all!"

Regaining control of herself, Rosalie asked indignantly, "Do you believe it, Mr. McCune? *Clarissa's* Confections?"

Susan asked innocently, "Who's Clarissa?"

Kenton answered, "A troublesome acquaintance of ours."

Rosalie said, "I can't believe she's actually tending shop herself."

Starting across the street, Kenton said, "I can't either, but I'm going to find out if she is."

Rosalie held back. "You don't really intend to patronize the place, do you?"

With a mischievous smile, he said, "It's time I treat Susan to some chocolates. No telling what that simple act might reveal."

Crossing the street with Kenton and Susan, Rosalie paused on the walk a few yards away from the confectionery. At least a dozen children were crowded around its front window. Though curious as to the reason, Rosalie remained determined to keep her distance. "You two go on in. I can't bring myself to step foot in a place with Miss Hackbardt's name on it after what she's already put Aunt Lottie and Uncle Benjamin through."

The bell on the screen door of the candy shop jingled constantly as Rosalie waited for Kenton and Susan to return. Rumors of an accident on the road and a delay of the parade floated around her as more people gathered along the street. A few minutes later Susan and Kenton were again at her side, the young girl licking an elephant-shaped red lollipop.

Susan paused in her indulgence to say, "They didn't have any chocolates, or any fudge, but the lady in there gave me this!"

Kenton explained further. "Miss Hackbardt was very much in evidence—not working, mind you, but acting as a sort of greeter and handing out samples. She said the dipped chocolates and fudge will be available again after your aunt and uncle come to work at Mr. Gowen's factory next week."

Susan said, "You ought to see the circus display in their window, Miss Foxe. There are hard candies in every shape and color showing the different acts. The center ring even has elephants that move in a circle, all linked together, trunk to tail!"

"No wonder so many children are pressed against the window," Rosalie concluded.

Kenton pulled a wrapped butterscotch from his pocket and offered it to her. "Miss Hackbardt inquired about you. When I told her you were right outside, she insisted I give you this."

Despite her aversion to the giver, Rosalie was tempted to accept the candy, remembering the delicious sample Mr. Gowen had provided the night of the carnival ball, but she put hand up. "You keep it."

Susan pulled her lollipop from her mouth long enough to ask Kenton, "What time is it? I thought the parade would have started by now."

Just then, the sheriff came riding down the center of the street making an announcement through a megaphone. "Please be patient! The circus parade will begin in thirty minutes!"

Rosalie expected a grumble from Susan, but the girl only shrugged. "I'm glad I've got this lollipop to pass the time, if we're going to have to wait."

Catching sight of Cutler Gowen approaching, Rosalie nudged Kenton. "It appears the boss has come to check on his new business."

Kenton watched with interest as the other man disappeared inside the confectionery. "If you ladies will excuse me, I have a sudden need for some hard candies."

When he had gone, Rosalie commented to Susan, "I guess that leaves the two of us to keep up conversation."

Susan took her lollipop from her mouth long enough to say, "I already told you most of my story, so I'd just as soon you did the talking. Besides, I never knew anyone from North Carolina. What's it like there?"

Rosalie described Old North State in generalities from the Atlantic Coast in the east to the Piedmont in the central section, to the Blue Ridge Mountains beyond.

Then Susan asked about Rosalie's family and schooling. The young girl listened with rapt attention, learning of the traditions at Tanglewood, and at Salem Academy—the birthday celebration of the president of the school each September, the candlelight service and love feast held on Christmas Eve in Old Home Church, and the celebration of Christ during Easter week with another love feast. Rosalie had begun a description of summers in the mountain resort of Blowing Rock when the sound of band music in the distance caught her attention.

"I believe the circus parade is coming!"

Susan tipped her ear, then cast a backward glance at the confectionery. "Mr. McCune had better come soon, or he'll miss the start of it!"

On cue the appearance of a red top hat—easily visible above the crowd—marked his emergence from the candy store. Cutler Gowen and Clarissa followed behind, blending into the crowd several feet to the left of Rosalie and Susan.

When Kenton took his place beside Rosalie, she said, "Mr. Gowen must have been quite talkative."

Kenton nodded. "He had plenty to say all right. And almost every word concerned the candy business."

"Did you ask him what he was doing before he came to Traverse City?"

Kenton nodded. "He said he traveled a lot, then he went right back to the subject of candy and what a fine job Clarissa has been doing."

With the strains of *Yankee Doodle* growing louder, Rosalie gave up on conversation and focused on the parade now coming into view. A huge bandwagon led the way, drawn by a team of six plumed white horses arrayed in silver-studded tack. The wagon itself, painted white with golden swans carved in high relief, was identified with the Wallace name arcing above the birds.

The band was followed closely by a float carrying a lovely tableau of young ladies clad in filmy white dresses and ballet slippers, their slim, elegant forms supported by the shoulders of strong young men in tunics and leotards. Behind them, a long flatbed wagon offered three pairs of acrobatic performers enough space to demonstrate a sampling of their gymnastic skills. The cartwheels and handsprings of the men reminded Rosalie of Bobby Dan. The mid-air somersaults of both the men and the young ladies who landed in their arms made Rosalie realize how talented circus performers must be to do it at all, let alone to execute their stunts on a moving wagon.

Next came a contingent of clowns weaving a humorous path from one side of the street to the other, colliding and falling down, then picking each other up so forcefully they would fall again. One clown carried a bouquet of balloons. He offered one to Susan, then quick as a wink, stole Kenton's hat! Making an effort to place it on his orange mop-like hair, he pranced around causing gales of laughter, teased Clarissa by temporarily setting it on her head, then returned it to Kenton's head with a bow.

Behind the clowns came three squads of spirited ponies in gilt bridles and reins, their equestrian performers riding bareback. Susan pointed to the smallest pony carrying the smallest rider—a little girl wearing leotard, tights, slippers, and a puffy little pink skirt.

"She can't be more than five years old, and look how well she rides!"

Kenton nodded and smiled. "She'll probably steal the show when the equestrian act takes the ring."

No sooner had the little girl ridden past, than Susan's attention was claimed by the animals in cages on wheels. A lion with a huge mane announced his presence with a roar. Tigers, leopards, and a gorilla followed in line. The next wagon, divided across the center, held three chimpanzees in the front half and several smaller monkeys in the rear. The chimps swung from their swings and the bars of their cage, squealing and laughing with raucous delight while the smaller monkeys hung by their tails or flitted about their quarters with ease and grace. The animals had just gone by when a gasp rose from onlookers to the right. Susan darted into the street to see what was happening before Rosalie or Kenton could stop her.

"The monkeys are loose!" she cried.

Someone else said, "The chimpanzees are out, too!"

Confusion reigned as the parade came to a halt. Suddenly, monkeys and chimpanzees seemed to be everywhere. One monkey leaped from person to person across shoulders stealing hats at will and tossing them aside until he came to Kenton. Swiping the tall red hat, he ran off down the street.

Susan jammed her lollipop into Kenton's hand. "I'm going after him!"

She took off before Kenton could protest. He shoved the girl's lollipop at Rosalie. "I'll fetch her!"

Behind Rosalie, someone said, "Look! The monkeys have gotten into the candy shop!"

She turned to find Clarissa trying unsuccessfully to chase monkeys and chimpanzees away from the front of the store with a broom while Cutler Gowen and one of his lady clerks tossed an unwanted invader--his fists full of licorice—out the front door.

A moment later the monkey carrying Kenton's hat reappeared, leaping from the sign on the neighboring store to the awning of the candy shop. He paused there to swing back and forth. When Kenton and Susan caught up with him, he taunted them with a hideous laugh.

Susan shook her finger at him. "You naughty boy! Come down this instant!"

Kenton reached slowly for the monkey. "Nice fellow. Now come to me."

Rosalie offered Susan's lollipop to the monkey as an enticement. "Here, boy, come on down and get a treat."

Clarissa pushed in front of them, claiming, "I can get that rascal down." She raised her broom and swung it at

143

the monkey.

The hat went flying.

The monkey fell into Kenton's arms.

When the rascal tried to scramble away, Kenton gripped him tightly by the wrists, claiming, "Your tricks are up, little fellow!"

Just then, Cutler Gowen opened the door to evict two chimps. Seeing an opportunity, the monkey Kenton was holding bit him on the hand to free himself, retrieved Kenton's hat from the walk, and scrambled inside.

Kenton rubbed the back of his hand. "That little scamp!"

Rosalie turned on Clarissa. "Now look what you've done!"

Clarissa dropped her broom to inspect Kenton's hand. "I'm sorry! I didn't mean for that to happen."

Rosalie wanted to pick up the broom and swat Clarissa's behind. The thought evaporated when a chimpanzee ran out of the store carrying Kenton's hat filled to the brim with candy.

Cutler Gowen followed in hot pursuit. "Catch that chimp!"

When Kenton and Susan took up the chase, Rosalie hurried after them, but the crowd was so thick she soon lost sight of the hat, the chimp, and both of her friends. All of Front Street was mayhem, the parade stalled in its tracks while every member of the circus and all those who had come to watch the parade set about returning the monkeys and chimps to their cage. Rosalie was working her way back to the confectionery to wait for Susan and Kenton when the young girl caught up with her, Kenton's hat in hand.

"Look what I found, Miss Foxe!" Susan beamed. "It's not very clean and half of the candy is missing, but at least I got it back."

Several hard candies and small lollipops remained in the hat—and the glimmer of something more. She reached in to pull out a chased gold money clip fat with bills. Flipping through them, she began to count the cash, but gave up when she lost count, realizing that most of the currency was in large denominations.

Shoving the money clip into her skirt pocket, she told Susan, "Mr. McCune will know what to do with it." Scouring the crowd for Kenton, she spotted him some yards away, headed toward her.

Moments later the young girl presented him with his half-full hat. "It's soiled, but it's not dented."

"Good job, Miss Reddick." Kenton glanced at the candy, then handed the hat back to Susan. "You'd better return the sweets to the confectionery."

When the young girl had departed, Rosalie said, "Come with me, Mr. McCune, there's something I want to show you." Away from the hub of the crowd, she gave Kenton the money clip. "This was inside your hat when Susan found it. I don't know how much is there."

Kenton whistled softly as he counted the money, pausing to study some of the bills as if determining their authenticity. His brow twitched at the discovery of a newspaper clipping buried in the center of the stack of currency. He tucked the money in his pants pocket and began to read the article to Rosalie.

"'Lazarus Ambrose Dead. New York Central Conductor Killed by Ruffians. Lazarus Ambrose, a twenty-year employee of the New York Central Railroad, was found dead this morning in an alley near his Cherry Street home, the apparent victim of assault and robbery. The suspects are still at large. The bachelor leaves one brother, two sisters, and several nieces and nephews in the city. Due to the brutal nature of his demise, a closed casket funeral will be held at the home of his sister, Mrs. William Spicer, Saturday at one o'clock, directed by W.S. Vincent. Mr. Ambrose was forty years old.'" Focusing on Rosalie, Kenton wondered, "Why would this be kept in a money clip?"

She shrugged. "Mr. Ambrose must have been a friend of the man who lost this money."

"A friend, or a victim?" Kenton asked as he refolded the article and tucked it into the gold clip where he'd found it.

Chills ran down Rosalie's spine. "That's a frightening prospect, Mr. McCune—that the man who lost this money might be a . . . "

"Murderer?" He slipped the cash back into his pants pocket. "I'm going to turn the entire problem over to Sheriff Rennie just as soon as I can find him."

Seconds after he'd spoken those words, Cutler Gowen appeared with Susan. "Miss Reddick says you found a money clip in your hat. It's mine, and I can identify it."

Kenton regarded him skeptically. "I'm listening, Mr. Gowen."

Rosalie reached for Susan's hand, drawing her away from Gowen while listening intently to his every word.

"If the monkeys didn't lose any of my money while they were on their rampage, there are . . . " he paused. Drawing Kenton near, he spoke in confidential tones.

Kenton stood back. "Your description is correct, as far as it goes."

146

Gowen thought a moment, his expression transforming from troubled to melancholy. "There was one other item in my clip, a notice of the death of . . . " he paused to swallow, his eyes growing misty. When he spoke again, it was with reverence and respect. " . . . my lifelong friend, Lazarus Ambrose. I loved him like a brother, may he rest in peace."

Kenton handed over the money clip.

Mr. Gowen started to put it away, then evidently thinking better of it, pealed off two bills and offered them to Kenton. "Your reward for finding and returning my money."

Kenton shook his head. "If anyone deserves a reward, Miss Reddick does."

Gowen stepped up to the young girl and stuffed the bills into her hand. "Don't spend it all in one place—unless, of course, you decide to patronize Clarissa's Candy!"

Susan stared at the pair of one hundred dollar bills in awe. "Thank you, Mr. Gowen! Thank you!"

As Gowen walked away, the last contingent of the circus parade was announced by clowns who proceeded down either side of Front Street, shouting "Hold your horses! The elephants are coming!" In the distance, the calliope could be heard.

Susan turned to Kenton, her face the definition of delight. "So much has happened already, I almost forgot! We haven't even been to the circus, yet!" Shoving her money into his hand, she asked, "Will you please keep this for me until I get home?" Not waiting for an answer, she hurried to the edge of the walk.

Kenton hadn't even had time to tuck her money into his own clip when she turned to beckon. "Mr. McCune, Miss Foxe, come look!"

Rosalie couldn't help smiling at Susan's enthusiasm. As she and Kenton took places on either side of the young girl, Rosalie noticed that Kenton, too, was grinning with satisfaction over Susan's obvious interest in the drove of elephants—huge mama and papa bulls followed tail to trunk by their baby offspring in fancy oriental coats.

Behind them, the street cleaners shoveled elephant-sized dropping into wheelbarrows while the calliope brought up the rear of the parade with a lively rendition of *Where Did You Get That Hat?*

When the rolling steam organ had passed by, Kenton offered an arm to each of his lady friends. "We'd best follow the music to the circus grounds. There are bound to be some interesting side shows to watch before the start of the performances in the rings."

CHAPTER

12

North Carolina

Vanda Mae struggled with herself all morning long, caught between wanting to cancel plans to go riding at the Steadmans', and her curiosity to see the race horse even if she couldn't get on its back. Her mind seemed to vacillate with every basketful of manure she cleaned from the stable floor, every bucket of corn and oats she dumped into the manger, every stroke of the brush as she groomed Hurricane. At two o'clock, when Bobby Dan came to fetch her, she made no mention of her promise not to ride the race horse from Saratoga. And the moment Porky led the filly from the stable, she knew she would break her word.

Lightning was a dark, dappled gray--a steely color unlike other thoroughbreds of Vanda Mae's acquaintance, which had all been some version of brown. The horse's head and neck had an elegant, long look that was carried out by the proportions of her body and legs. Even her tail was pretty, not thin and shabby like some retired racers.

From the first moment Vanda Mae patted the filly's shoulder she felt as if they belonged together. Lightning nickered and bobbed her head up and down, then she nuzzled Vanda Mae's neck and tried to stick her nose into the pocket of her breeches.

Porky, who had the build of a fighter and the congeniality of Santa Clause, laughed. "She didn't warm up to me nearly that fast. What's your secret, Vanda Mae? Got sugar lumps in your pocket?"

She pushed Lightning's nose away from her breeches then stroked her cheek. "I don't have a thing for her except a gentle touch and soft words. I hope she'll let me get on her now that we've made an acquaintance."

Keeping a tight grip on her lead rein, Porky said, "I'll hold her steady, 'less she decides to buck or rear. Then, you're on your own!"

Bobby Dan gave Vanda Mae a hand up. She slid into the saddle as gently as possible, keeping up a soothing patter. "Good girl. Steady now, girl. You're doing fine. You and I are going to be good friends, aren't we?"

Lightning remained calm while Bobby Dan adjusted her stirrups. Evidently apprehensive still, Porky said, "I'll walk you 'round some, case she forgets her manners." He started to make a small circle in a counter-clockwise direction around the meadow—the direction the horse was accustomed to traveling from her racing days.

Vanda Mae continued to pat her neck and praise her. "Good girl, Lightning. You're doing fine. You just take me on a nice, slow tour of your pasture."

When they had returned to the starting point, Porky asked, "Want to try her alone now?"

Vanda Mae consulted Lightning. "What do you think, girl? Can you behave yourself if Porky lets go?"

She nickered contentedly.

Bobby Dan said, "I take that for a 'yes.'"

Vanda Mae told Porky, "You can leave us on our own."

He patted Lightning on the neck. "Mind your p's and q's. Don't want Vanda Mae coming off your back 'fore she's ready." He unclasped the lead rein.

Vanda Mae said a silent prayer then gave a gentle nudge with her knees. "Lightning, walk."

The horse immediately obeyed. Vanda Mae tried a wider circle this time, praying Lightning would do as she asked, and wouldn't sense her apprehension. Keeping up a constant patter of praise, they soon returned to the others.

Porky patted Lightning's neck. "Good girl. That's the best you've ever done!" To Vanda Mae, he said, "Better let me unsaddle her. Then we can go for a ride on horses we trust."

Without even thinking, Vanda Mae told him, "I'd like to work with Lightning a little longer, if you don't mind. I want to try her at a trot."

Porky hesitated. "She might take off."

"I'll keep a tight grip," Vanda Mae promised.

Bobby Dan told Porky, "If you and I ride just ahead of Vanda Mae on either side, Lightning's more likely to behave."

The fellows mounted their horses and preceded Vanda Mae around the pasture. They made several circles, then a figure eight pattern. Twenty minutes later, Lightning had shown no sign of wanting to break into a canter.

Porky pulled up in front of the stable. "That's enough for one day."

Confident on Lightning and unwilling to dismount, Vanda Mae said, "Let's ride the trail through the woods. It's impossible to do more than trot there. Lightning will be fine, I'm sure of it!"

Porky shook his head. "Had her in the woods the other

day. Spooked at everything except the cicadas!"

Bobby Dan said, "She'll never make a good saddle horse if you don't give her a chance to get used to the trail. Vanda Mae seems to have a real way with her."

Porky sighed. "All right, but we're coming back the second there's any trouble."

He led the way off his daddy's farm into the adjoining woods. Vanda Mae rode at the rear, behind Porky and Bobby Dan. At times, she thought she heard someone behind her, but each time she turned to look, she found nothing.

Lightning behaved like a perfect lady. Two or three miles later, they arrived at an open field, proceeding across it three abreast at a walk.

In the distance Vanda Mae could hear dogs barking. Lightning's ears twitched. Beneath her, Vanda Mae felt the horse tense up. Suddenly, Lightning laid her ears back and took off.

Fear coursed through Vanda Mae. She pulled back on the reins with all her strength.

"Whoa, Lightning! Stop!"

The thoroughbred ignored her.

Again, she cried, "Whoa, girl! Whoa!"

Lightning galloped on.

Vanda Mae checked hard, jerking the reins sharply.

The horse paid no heed.

Desperate, Vanda Mae see-sawed the reins.

Lightning continued her charge—straight for a split rail fence!

Panic seized Vanda Mae. This horse had no training to jump the fence. Surely she would balk and Vanda Mae would go flying over the rail the same way Rosalie had been thrown from Hurricane years ago.

Vanda Mae squeezed her eyes shut and prayed, *Lord, save me!*

CHAPTER

13

Michigan

"How can he swallow fire?" Susan asked Kenton as one of the Alphonzos inserted a flaming stick into his mouth at the circus side show.

He shrugged. "I've always wondered that myself. Miss Foxe, do you know?"

"I'm afraid I don't know anything at-all about fire eaters. But even if I did, I wouldn't tell. It would spoil your fun!"

A larger flame disappeared down the throat of the performer garnering Susan's enthusiastic applause. "This is the best show I've ever seen!"

Kenton chuckled, pleased that his young charge was enjoying a break from the daily chores and training at her father's stables. "This is only the side show. Wait until you see the performers in the rings!"

When the ventriloquist, contortionists, puppeteers, snake charmer, strong man, knife and hatchet throwers, and minstrels had completed their acts, Kenton escorted Rosalie and Susan to front row seats by the center ring.

Having purchased a candy apple for Susan, a bag of popcorn for Rosalie, and some peanuts for himself, Kenton settled down beside his lady guests to watch in awe as the lion trainer entered the cage with several lions, a small buggy whip in hand. With precise cracks, the trainer signaled his animals onto stools, through hoops, and over one another leap-frog style. Then he set a ring on fire. All the cats jumped through on command except one. The last lion, the largest of all, pawed at the trainer, knocked his whip from his hand, then gave chase. The trainer ran from the cage, slamming the door shut just in time to prevent the lion's escape, then returned to successfully coax the lion through the hoop before dousing the fire.

Susan clapped furiously.

Kenton exchanged glances with Rosalie who was smiling at the young girl's reaction, just as he was. Silently, he gave thanks for a day which, despite early setbacks, was turning into real fun for the Reddick girl and a pleasant outing for Rosalie and himself. He was thankful, too, that new light had been shed on the mystery surrounding Gowen.

His private thoughts ended when Susan pointed to the ring to their left.

"Look! The equestrians! I've been waiting all day for this!"

A white Lippizaner pranced into the ring and began circling it. The little girl who had ridden in the parade, now ran into the ring, paused to curtsy, then ran to a launching platform and sprang to a standing position on the horse's bare hind quarters. Susan turned to Kenton and Rosalie, her face a puzzle.

"How does she stay on?"

Rosalie answered, "With resin. Equestrians put lots of resin on their slippers and on their horses' backs. They have a special name for their horses, too. Resinbacks!"

Kenton said, "You know a lot about circus horses."

"Gaspar told me about them." To Susan, she explained, "Gaspar is my Daddy's hired man who used to travel with the circus."

The girl nodded in understanding, her attention again riveted by new horses and performers entering the ring. A woman dressed in white satin, possibly the girl's mother, created a lovely tableau with her, posing on the points of her ballet slippers. Their stunts were enhanced by the addition of a white dog jumping on and off the horse's back, and white doves which perched on their shoulders.

Their feminine expertise was followed by a young man with a vaulting act. Running alongside his horse, he held a handgrip that was attached to the harness. Executing somersaults and cartwheels, he then sprang onto the horse in a back-facing position and scissored around to the front.

When the gymnast exited the ring, an older man entered, standing astride two white horses. Rosalie told Susan, "That's called *La Poste*, after the French word for courier. Watch what comes next."

Another horse entered the ring following closely behind the first two. They split apart and the third horse passed between the rider's legs while he picked up its reins. The process was repeated again and again until the rider was in control of an eight-horse team. They exited the ring to thunderous applause.

Susan turned to Kenton, her face bright with enthusiasm. "That's the most exciting horse riding I've ever seen in my life! I wish Papa could have come. He'd have loved it!"

Kenton smiled. "Maybe next time *he'll* bring you."

She shook her head. "All he ever wants to do is work."

As a bear act filed into the ring to the far right, Susan

told Kenton and Rosalie, "I don't think the rest of the circus could be as good as the horses."

But she applauded just as loudly for the bears that balanced on balls and tight ropes; the Dellameades who posed in scenes of history and mythology; the Stirk family who performed hand stands and other feats on moving bicycles; the tramp bicyclist, Edie Penaud; the Japanese jugglers who kept five pins in the air simultaneously; the trapeze artists who somersaulted backward to be caught in mid-air; and the high wire walkers who leaped over one another.

And there was no indication that the final act, the elephants, was any less extraordinary or amazing to Susan than its predecessors. She appeared utterly fascinated by the mammoth animals who could stand on their front legs or their back legs, turn pirouettes on tubs, push one of their offspring around the ring in an oversized buggy, and ride bicycles.

When an elephant held a beautiful woman in his mouth and spun around, Susan told Kenton and Rosalie, "The elephants are just as good as the equestrians!"

Rosalie said, "And they're not finished yet. Watch closely."

While one elephant stood stationary, another elephant placed front feet on his hind quarters. One, by one, other elephants stacked up in a row until ten huge animals formed an impressive line.

Applauding with gusto, Susan said, "I was wrong. The elephants are even *better* than the horses!"

Kenton grinned. "That's quite an admission, coming from you!"

As the band played a rousing exit piece, Kenton escorted Rosalie and Susan out of the tent. The young miss was full of chatter all the way to Washington Street. He was thankful that she kept Rosalie entertained on the gazebo while he managed a secret conference with the Marshalls and Mrs. Buckley, hitched Nick to his buggy, then returned to the house to collect a chipboard box which he stowed in the compartment at the rear of the carriage.

Susan's enthusiasm for the circus didn't wane even on the drive home. When Kenton helped her out of his buggy, she was in such a rush to tell her father about her day that she hurried off without her reward money.

Kenton called after her. "Miss Reddick, aren't you forgetting something?" He took the bills from his pocket and held them in the breeze.

At the same time, her father emerged from the stable. When the two of them arrived at the carriage, Susan was still bubbling over with descriptions of her day. ". . . and you should have seen the elephants and the horses!"

Mr. Reddick smiled, but Kenton could see the same weariness on his face as before, and hear it in his voice when he spoke to his daughter.

"You had a good day, I take it."

"Oh, yes! And I've got to tell you what happened at the parade! The monkeys—"

Her father cut her off. "Enough for now, Susan. Go change and do your chores. Day's almost done."

Her face fell, her exuberance traded for resignation as she reluctantly turned away.

Rosalie stepped out of the buggy. "Miss Reddick, wait!" To John, she said, "Begging your indulgence, sir, but your daughter and Mr. McCune have some news that's guaranteed to make you feel more terrific than a turkey in young corn."

Holding Susan's reward money for John to see, Kenton said, "Your daughter earned cash money today. Two hundred dollars." He handed the bills to his friend.

John gave them a good looking over as if suspicious of their authenticity. Seemingly convinced they were genuine, he focused on Susan. "Money like this don't grow on trees any more than horses do. Where'd you get it?"

Evidently unsure where to begin, Susan turned to Kenton. "You tell him, Mr. McCune!" Not waiting for his explanation, she hurried toward the house.

Rosalie went after her.

Alone with John, Kenton briefly told about the escaped monkeys and his stolen hat. "Mr. Gowen, the owner of the new candy factory in town, lost his money clip, and Susan found it in my hat along with some candy. This is her reward."

A silent moment lapsed—a long moment in which John's skeptical look melted into one of gratification. His eyes clouded over as he folded the bills and pressed them into his breeches pocket. His voice quiet with emotion, he said, "Thank you, Mr. McCune. You know I was in bad need of this."

"Don't thank me. Thank God," Kenton advised reverently. "This money is answered prayer."

John's fair cheeks began to flush. "Answered prayer? It was a passel of monkey business, if you ask me."

"God used monkeys to answer prayers," Kenton explained.

"I didn't do any prayin'," John asserted.

Kenton grinned. "No, but I did, and so did Miss Foxe and her aunt and uncle."

John's color deepened. "You didn't—"

Acutely sensitive of John's pride, Kenton interrupted before his friend could grow angrier. "No point in working yourself into a stew. None of them knew you were short of money, they only knew you needed help with your business, and that the Lord would know best how to supply it."

John rubbed his boot in the dirt, contemplating the thought. His cool blue eyes meeting Kenton's, he said, "I think it was coincidence. But I'm thankful to you for takin' Susan to the circus." Taking the bills from his pocket to look at them again, he chuckled softly. "Just thinkin', two days back I was convinced it would be a waste of time."

Kenton wanted to press his point about answered prayer, but decided against it when he saw that Rosalie was about to join them. Addressing John, she said, "Do you remember telling me the other day that you have plenty of riding horses in brown?"

He nodded. "You're welcome to make use of 'em anytime you want. Got a real gentle chestnut mare that'd be just right for a lady such as yourself. Want to see her?"

A moment of panic cut in. Suddenly, the notion of riding again took flight. "I . . . uh . . . maybe another time. It's getting late." To Kenton, she said, "Mrs. Buckley will be angry if we're late for supper."

On the drive to town, it was all Kenton could do to keep from bringing up the subject of riding. Rosalie remained quiet, and he suspected she was contemplating the prospect still. His suspicions were confirmed when she finally broke the silence several minutes later.

"I've been thinking, Mr. McCune, and I've come to a profound conclusion."

A long pause ensued during which Kenton held his

breath and prayed that Rosalie would overcome her estrangement from horses. He was about to prompt her when she continued.

"I've come to the conclusion that courage can't be borrowed. It can be contagious for a time, in a superficial sort of way, but real courage definitely cannot be borrowed."

"Then you agree somewhat with a man named Prentice. He once said, 'Courage, like cowardice, is undoubtedly contagious, but some persons are not liable to catch it.' I think your perception is much deeper and wiser." Kenton continued to ponder the thought, adding, "I have a belief about the true source of courage."

When a silent moment had lapsed, Rosalie said, "I'm waiting for you to enlighten me! Goodness knows my understanding is less than complete."

"And so is mine," Kenton warned her, "but there is One who has all the answers. One who's the source of courage if we ask, and His help is never superficial."

Rosalie knew he referred to her Father in heaven. And she knew Kenton was right. God was the source of real courage. She knew also that since her fall from Hurricane six years ago she had never once asked in prayer for God to give her the courage to get up on a horse again. Perhaps such a prayer was long overdue, but within herself, she found she lacked even the courage to pray it.

Though it took all the self-control Kenton could muster to keep from launching into a speech on the advantages of overcoming fears and personal demons by summoning the help of God, he forced himself to lay the topic aside and focus on his driving. Rather than turning right as he would normally have done on his route toward Washington Street, he kept Nick on a straight path toward the bay and the docks, raising comment from Rosalie.

"I assume you have a purpose for taking a longer way home, Mr. McCune. I hate to think we'll be any later than necessary for Mrs. Buckley's dinner. She can dish out quite a serving of wrath when occasion warrants."

He couldn't hide a grin. "Miss Foxe, I have a confession to make. We're not eating supper at home tonight."

"But what about—"

"It's all arranged with Mrs. Buckley. I apologize for not saying so when we were at the Reddicks', but I didn't want to mention then that I've planned a surprise for you tonight—an evening cruise and concert on the bay and a box supper on the grounds of the Ne-ah-ta-wanta Resort. I hope you're not too tired to enjoy it."

"Too tired? Of course not! It sounds like a perfectly lovely way to finish our day." As he parked near the end of a long, wide pier and retrieved their box lunch from the storage compartment, her thoughts drifted back to that morning on the gazebo. She'd had fleeting thoughts of a day alone with Kenton, but his plans for this evening were far nicer.

He escorted her onto a dock she'd visited several times on her missions to scare up candy customers. On the left was a huge lake steamer, the *Illinois*, taking on overnight passengers and cargo for distant ports. She'd stood in awe of it many times before, and tonight's close-up view of its dark hull and stack, rows of lifeboats perched on the top deck, and line of cabins beneath was no less fascinating.

Opposite the *Illinois* on the right side of the pier floated the Traverse Bay Line's smaller boat, *Columbia*, ready for excursion passengers to come aboard. In the center of the

dock between the two vessels stood the little square building where tickets were sold, a sign above its door reading,
Crescent Band Moonlight Cruise Tonight—6:30. Kenton
had soon purchased two twenty-five cent tickets and
ushered her onto the upper deck of the boat, choosing seats
inside the lounge a comfortable distance from the band and
affording a good view of the scenery.

But Rosalie couldn't stay seated for long. Once under-
way she roamed the deck, studying the landmarks on shore.
Kenton identified them for her as they grew smaller—the
Wequetong Clubhouse just east of the Boardman River; the
three stacks of the Oval Wood Dish Company and the
single stack of the Beitner Company, all on distant Boardman Lake; and the Greilick Sawmill at the foot of Division
Street.

In the opposite direction, a small island in the center of
the bay came slowly into view, its wooded shores transforming from a gray-green haze in the distance to a deeper
forest green as the *Columbia* steamed past. A few minutes
later a point of land drew Rosalie's attention, and the
Ne-ah-ta-wanta Resort distinguished by white siding, dark
roofed gables and a multi-windowed center tower.

Once onshore, Kenton led her to an umbrella table with
a perfect view of the bay, the island, and the setting sun.
Placing the box lunch in front of her, he said, "Why don't
you start unpacking supper while I fetch us suitable beverages."

While Rosalie set out the roast beef sandwiches, celery
and carrot sticks, fresh peaches, and jam-filled sugar cookies Mrs. Buckley had packed, she noticed that other passengers had chosen to spend their time strolling the beautifully manicured lawn or partaking in games of croquet and

badminton. The happy voices of children at play in a distant side yard blended delightfully with the evening songs of the robins and sparrows flitting from tree to bush, and the calls of gulls over the water. She watched them soar low, then dive into the water for their dinner, thinking how different was Grand Traverse Bay from her home in the Piedmont of North Carolina. Her thoughts had drifted from North Carolina, to the circus, to the strange happenings with Cutler Gowen when Kenton returned with two glasses of root beer.

He sat beside her and asked a blessing on their meal, then reached for a carrot stick, chewing contemplatively, until sharing his thoughts. "We learned some things about Mr. Gowen today."

Rosalie set aside her roast beef sandwich. "I was thinking that very thing when you were fetching the root beer."

"He had a lifelong friend by the name of Lazarus Ambrose," Kenton recalled.

"An Ambrose who lived on Cherry Street and was a conductor for the New York Central," Rosalie added.

"Now if we only knew what city. I'm willing to guess that just about every town connected to the New York Central has a Cherry Street."

"But only one has a Mrs. Spicer who would have been Ambrose's sister. I could write letters of inquiry on Monday," Rosalie offered.

Kenton jabbed the air with a celery stick. "Or better yet, send telegrams."

Rosalie pondered the suggestion. "Mr. McCune, I hope you won't take me wrong in what I'm about to say, but I still think Clarissa Hackbardt was mainly at fault for Aunt Lottie and Uncle Benjamin's troubles. Now that Mr.

Gowen has been willing to make amends, is it really so important to delve into his past?"

Kenton remained firm. "No man covers his tracks as well as Gowen has unless he's got something very important to hide. We spent all of Thursday and Friday checking with Mr. Johnson at the bank and Miss Welsh at the Western Union Office, and what did we find?"

Rosalie sighed, recalling the futility of their efforts. "No out-of-town bank drafts, no telegrams sent or received aside from those pertinent to the building and running of his candy factory."

"Exactly. Something's amiss and I won't be satisfied until I find out what it is."

Rosalie nibbled on her sandwich. Despite Kenton's concentration on Gowen, she was still pondering the conundrum of Clarissa. "I'm curious as to how Miss Hackbardt linked up with your nemesis. Did they know each other before Mr. Gowen came to town?"

"No, they didn't, and please believe me when I say you don't want to know the occasion of their meeting." Delving into his sandwich with gusto, he paused between bites to push a cookie in her direction. "If you don't like your sandwich, at least eat a cookie."

A sick feeling settled in the pit of her stomach. She pushed the cookie away, watching him finish his sandwich and begin on his own cookie before commenting, "You must have somehow fostered Gowen's and Clarissa's association."

Polishing off the last bite of his cookie, he warned again, "You don't want to know." Conjuring up a mischievous smile, he scolded playfully. "Miss Foxe, do you realize you are wasting a perfectly lovely Saturday evening at the Ne-ah-ta-wanta Resort talking about unpleasant business that will only lead to indigestion?"

"You brought it up—the talk about business, I mean."

Raising hands palm out, he admitted, "Guilty as charged! Now let's put it aside until Monday and concentrate on a subject more pleasant and sweet, such as Mrs. Buckley's raspberry jam-filled sugar cookies. You really should try yours." He slid it in front of her again.

Though tempted to argue, the contrite look on his face, now being drawn into an exaggerated, pleading expression, made her chuckle.

Reaching for the cookie, she conceded, "Until Monday."

CHAPTER

14

North Carolina

Alone in her room after returning from the Steadmans', Vanda Mae unbuttoned her shirt and studied her right shoulder in the cheval glass. A bruise was already beginning to show and the joint had begun to swell. At least it wasn't crushed the way Rosalie's had been. The pain was almost enough to make her cry. She told herself it would feel better once Shani brought the ice pack she'd asked for on her way up to her room.

She buttoned her shirt, sat on the window seat, and looked out at the huge oak in the front yard. As she watched squirrels chase one another across the branches she wondered how she'd keep her injury a secret when every move of her right arm hurt from her shoulder blade to her fingertips. It had been too painful to even pull herself onto Hurricane's saddle. Porky and Bobby Dan together had boosted her up so she could ride home.

Gaspar had given her a curious look when she'd asked him to unsaddle and groom her horse rather than doing it herself, but he hadn't asked questions. And her mother, who would have been full of curiosity about the afternoon outing and would have known intuitively that something was wrong, had already gone to her room to dress for dinner before Vanda Mae came in.

Now her daddy's carriage was rolling up the drive. Soon, she'd have to face him with the truth. And what acceptable reason could she give for breaking her word? *None!* He got out and came in through the front door carrying a package from the butcher shop beneath his arm while Willy Jo drove the buggy around back.

Willy Jo. She dreaded telling him what she'd done more than telling her father. The prospect gave her a headache knowing one wrong was leading to another and that it all had started when she'd broken her promise by riding Lightning.

A knock sounded and Shani entered with the cold pack. "Hope you be feelin' better in time for dinner, Miss Vanda. I be puttin' steaks on the griddle in an hour—nice, thick filets your daddy just brought home." She turned to leave.

"Shani, wait." Vanda Mae pressed the ice pack to her shoulder. "I don't feel well enough to come down for dinner tonight. Could you please bring it up?"

Shani sighed. "I s'pose."

Vanda Mae's joint was so tender it was hard to say whether the pressure of the ice pack was worth the small amount of relief it brought. A few minutes later she pulled back the chenille spread on her canopy bed and lay down on her left side plumping pillows in such a manner as to keep the ice pack in place. She had prayed for God's forgiveness, asked for his healing, and repeated several Bible verses from memory in an effort to ignore the pain when she heard a gentle knock and her mother's voice.

"May I come in, honey?"

"Yes, Mama."

Her mother's expression when she entered the room was one of immediate concern. She set a letter she was holding on the bed stand. "Shani said you asked for an ice pack. What happened?" She indicated the hurt shoulder.

Vanda Mae sighed. "I rode the horse from Saratoga and fell off."

"Vanda Mae . . . " The disappointment in her mother's voice was tempered with sympathy.

Rallying, Vanda Mae hurried to explain. "Everything was fine. Then, of a sudden, she took off! Went straight toward a fence. When she swerved, I hit a fence rail like a sack of yams."

Minnie removed the ice pack and unbuttoned Vanda Mae's shirt far enough to reveal her shoulder, more swollen and bruised than before, despite the cold pack.

Her mother stood. "I'm ringing up the doctor."

She was nearly to the door when Vanda Mae protested. "I'm only bruised. I don't need a doctor!"

Her mother's voice grew panicky. "How can you know? You might end up with a shoulder that doesn't work anymore, just like Rosalie!"

"Mama, wait!" Vanda Mae cried, but her mother was already out the door and on her way downstairs to the phone.

A moment later she heard her father's footsteps in the hall and called to him. "Daddy, would you come here, please?" The instant he crossed her threshold, her guilt increased ten-fold. He appeared refreshed and relaxed from his bath and was almost smiling until his gaze fell on her shoulder.

His brows furrowed and he was clearly on the brink of a question when she spoke again. "I disobeyed you, Daddy. I rode Steadmans' race horse and . . . " Her throat clogging with shame, she forced out the next words. "I fell off. I'm sorry."

His distress, apparent in both his silence and his scowl, brought her to tears that leaked out, running across her nose. He offered her his handkerchief, his expression softening as he pulled up a chair to sit and face her. "I'm sorry, darlin'. Sorry you got hurt, and sorry you broke your promise."

She sobbed quietly. When her crying was in check she looked again into her daddy's face, now pensive.

He spoke softly. "I suppose what's bothering me as much as anything is wondering how honest you'd have been if you hadn't gotten hurt today. Would you ever have told me that you'd disobeyed?"

She closed her eyes letting her silence and more tears answer for her.

He brushed his hand across her damp cheek. "Vanda, honey, look at me."

She choked back her sobs regaining fragile control as she focused on his soft brown eyes.

"I love you, darlin', but I'm going to have to punish you. You know that, don't you?"

She nodded against the pillowcase.

"Your mother and I will talk it over and decide what's fair."

Her throat was too tight to reply. More tears leaked out.

He bent and kissed her on the head, then turned to go, pausing to tap his finger against the letter her mother had left on the bed stand. "Here's news from your sister. It'll surprise you."

Her mother returned a minute later to say the doctor would arrive in about an hour. She managed to get into the tub for a bath and eat a few bites of the filet Shani brought despite constant pain. When the woman had taken away the dinner tray and supplied her with a fresh ice pack, Vanda Mae reached for the letter from Rosalie.

She was indeed surprised to learn that her sister had moved to a new address and that their aunt and uncle were no longer keeping shop. But she had little time to ponder the news, for the doctor arrived the moment after she had finished reading the letter.

Upon a careful—and painful—examination of her shoulder, he was able to convince her parents that no bones were broken and that she was *not* crippled for life like Rosalie. He predicted that in two weeks she would be over the worst of it, and eventually she would be completely mended. In the meanwhile, she could ease her pain with cold packs and the pills in the tiny bottle he left on her bed stand.

Through her open door she could hear her parents in conference with the doctor in the hallway but she couldn't make out the words. Minutes later, her folks came back into her room. Her daddy spoke first.

"Your mama and I have discussed your punishment and come to a decision."

Her mother said, "You're confined to your room. Tomorrow, you're to start packing your trunk. You and I are going north to visit Rosalie and your aunt and uncle. We'll stay in Michigan until month's end."

Michigan! The thought of leaving Tanglewood compounded her misery—no more evening outings on horseback with Willy Jo and her daddy. She wouldn't even be able to watch Jewel grow. But she dared not complain.

Her father must have read her thoughts. "I know it'll be

hard on you, but maybe next time you'll consider the consequences before breaking a promise."

They had been gone the better part of an hour when she heard Willy Jo's footsteps in the hall. Moments later he stood in her open doorway, his expression sober.

She made a vain attempt to smile. "Come on in."

Accepting her invitation, he repositioned the chair by her bedside, straddling it to lean his arms across the back.

Vanda Mae didn't need words to know what Willy Jo must be thinking. Nor did she wish to broach the subject of her fall while he was looking so cross. She avoided the topic by posing a question. "Did you ride down by the river tonight?"

He shook his head. "Didn't feel up to it." Again, he grew silent with thought.

Vanda Mae knew from the expression on Willy Jo's face that his displeasure was mounting. Unable to ignore it, she grew contrite. "I really made a mess of things. I should have listened to you."

He grumbled.

A quiet moment lapsed--a moment in which Vanda Mae could well imagine the angry thoughts running through Willy Jo's mind. He rose from his chair and started to leave.

"Willy Jo, wait!"

He paused, regarding her over his shoulder.

"Mama and I are going to visit Rosalie. Did you know?"

He nodded. "Give your sister my greetings."

"Promise you'll exercise Hurricane for me while I'm away."

He turned to face her again, his expression one of incredulity.

"Please. You don't have April to ride anymore, and he'll miss his outings terribly."

After a moment's thought, he mumbled, "I can't promise." Then he disappeared.

The poison of anger filled Willy Jo's heart as he cinched Hurricane's saddle in place and started for home. He cared not a whit that his daddy had banned him from the family farm. His quarrel now was with Bobby Dan, the spoiled, selfish, shortsighted younger brother who cared for no one and nothing but himself, and had caused all manner of hurt in the process.

As Hurricane trotted along the dark driveway, Willy Jo barely noticed the oppressive night air too moist to dry the perspiration on his brow, or the musty essence of the piney woods. A concert of cicadas and crickets filled the night with a relentless rhapsody, but they played only a quiet accompaniment to the loud, heated words buzzing in Willy Jo's head.

Light spilled from the open door of his father's stable as he approached. Inside, Bobby Dan was practicing handsprings down the center aisle. Quietly, Willy Jo slid off Hurricane's back, stepping inside to confront Bobby Dan as he sprang his way toward him.

Abruptly, the fair haired one halted, instantly trading a momentary look of surprise for a smile that couldn't completely hide his apprehension.

"Willy Jo, what brings you home?"

"Why'd you do it?" he demanded in a low, bitter tone.

Bobby Dan put on a mask of innocence. "Do what, big

173

brother?"

Willy Jo shoved him hard. "Why'd you let Vannie-Mae get on that horse?"

Bobby Dan backed away. "She insisted! You know as well as I do, you can't tell that girl anything where horses are—"

Willy Jo pushed him so hard, he fell. "I've half a mind to hurt your shoulder the way you did Vannie-Mae's!"

His brother scrambled backward across the dirt floor of the stable. "This isn't about horses, is it? You're sweet on her!"

Willy Jo pursued, tempted to plant the toe of his boot in his brother's midsection.

Before he could act on the urge, his daddy's voice boomed forth from the doorway behind him. "Willy Jo! Leave him be!"

He turned to face the man.

Cheeks scarlet, eyes flashing, his father came toward him. "You've got no place here! Now, get out!"

Willy Jo stood firm. "Not till I've settled my differences with Bobby Dan."

Jabe gave Willy Jo a hefty shove. "Is this the way I taught ya to get along with your little brother?"

Sparks of anger ignited. Without thought, Willy Jo planted his fist in his father's gut.

Jabe doubled over, windless.

Willy Jo towered over his old man for the first time in his life. "Bobby Dan's your favorite. That's what you taught me about my little brother!" He turned to Bobby Dan, yanking him up by the front of his shirt. "You may have Daddy fooled, but you don't fool me. You're nothing but a spoiled brat without a farming bone in your body.

The sooner you make Daddy understand that, the better!" He tossed him down again.

His mind in a spin, he hurried outside and leaped onto Hurricane's back, digging his heels into the gelding's flanks. Beneath a starless, moonless sky, he galloped off, the rumble of thunder at his tail.

CHAPTER

15

Michigan

The following Wednesday, as Rosalie helped Vanda Mae unpack in her bedroom in their aunt and uncle's upstairs apartment, her anger over the recent discovery that Kenton had indeed brought Clarissa Hackbardt and Cutler Gowen together was long gone from mind. Her entire focus now was on news from home, and she could hardly wait to hear more. On the ride from the train depot, she'd learned how her sister's favorite horse had been stolen on Friday night when Willy Jo had ridden it to Salem, and how she'd hurt her shoulder the following afternoon, thus causing her father's hasty plans to send her mother and sister to Traverse City. Now, Rosalie was eager for other news.

"Aside from Daddy being terribly disappointed about your horse and your accident, how is he?"

Vanda Mae paused as she lay her underthings in the drawer Rosalie had cleared for her. "Daddy's fine—at least as far as his health is concerned, but he's been cross as a bear with two cubs and a sore toe since he heard the news Gaspar gave him Sunday morning."

Having hung one of her sister's dresses in the closet, Rosalie turned with curiosity to Vanda Mae. "The only way Gaspar could displease Daddy is if there's something wrong with his driving horses. Did one of them take sick?"

Vanda Mae shook her head. "Worse. They were both missing from the south pasture that morning. There weren't any holes in the fence, either. They just vanished without a trace!"

A few quiet moments lapsed while Rosalie rearranged hat boxes on her closet shelf to make room for Vanda Mae's. Her sister tried to help, but in her injured state, her assistance caused more problems than it solved.

Laughing at her own ineptitude, Vanda Mae said, "I'm just going to get out of your way and let you arrange things. You're far more practiced using your left hand than I shall ever be." She had started to back out of the closet when she paused to inspect a pair of ladies' knickerbockers hanging on the rod. "I've never known you to own a pair of these. Have you taken up cycling since you came north?"

Rosalie's face grew warm. "No . . . I . . . uh . . . Mr. McCune bought those for me thinking it would help me gather the courage to . . . "

"To ride tandem with him? What a romantic notion, touring the city on a bicycle built for two. Of course, balancing will be—"

"The knickerbockers aren't intended for the purpose of cycling," Rosalie said, trying to shoo Vanda Mae out of her way.

The young girl remained planted, hand on hip. "What then?"

Knowing her cheeks were crimson as poppies, Rosalie explained. "If you must know, I'm considering getting on a horse again."

"Rosalie!" Vanda Mae gasped with obvious delight.

"Mr. McCune wanted to buy me a fancy, expensive riding habit but I told him that might be a complete waste,

177

if I never actually put my foot into a stirrup."

Leading Rosalie away from the closet to a straight-backed chair, Vanda Mae pulled up another one for herself. "Sit down this minute and tell me how Mr. McCune managed to revive your interest in horseback riding."

Rosalie did as she was asked, sharing the story of Susan Reddick, finishing with, "I know you'd like her. Perhaps Mr. McCune will take us all to the Reddick place soon, so you two can meet."

Vanda Mae scowled.

"Now, you've got a face like a mule eating briars," Rosalie gently scolded.

With a sigh, Vanda Mae explained. "As punishment for riding the Steadmans' racing horse when I promised not to, Daddy has forbid me to get on a horse again for a month." Suddenly brightening, she added, "But I want to meet Susan and her daddy and see their horses, and I surely want to be there when you ride again."

"Don't get your heart set on my doing it anytime soon. I'm about a ton short on courage."

With a mischievous wink, Vanda Mae said, "Then I'm going to start praying for that ton to be delivered post haste."

Rosalie reached for Vanda Mae's hand, giving it a squeeze, then took up conversation on a new topic. "Tell me, how is Bobby Dan?" When Vanda Mae rolled her eyes, Rosalie quickly amended her question. "You know what I mean, other than the usual handsprings, cartwheels, and crazy antics he's always pulling."

Unsmiling, Vanda Mae replied, "He pulled the biggest antic of them all three days ago."

"I hope he didn't hurt himself doing acrobatics."

Moving to the fainting couch, Vanda Mae leaned back. "I'll tell you what happened." Rosalie listened intently as her sister relayed Willy Jo's description of the spat concerning himself, Bobby Dan, and his father, ending with the words, "So Bobby Dan up and ran away from home the very next night, and nobody knows where he's gone. Of course, Mrs. Winthrop is beside herself, and Willy Jo is taking it real hard, giving himself all the blame. In my opinion, it's their daddy who's at fault. He ought to know his chances of making a farmer out of Bobby Dan are about as good as sneaking dawn past a rooster."

"Maybe he'll see that, now that both sons are away from home." Rosalie got up to put her sister's gloves away in her top drawer, mulling over all that had been shared. Tentatively, she turned to her sister. "I don't suppose Willy Jo sent any greetings for me—I mean, with all that was happening, it probably didn't cross his mind." At least, she hoped it hadn't. Talk of the Winthrops was stirring guilt over her growing friendship with Kenton.

"Willy Jo *did* send his greetings!"

Rosalie almost dreaded the words to come.

"He said, 'Give your sister my greetings.' That was his precise message."

Inwardly, Rosalie sighed with relief.

Vanda Mae paused but a second before delving with hushed enthusiasm into a new topic. "Now tell me about this Mr. McCune. In your letters, you said he's a friend, but I think there's more to it than that."

"Vanda Mae!" Rosalie scolded. Closing the bedroom door to ensure privacy, she began a long description of her association with Kenton that included the day he kept her from running away, their current efforts to trace the history of the infamous Cutler Gowen, and all the events in between.

Although Lottie and Benjamin had been required to report for a half day's work early the following Saturday morning, Rosalie was enjoying a later, unhurried meal with Kenton, her mother, and sister. She had devoted the previous two mornings to working with Kenton at his office while her sister and mother made acquaintance with the Doyle sisters. Kenton had wanted her to spend the entire day with her family, not just the afternoons, but she was too frustrated by lack of progress in tracking down Cutler Gowen's past to let that task go unattended. She broached the subject now with Kenton.

"What do you make of the letter that arrived yesterday from Mrs. Spicer saying her brother never knew anyone by the name of Cutler Gowen? If that's true, it seems mighty strange to me that Mr. Gowen himself referred to Lazarus Ambrose as his dearest friend."

Kenton set down his coffee cup. "Someone is obviously not telling the truth."

Minnie, who had been aghast to learn full details of the manner in which her brother and sister had been cheated out of their shop, said with disgust, "And I can tell you who's lying. It's a good thing I've never met this Cutler Gowen. I'd be sorely tempted to wring his neck."

With a question aimed at Rosalie, Vanda Mae wondered, "What are you going to do next?"

Rosalie shrugged, turning to Kenton. "Yes, what *are* we going to do next?"

After a moment's thought, a smile crept over his face. "We're going to forget about Cutler Gowen and Lazarus

Ambrose and take that ride out to the Reddicks' just like we promised Susan when we rang her up last night. I could do with a few hours in the country on a good riding horse."

Minnie smiled. "And I, the same." To Rosalie, she said, "No offense, dear, but after one day of euchre with Miss Ava and Miss Eda, and another day walking all about this fair city, I'm ready to climb aboard a good horse and ride."

To Rosalie, Vanda Mae said, "Be sure to put your knickerbockers on beneath your skirt before we go. You never know when that ton of courage might come tumbling down on you."

Rosalie set her napkin aside. "I'll wear them, but don't get your hopes up. That ton of courage you've been praying for seems to be on an ounce-at-a-time delivery schedule."

On the drive to the Reddicks', Rosalie was unprepared for the enthusiastic manner in which her mother and sister spoke of her riding again. They seemed to assume that this time, it would really happen. Fear of disappointing them after all these many years of avoiding the saddle only added to the chills that sometimes galloped up her spine, ending in bristled hairs on the back of her neck. Despite the warmth of the day—already seventy-five degrees by mid-morning—her hands were cold and clammy, and the songs of the sparrows along the country road sounded more like a prelude to problems than a precursor of success.

Susan and her father welcomed them the moment Kenton brought his carriage to a halt in the driveway. With introductions accomplished, Mr. Reddick led them toward the stable, his comments directed at Rosalie.

181

"Susan has taken the liberty of saddling up Penny for you."

The young girl said, "She's so tall, it'll be easiest to use the mounting platform to get on her." She indicated a wooden structure near the end of the building. "But Daddy and I will be right there to steady her and adjust your stirrups once you're in the saddle."

Inside the stable, Penny was cross tied in the aisle, all brushed, bridled, and saddled as had been promised. Standing there, outside of her stall, the horse suddenly seemed larger than Rosalie had remembered, and far more intimidating. Her heart began to flutter.

"I . . . I've changed my mind about riding today. Maybe some other time." She started to back away, but Vanda Mae prevented her, slipping her arm about her sister's waist.

"I'm not going to let you run away this time, Sis. Penny is the perfect horse for you, I can tell just by looking at her. And you're going to get on her."

Minnie stroked Penny's neck, giving her tack a cursory inspection. "Vanda Mae's right, Rosalie, Penny's a good choice, and getting on her will be easy as shoofly pie. You'll see."

John began unfastening the animal. "Like Susan said, we'll be right beside you every second. There's nothin' to worry about."

Despite the reassurances, Rosalie's mouth went dry with fright. She wanted nothing more than to bolt out of the stable and away from the Reddick farm. Only Kenton's encouraging smile and her sister's firm hug kept her from doing so.

Mercifully, the mounting platform was situated beneath

the shade of an oak. Vanda Mae led her up the steps.
Now, looking down on the saddle, visions of her fall off
Hurricane came rushing back. Vanda Mae, her mother, and
Susan, encouraged her in turn.

"It's just one little step from here, Sis."

"There's no better time than now, to get on a horse
again, dear."

"You can do it, Miss Foxe, just like I did!"

The longer Rosalie stood staring at the saddle, the more
impossible the last step seemed.

Her mother grew impatient. "Don't keep the Reddicks
and poor Penny waiting forever, dear. Just say a little
prayer and lower yourself onto the saddle."

At her mother's suggestion, Rosalie's mind and body
went numb. She needed time to expel the last of her fears
and replace them with some frail semblance of confidence.
Her mother's urgings seemed only to impede the process.

Kenton must have understood, for he took Minnie by
the elbow. "Mrs. Foxe, perhaps Rosalie will do better with
fewer people looking on. Come, let me show you my pride
and joy, my horse, Judge."

As he led her off toward the stable, she called over her
shoulder, "You can do it, dear, I know you can!"

With her mother gone, Rosalie prayed for the fortitude
to bend down, reach for the saddle horn, and settle herself
on Penny, but every last remnant of courage seemed to
have taken flight like the sparrows.

CHAPTER

16

North Carolina

Full from the catfish dinner Shani had served this Friday night, Willy Jo leaned back on the grassy cushion of the riverbank, pulled his cap down over his eyes, and inhaled deeply of the magnolia essence before expelling it with a sigh. While locusts droned their tedious tunes, he pondered his circumstances since Vanda Mae's accident.

Thirteen days had lapsed—thirteen evenings since she'd gone riding with him. And nine days had passed since he'd heard her voice or seen her face. Tanglewood wasn't the same without her.

Now, at the end of his sixth week at Foxe Brothers, he couldn't help wondering if or when he would get back to the farm chores he loved. He'd prayed God would forgive him for the fight with his brother and father, but he hadn't been able to bring himself to go to his daddy and apologize. With Bobby Dan's departure, he knew his daddy needed help. He'd hoped his father would ask him to lend a hand, then he'd be able to say he was sorry, but it was a foolish thought.

He recalled the fact that Fergus had spoken with his daddy just two days ago, and the exact words. *Your daddy is claiming you're all to blame for Bobby Dan leaving home. When I told him it was just as much his fault for trying to force the boy into farming, he raised more fuss than a weasel in a hen house and told me to mind my own business. Guess you'll be staying on here awhile, son.*

The mere recollection made Willy Jo smolder within. Getting to his feet, he mounted Hurricane, walked him out of the woods, then dug his heels into his belly, racing as fast as he could across the pasture. When he slowed to a walk to cool the horse down, he realized he couldn't outrun anger or frustration, but perhaps with God's help he could find a way to put it behind him. He prayed it would be so.

When he had unsaddled Hurricane, fed him a ration of oats, and turned him out to pasture, he walked back to the house. Shani was working in the kitchen, and greeted him as he removed his boots in the back room.

"Mr. Foxe said to tell ya he done turned in for the night. Is there anything I can get ya 'fore I do the same?"

"No, thank you, Shani. I'm going up and take my bath soon."

She wiped her hands on her apron. "I'll go on up and draw the water for ya."

"No need. I'll draw my own bath," Willy Jo told her, intending to sit in the library and read the paper for a spell. But when he walked into the room, he found an open letter atop the newspaper on the table between Fergus's chair and his. He remembered then that a letter from up north had been waiting for Fergus on the table in the front hall when they'd arrived home, but he'd saved it for later knowing Shani was ready to put dinner on the table. He evidently intended for Willy Jo to read it, too. He recognized Vanda Mae's hand at the top of the page.

> *Dearest Daddy,*
>   *How I wish you had been here today! Mr.*

McCune, the lawyer friend of Uncle Benjamin and Aunt Lottie, took Mama, Rosalie, and me to a horse farm and Rosalie actually sat on the back of a horse! She only stayed there a minute or two, and wouldn't let Mr. Reddick—he's the man who owns the farm—lead the horse around at all, but at least she made a start at getting over her fear.

Daddy, I know I'm not supposed to ride a horse while I'm here, but I hope you'll reconsider. My shoulder is much better than it was, and in one more week, I'm sure it will be good as new. If you would let me ride at the Reddicks', I think I can convince Rosalie to ride along beside me with our horses at a walk. <u>Please</u> give me your permission. Mama absolutely will not allow me to mount a horse without your blessing.

I must end here and let Mama write the rest of our news. Give my greetings to Willy Jo if he is still with you at Tanglewood, or when you see him next, if he is not.

Your dutiful daughter, Vanda Mae.

Dearest Fergus,

As Vanda Mae has informed you, Rosalie is progressing toward the day when she will once again ride horseback! Please let us hear from you soon regarding Vanda Mae's request to ride beside her sister. She may well be able to give Rosalie the extra measure of confidence she so sorely needs to take the next step.

As for other news, our stay here has been very pleasant—and interesting. Mr. McCune has *enlisted Rosalie's help in untangling the problems that put my sister and brother out of their shop. I don't know if they'll ever succeed at getting to the bottom of the mess, but Rosalie and Mr. McCune seem to be making an excellent success of their friendship. In fact, Rosalie has already hinted that she might like to stay on up north past summer's end and I wouldn't be at all opposed, should it come to that.*

Is Willy Jo still with you? I pray he has made amends with his kin and moved back home. Virginia would take great solace in his return, especially since the disappearance of Bobby Dan. Did he come back home yet? By the time this reaches you, perhaps my prayers for both boys will have been answered and the wayward sons will have returned. I'm eager to know if Winthrops have had cause to celebrate a family reunion.

I must close now and put this in the mail. I miss you, my darling, and pray the August heat hasn't been too hard on you. The climate is very pleasant here by the big lake, but after all my years in Old North State, I find I miss the mountains at Blowing Rock. Perhaps we can take a holiday together there this fall, when Vanda Mae has returned to the Academy and family and business matters are less pressing.

Your loving wife, Minnie.

Willy Jo read the portions about Rosalie a second time before setting the letter down. A strange sense of relief came over him that, despite the longtime assumption he and

Rosalie would someday marry, she was now enjoying the friendship of another man, freeing him of guilt over his attraction to her younger sister. But relief was not the only emotion deep within his heart right now. An emptiness had set in, and a longing for as much love in his own family as he sensed among the Foxes.

Feeling a need to ponder these thoughts and more, he wandered out to the pasture, soon riding bareback atop Hurricane whom he walked along the road toward his daddy's place. As dusk set in and whippoorwills soared overhead making their plaintive pleas, he longed to turn up the drive toward home, but instead, he kept to the road, passing his father's largest cornfield. Even in the dim light he could see that the stalks were not as high as they should be this time of year. Weeds were encroaching on some of the rows he'd helped cultivate and plant during spring recess from school, but other rows had been recently hoed.

Arriving at the path to the hog pen and barn, he turned up the two-rut trail. Off to the side stood his daddy's wagon, one wheel missing. He wondered why Lincoln hadn't fixed it. Daddy never left equipment in disrepair, but always put Lincoln, his trusted farm hand with wheelwright and blacksmith skills, right to the task.

He continued on, toward the hog pens. Even from a distance he could hear the anguished roars and moans of hungry pigs. Drawing nearer, he saw that the trough in the pen of feeder pigs was empty and their wallow dry. He dismounted, tethered Hurricane, and went into the barn in search of feed. A basket stood beneath the chute of the potato cleaner, half-full. Willy Jo cranked the handle, sending more cleaned potatoes down the chute until the basket could hold no more, then he carried it out and dumped it in the trough. The pigs grunted and squealed in their rush to feed. Making more trips to the barn, Willy Jo fetched basket after basket of corn until the trough was full.

As he stood back to watch the hogs feed, he noticed that some of the animals were maturing well, but others were downright scrawny. He wished he'd been there to make sure they were *all* receiving sufficient feed. Surely each and every hog would have prospered under his care. As it was, several of them needed considerable fattening up to attain a normal weight for their age.

On his way back to the barn, he paused at the sty of the sow who'd been lame at the start of July. At least now, she appeared to be moving normally on all fours.

In the barn once more, he gathered water buckets in hand, headed for the well, then carried several gallons of water to the wallow until it was thoroughly muddy again. Leaning his foot on the fence rail, he watched as the satiated pigs rolled in the cool, wet earth, acquiring a muddy coat of protection against flies, mosquitoes, and parasites. Their satisfied grunts were music to his ears, but he couldn't help wondering why his father hadn't properly tended the hogs himself.

With a heavy heart he mounted Hurricane and continued on, taking a hard clay path toward the hired man's house. Maybe Lincoln could tell him why the wagon had gone unrepaired, the cornfield wasn't hoed, and some hogs were underfed. Several yards from the house he heard a man's voice, song-like. The sound grew louder and bawdier as he moved closer. The words and tune were unrecognizable, but the voice was easily identified, as was the state of its owner. Lincoln was obviously in a bad way, the victim of too much whiskey.

Now, Willy Jo knew why the cornfield was neglected, the hogs underfed, and the wagon in disrepair. Lincoln had lapsed into his old, bad habit, one he had overcome years ago, but had evidently taken up again. Without Lincoln's help, or that of either son, there was only so much Willy Jo's daddy could do.

Sympathy did battle with resentment in Willy Jo's heart. He hated seeing the family farm in decline. He hated more his father's stubbornness that kept the two of them apart. Swinging Hurricane around, he trotted down the clay path onto the road and nudged the horse's flanks with his heels, setting him into a canter toward Tanglewood.

CHAPTER

17

Michigan

"Don't forget these!" Vanda Mae reminded Rosalie, holding up the knickerbockers she'd worn to the Reddicks' one week ago.

As Rosalie dressed to go downstairs for breakfast, she was dreading the visit they would soon make to the horse farm. Her fear of this day had plagued her all week long, giving her nightmares last night. By the time she'd crawled out of bed this morning, a butterfly ballet had begun in her stomach and she was incapable of stopping the performance.

Her sister and mother had made it perfectly clear all week long that they expected her to do more today than simply sit on Penny's back. The problem was, each time she envisioned herself actually riding a horse, Vanda Mae was riding horseback beside her, urging her on with words of courage and confidence. But her sister would not be allowed to mount a horse today.

Releasing an apprehensive sigh, Rosalie pulled the pant-like garment up beneath her skirt and stepped in front of the mirror. She was arranging the folds of blue serge over the knickerbockers when Vanda Mae came up behind her.

"You're going to do it today, Sis. You're going to ride

Penny around the ring and nothing bad is going to happen."

Rosalie met Vanda Mae's gaze in the mirror. "I'd be a lot more sure of myself if you could ride beside me." Turning to face her sister, she admitted solemnly, "As it is, I'm so tied in knots, I'm not even sure I can manage to get in a saddle again."

"Oh, go on!" Vanda Mae offered an impetuous hug. She was releasing Rosalie when the sound of a buggy coming to a stop in front of the house caught their attention.

Vanda Mae hurried to the window, pushing back the curtain. "It's the Western Union hack."

Rosalie turned to the mirror again. "News for Kenton about Cutler Gowen, I hope. I'm more convinced every day that he sprang full-grown from behind a rock." She fussed with her hair, trying to tuck a loose strand into her topknot and finding little success.

Vanda Mae headed for the door. "I'm going down and find out." She returned moments later, a grin stretching the limits of her face as she shoved the telegram into Rosalie's hand. "This is the best news since Tassie had her foal!"

"Did Gaspar find Daddy's missing horses?" Rosalie wondered aloud. Focusing on the message addressed to Vanda Mae Foxe in care of Kenton McCune, she read, "'Permission granted to ride with Rosalie. Only. Letter to follow.'"

At her puzzled look, Vanda Mae quickly explained. "I wrote Daddy last week and told him you were considering riding again, and that I thought you'd be more likely to follow through if I could ride with you."

The butterflies in Rosalie's stomach seemed to be leaping across their stage in unison. "Now, you've done it, Vanda Mae! Now you've really put me on the spot!"

192

Vanda Mae wagged her finger. "Only a few minutes ago you told me you'd be more sure of yourself if I could ride with you. Well, you got your wish! Nothing's going to stop you, now!" Going straight to her trunk, Vanda Mae pulled out the riding breeches and shirt she'd brought north just in case, but hadn't bothered to unpack.

As Vanda Mae changed her clothes, the butterflies in Rosalie's stomach seemed to do one last leap before exiting the stage.

But as she learned an hour later when Kenton pulled into the Reddick's drive, the winged troupe had only taken an intermission. Now, they were back for the final act, and their performance was causing a minor case of nausea. Rosalie tried desperately to put her mind elsewhere—on the white clouds with their heavy grey bottoms portending rain before the day was through; on the skunk essence still lingering from a previous night's encounter with a foe; on the scolding of a blue jay and taunt of a grackle as a squirrel scurried over the branches of their old oak home. Still, her hands were cold and damp and her mouth dry and distasteful as though she'd been breakfasting on cotton batting.

As the carriage drew near the stable, Rosalie felt immobilized by fear. Looking down at her left hand, she realized she was gripping the seat so tightly, her fingers had turned white. In desperation, she sent up a silent plea for help. *Dear Lord, send me courage, and send it now!*

She waited for her mother and sister to step out of the carriage before releasing her grip and allowing Kenton to help her down. His hand was warm and dry against her cool, damp one. His touch, and the smile of encouragement he offered, began to thaw her fears.

Somehow, she managed to make light conversation while the horses for Kenton and her mother were led from the stable, all saddled and ready. They mounted and rode off, then she and Mr. Reddick led Penny out of the stable followed by Susan and Vanda Mae, each atop chestnut mares. As Rosalie drew near the wooden mounting platform, a lesson from the Bible came to mind. She repeated it silently again and again and again. *I can do all things through Christ, I can do all things through Christ, I can do all things through Christ . . .*

The courage she had sought from God seemed to come a drop at a time, one for each step as she mounted the platform, and it fell far short of the dose needed to do what was expected of her. Stalled beside the huge horse, she felt a strong urge to abandon the scene when Vanda Mae's words penetrated the fog of fear swamping her mind.

"Do this for yourself, Rosalie. You can, if you *want* to!"

Rooted in place, she tried to make herself bend toward the horse, but could only remain stiff as a mannequin.

Her sister spoke again, this time in hushed words of prayer that floated to Rosalie on the soft summer breeze. "Dear Lord, my sister's a tad scared just now. Wrap her in a mantel of courage. Bind her fears and cast them out. Take her in your arms and set her on Penny's back, then carry her there until she knows no doubt or apprehension. In Jesus name, Amen."

Her movements no longer her own, Rosalie lowered herself onto Penny's back, took up the reins, and relaxed into the gentle jostling of the saddle, recalling after six long years the habit of moving with the horse's gait.

Having surmounted the toughest challenge, she managed to complete her first trip around the riding ring—led by Mr. Reddick and flanked by Susan and Vanda Mae—with no untoward results. Her courage building, she took the second trip around without his help, the younger girls keeping her fortitude in tact. By the end of the hour, she was riding around the ring alone, a goal she'd assumed would require another week or two to accomplish.

The sense of satisfaction she felt when showing Kenton and her mother her achievement made her wish she wouldn't have to wait a full eight days before repeating the experience, but the Reddicks were going away to a horse auction in Chicago and she wouldn't be able to ride Penny until next Sunday. Nevertheless, the glorious feeling of success stayed with her all the way home. She was still basking in it when Mrs. Buckley met them at the door, a letter for Kenton in hand.

"This came for you special delivery not an hour ago, sir. It's addressed to your office, but the postman brought it by thinking you'd like to have it before Monday morning."

Kenton quickly set his riding crop and helmet on the hall table. "Thank you, Mrs. Buckley."

With a nod, the hired woman retreated to her kitchen.

Rosalie studied the address over Kenton's shoulder. "It's from Mrs. Spicer."

Minnie said, "I've been praying for news from out East."

Vanda Mae said, "Read it aloud, Mr. McCune. We all want to know what the woman has to say."

Removing the missive from the envelope, Kenton began. "'Dear Mr. McCune, I was visiting my dearly departed brother's grave a few days ago when I happened to read the inscription on an old headstone I had never

195

noticed before. It says, "Cutler Gowen, born 1848, died 1872." At first, I thought the man in your city must be a descendant, but the granite marker made no mention of family, and I found no evidence of relatives buried near his grave site. My curiosity aroused, I searched records at the county office thinking I would find something about the man buried here that might shed light on the fellow by the same name in your city, perhaps information regarding a Cutler Gowen, Jr. Oddly enough, no birth or death records bearing the name "Cutler Gowen" can be located! The clerk said they are probably in the wrong file, but when I asked him to look more thoroughly, he became very irritated with me. I have an uneasy feeling about it that I cannot explain. I am asking around the city to see if anyone remembers Cutler Gowen, but so far, I have found none who knew him. Sorry I could not be of more help in the matter. If you think of any way in which I could be of further assistance, do not hesitate to ask. Sincerely, Mrs. Spicer.'"

Rosalie reached for the letter. "Do you think our Mr. Gowen is the son of this dead man?"

Minnie said, "Perhaps he's a nephew."

Vanda Mae asked, "What are you going to do now, Mr. McCune?"

In the thoughtful moment that followed, thunder rumbled over the bay. Taking the letter in hand again, Kenton said contemplatively, "I don't really know what I'll do . . . except to pray that Mrs. Spicer finds someone who knew Cutler Gowen and his kin."

In the wee hours of the morning, with the house dark and everyone sleeping to the patter of steady rain on the roof, Kenton lay awake, still thinking about the letter from Mrs. Spicer. He pondered again the conundrum of Cutler Gowen. Thunder cracked, then lightning flashed outside his window, momentarily illuminating the collection of photos occupying the table opposite his bed. Suddenly, a new thought bolted into his mind. Hopping out of bed, he hurriedly dressed, pulled on his macintosh and galoshes, grabbed his umbrella from the hall stand, and made haste to the Western Union office. He was certain Mrs. Spicer could be of further assistance, and he wasn't about to waste a moment letting her know how.

Realizing his hunch could prove false, he decided not to mention this communication to anyone lest he foster disappointments. Nevertheless, he could hardly wait for the woman's response.

CHAPTER

18

North Carolina

Willy Jo was thankful that Fergus had closed up shop and brought him home a couple of hours earlier than usual on this still, sultry, Saturday afternoon. In his spare time before dinner, he mounted Hurricane and headed for his daddy's farm, perspiration rolling down his face and dripping off his chin with each sluggish step of the grey gelding. But he gave little thought to the heat now, and was only slightly aware of the musty essence of the woods that shaded this stretch of road. Foremost on his mind were last night's images of neglect on his daddy's hog farm.

As Willy Jo rounded the bend, the woods gave way to a clearing. In the distance he could see his daddy laboring alone at the axle of his broken-down wagon, struggling to replace the wheel that had been missing the night before. In the shade of a nearby poplar stood his team, waiting to be hitched.

With a nudge of his heels, he urged Hurricane to trot. His father seemed unaware of his approach, grunting and straining as he toiled to position the heavy, iron-rimmed wheel on the axle. Willy Jo quickly dismounted and grabbed hold of the spokes, lending enough muscle power to mate the hub to the axle.

Jabe straightened and heaved a sigh. His hand on his

back, he slipped off his straw hat and mopped his sweaty forehead on his rolled-up sleeve. With barely a glance at Willy Jo, he pulled the wide, fringed brim down over his eyes again, mumbling, "Didn't hear ya comin'."

Lacking a reply, Willy Jo began tightening down the wheel. Without so much as a word of thanks, his daddy went to fetch the team. Willy Jo waited while he backed them into position, then helped hitch them up, attaching the right tug to the wagon while his daddy secured the left.

When Jabe swung up onto the driver's seat, the urge of an old habit made Willy Jo want to climbed aboard beside his daddy as he'd done hundreds of times since he'd been a small boy. Instead, he forced himself to walk away, toward Hurricane.

He was about to mount up when Jabe spoke up. "Tie that rascal to the wagon and ride up to the house with me. I'm sure Kezia has enough lemonade for us both."

The soft rhythm of the horses' hooves on the dusty roadbed, the quiet creaking of the wooden wagon wheels, the unremitting buzz of locusts in tree limbs high above the road proved a poor substitute for conversation. Nevertheless, Willy Jo was mighty thankful for the few sentences already spoken, and he searched his heart for appropriate words of his own. Sadly, he concluded that no matter what subject he might broach, he was sure to say the wrong thing. So he kept his silence all the way to the house, as did his daddy, speaking only words of thanks when Kezia brought cooling beverages to them both in their repose beneath the fronds of the huge willow in the dooryard.

Willy Jo didn't miss the look of keen interest in the dark-skinned housekeeper's eyes when she saw him, nor the way she pressed her lips together to keep from speaking out of turn. He was wondering why his mother hadn't come out to greet him when his daddy spoke again.

"Your mama's out to a sewin' circle meetin'. She'll be right sorry she missed ya."

"Give her my love," Willy Jo promptly replied, wishing affection for his father were as easily felt and expressed.

Their lemonade glasses were half-empty when Jabe saw fit to speak again. "Been a lot of horses stolen hereabouts this month. Two of Benders' came up missin' just last night." He named neighbors on a nearby farm. "I've been keepin' my roans tied up outside my bedroom window at night." He paused, then his gaze met his son's and Willy Jo was certain the sore subject of April would come up. Instead, conversation took a new turn. "Heard from your brother the other day."

"How—"

Jabe hastened to explain. "Fool kid up and joined a travelin' show. He's doin' acrobatics at fairs up north—in Wisconsin last I heard."

Willy Jo was still absorbing the news when a grin bloomed on his father's face. "Should've known I'd never make a farmer out of him. At least he's happy."

At least he's happy. The sentiment rang in Willy Jo's head. Anger reared in his heart and words leaped off his tongue before he could stop them.

"All you care about is Bobby Dan! What about *me?* What about *my* happiness?"

Jabe's mouth fell open. Color invaded his cheeks. Willy Jo surged on before his daddy could reply.

"Bobby Dan never does wrong in your eyes. And I never do right! No matter how hard I try, I never hear a word of thanks or praise!" Tossing the remaining lemonade and ice from his glass, he plunked it down beside his father and sprang to his feet. "I wanted to come home. Goodness knows you need my help. I hoped things could be different between us, but I can see now, nothing's changed!"

Untying Hurricane, he swung into the saddle.

"Willy Jo! Wait!"

Ignoring his father's plea, he set a course for Tanglewood, putting the gelding into a canter despite the heat.

The full moon was a large, white treasure amidst a collection of lesser gems that shone through a hole in the clouds when Willy Jo gave up the notion of sleep, pulled on work pants and shirt, and ventured out of the manor house at midnight. The air was still heavy with moisture despite the passing of the thunderstorm that had moved through in the last hour. The continued heat and humidity, along with troubling thoughts of his latest encounter with his father, had kept him from finding entrance to dreamland.

Leaning against the fence, he gazed at the row of outdoor boxes alongside the stable. A restless Hurricane stood visible until clouds moved in to obscure stars and moon again. As warm winds breathed down his collar, he contemplated the hasty ending to his afternoon ride. He shouldn't have stormed off. He should have given his father a chance to talk. But pent-up anger, resentment, and yes, even jealousy, had destroyed the last fragment of tolerance he might have summoned for any words his daddy could have offered.

Without aforethought, he fetched Hurricane's bridle from the tack room, slipped them onto the horse, and mounted his bare back. Responding to some inner, magnetic force, he headed in the direction of his daddy's farm. There, following instinct rather than plan, he lit a lantern and tended the hog pen, carrying basket after basket filled with potatoes and corn.

Seeing a large abscess on one of the pigs, he removed the animal from the pen, then cleaned, lanced, and drained the infection. Afterward, he inspected the pen thoroughly, and by lantern light repaired a rough board that could have caused the break in the one animal's skin, allowing infection to set in.

From the barn, he fetched a hoe and basket, carried them along with an extra lantern to the nearby cornfield, and began digging weeds from between the stalks. Though he knew he couldn't hope to finish the work required in the field tonight, at least he could make a start, labor until fatigue overcame him, and return some other time. As he loosened the dirt, pulled out the grassy weeds, and laid them aside to collect later, he realized how much he'd missed putting his hands in the soil, turning the earth, cultivating the crop that was essential to a hog farmer's success —almost as much as he'd missed caring for the hogs. Down one long row and up another, he worked back and forth across the field until thunder rumbled. In the distance, lightning flashed. Another thunderstorm was moving in, making it unsafe to remain in the field. Quickly, he gathered uprooted weeds into his basket, took up his hoe, and headed for the barn where Hurricane was tethered, but uneasy.

The wind picked up, gusting in his face as they headed for Tanglewood. Rumblings of thunder made Hurricane shy and side-step.

"Get on, boy. It's all right," Willy Jo reassured him. "We'll be home soon, then you can hide in your box if you want."

Hurricane remained uneasy, so Willy Jo kept up a mindless, soothing patter until they reached the pasture gate where he dismounted to swing it open.

Lightning flashed.

Thunder boomed.

Hurricane bolted, ripping his reins free of Willy Jo's grip and taking off down the road as rain let loose.

"Whoa, boy! Come back!" Willy Jo shouted, running after him.

Another crack sounded—of gunfire, this time.

Then he heard Gaspar shout, "Stop, you thief!"

Before Willy Jo could identify himself, a second shot sent searing pain into his side. Clutching his wound, he slumped onto a hard, slippery bed of wet clay.

CHAPTER

19

Michigan

As Kenton drove home from his office the following Friday afternoon, he couldn't help feeling disappointed at Mrs. Spicer's lack of response. He'd expected to hear from her before now, and was growing impatient. Even Rosalie noticed, adding she was glad he had given her two days off to take her mother and sister on an excursion to Northport aboard the *Columbia*. When she asked what was bothering him, he put her off. The wire sent East remained his secret.

He pulled into the carriage barn, unhitched and fed Nick, and started for the house when he saw a postal delivery hack stop out front. He hurried to intercept the postman halfway up the front walk.

"Special Delivery for you, Mr. McCune. I missed you at your office and figured I ought to bring it by."

"I left a few minutes early today. Much obliged," Kenton said, his heart skipping a beat when he recognized Mrs. Spicer's handwriting. He was further encouraged by the stiffness and thickness of the envelope. Seeking a chair on the front porch, he could hear Benjamin and Lottie in conversation in the parlor discussing their day at the candy factory as he ripped open the flap of the envelope and pulled out the contents.

A one-page letter enfolded two enclosures. He set it

aside along with a news clipping, and stared down at the photograph of Mrs. Spicer's brother, Lazarus Ambrose. Kenton's blood rushed with excitement. He turned it over, finding the man's name and the date his picture was taken penned in Mrs. Spicer's hand. He set it aside to read the newspaper article, his mind spinning with the information contained therein. Finally, he read the letter. It opened with a brief statement that Lazarus Ambrose had died a loner without heirs. In the paragraphs that followed, Mrs. Spicer eulogized her honest, trustworthy, beloved late brother.

Kenton was still pondering all that he had discovered when Rosalie, Vanda Mae, and Minnie came up the walk, singing a harmonious rendition of *Daisy Bell* in blended soprano voices. He rose from his chair to greet them as they climbed the porch steps.

"It's nice to see you're in such good spirits, ladies, and I have news that will make them even better!" He held up the envelope from Mrs. Spicer.

Rosalie, Minnie, and Vanda Mae spoke in quick succession.

"Is our Cutler Gowen the son of the man in the cemetery?"

"Is he the nephew?"

"Tell us quick, Mr. McCune, before I expire of sheer curiosity!"

Kenton held the door open. "Come inside. I want Benjamin and Lottie to be in on this, too." In the parlor, he directed Rosalie to sit between her aunt and uncle on the sofa, then he stood before them. "This is a photograph of Mrs. Spicer's brother, the late Lazarus Ambrose." Pulling the portrait from the envelope, he held it at eye level.

Lottie gasped, hands flying to her cheeks.

Ben scowled and mumbled under his breath.

Rosalie's mouth dropped open. She took the picture in hand to study it more closely, finally asking, "Do you think . . . could this possibly be . . . a fair-haired likeness of our dark-haired Cutler Gowen?"

With words quicker than logic, Vanda Mae said, "If it is, then Uncle Benjamin and Aunt Lottie are working for a dead man!"

Minnie laughed. "Obviously not, but something's rotten as a basketful of spoiled eggs if the deceased Lazarus Ambrose has risen from the dead to live a second life as Cutler Gowen. Are you all certain the two are one and the same?"

Lottie studied the portrait a second time. "It *must* be."

Benjamin stated, "There's little doubt."

Rosalie said, "I think Mr. Gowen's using shoe polish on his hair to change his appearance."

Kenton said, "There's more. Mrs. Spicer sent a newspaper article that came out about a month after her brother's death. I'll read it to you." He perched on the edge of his winged chair. "'Embezzlement at New York Central. Accounts empty. Auditors at a loss to explain. A recent audit of accounts of the New York Central has revealed considerable irregularities. Banking deposits that were posted to the railroad's accounts were, in fact, never made. Railroad ledgers and bank books appear to have been falsified to cover the embezzlement of thousands of dollars. The exact amount is not known.

"'It is certain, however, that the late Lazarus Ambrose had charge of the accounts for the railroad. As you will recall, we reported in this newspaper one month ago that

Mr. Ambrose was brutally murdered outside his Cherry Street home.

"'Mr. Ambrose was known by his fellow employees to have been meticulous with his bookkeeping. According to his supervisor at the Central, Mr. Ambrose's accounts were never out of balance in all the twenty years he was employed by the railroad.

"'Police fear that Mr. Ambrose stumbled on an embezzlement scheme and was killed before he could bring it to the attention of his superiors. Although they have thoroughly questioned employees at the Central and at the bank where the money was supposedly on deposit, they have no leads in the case.'"

Rosalie said, "It's obvious Mr. Gowen—Ambrose, or whatever his name is—used money he embezzled from the railroad out East to set up a candy factory here in Traverse City."

Her mother theorized further. "He evidently assumed that by moving so far away, no one would discover his crime."

Lottie grew urgent. "We must go to the Chief of Police immediately!"

Ben reached for the photograph. "I've a mind to take this straight to Mr. Gowen, shove it in his face, and see what he has to say!"

Kenton grew cautious. "You'd better not."

"But he's a scoundrel! Stole huge sums of money! He must be called to account!"

His lawyer's mind taking over, Kenton warned, "But we haven't one iota of proof."

Minnie reasoned with her brother. "He's one cunning critter, putting you out of your store the way he did. The first instant he thinks someone's caught onto his ruse, he'll be off to parts unknown, never to be found again."

Vanda Mae sighed. "Lazarus Ambrose may have been an honest man when he was alive, but since he died, he certainly has proven himself to be one perfidious lout."

Kenton pondered aloud, "I wonder who's buried in Lazarus Ambrose's grave."

Lottie focused a squinted eye on him. "Do you think someone was . . . murdered . . . maybe even by Mr. Ambrose . . . and buried there instead of himself?"

Kenton shrugged. "It's impossible to say until the body is exhumed." After a moment's silence, he added, "And now that I think back on the death notice in Mr. Gowen's—or Ambrose's—wallet, it said that he had a closed-casket funeral."

Rosalie offered a wry smile. "That surely explains why Cutler Gowen called Lazarus Ambrose his very best friend."

Lottie chortled. "The best friend who made him wealthy."

Minnie grew contemplative. "Poor Mrs. Spicer. She thinks her brother died an honest accountant. How will she take the news that he's alive and not . . . "

Kenton supplied the words, read from Mrs. Spicer's letter, "' . . . a gem of a man. Upright, honest, and completely devoted to the New York Central.' At least she won't have to know for awhile—not until investigations uncover enough proof of his secret criminal activities to warrant his arrest."

Rosalie spoke thoughtfully. "You'll have to send word to the police out East who investigated Ambrose's so-called murder and the embezzlement."

Kenton nodded. "I'll send a wire to the New York Central as well. They'll want to know of new leads in the case."

Lottie pondered the situation out loud. "I suppose this means we all have to go on treating Mr. Gowen as if nothing's changed."

Ben almost smiled. "Actors. We'll all be actors. Before you know it, we'll be appearing on stage at the Opera House."

Minnie's head moved slowly from side to side. "I still can't help thinking of the shock Mrs. Spicer will suffer when she learns about her brother. There seems no easy way to apprise her of the truth."

Kenton said, "We'll cross that bridge when we come to it. In the meantime, we can pray for some merciful method of breaking the news."

Two days later, Vanda Mae gazed with pride at her older sister as they prepared to spend a Sunday afternoon horseback riding at the Reddicks'. Dressed in the new riding breeches and boots she had bought from Millikens the previous day, she looked every bit a horsewoman—except for the slight frown creasing her forehead.

Making reference to Susan, who had rung them up the previous evening, Vanda Mae tried to distract her sister from her worry. "Did I mention, she said her daddy bought a new mare at the auction in Chicago?"

"Only half a dozen times since last night," Rosalie said with a wry smile.

"To hear Susan tell it, that new horse of hers is the finest mare this side of the Mason-Dixon line. I'd never say a word to disappoint her, but that mare can't be as nice as my April was."

"That's what you said last night," Rosalie reminded her.

Vanda Mae went on. "April was the finest riding horse I've ever seen. Daddy liked her so much, he—"

"—wanted to make her into a brood mare," Rosalie finished for her.

"I guess I told you that before, too."

Picking up her new riding gloves, Rosalie headed for the door. "If we don't get started soon, you'll have repeated your entire life's story before we get to the Reddicks', and it would be a pure shame to deprive Susan and her father of the pleasure of hearing it."

Vanda Mae grinned. The worry wrinkle was gone from her sister's brow, and that was all she cared about for now.

A quarter of an hour later, when Kenton pulled into the Reddicks' drive, she could see Susan in the distance, riding around the ring atop her new mare. The dark chestnut color reminded her of April, making her mildly jealous. She quickly prayed the feeling away, wanting only to be happy for Susan, who had expressed such excitement over the new addition to her daddy's horse farm.

But when Susan left the riding ring and headed toward Kenton's rig, Vanda Mae saw a blaze on the mare's forehead that was identical to April's, flaring out narrowly on the right side only. Three white socks matched the ones that marked April. The moment the buggy came to a halt, Vanda Mae jumped out and ran to the horse. Seeing a telltale sprinkle of white hair at the mare's brow line, she cried out with glee.

"April, it's you!"

The mare nickered and bobbed her head.

Vanda Mae reached for her bridle, stroking her nose,

then hugging her neck. "I found you, girl! I can hardly believe it! I found you!"

April nuzzled Vanda Mae's neck, her soft whinny revealing her joy.

Susan backed the horse away with a firm command, then addressed Vanda Mae. "What are you talking about? This is Queenie, *my* horse, the one Papa bought for me at Chicago!"

"But she was stolen from me earlier this month!" Vanda Mae insisted.

"We have the papers to prove this horse is ours!" Susan claimed.

The argument grew louder until Susan's father and the others joined them, John intervening with a minimum of words.

"Whoa, young ladies! What's this all about?"

With tears in her eyes, Susan turned to her father. "Vanda Mae says Queenie is hers, that she was stolen, and we don't really own her. *Please* show her the paper that says we bought her, fair and square!"

Vanda Mae addressed her mother. "This is *April!* I'd know her anywhere! See the shape of her blaze, her three white socks, and the frost in her eyebrows?"

Minnie took hold of April's bridle. She spoke softly to the animal, stroking her nose and inspecting her teeth and markings before turning to John. "My daughter's right, Mr. Reddick. My husband can prove this horse belongs to him, and she *was* stolen from us about three weeks ago."

John's expression hardened. "Then let your husband replevy the animal—put up security and take me to court." To McCune, he said, "You'll represent me in this matter, won't you?"

Kenton seemed to look past him, at the stables in the distance, before focusing on his good friend. "I'm suffering from conflict of interest, being a family friend to both you and the Foxes. I'd be foolish to take either side in a dispute between you. But John, I'll give you this advice for free. If Mr. Foxe documents his ownership to the court's satisfaction, the animal will be returned to him."

Minnie added, "And there's no doubt in my mind, Mr. Reddick, you'll lose."

Kenton rested a hand on John's shoulder. "From one friend to another, I believe your best recourse is to locate the fellow who brought the horse to auction."

John gazed at April, then at Susan, his blue eyes clouded with concern.

His daughter brushed away a tear with the back of her riding glove, pleadeding quietly. "Don't let them take Queenie, Papa! You said yourself, she's just the mare we need to build up our stock and keep the place going."

He reached up, caressing Susan's moist cheek. "We've got to do what's right."

"I won't give her up! I *won't!*" The young girl dug her heels into April's flanks and rode off in a cloud of dust.

Rosalie spoke up as the air cleared. "Mr. Reddick, I'll be glad to type up a letter to the auction house from Mr. McCune informing them that they've been party to traffic in stolen property and inquiring as to the seller's whereabouts. It might help you recover your investment so you can purchase some other animal."

Minnie said, "Something must be done to catch the thief, and the sooner, the better."

A hand shading her eyes, Vanda Mae watched Susan and April disappear across a wide meadow and into the adjoining woods. "One thing's certain, I've just lost my hankering for a horseback ride. Maybe Mr. McCune should take us straight to his office so Rosalie can use his typing machine, instead."

Her mother nodded. "And we should wire my husband about April."

John remained troubled. "I'd be much obliged for the help, but I don't think it'll make a difference. If the horse was stolen, the thief 'd be long gone from Chicago by now."

Kenton replied with a quote. "'Nothing venture, nothing win,' William Gilbert, *Iolanthe*, Act II. If you'll fetch the address of the auction house and the papers on the horse, the Foxe ladies and I will post a letter before the day is through."

CHAPTER

20

North Carolina

Like the restless grey clouds in the sky above, Willy Jo couldn't suppress the uneasiness he was feeling as Fergus pulled onto the main road and turned toward his daddy's place to honor their invitation to Sunday dinner. A week ago, upon receiving a telephone message from Fergus that Willy Jo had suffered a gunshot wound, his daddy had come to pay him a visit. The injury was nothing serious, the bullet having only grazed his flesh, but the incident had brought about direct communication between them. For the first time in years, his daddy had seemed a mite sympathetic. For the first time in years, he hadn't jumped at a chance to condemn Willy Jo for the calamity that had befallen him. For the first time in years, Willy Jo had heard his father speak not one word about Bobby Dan.

But neither had his daddy thanked him for the help he'd given him with the wagon wheel, or the work done in the cornfield and the hog pen just before he was shot. The circumstances of the accidental shooting had been carefully explained. His daddy knew where he'd gone on Hurricane in the middle of the night, and why Gaspar had mistaken him for a horse thief on his return to Tanglewood. Even if his father had chosen to ignore the explanation, surely he couldn't ignore the hoed rows of corn, the full trough in the

214

hog pen, and the repair he'd made. But no expression of gratitude had been forthcoming.

Perhaps Willy Jo was expecting too much. His father was slow to change. He should be thankful for the improvements he'd already seen. He tried to think less about his disappointment and more about the opportunity at hand.

As Fergus turned off the main road, the essence of phlox along his father's fence-lined drive filled the air. The perfume of the delicate flowers brought to mind his mother's sweet nature. He silently prayed that her gentle spirit would rule this day. And with the appearance of the sun through a rare hole in the grey heavens, hope sprang within that his petition was about to be answered. The sight of his daddy stepping out the door to greet him and Fergus with an equally rare smile seemed to confirm the fact.

"Fergus, Willy Jo, you're right on time. Kezia is ready to serve up." He rested his arm atop Willy Jo's shoulders as they went inside. Such displays of affection had been absent from their relationship since—Willy Jo couldn't remember when—and seemed unnatural now.

In the front hallway, he greeted his mother with his customary peck on the cheek. Her eyes were welling up, her voice a tad shaky when she greeted him.

"Good to see you, son."

He could only mumble a reply, his own throat growing tight as he cherished the familiar surroundings he'd missed for so long—the shadowbox of dried roses his mother had created years ago and hung on the foyer wall; her rose petit point chair cover when he seated her at the dining table; the polished oak sideboard his father had refinished when Willy Jo was still a boy in short pants. Now it was laden with the results of Kezia's culinary efforts. The sense of homecoming he'd experienced each time he'd returned from a long stay at school, he would like to have known again, except now he felt like an outsider.

When they had settled around the table, Jabe offered his standard prayer. "Blessed be the Lord, and bountiful thy hand. For these, thy gifts, we give thee thanks. In Jesus name, Amen."

Kezia set before him half a clove-studded ham covered with pineapple rings. Despite the pretense of normalcy as it was carved and served along with her grits, yams, and sticky buns, Willy Jo recognized the tension underlying the polite dinner table conversation. When the main course had come to an end and Kezia headed for the kitchen with a promise of cobbler made from home-grown peaches for dessert, a lull in the flow of words brought about a prompting from his mother.

"Jabe, you had something you wanted to ask Willy Jo today. Now's a good time."

Barely hiding his disquietude, his father focused on him. "Son," he paused as if the words he was about to say were not his own, "it's time ya moved back here—that is, if you're still of a mind to."

The invitation lacked conviction, and Willy Jo's first instinct was to refuse, but Fergus intervened with a smile that seemed unwarranted.

"I'll be hard put to replace Willy Jo at the lumber yard, Jabe, but I've been praying for weeks that this day would come." To Willy Jo, he said, "Of course, Tanglewood will be a mighty lonely place till my women come home from up north, but I'll have Gaspar help you move back home this very day."

Virginia's eyes sparkled with a mist of gratitude. "I'll

be so thankful to have at least one of my boys under my roof again."

Jabe's mouth curved in a half-smile. "Then it's settled." With barely a pause, he continued on another subject.

As conversation flowed between Jabe and Fergus, Willy Jo entertained private reservations about moving back into his father's house that bore a tart contrast to Kezia's sugary sweet cobbler.

He was still considering his impending move home when he and Fergus arrived at Tanglewood. His troubled thoughts were interrupted when Shani came hurrying out the back door of the house, waving Fergus down as he headed toward the carriage barn.

"Mr. Fergus, Mr. Willy, wait up!" A smile stretched the limits of Shani's generous mouth as, huffing and puffing, she waddled up to the carriage and shoved an opened Western Union envelope into Fergus's hand. "Forgive me for . . . readin' your message, but . . . I had to know if it was news that could wait . . . or if—"

"It's all right, Shani." Fergus eagerly extracted the telegram and read the few words out loud. "'April has been found here, in Traverse City. Letter with details follows. Love, M-R-V,' Minnie, Rosalie, and Vanda Mae," he explained before slapping Willy Jo on the back. "What do you know! April's been found way up in Michigan! At least now, we can put our minds to rest over that perplexity." When Willy Jo failed to smile, he asked, "What's the matter, son?"

"I can't help thinking . . . "

"Thinking what?"

"Eck Danvers is involved."

217

Fergus grew thoughtful. "Eck Danvers, your old nemesis? What makes you suspect him?"

"I'm sure he was lying to me the night April was stolen. I'm convinced he took her, and the other horses that have turned up missing hereabouts. I'd like to prove it."

Having pondered the suggestion, Fergus concluded, "I think you'd best tell your suspicions to my brother, since he's the sheriff. You're going to be too busy helping your daddy with the harvest to catch Danvers—if he *is* the thief."

As the buggy rolled into the carriage house, Willy Jo knew Fergus was right. Now was not the time to trail a horse thief. His daddy needed him, and no matter what his misgivings about moving home, he would not renege on the promise to return to the family farm.

CHAPTER

21

Michigan

As Kenton pulled off the road at a scenic lookout a few miles north of the city on the Mission Peninsula, Rosalie was thankful that he'd suggested the Sunday afternoon drive as an alternative to the horseback riding plans that had fallen through at the Reddicks'. This was her first carriage ride on the strip of land that separated the west side of Grand Traverse Bay from the east, and she was pleased that her mother and sister seemed to be enjoying the outing as much as she was herself. With pastoral views to the east and watery vistas to the west, thoughts of the letter they had posted to the Chicago auction house earlier that afternoon took flight.

Her entire attention was now on the visual delights surrounding her, as well as the scented ones, for the road was trimmed with a heavily perfumed, pink edging of phlox. She wanted to enjoy the moment fully, for one day soon she would be aboard a train heading south with her mother and sister so that Vanda Mae could start school at Salem Academy on the fifth of September.

Standing on the sandy shore, gazing at the rippled expanse of blue dotted by white triangles, feeling the warm breeze, was making her regret her impending departure. Little by little, she'd grown accustomed to Grand Traverse Bay and the Queen City on its shore, and she now had to admit to herself she was actually fond of the region—and fonder yet of the man beside her who called it his home.

She ventured a furtive glance at Kenton. He was looking in the direction of Bassett Island, a sand-rimmed patch of green a short distance offshore, but his gaze seemed to go beyond the tiny isle. She was wondering what thoughts gave him such a faraway look when he turned to her, uncertainty creasing his brow.

"I hope I'm not speaking out of turn, but I've been thinking." His focus now taking in her mother, he continued. "Mrs. Foxe, would you consider permitting your eldest daughter to remain longer in Traverse City?" To Rosalie, he said, "That is, if it's agreeable to you." Words now tumbling from his mouth, he explained. "I still need your help with the Gowen case, and there's the new problem over the Morgan, as well as my regular work load and—"

Vanda Mae interrupted. "Sis, you've got to stay!"

Rosalie was momentarily tongue-tied.

Her mother said, "It's up to you, dear."

She turned to Kenton, her heart far lighter than just moments ago. But she kept her smile modest and her answer simple. "I'll stay."

Vanda Mae beamed. "Good! It's settled!"

Rosalie's sense of elation was with her still when she lay her head on her pillow that night. For awhile longer, she could linger in the home of the man for whom she'd developed a real fondness, and continue to assist him daily at his office. But a troubling question lurked briefly in her mind. Was she only postponing the inevitable, making it harder to part when the time came? She sent up a quick prayer.

"Father in Heaven, guide me in the path you would have me take, and in my feelings for those around me, especially where Mr. McCune is concerned. In Jesus' name, Amen."

Though a sense of peace came immediately following her prayer, a new concern haunted her—that Susan Reddick's recently acquired horse was rightfully the possession of Vanda Mae. The young girl's words repeated in her mind, words she had quoted from her father. *. . . she's just the mare we need to build up our stock and keep the place going . . .* an indication that John Reddick was struggling still.

On the heels of that thought came the prayer she'd said weeks ago on John's behalf, asking the Lord to provide his need. She'd thought the answer had come the day of the circus when Susan had recovered Cutler Gowen's money clip and earned a $200 reward for her good deed. A question now hit her like a bolt from heaven—was Vanda Mae's horse another answer to that prayer?

Rosalie had never expected her sister to suffer because of it. Logically, she could easily conclude that April's appearance at the Reddick farm was strictly coincidence. From deep within, she had to ask herself if coincidence was really the case, or if Divine intervention provided a truer definition for the strange circumstances?

Prayer seemed the only hope for answers. She quietly asked the Lord to guide her in her search for the horse thief, and to give all involved in the matter both the wisdom and the grace to recognize and accept his will.

Moments later, she fell into a pleasant dreamland that was not only free from worry over April, but filled with images of her pleasant afternoon by the bay and the man who had made them memorable.

Six days later, as Kenton drove home from the Boston Store sale, Rosalie could barely see above the boxes and paper-wrapped packages stacked on her lap. Beside her on the rear seat of the carriage, her mother and sister were equally laden with purchases. Rosalie chuckled to herself, thinking it was so like her mother to postpone her departure for Tanglewood by a day in order to take advantage of the Saturday bargains offered in the newspaper ad.

For Rosalie and Vanda Mae, Minnie had purchased silk waists reduced from $8 to $2.48. For their father, she found an umbrella reduced from fifty cents to twenty-nine cents, and several ties for a quarter apiece—half their regular price. For herself, she had purchased four-yard lengths of silk at fifty-nine cents a yard—down from a dollar—and dozens of one-, two-, three-, and five-cent values including Valenciennes lace, a curling iron, darning cotton, handkerchiefs, embroidery floss, buttermilk and almond meal soap, white pearl buttons, and other notions. The trick now would be to fit everything into their trunks and onto the train! But somehow, her mother would manage.

Now, as Kenton turned onto Washington Street, Rosalie's mind turned to other thoughts as well. Despite the distraction of the shopping trip, she could tell that Kenton was troubled by the lack of response from both the police department in Rochester and the New York Central Railroad regarding his speculation that Lazarus Ambrose was likely operating under the alias of Cutler Gowen. He was concerned, too, that the auction house in Chicago had been quick to deny any indiscretion regarding the sale of the Morgan to John Reddick, and had refused to divulge the name and address of the former owner. She hated to see her own father and Susan's in a court fight over the animal, and prayed again that the Lord's will would be done.

When Kenton pulled into the driveway and helped her down from the carriage, she tucked a package beneath her arm and shoved troubling thoughts aside. Despite legal challenges and worries, she was still pleased that she would be remaining in his company for the weeks to come.

This notion was dislodged, however, by the sound of a stranger's voice—a male voice—which was flowing from the parlor window, and the quiet tone of her mother when she alighted from the carriage.

"Mr. McCune," Minnie cocked her head, pausing to listen to Lottie's cascade of chuckles and Ben's quiet laughter in response to something the fellow had said, "it seems a gentleman has come calling. An acquaintance of yours, perhaps?"

Kenton listened to more of the congenial masculine tones and feminine laughter. "I don't recognize the voice, but from the sound of it, he's a friend of your sister and brother."

With an inquisitive little smile, Minnie lifted her skirt and stepped off toward the front porch. Rosalie and Vanda Mae followed her into the house, leaving Kenton to put away his rig.

In the front parlor, Ben occupied the couch and Lottie the love seat, her attention focused on the gentleman who amply filled the chair beside her. His round cheeks were pink with joviality, and he rose the moment the women entered the room.

Lottie made introductions. "Minnie, Rosalie, Vanda Mae, this is Detective O'Shea, come all the way from the police department in Rochester, New York to investigate Mr. Gowen. Detective O'Shea, meet my sister, Mrs. Fergus Foxe, and her daughters, Rosalie and Vanda Mae, from North Carolina."

His blue eyes sparkled beneath dark, thick brows. "My, my! A right pretty bouquet of southern roses you ladies make!"

Minnie smiled. "Thank you, sir!" She took a seat beside her sister. While Rosalie and Vanda Mae settled on the couch beside their uncle, Minnie continued. "Now that you're here, Detective, I truly hope you won't waste any time arresting that awful Cutler Gowen--or Lazarus Ambrose, as he was evidently known in your neck of the woods."

Lottie spoke up. "The detective wants to talk with Kenton first."

Ben rose. "I'll go out and tell him Detective O'Shea is waiting to see him."

While he was gone, Lottie explained that the detective had taken a room next door with the Doyle sisters. When he'd asked directions to Kenton's office, they'd brought him to Kenton's home, and in his absence, had introduced him to her and Ben, leaving the policeman there to await Kenton's return.

A few minutes later, Kenton shook the detective's hand, then reviewed the information he'd obtained which had prompted him to send a telegram to the Rochester Police Department, including the newspaper clipping and photograph from Mrs. Spicer. Detective O'Shea pulled Kenton's missive from his pocket and tapped it on his palm.

"This sent me on a course straight to the New York Central authorities. They obliged me with train tickets to Michigan, but we've a long way to go, collecting evidence, before an arrest can be made. First, I need to get a look at Cutler Gowen myself and make a determination if he's actually Lazarus Ambrose, like you think."

Ben added, "Since the two of you were acquaintances back East, you can't be seen in the process."

Lottie said, "If he *is*, you can get Police Chief Rennie to help make the arrest so you can take him back to New York for his trial."

O'Shea chuckled. "Whoa, lass! You're gettin' the cart way out front of the pony. Like the newspaper said, we investigated about a month after his so-called death when certain accounts came up empty, but we couldn't get to the bottom of it. If the man truly is alive and not buried in his grave, we've got to find out who or what lies in his coffin and proceed from there."

Kenton added, "All without his sister growing suspicious. She still visits his grave, you know."

Minnie said, "She'll be mighty upset if you don't allow her sainted brother to rest in peace."

The detective gave a wink. "God forgive me if I tell dear Mrs. Spicer that we've discovered new information about her brother's murderer and need to examine his poor, mutilated body once more before making an arrest."

Vanda Mae spoke up. "Since Lazarus Ambrose killed himself, you won't be fibbing."

Rosalie added, "You just won't be telling her everything you know—for her own good."

The detective raised a pudgy finger. "First things first.

I've got to get a good look at the fellow."

Ben said, "His office at the factory has a big window to the right of the front door. You could come there Monday morning, about nine, and take a peek."

Lottie shook her head. "Monday is Labor Day, Ben. Everyone will be at the parade, but I have an idea. Mr. Gowen's already planning to drive his fancy wagon down the center of Front Street with Miss Hackbardt playing Candy Queen like she did on the Fourth. Detective O'Shea would be just another face in the crowd."

Mention of Clarissa stirred latent curiosity in Rosalie. "I'm still befogged by the missing coin. That Hackbardt woman's got to have it somewhere."

O'Shea's brow twitched. "Missing coin?"

Kenton appeared on the brink of a reply when the sound of Miss Eva's voice floated through the front screen door.

"Hello? Mr. McCune? Detective O'Shea?"

Their answer brought her to the front parlor where her gaze took in the entire company.

"I've come to invite you all to supper with Ada and me and our newest guest." She beamed at the detective. "I'm sure you could use more time with Mr. McCune."

O'Shea nodded. "He owes me an explanation about a missing coin."

Kenton's look of dismay was obvious, but Eva forestalled any possible complaint when she focussed on Lottie. "It'll save you a fuss in the kitchen, seeing as how it's Mrs. Buckley's night off. Would half past six suit?"

Lottie replied with haste. "Miss Eda, we'll be glad to accept your invitation, providing you allow me and my kin to help you get the meal on."

*   *   *

At supper, Rosalie couldn't help noticing certain amicable looks passing between Detective O'Shea and Lottie, who was seated directly across from him. When the Rochester native had dug into his potato salad and ham and delivered profuse compliments to his hosts, he again raised the question of the missing coin. Kenton wisely suggested Rosalie's aunt fill him in on the details. Lottie's explanation of the purloined double eagle and her frequent mention of Cutler Gowen's name in conjunction with Clarissa Hackbardt's, brought a thoughtful look to the man's brow. He listened to the complete story, then replied.

"You were tellin' of a parade on Monday where I might get a good look at this fellow, drivin' his candy wagon."

Lottie nodded. "Just remember, he's blackened his hair since he was Lazarus Ambrose."

O'Shea smiled confidently. "His color 'o hair won't fool me. I *would* like to get a close look at him. Hear the sound of his voice."

Rosalie asked, "How can you do that without being recognized, yourself?"

Eda dabbed the corners of her mouth with her napkin. "You must be careful. It'd be a shame to spoil things, when you've come so far."

Ava blinked rapidly. "It most assuredly would. If only we could help you somehow . . . "

The detective's blue eyes twinkled. "I've a plan, a notion clever as a leprechaun's. But I'll need plenty o' help 'tween now and the top o' Monday mornin' to carry it off."

Detective O'Shea described his secret hobby. Even in Rochester, few people aside from his brothers and sisters, knew that the lifelong bachelor spent many an off-duty Saturday, and each and every parade day, playing the part of a clown, his greatest joy being to make children laugh.

In Michigan, however, he had none of his clown para-phernalia—no costume, no make-up, no props. And even if he'd brought them, which had never crossed his mind, he'd have been unable to use them since Lazarus Ambrose could recognize him as the clown from the Rochester parades, thus growing suspicious.

So the detective proposed that he dress himself as a different clown character from the one he portrayed back East. From Kenton, he solicited an old jacket that was several sizes too small, stretching ridiculously over his ample belly. From Ben, whose feet were nearly the same size as his own, he borrowed an old pair of shoes that could be painted white with bright red and yellow spots.

Ben supplied him, too, with a pair of white pants—the type worn by a candy maker—and Ava and Eda offered to sew bright red and yellow trim on both his pants and jacket.

As for his head, Rosalie and her aunt fashioned a red yarn wig. And Vanda Mae loaned him her straw boater. The too-small hat, perched on top of the yarn hair, lent the right touch of whimsy to the developing character.

Work was progressing well on the detective's costume by the time Rosalie kissed her mother and sister good-bye at the depot early Sunday. She wished Vanda Mae success with the start of a new year at Salem Academy come Wednesday. Though she felt a momentary longing to see Tanglewood and her old school again, the feeling passed quickly when she thought of actually leaving Kenton and Traverse City. Confident that she was right to stay behind, she prayed for traveling mercies during worship service at St. Francis.

By late that afternoon, the clown costume was in readiness except for the shoes, which still needed paint, some spirit gum and putty to fashion a large round nose, and props. Detective O'Shea desperately needed balloons in red, white, and yellow, and long, thin sticks to tie them to. So at four o'clock, Rosalie accompanied Kenton on a mission to obtain the missing items from Wilhelms' Mercantile, looking the shopkeeper up at his home. A special trip to the store provided the coveted necessities, and an evening of blowing up balloons resulted in a huge, colorful bouquet.

Early Monday morning, following Detective O'Shea's directions, Rosalie assisted her aunt and the Doyle sisters in concocting clown make-up from common pantry ingredients. She then watched in awe as the jolly Irishman transformed his facial features.

He began by applying large patches of white about his eyes, covering his eyelids as well. Another patch of white rimmed his lower lip and chin. When the white had been powdered down, he applied pink to the remaining areas of face and neck. Then, with great skill, he began outlining with a thin brush. First, red was applied to his exaggerate his mouth. Then, black was used. With it, the detective first rimmed his white eye patches and added laugh lines. He then turned his ordinary mustache into a handlebar. And lastly, he outlined the white surrounding his chin. When he had finished, he applied his bulbous red nose.

Minutes later, in full costume, he took up his bouquet of balloons and stood in the center of the parlor for all to admire his completed costume.

Lottie's head moved from side to side in awe. "Detective O'Shea—"

"Freddy, the Clown!" he corrected her.

"Freddy, if I hadn't seen for myself, I'd never have known you and the detective are one and the same."

Rosalie said, "Cutler Gowen, or Lazarus Ambrose, whichever he is, will never know you, either."

Kenton, Ben, and the Doyle sisters concurred.

To Kenton, O'Shea said, "I'd like to get to the startin' point o' the parade plenty early—get a close look at this candy man, hear him talkin' before he rolls down the street atop his wagon."

Kenton checked his watch. "We can go now, if you like."

The detective nodded, then approached Lottie, alternatingly lifting feet and elbows high with clownish exaggeration. "Miss Marshall, when I see you at the parade, I'll be givin' you a balloon—white if our suspect's not Lazarus Ambrose, red if he is."

Solemnly, she replied, "I'll be praying for a red balloon, Freddy."

Tipping his helmet, he turned and headed out the door, his comic clown walk banishing sober thoughts to leave Rosalie, Lottie, and the Doyle sisters laughing.

CHAPTER

22

North Carolina

Vanda Mae rose at dawn, drew back the curtain, and sent up a silent prayer of thanks that this, the last Saturday in October, promised to be a day of sunshine. On her weekend visits home from the city, she needed every opportunity possible to prepare Topaz for the upcoming Fall Fair, and she couldn't afford a weekend of rain with the big horse show only six days off.

Sometimes, she still longed for April. The Morgan had been an exceptional horse, compliant and easy to work with. She wished April were here now, but she no longer begrudged Susan Reddick her ownership of the filly, nor her father's decision not to take the matter to court. Topaz had excellent qualities, and with her unusual markings, she just might find favor with the judges and win first place in the ladies' division.

Pulling on riding jacket, jodhpurs, and boots, Vanda Mae quietly slipped out of the manor house into the cool morning air and hurried toward the stable. Voices caught her attention before she even reached the open door—Gaspar's and another male voice she thought she recognized, though she hadn't heard it in more than two months. Then, the talking stopped, replaced by the sound of feet lightly landing on the wooden floor.

She stepped into the stable to discover the graceful acrobatics of the neighbor who'd disappeared back in August. Only now, Bobby Dan was performing more than simple handsprings down the center aisle, and he wasn't dressed in everyday shirt and pants. Clad in tights that revealed the muscular curves of his well-toned physique, he turned flips, back flips, twists, and handless cartwheels, threading himself through a huge ring held aloft by Gaspar, then coming to a halt two feet from her. As she and Gaspar applauded his tumbling run, the young fellow gave a bow, tossed back his fair hair, and offered her his winning smile.

"Bobby Dan! You're back!"

Quick as a wink he grabbed her by the shoulders, pecked her on the cheek, then set her free before she could register a protest. "Good to see you, Vanda Mae!" His blue eyes sparkled like never before, lighting up his entire countenance.

Slightly embarrassed by the sight of him in his skin-tight costume, she stumbled over her next words while keeping her gaze from wandering below his neck. "Are you . . . have you . . . "

Gaspar came up behind Bobby Dan, resting his hand in a fatherly fashion on the lad's shoulder. "Mr. Bobby and me, we make an act for the fair, *si?*"

Indicating a large wooden box at the opposite end of the aisle, Bobby Dan waxed enthusiastically. "Gaspar's reviving his famous escape act. I'm his assistant, then he's mine, when I do my acrobatics."

Grinning, Gaspar leveled his finger at her. "The Amazing Gaspar and Mr. Bobby every afternoon at Piedmont Park. Friday after horse show, you'll see!"

Vanda Mae clapped her hands together with anticipation. "I can hardly wait! Do your folks—"

Bobby Dan shook his head vigorously. "I haven't been home yet. I only got off the road last night. I came straight here to ask Gaspar if he'd team up with me."

"You've got to visit your folks. And Willy Jo. They'd love to see you!" she insisted.

The light in his eyes faded. "I can't. Not yet. If they want to see me, let them come to the fair and see my act."

One hand on hip, finger wagging, Vanda Mae pinned him with a steadfast gaze. "Daddy won't stand for you hiding out here while your own mama and daddy are wanting to see you. I'm going right inside and tell him who I discovered in his stable."

No sooner had she pivoted on her heel than Bobby Dan caught her by the elbow and swung her back around. "All right, I'll go see them, but give me till tonight. Gaspar and I have a lot to do today, working up our act for the opening of the fair on Tuesday."

Willy Jo was helping his father fill the corn crib when he first saw the rider approaching. The long shadows of the magnolias in late afternoon obscured the stranger from view at first. But when the fellow emerged in the sunlight at the end of the drive, Willy Jo knew the rider was no stranger after all.

"Daddy, look! It's Bobby Dan!"

Jabe's head snapped around. A grin burnished his tan features. Dropping his basket where he stood, he started toward his younger son with long, eager strides.

Willy Jo stayed put. As his brother drew closer, he could see that Bobby Dan appeared to be both fit and fine. The fact that he was on Topaz said that home hadn't been his first stop in the Piedmont. Willy Jo hurried to the house to fetch his mother from the kitchen where she and Kezia were preparing the evening meal. When he emerged with her a minute later, Bobby Dan had dismounted and was standing in the dooryard, his daddy's arm about his shoulders.

Virginia smiled through her tears, too overcome with happiness to do more than murmur his name before wrapping her arms about him. Releasing her embrace long moments later, she slipped one arm through his, the other through Willy Jo's. Her face shimmering with moisture, she looked up into her younger son's face.

"This day is answered prayer. At last, my two boys are home with me again!"

Jabe's beaming smile lingered, too, and Willy Jo couldn't remember when he'd seen his folks this pleased. The years-long friction between him and his daddy had all but disappeared since his return from Tanglewood, and now the younger wayward son had come home. Even Willy Jo's own harsh feelings about Bobby Dan had dissipated with time, allowing him to forgive and forget past differences, and pray for his brother's wellbeing. Deep within, this reunion brought him peace—a peace instilled with the knowledge that God knows every need, and hears and answers prayers. The only flaw at this happy moment was the uncertainty in Bobby Dan's expression as his gaze met Willy Jo's.

He hastily offered words of reassurance. "Glad you're home, little brother. You'll stay to dinner—" Suddenly remembering his brother had just come off the road, and the sparse, primitive conditions of a traveling show, he amended his invitation. "You'll stay the night, won't you?"

"I'd like that," he quickly replied. Skepticism still evident on his brow, he quietly announced, "I've . . . got news."

Suddenly dreading word of a betrothal to a trapeze artist, or some equally outlandish notion of his crazy little brother, Willy Jo forced himself to remain calm. "What's that, Bobby Dan?"

Lifting his nose to sniff the air, he winked mischievously. "I'll tell you over dinner. Right now, the smell of Kezia's sauteed onions and fried pork chops is making my mouth water. Do you know how long it's been since I've sat down to one of her home cooked meals?"

Thin clouds veiled the morning sun, dulling the reds and golds of the hardwoods trimming the road to Winston, but Willy Jo's vision remained clear regarding the race he intended to enter and win today at the fair.

In hand he held the reins to an exceptionally fine burnt chestnut stallion, Piedmont, a cross between a Morgan and an Arabian he had recently purchased with the money his father had paid him for his work on the farm. He wasn't quite the horse April had been, nor as expensive, but he was paid for in full, and he just might be fast enough to outrun the competition in the wagon race he'd decided to enter when his mother had refused to ride Piedmont in the ladies' competition.

With her decision firm and incontrovertible, Willy Jo had focused his efforts on the gentlemen's wagon race. The wagon in which he sat was very special without a doubt, an early birthday gift his folks had ordered built to specification at the Nissen Wagon Works. For a moment, his mind drifted, and instead of the cool, morning breeze

teasing at his open collar, he felt the rush of warm afternoon air as he raced around the oval. Instead of the noisy,
scolding grackles flocking to the maples as he drove along
the country road, he heard the crowd at Piedmont Park
cheering him for coming in first at the finish line.

And he saw the fine, new buggy that would reward his
success. His first buggy. His own buggy. A memento of
practical worth that he could drive for years to come. How
proud his daddy would be of him if he came away the
owner of the best prize offered at the fair!

Smiling to himself, he gazed heavenward and spoke
reverently. "Lord, thank you for answering prayers, and
teaching daddy and me to get along. I didn't think you
were listening, but now I know different." Seconds later,
he added, "And Lord, if it wouldn't be too much to ask,
help me get over the finish line before those other drivers."

Realizing how selfish his request sounded, he continued
to pray in silence. *Lord, even if I don't win the wagon race,
I know Daddy will still be proud of me. A few months back,
I wouldn't have felt this way, but things are different now.
Daddy's different. Sometimes, he even praises me. I know
the words come hard for him. But thanks for putting them
in his heart, and in his mouth.*

*And like I said, I'd be mighty glad if I could win this
race today, just so I could go up to him afterward and say,
"Daddy, I did it for you!"*

His focus shifted from private prayer to the handsome
coach several yards in front of him carrying his daddy and
mother. The carriage, with its double collar axles, patent
leather dash, and Norway iron bolts, was drawn by the
finest roans in all of Forsyth County. His daddy would
enter the competition for the best pair of coach horses,

outfit taken into account. The harness ornaments and plumes really made his rig stand out. Willy Jo was hoping his father would come away with the $15 prize being offered. If he did, he was certain his daddy would present his winnings to the woman on the seat beside him.

But winning was no sure thing with Fergus Foxe entering his own coach and horses in the Forsyth County event. Since horse thefts from Tanglewood had robbed him of his best team, Fergus had come up with a new pair. Willy Jo had seen them out on the road, and they were stylish indeed!

Willy Jo's musings of Tanglewood recalled his brother's appearance on Topaz and his surprise announcement. Thankfully, it had nothing to do with a young lady trapeze artist, or other betrothal. Instead, Bobby Dan had informed his family that he'd got up his own show in partnership with Gaspar, and they had contracted with the fair to give performances every afternoon at Piedmont Park. Then Bobby Dan had promptly insisted his folks wait until the end of the week when their act would be at its best before coming to see it.

So as Willy Jo neared the twin cities of Salem and Winston, this day was full of promise. Right away, he noticed a definite increase in the usual amount of traffic heading into town on Main Street. Even Academy Square, several blocks from the hub of activity at the courthouse, seemed far busier than normal.

He couldn't pass Salem Academy, its brick Main Hall or neighboring Home Church and steeple, without thinking of Vanda Mae. Bobby Dan had said she'd been home each weekend training to enter Topaz in the ladies' division of the horse show today, but Willy Jo hadn't seen or spoken with her since school had begun in September.

Willy Jo fondly recalled the rides he and Vanda Mae had taken together at Tanglewood. Her enthusiastic, eternally optimistic approach to life had set sunbeams dancing during days of discord with his father. But he hadn't forgotten the considerable frustration and worry inflicted by her daredevil nature. He supposed he never would understand why she would take chances on Steadmans' horse despite his—and her father's—warnings against it. But such was the way of Vanda Mae.

Despite her confounding spunkiness, thoughts of the young lady stirred an uneasiness deep within. Whether it was fondness, or guilt over his longtime friendship with her older sister, he couldn't tell. He'd been too busy with harvest on his daddy's farm to think much about Tanglewood women.

And thoughts of them now gave way to concerns for heavier traffic, both on foot and in wagons. The intersection at First Street, marked by the double porticos of the Sallade home, was bustling. Proceeding carefully, he negotiated the intersection at Second and approached the courthouse. Gaily decorated with a huge red and white bunting, it stood sentinel at Third and Main over an assortment of merchant booths that had been erected on the square. Even from the seat of his wagon, he could see Mr. Seabott touting the finer points of his Garland stoves to a woman with a white ruffled parasol and her silk-hatted husband. Beside them, the town optician, Mr. Harger, was examining the eyes of a frosty-haired prospect sporting bright red suspenders. Adjacent, Mr. Vogler promoted the finer points of his walnut sweetheart chest to a young couple more interested in gazing into each other's eyes, than into their reflections in his glossy varnish finish.

The fragrance of freshly pressed apple cider at Mr. Winkler's booth mingled with the less appetizing odor of horse and mule droppings in the congested street and the enticing aroma of freshly popped corn drifting from the popcorn wagon parked at the opposite curb.

No-name tunes from penny whistles, chimes of cowbells, and the occasional pop of a firecracker or discharge of a torpedo accented the symphony of happy voices, rattling wagons, and horses' hooves.

Slow going marked the block north of the courthouse where tobacco wagons lined both sides of the street in anticipation of offloading a new harvest at Brown's Warehouse. Willy Jo crept past Gentry's watchmaking shop, Farabee's restaurant and grocery, and Marler and Dalton's drygoods.

Once past the busiest section of Winston, Willy Jo followed his father's coach up Liberty Street, gaining a view of Pilot Mountain with its biscuit-like top. Thereafter, traffic moved at a better pace toward Piedmont Park. Though this end of town was busier than normal with dozens of extra hacks hired to shuttle folks from the city center to the outlying fairgrounds and back, Willy Jo was soon able to turn onto the county grounds.

While his father parked his coach near the show rings, he turned in the direction of the race track. Entering through the passageway between the banks of bleachers, he saw the winner's prize on display at the center of the infield—a brand new buggy with solid silver trim, shiny brass lamps, and silky black fringe. Excitement laced through Willy Jo at the prospect of driving the classy carriage home.

As he approached the starting line, he saw that six other wagons had already lined up on the half-mile oval. He pulled even beside them. The driver to his left had his back to him as he performed a last-minute check of his tack. Willy Jo jumped down to do the same. He was inspecting Piedmont's belly band when the other fellow spoke, his voice both familiar and unwelcome.

"Young Winthrop, I expected you'd be driving a purebred Morgan, knowing your fondness for them."

In no hurry to respond, Willy Jo sensed Eck Danvers studying every detail of Piedmont and the new Nissen wagon. Deliberately, he turned to face him. Greeted by a sinister smile that said more than words, Willy Jo remained cool.

"Where you been, Danvers? Haven't seen you around these parts in awhile."

Danvers met his gaze briefly, then continued his assessment of Piedmont. "I've been away up North, but that ain't none—isn't any of your business."

Willy Jo suffered a near uncontrollable urge to grab the fellow's shirt with both fists and scream into his face, *You went to Chicago to auction off the horses you stole from Forsyth County, didn't you?* But calmer thinking brought an intriguing idea, and wiser course of action to mind.

Turning his attention to Danvers' outfit, he discovered a wagon that was small and light, and a bay Thoroughbred filly built powerful and lean enough to give it speed aplenty. Certain the horse couldn't have been off the track more than a few weeks, Willy Jo began to suffer misgivings over Piedmont's ability to match her. He spoke with complete confidence, nonetheless.

"I'll wave to you from the winner's circle when this is

over, Danvers."

With a raised brow, Danvers replied, "*I'll* wave to *you* from the seat of that buggy when I drive it out of here, young Winthrop."

As the announcer warned contestants to prepare for the start of the race, Willy Jo said casually, "I understand the Foxe girl is entering her new Morgan in the ladies' competition. Blue ribbon horseflesh, from what I've seen."

With an air of studied disinterest, he replied, "I wish her well."

Aboard his wagon, Willy Jo tried not to hold Piedmont's reins too tight, but nerves tensed his grip. Before he could relax, the starting gun sounded.

Danvers bolted down the track. The others followed close behind. But Piedmont remained frozen, blinded by a cloud of dust!

Willy Jo slapped the reins firmly against him. "Go, boy, *go!*"

With a mighty lurch, he shot across the starting line and surged forth in a spirited gallop, pulling quickly into the middle of the pack.

But he was far back from the first turn when Danvers rounded it alone, his Thoroughbred pulling his wagon as if it were so much fluff.

Piedmont kept his stride, working his way to the front of the pack. By the second turn, he'd started to close in on Danvers.

Down the straightaway they flew, running neck and neck as Piedmont took the outside at the third turn.

Ahead briefly on the next straightaway, he attempted to pass the Thoroughbred.

She gave no quarter. Hugging the inside, she matched

Piedmont's speed and bested it by a shoulder.

But Piedmont pressed hard. Going into the last turn, he ran even with the Thoroughbred, pulling ahead as they came out of it.

With the finish line in sight, Danvers continued his fight for the lead, pulling ahead by a nose. Then Willy Jo inched past him. Nose and nose, the lead alternated time and again. At the end, Willy Jo couldn't tell who was the winner.

Then he heard the voice of the announcer.

"And the winner is Willy Jo Winthrop!"

The crowd cheered. Willy Jo rounded the track in a victory lap. In the front row of the stands, his daddy waved his hat wildly, his face beaming with a pride of which Willy Jo had only dreamed.

Pulling onto the infield, he watched with satisfaction as the judge pinned a blue ribbon to Piedmont's bridle. Promising to collect his prize at the end of the day, he headed toward the exit where others were leaving to clear the way for the race to follow.

As he reached the passageway between the bleachers, Eck Danvers cut in front of him, pausing to doff his straw boater. "Hats off to you, young Winthrop. I didn't think that crossbreed horse of yours had it in him to win."

Willy Jo smiled. "You'd better find something faster than that Thoroughbred if you expect to take the prize next year."

With a covetous glance at Piedmont, Danvers asked, "You wouldn't be in the market to sell, would you?"

Willy Jo hooted in disbelief. "You never give up, do you?"

"Just thought I'd ask."

As Danvers drove out ahead of Willy Jo, more ideas emerged regarding his notion to catch a horse thief. But he couldn't dwell on them now. His daddy would soon be competing for the best pair of coach horses in ring eight, then Vanda Mae would be vying for Best Lady Rider in ring five.

He joined his mother and Minnie Foxe to watch each coach and team take its turn as the center of attention. The first three carriages had been manufactured locally by Mr. Meinung, known for his drays and business wagons. Willy Jo concluded that these vehicles were practical and sturdy, but lacking the styling that could have made them stand out.

Next, his daddy entered the ring in his Cook carriage from New Haven, Connecticut. Its silk fringe tossed winsomely in the mild breeze, and his roans had never looked finer—their coats clean and shiny, their heads high and proud, their manes brushed to perfection. From the applause, he had easily won favor over the previous contestants.

Then Fergus Foxe made his grand entrance in a new Graham carriage from Rochester, New York. Its etched windows, sweeping fenders, and tall body made it a standout above all others, but Willy Jo was even more impressed by his neighbor's new team. They were the prettiest pair of matching dappled greys he'd ever seen, with their manes carefully braided, white plumes atop their heads, and silver studs on their harnesses and bridle fronts.

Onlookers clapped enthusiastically, and when the remaining contestants had been given their turn around the ring, the judge presented Fergus Foxe with the $15 prize.

He and Jabe joined their wives a few minutes later,

Fergus offering Willy Jo a hearty pat on the back.

"Congratulations on your win, son!" To Jabe, he said, "Doesn't he make you proud?"

His daddy's face lit in a wide smile. "Proud as the day he was born." Playfully, he tapped Willy Jo's cheek with his fist, something his father had done hundreds of times to Bobby Dan, but never to him.

Suppressing an urge to hug his daddy right then and there, Willy Jo quickly changed topics. "We'd better get over to ring five if we want to see Vannie-Mae in the ladies' competition."

With new joy and a prayer of thankfulness in his heart, Willy Jo stood just outside the ring with his folks and the Foxes to watch each of the lady riders circle around at a walk, trot, and canter both in a clockwise and counterclockwise direction. The first four competitors were all much older than Vanda Mae. But each of their routines was flawed in some way—one had difficulty switching directions in the ring; another couldn't convince her horse to canter; the third horse balked, then nearly bolted into a canter; the fourth started to rear up, nearly dismounting its rider before going into its routine.

Throughout it all, Willy Jo had noticed that each rider had a cluster of family and friends watching, and that all of the onlookers outside the ring belonged to one of these groups—all except one. A fellow wearing a straw hat with a brim wide enough to shade his entire face changed his position each time a contestant finished her routine, lurking near the supporters of the new competitor, engaging them in casual conversation.

Now, Vanda Mae was standing just outside the ring. Her folks, and his alike, gave her their rapt attention,

Minnie waving and blowing a kiss to her daughter. Seconds later, the curious stranger stood but a few feet behind them.

Willy Jo turned to get a better look at the man, noting his full-bent pipe and the essence of his vanilla tobacco. Eager to engage the fellow in conversation, he edged nearer. "Have you got kin in this event?"

The stranger pushed back his hat, wiped his sweaty forehead with the cuff of his plaid shirt, and shook his head. "Ain't from these parts." Indicating Vanda Mae, who was just entering the ring, he asked, "Your sister?"

"Neighbor," Willy Jo replied, "from a farm called Tanglewood, on the line with Davidson County."

Though the fellow nodded casually, Willy Jo sensed he was making note of the information even while easing away.

Having accomplished his objective, Willy Jo now turned his complete attention to Vanda Mae. The young woman was even more appealing than he remembered. She was dressed in a striking blue velvet jacket, jodhpurs, and riding helmet, her hair in a braid down her back that bounced softly with each step of her mount. Topaz's mane and tail had been braided also, with brightly colored satin ribbons. Together, horse and rider created the prettiest picture Willy Jo had ever seen.

And Vanda Mae's form was flawless. Her back was straight and tilted forward at precisely the right angle; she moved in perfect synchronization with Topaz, seeming one with her horse; and the Morgan proceeded effortlessly and flawlessly through each phase of her routine, following Vanda Mae's quiet voice commands. When Topaz pranced out of the ring, respectful applause registered the approval of her audience, including the curious stranger.

When two more contestants had performed in the ring, the judge called Vanda Mae's name as the winner, presenting her with the blue ribbon, a set of books containing classic literature, and the ten dollars that had been designated the prizes for the ladies' competition. More applause followed. As she exited the ring, the stranger moved off.

Prizes in one hand, her horse's rein in the other, Vanda Mae joined her family and neighbors, her pretty oval face and shining blue eyes alight with happiness over her win. But she nearly ignored the compliments from her folks to focus with excitement on Willy Jo.

"You did it! You won the buggy! I'm so happy for you!" Impetuously, she dropped Topaz's rein, shoved her books and money into her father's hands, and put her arms lightly about Willy Jo's neck to peck his cheek.

Willy Jo was too stunned for words, his face burning in response.

Fergus chuckled. "That's one prize you hadn't counted on, eh, son?"

Vanda Mae waved her hand. "Don't pay Daddy any mind, Willy Jo."

Jabe said, "Seems to me, for a kiss like that, the least a fella can do is give the young lady a ride in his new buggy."

Vanda Mae was a picture of anticipation. "Would you, Willy Jo? This weekend, before I go back to Aunt Ophelia and Uncle George's for school?"

Willy Jo nodded.

Minnie said, "Maybe he'll carry you back to your aunt and uncle's, come Sunday afternoon."

Virginia said, "I'm sure he would. Wouldn't you, dear?" She touched her gloved hand to his wrist.

Still recovering from his embarrassment, he replied, "I'd be honored to carry you, Vannie-Mae. What time should I fetch you?"

She shrugged. "Two o'clock?"

As quickly as her enthusiasm had swelled for the buggy ride, it seemed to die, her attention now distracted by activity in the ring to their left. "Look! It's Bobby Dan and Gaspar! They're about to start their act!" Taking Topaz's rein in hand once more, she headed in that direction.

Willy Jo and the others followed, forming the nucleus of an audience that grew as Bobby Dan, clad in leotard and tights, performed a series of handsprings the circumference of the ring to music performed by an accordionist. As the tempo increased, so did the speed of his handsprings, until he made his way to a trunk set in the center of the ring, performing a back flip, then a front flip over the wooden chest.

With a chord sounding like "ta-da" from the accordionist, the audience applauded, then Bobby Dan made an announcement.

"Good afternoon, ladies, and gentlemen! I'm Bobby Dan, and I'd like to introduce to you my partner, the amazing Gaspar, escape artist extraordinaire!"

Dressed in black pants, a red silk shirt, and a sash reminiscent of the garb worn by bullfighters, Gaspar hurried to the center of the ring, bowing deeply to another smattering of applause while flourishes sounded from the accordion.

Gaspar then opened the trunk and removed a rope, a canvas bag, a chain, a padlock, and a silk sheet. To the suspenseful notes of the musician, Bobby Dan tied Gaspar's hands behind his back, chained and locked the canvas bag, and closed him inside the trunk. He then wrapped a

247

chain around the trunk and secured it with a padlock, finally draping it with the silk sheet. While the accordionist began to slowly play *Pop! Goes the Weasel*, Bobby Dan started performing cartwheels around the circle, slowly at first, then faster as the music gained tempo.

Willy Jo found the acrobatics simple and unimaginative—far below his brother's capabilities. But as the tempo of the music picked up, so did the speed of his brother's gymnastics until Bobby Dan was speeding toward the center of the ring in a series of handless cartwheels. Hurling himself in a high forward flip over the trunk, he'd barely cleared it when Gaspar burst forth from beneath the silk sheet to the *Pop!* at the end of the song!

The audience applauded enthusiastically, especially the children. Then the accordion player struck up a new melody while Bobby Dan and Gaspar carried a lightweight folding screen to the center of the ring. Starting behind the trunk, they set it in place around three sides, leaving the chest visible only from the front. To the notes of a haunting melody, Bobby Dan again tied Gaspar's hands behind his back, chained and locked him inside the canvas bag, then closed him inside the trunk, chaining it and locking it no less than four times.

Now, to low and mysterious tones from the accordion, Bobby Dan drew the silk screen closed and stepped behind it. After a moment's pause, the accordionist played a chord filled with expectation. When nothing happened, he progressed to a chord one step higher. More silence. Then he sounded a third, triumphant chord, fortissimo, but still, no one appeared from behind the screen!

Willy Jo grew warm with concern. Obviously something had gone terribly wrong. The musician, appearing much distressed, sounded his chord again.

Just when murmurs of skepticism began rippling through the audience, Gaspar pulled back the screen and revealed himself to the crowd with great finesse, the accordionist enhancing the moment with his most triumphant chord yet!

But only moments later, some in the audience began calling out to Gaspar.

"Where's Bobby Dan?"

"Where's your partner?"

With great pretense to sudden memory, Gaspar hurried to the trunk. Using the flair of a seasoned showman, he unlocked the four chains, raising his hands in the air after each one, then again when he opened the lid of the trunk. Inside, a figure in the canvas bag tried to poke his way out. Gaspar helped the shrouded fellow to his feet and unlocked the chain at the top of the bag.

Out stepped Bobby Dan, his hands tied behind his back!

Applause, loud and furious, filled the air! The accordionist lit into a series of ruffles and flourishes. Gaspar untied Bobby Dan's hands. Performing one last cartwheel and flip, he and his partner bowed, then made a swift exit, props in tow.

Jabe hollered, "Good show, Bobby Dan!"

Willy Jo had never seen such delight in his mother's eyes, nor heard such loud applause from a pair of gloved hands.

Vanda Mae's folks were nearly as enthusiastic as his own, Fergus commenting, "I hope Gaspar doesn't take a notion to go back on the road. I could never replace him at the stables."

Vanda Mae was the last to stop clapping. Her face

aglow, she told Willy Jo, "I'm so proud of Bobby Dan! Aren't you?"

He only nodded, certain that the grin on his face was enough to convey the sentiment in his heart. For years, he'd considered Bobby Dan's shenanigans and acrobatics a pure waste, just a way to avoid his share of chores around the farm. He couldn't be more pleased to know that the tumbling tricks and practical jokes had paid off.

Fergus checked his watch, then drew his wife and Vanda Mae to him. "It's getting late, ladies. What do you say we call it a day at the fair?" Seeing their nods of agreement, he turned to the Winthrops, his gaze taking in the three of them. "How about following us to Tanglewood for dinner? I'll stop by the lumber yard office so Minnie can ring up Shani and tell her to toss three more yams in the pot."

Willy Jo was eager to spend the evening at Tanglewood, and it had little to do with Vanda Mae, though her company would be a welcome pleasure. He waited hopefully for his father's response.

Jabe's focus taking in his wife and son in turn, he said, "That'd be a right hospitable end to our day, don't ya think?" Receiving their approval, he told Fergus, "Why don't ya head over to the lumber yard to ring home. Meanwhile, I'll help Willy Jo hitch his new buggy to the back of his wagon, then we'll be right along."

As Willy Jo followed the Foxes and his daddy out of town, he couldn't help remembering traversing the same road several weeks earlier, on the first weekend in August, when he was returning with his mother, brother, and Vanda Mae from the trolley party. Crossing paths with Danvers today, then seeing the stranger lurking near the lady competitors conjured up bad memories—thoughts of Vanda Mae's first Morgan being stolen in Salem; the pure terror that had ripped through his heart when a crazy horseback rider had come up behind him shooting off a gun; the immediate arrival of Danvers on the scene; and his suspicious-sounding denials when asked about the rider and Topaz.

Of course, there was no danger of Topaz being stolen tonight. She was safely hitched to the back of Fergus's coach. And as for being run off the road, dusk was only starting to fall. A gun-toting horseman wouldn't strike without full cover of darkness. Besides, Willy Jo's wagon wasn't a lone vehicle on a deserted road as had been the situation in August.

More than ever, he was certain Danvers, the lone horseman of that fateful August night, and the stranger lurking about at the horse show were somehow related, and responsible for the thefts of many Forsyth County horses in earlier months. The problem was catching them in the act. And Willy Jo had been laying bait for that very possibility all day.

After dinner, when his daddy and Fergus withdrew to the library, he'd talk to them. Despite the fact that Danvers had caused a great rift between him and his daddy in the past, he believed their respect for one another had grown deep enough now, that Jabe would listen to what he had to say about the man.

Sipping hot mulled cider after a filling meal, Willy Jo set his cup on the library table and waited for the banter about the prices of hogs and lumber between his father and

Fergus to break off. Drawing a breath of air heavy with smoke from their cigars, Willy Jo squared his shoulders and took advantage of the rare moment of silence following the men's laughter.

"Daddy, Mr. Foxe, there's something I'd like to discuss with you."

Fergus flicked the ashes from his cigar into the tray beside his winged leather chair and leaned forward, his smile fading. "Sounds serious."

Jabe exhaled smoke in tiny rings that drifted toward the plaster medallion above the fan and chandelier, then focused on Willy Jo. "Go ahead, son."

"Today, I noticed a real suspicious-looking fellow at the ladies' competition." He explained the hints he'd dropped to the fellow about Tanglewood, and to Danvers about Vanda Mae's new Morgan, because of his long-held conviction that the man was behind the previous thefts. Then he told of his concern that the fellows could be in cahoots to steal Topaz this very night.

Creases of doubt drew his father's brows together. "We've got no real evidence that Danvers steals horses. And as for that other fellow, he's probably just a stranger in town for the fair like hundreds of others."

Fergus said, "Even if he *is* planning to get his hands on someone else's horse, how do we know he'll come *here* tonight? He could have his sights set on any one of those other ladies' mounts."

Willy Jo pressed ahead despite their arguments. "You could be right, but I think he'll go for the best horse first. What I'd like to do is turn Topaz out to pasture for tonight and set up a blind there, a haystack beside the far gate. That way, I can keep my eye on the horse, and on anybody coming to steal her."

Fergus and Jabe exchanged glances, their skepticism obvious. Then, with a chuckle, Fergus said, "You're young. If you want to give up a good night's sleep, I won't object, but I think it's all for naught."

Two hours later, while his mother and daddy were engrossed in their game of charades with the Foxes in the manor house parlor, Willy Jo took up his lone watch in Topaz's pasture from within the confines of a mound of hay. He'd been settled inside his haystack by the gate farthest from the stables for less than an hour when he began to question the wisdom of his plan. He could see very little in the dark of night, clouds obscuring moon and stars, and the bare skin on his hands and neck had begun to itch. He'd suffered a sneezing fit that had turned his handkerchief into a wet rag, and despite the layer of clothing protecting the rest of his body, he imagined pinhead-sized bugs crawling all over him, making him itch like mad and eager to head for the nearest tub of bath water.

He'd played in haystacks plenty of times as a small boy and never felt this way. And as an adult, he hadn't been particularly bothered by hay when feeding horses, with the exception of an occasional sneeze which he'd blamed on dust. But this close, prolonged contact was definitely bringing out the worst in him.

To pass the time and put discomfort from mind, he began silently recalling Bible verses he'd memorized as a child. Several had come to mind when he paused to ponder one of his favorites.

For God so loved the world, that he gave his only begotten Son, that whosoever believeth in him should not perish, but have everlasting life. John 3:16.

He considered this to be the greatest message in all the Bible—that long ago, God had become the father of Jesus, nurturing and loving him from infancy to manhood; that God had endowed his son with an important mission—to bring His love to all the world; that God had sacrificed his precious son in a cruel, painful death on the cross.

Willy Jo closed his eyes and thanked God for his own redemption through Christ, the enduring friendship Jesus offered to all, and the workings of the Savior's love in his own heart, and his daddy's. Truly, through Christ all things were possible, even the reconciliation with his daddy that had seemed inconceivable. Dark days and nights of conflict had given way to brighter, happier times for them both.

His thoughts were interrupted by the faint rumbling of thunder in the distance. Topaz was growing uneasy, pacing back and forth inside the closed gate that kept her from entering the stable. Sprinkles of rain began to fall, then larger drops. The wind gusted stronger, tugging at the hay mound.

Lightning flashed, thunder cracked loud overhead, and rain fell hard. A mighty gust of wind stole the last of Willy Jo's hay mound leaving him totally exposed. Head down, he ran across the pasture and whipped open the gate for a frantic Topaz, following her into the stable where he put her in her box and wiped her down. Damp and discouraged, but not defeated, he was determined to return to the pasture when the storm had passed.

He checked the time—nearly one in the morning. The lights in the windows of the manor house told him the parlor games continued on. The same was true an hour later when he turned Topaz out to pasture again and reconstructed his hay mound, this time under clear skies in a field lit by both moon and stars.

The temperature dropped as the hours passed. The storm had brought cooler air, and despite the thick layer of hay blanketing him on all sides, Willy Jo grew chilled in his damp clothing.

With an hour left till dawn, he realized he was coming down with a sore throat. Surely a head cold would follow. His eyes were blurry from exhaustion, his neck and back tight with knots, and his patience strained to the limit.

His father and Fergus had been right. He'd wasted a good night's sleep. He rubbed his eyes. Visions of the warm, dry bed waiting for him at home came to mind. Ready to admit defeat and give up his foolish vigil, he made one last perusal of the pasture.

And he saw the man sneaking past the far gate.

Willy Jo's heart skipped a beat. Wide awake and keenly alert, he watched the fellow carrying something toward Topaz where she stood sleeping at the opposite side of the pasture. In the blink of an eye, he'd slipped a halter over the Morgan's head, a bag over that, and began leading her away.

When he passed close to the haystack, Willy Jo could smell his vanilla pipe tobacco, and see the silhouette of his wide-brimmed straw hat, and was certain the man was the same fellow he'd seen lurking about the ladies' competition. After he and Topaz had left the pasture, Willy Jo began shadowing them, hiding himself in the fringe of trees along the road. He'd followed for a quarter of a mile when the thief headed off the road into the woods.

Willy Jo hurried to catch up. There, in a small clearing lit by dim lantern light, stood a large livestock van. Three horses were already aboard, and beside the rear entry ramp waited another man.

Eck Danvers.

He opened the gate to the van while his accomplice started leading Topaz up its ramp. Unconcerned that the thieves outnumbered him, Willy Jo charged into the open.

"Stop! You can't get away with this!"

In a flash, Danvers pulled a pistol from beneath his jacket and turned it on Willy Jo. "Hold it right there, young Winthrop!"

Willy Jo froze.

To his assistant, Danvers said, "Fitch, get the Morgan aboard. We've got to do something about young Winthrop, here." He smiled wickedly.

Willy Jo started to back away.

"Stay put!" Danvers ordered, cocking the hammer of his gun. "Do as I say, and you won't get hurt. Run, and you're a dead man."

Willy Jo's mind raced, desperate for a means of escape. If only he could run back to the house and call for help! But with Danvers' focus steady upon him, he couldn't move.

Then, he heard horses coming down the road. Danvers heard them too. The instant his gaze turned toward the sound, Willy Jo rushed at him, tackling him by the legs.

Danvers hit the ground with a thud.

A shot went off.

A horse wailed as if with pain.

Willy Jo looked up, afraid Topaz had been shot.

Danvers took advantage. Still holding the gun, he rolled on top of Willy Jo and forced the pistol against his neck. "I'm losing patience with you, young Winthrop!

Your next move is your last!" To Fitch, he said, "Get me the rope in the van!"

A few feet away, a horse continued to whinney with pain and Willy Jo could hear Fitch still struggling with Topaz.

"Get the blame rope yourself!" Fitch retorted.

Miffed, Danvers hollered, "I said get the rope! *Now!*"

Before Fitch could reply, Jabe and Fergus burst into the clearing aboard Hurricane and Firelight.

Danvers turned his gun on them.

With a mighty effort, Willy Jo pushed him off, knocked his pistol away, and straddled him, pinning his shoulders to the ground.

Jabe dismounted in an instant, lending his strength to hold Danvers still.

Fitch scrambled to shut the van gate.

Fergus retrieved the pistol and pointed it at him. "Get away from there, you thief!"

Fitch put his hands up. "I only did what Danvers told me! It was all his idea!" He took a step back.

"Stop right there!" Fergus warned.

Jabe brought Danvers to his feet and slammed him up against the side of the van. "You rotten, good-for-nothin' ... " To Willy Jo, he said, "I should've listened to ya from the start, son. Ya were right all along about this no-account."

Fitch spoke again. "He's been stealin' from places all 'round this county for months."

Danvers strained against Jabe's hold. "Shut your mouth, Fitch!"

Jabe tightened his grip. "*You* hush!"

To Willy Jo, Fitch said, "Danvers made me spy on you

and the young lady in the woods last summer."

With alarm, Willy Jo, recalled his sense of being trailed during his rides with Vanda Mae.

Fitch continued. "And the night he made me steal that Morgan from Salem, he saw a chance to heist your daddy's drivin' team and told me to run ya off the road."

Danvers protested. "It's a lie!"

"No, it ain't! You figerred to make a big accident. Told me to unhitch the horses while the folks was too hurt to stop me."

Jabe went for Danvers' throat. "You . . . !"

He struggled for air, his eyes bulging.

Willy Jo moved to ease his daddy's grip. "No good will come of strangling him."

Jabe loosened his hold.

Fitch went on. "When the buggy didn't turn over, he rode by and offered to help ya just to make ya think he was a good S'maritan."

Willy Jo pinned his gaze on Danvers. "You took the Morgan to Chicago and sold her at auction, didn't you?"

Fitch answered for him. "He did! And a carload of other horses, too. Put hisself in tall cotton!"

Jabe put his face inches from Danvers. "There's one thing I don't understand. In the beginnin', ya were willin' to buy that Morgan and pay a mighty big price for her."

Danvers' mouth twitched but he made no reply.

His accomplice explained. "He'd a paid somethin' down and given ya a promissory note for the rest."

"I'd have never taken a note," Jabe declared.

Fitch chortled. "Ya woulda from *him*. He can talk the bone away from a dog! And that woulda been the last y'd a seen of him, *and* your horse."

Puzzled, Willy Jo asked, "If Danvers wanted the Morgan so much, why did he auction her off?"

Again, Fitch's derisive laugh cut the air. "He changes his mind 'bout horses quicker 'n flames scorch feathers."

With a wave of the pistol, Fergus motioned Fitch toward his boss. "Get over there so we can tie the two of you together. One thing's not going to change. You're both on your way to the pokey and my brother--the sheriff—will be mighty glad to see you."

Willy Jo quickly found the rope in the van, discovering with relief that Topaz had not been shot. Rather, the horse in front of her had been grazed in the rear.

As he helped his father tie the culprits together, a puzzling question came to mind regarding Fergus and his daddy.

"How is it you happened to show up just when I needed you?"

With a wry smile, Jabe admitted, "A couple of hours ago, three worried women shamed us into watchin' the meadow from the stable."

In his heart, Willy Jo interpreted the answer to mean *three worried women with the voice of God.*

CHAPTER

23

Michigan

Nearly two and a half months had passed since the Labor Day Parade. Traverse City was quieter, and a good bit cooler than it had been on that last holiday of the summer season. But Rosalie couldn't ride down Front Street with Kenton even now, on the second Sunday in November, without recalling the moment Detective O'Shea in his "Freddy, the Clown" costume had walked up to Lottie. One foot after the other lifted high, he paused and handed her not one, but *three* red balloons!

As Kenton drove on, past the American Candy Company factory and out of town toward the Reddicks', Rosalie wondered why no effort had been made to arrest the notorious Lazarus Ambrose, alias Cutler Gowen. The detective had warned before departing for Rochester that he would need time to develop a solid case against all those he suspected of being involved in embezzlement from the New York Central, but she hadn't expected more than two months to pass without a word from the jolly Irishman.

Such thoughts troubled her, as did her curiosity over Kenton's out-of-town trip this past week. He'd told no one of his destination, nor the exact day of his return. When she'd asked if he was headed to Rochester, he'd only smiled. At least, when he arrived home four days later, he was in excellent humor, though tired.

She was silently speculating on what might have conspired during Kenton's sojourn when he pulled into Reddicks' drive for the horseback ride the two of them had planned for the afternoon. They had already chosen a route, one that would take them to a high hill on another road south of town. There, Kenton promised her an impressive view of West Bay and the Mission Peninsula. But when he turned to her, a look of skepticism in his hazel eyes told her even before his words did, that he was again pondering a question he'd already asked her five times in the previous twenty-four hours.

"Are you *sure* you want me to return Nick to the Reddicks and go back to driving Judge?"

"I'm sure!" she told him with a smile. Though she was certain of her own confidence in the grey horse, established gradually over the past two months of regularly riding Penny alongside Kenton and Judge, the lawyer evidently couldn't resist one last opportunity to cross-examine her.

Thoughts of Penny and Judge took flight when Rosalie noticed Susan atop April in the riding ring at the end of the driveway. The young girl paused to wave hello, then continued with her training routine, causing Rosalie to comment, "Every time I see that young lady with April, I'm thankful Daddy had the wisdom not to press claim to her."

Kenton smiled. "He saved several friendships and a horse farm by purchasing Vanda Mae a new mare, instead."

His comment provoked a question. "Did I tell you, she and Susan are sharing stories about April and Topaz through the mail?"

Kenton chuckled. "A few times."

"It's hard to believe Vanda Mae nearly lost Topaz to

that horse thief, too. Willy Jo must know he's worth his weight in wildcats for catching the bandits."

Mention of Rosalie's North Carolina friend ignited a flicker of jealousy within Kenton, one he squelched quickly as he parked his rig outside the stable and focused on their purpose at hand. "Enough about the Morgans. Let's go get Penny and Judge. John's probably got them saddled and waiting inside."

Half an hour later, having told John where they were headed and when to expect their return, they cantered into the hilly region south of town. Kenton kept Rosalie on his right to cushion her from oncoming traffic. At least, that's what he told her, but he had other reasons. He loved to watch her while she watched the countryside. He loved the way the breeze blew tendrils of her hair loose from the little felt hat that was perched on her head. He loved the way her grey wool riding habit fluttered about her ankles. And he especially loved the way she sat erect and confident upon her side-saddle, a skill she had acquired through dedication and training these last several weeks.

The fact that she was on a horse at all made him proud enough to crow, but he kept a tight lid on such emotions. Her confidence and her form had improved so much from that first day when she had tentatively mounted Penny, he needed to remind himself she was the same person. For a woman who had refused to get on a horse for six years, she was now riding beside him as if she'd been born to it. She appeared as if she'd never fallen in her life, nor suffered from a crippled right arm, and he couldn't help but admire her for it.

Of course, that wasn't all he had come to admire in this young miss from North Carolina. He anticipated the start

of each and every day, hearing her mild southern drawl—
which was softening with her tenure in the North. And he
enjoyed working with her in his office. Her schooling at
Salem Academy had provided a solid education, and with a
dogged tenacity, she had mastered typewriting and stenog-
raphy better than others not challenged by an imperfect
right arm.

Nearing the lookout, he pulled ahead, leading her off
the main road along a winding path to a higher hill that
peaked in a lookout over the bay. He dismounted, then
held Penny steady for Rosalie to do the same. They stood
side by side in silence, each taking in the panorama of blue-
grey waters bound at the bottom by a small jewel of a city,
and on its sides by land made barren in preparation for
winter snows.

Wind rustled through the brown meadow grass at their
feet, and far off, a train whistle blew. The haunting sound
served as a reminder that Rosalie would soon be on her
way home to Tanglewood for Thanksgiving. The thought
dampened his spirits. After five months of having her near,
he was unwilling to let her go, even though she planned to
return immediately after the holiday and stay in Michigan
through Christmas and the New Year.

But supposing she changed her mind? Her old friend
and neighbor, Willy Jo, would undoubtedly be very much
in evidence. He could influence her to see out the year
down South.

Feeling possessive and protective, Kenton did something he'd never done before. He slipped his arm about
Rosalie's waist and drew her firmly to his side.

The startled look that met him transformed instantly to
a questioning smile, but he made no comment, letting

silence reign as she relaxed against him, her head on his shoulder, her sweet essence of peach blossoms comforting him.

Rosalie savored the new closeness Kenton offered. She could only guess at the reason for his sudden show of affection, and the uncharacteristic worried look in his eyes. It was not unlike the troubled waters of the bay, growing grayer with foreboding as dark clouds built in, precursors of a storm to come. She believed Kenton's concern was caused by the same thoughts that distracted her more frequently as each day passed—the knowledge that she would soon be departing for North Carolina—though temporarily.

In many ways, she was not looking forward to another separation. Reluctant as she had been to remain in the North five months ago, she was now equally reluctant to head south. Kenton's brief trip out of town had made her realize he'd come to mean more to her than simply a lawyer who had negotiated passage through the difficult straits of foreclosure. More, too than an employer who had invited her to sail with him daily on the challenging waters of a city law practice. He had come to be her special friend, both patient and strong enough to guide her past her fear of horses just as he was guided himself by a firm faith in the Lord. His routine of attending worship services each Sunday morning was more than an outward habit. Rosalie knew Kenton well enough after all these months to understand that he carried the Lord in his heart all the week through.

In fact, the more she knew of Kenton, the more remarkable she found him. Who else would have bought a home just to share it with friends who were in need? He had made light of the gesture, claiming he'd done it for Ben and

Lottie because they were like family—the kindest folks he'd known since leaving the orphanage family represented in the photographs in his room. Nevertheless, Rosalie considered him wonderfully magnanimous.

She admired his generosity toward one particular motherless girl, as well. That Susan Reddick idolized him was both understandable and justified. He had shown true Christian love, seeing Susan through the trauma of a broken leg and the challenges of riding again, and helping with her mother's needs. And his caring hadn't stopped there. He'd been willing—even eager—to spend the day with her at the circus, an experience her father would never have provided. Surely, the many kindnesses Kenton had shown to others was a clear indication that his capacity for love and affection ran deep and abundant.

And the tenderness he was showing her now, holding her close, spoke subtly of his feelings for her where words remained unsaid. How she wanted to put voice to the feelings in her own heart and tell him that she had grown to care for him more than she had ever thought possible, but she dared not utter a word of such sentiments now. She dared not assume such feelings were mutual. When the time was right, she was certain they would express their true regard for one another. For now, it was enough to stand close, to lean on his strength and support. She was thinking she could stay there forever, indulging the new sensation and studying the scenic view, when the sound of hooves wending up the hill caused them to part.

Susan's voice preceded her to the lookout. "Mr. McCune? Miss Foxe? Are you there?"

Kenton quickly responded for them both. "Up here, Susan!"

She emerged atop April, her expression a picture of excitement. "Mr. Marshall rang up. He said you're to return home immediately. Mr. Gowen's been arrested and the authorities want to talk to you!"

Rosalie gasped, her heart rushing at the news.

Kenton beamed at her, impulsively kissing her on the cheek. "Let's go! This is what we've been waiting for!"

Susan followed Rosalie and Kenton to his house at a gallop, heading back to her father's stable with their horses after assuring Kenton she would soon return with Judge and his rig.

He ushered Rosalie inside. No sooner had they entered the foyer than Detective O'Shea hustled forth from the parlor to greet them.

"There ye be! Come! My associate is more than eager to see you!" He nudged Rosalie toward the parlor, pausing momentarily to confer in whispers with Kenton.

In the parlor, Rosalie barely managed to catch the name of the silver-haired representative from the New York Central, Lawrence Lyons, who unfolded his long legs and rose from the sofa to shake her hand. She was vaguely aware that Kenton acknowledged previous acquaintance with the man from his secretive out-of-town trip only days before.

Her attention had been greatly distracted by the despised woman sitting beside Lyons—Clarissa Hackbardt—looking for all the world like the cat who swallowed the canary.

Rosalie narrowed her gaze on her nemesis. "What are *you* doing here?"

Lottie offered a quick explanation from her place beside Ben on the love seat. "Miss Hackbardt helped Detective

O'Shea get the evidence he needed to arrest Mr. Gowen."

Clarissa held up a bank draft. "And as you can see, I've been amply rewarded for my efforts."

Rosalie read the figure on the check, nearly choking at the generous amount. "You don't deserve a penny of that money! You're nothing but a devious, deceitful—"

Ben interrupted. "Rosalie, enough! Mr. Lyons has other business to discuss."

Lottie motioned to the pair of unoccupied wing chairs. "You and Mr. McCune make yourselves comfortable. Mr. Lyons assures us we'll like what he's about to say, now that we're all here."

Barely holding her anger in check, Rosalie did as she was asked. Seated beside her, Kenton reached for her hand, giving a reassuring squeeze while Mr. Lyons focused his attention on Ben and Lottie. "Now that Mr. Gowen and his twelve accomplices in Rochester are under lock and key, Mr. Depew—Chauncey Depew, that is, head of the New York Central—has authorized me to award temporary possession of the American Candy Company factory and store to you, Mr. Benjamin and Miss Lottie Marshall, such possession to become permanent pending the outcome of Lazarus Ambrose's trial."

O'Shea quickly added, "And guilty, he'll be found. We've way more than enough evidence to be assured o' that." He glanced Clarissa's way, bringing a smug smile to her face that soured Rosalie's stomach, tempering her happiness over the good news.

Lottie turned to Ben, her forehead wrinkled with un-asked questions.

He adjusted his glasses and gave a little shake of his head. "Did I hear you right? My sister and I are to own the store, *and* the factory?"

Lyons nodded, slipping two sets of identical papers from the portfolio at his feet. He handed one to Ben and Lottie, the other to Kenton, which he shared with Rosalie. Still addressing the Marshalls, Lyons admitted, "Your attorney, Mr. McCune, here, is the toughest, most philanthropic negotiator I've ever come up against in all my experiences at the New York Central."

Rosalie spoke up. "Begging your pardon, sir, but the two words don't seem to describe the man I know. Mr. McCune has shown no end to his kind and generous nature, but . . . tough?"

A wry smile tilted the railroad official's mouth. "At the Central, we were willing to grant that Mr. McCune was entitled to a reward for discovering the whereabouts of Mr. Ambrose. Especially considering the vast sums he embezzled and our recent recovery of the majority of them. But no lawyer has ever been granted terms that would result in ownership of an entire factory and retail establishment, then insisted the properties be put in the names of his friends!"

Rosalie held tight to Kenton's hand, her appreciation for him soaring as she absorbed the meaning of Mr. Lyons' words, and the grateful smiles they brought to her aunt and uncle's faces.

To Kenton, Lyons said, "Mr. Depew, himself, approved the terms you demanded when we met in Rochester earlier this week. The agreement is all laid out here, requiring only the signatures of your clients, Benjamin and Lottie Marshall, and a small token showing their desire to retain permanent possession of the businesses when Ambrose has been convicted." To Ben and Lottie, he explained further.

"Mr. Depew is delighted to make you the owners of the shop and factory—provided you don't intend to simply sell them at the first opportunity. He's a firm advocate of longevity in business in the Vanderbilt tradition."

Rosalie and Kenton read the papers in silence until the very last line, which she read a second time, out loud. "'This agreement shall be in force upon payment of one twenty-dollar gold piece by Benjamin and Lottie Marshall, and signatures of same.'"

Lyons explained. "You have to understand Mr. Depew. He has a penchant for sealing agreements with the exchange of a gold coin. In this case, he's specified a double eagle."

Ben turned his pockets inside out and searched through a fistful of coins, finding only pennies, nickels, dimes, and a half dollar. "Wouldn't you know. For want of a double eagle, a candy store and factory are lost."

Rosalie's heart sank. "Surely you must have some money tucked away upstairs."

Lottie's joyful look began to fade. "We don't usually keep such valuables in our apartment, but I'll look."

While she was upstairs, Detective O'Shea described the events that had unfolded in the past two months including Kenton's visit as the investigation was nearing its close, and the arrest of the twelve accomplices to Lazarus Ambrose's elaborate scheme, from the coroner to the undertaker to the bank teller—even a member of the police department.

"Mr. Ambrose was the mastermind, the others were his disciples, and a cunning lot they were. But we got them all, and most of the money they'd swindled. But we'd 've gotten nary a one if Mr. McCune hadn't put us on the right track, so to speak!" He winked.

Lottie returned from upstairs, her brow troubled. "I was right. I deposited all but a few silver dollars in the bank two days ago."

Kenton reached deep into his own pockets, a strange look passing between him and O'Shea as he did. Producing a money clip of bills and half a dozen small coins, Kenton said, "Sorry I can't help. Perhaps we can postpone execution of the agreement until tomorrow morning when the bank opens."

Lyons shook his head. "I'm leaving on the first train out tomorrow. If we don't act on this today, the operation of the candy factory and shop will have to cease until such time as I can return, two weeks or more from now."

Detective O'Shea's sunny humor flagged. "Such a shame to put so many good people out o' work with the holidays comin' on, and all." He turned in earnest to Clarissa. "Miss Hackbardt, you've been God's own blessin' to me and Mr. Lyons in this case. Might there be the least little chance you or someone you know would have a double eagle to lend?"

She smiled graciously. "Allow me." Bending down, she reached beneath the hem of her navy serge skirt to remove her *left* shoe, plucking from it a shiny double eagle.

Rosalie shot out of her chair. "Let me see that!" Snatching the coin away, she immediately recognized the nick in the edge near the word "God" in the phrase, "In God We Trust." So Clarissa had kept the coin hidden in her *left* shoe all along, not the *right* shoe as Rosalie had suspected the night of the ball last July. Hot anger rose within.

"You stole this! It's the exact same coin I paid you against Aunt Lottie and Uncle Benjamin's mortgage last summer. You took it just so Mr. Gowen—Ambrose—could repossess the store!"

"I did *not* steal that coin!" she asserted. "But even if I *had*, your aunt and uncle would be much better off paying for an entire factory and shop with it today, than if they'd made one month's payment on the candy store last summer."

Rosalie grew adamant. "You stole it! You stole it and caused all manner of upset, and I won't let you get away—"

Kenton intervened, his words resolute. "Miss Foxe! In the interest of sealing the agreement with Mr. Lyons and the New York Central, we must postpone this argument until another time."

Piqued at Kenton and frustrated beyond words, Rosalie sat down and folded her arms against her chest.

When signatures had been witnessed on both copies of the original agreement and the controversial coin placed in the possession of Mr. Lyons, Lottie favored Clarissa with a puzzled smile.

"Miss Hackbardt, I'd be most grateful if you could explain something. After Mr. Gowen put us out of home and business, why did he offer us good jobs and part ownership of this beautiful home?"

She chuckled. "Mr. McCune convinced him he'd never really succeed in the candy business in this city unless he added *your* fudge and chocolates to his line of confections. Then he told Lazarus what it would cost, and assured him that if he didn't have you on his payroll, you'd be back in business with someone else, stealing the bulk of the candy trade." With a fleeting glance at Mr. Lyons, she continued. "At the railroad, Lazarus learned the importance of eliminating the competition. 'The way of the Vanderbilts,' he's fond of saying. Lazarus put you *out* of business to establish his monopoly. He *hired* you to guarantee its future."

Ben scratched his chin. "That explains our jobs and our fudge recipe. What about our share in this house?"

Bestowing a grudging look of admiration on Kenton, Clarissa focused on Ben. "Lazarus says your lawyer is the only person he's ever encountered who caused him to suffer a temporary lapse of greed."

During a moment's pause while Ben digested the information, Kenton turned to Clarissa. "And what about you, Miss Hackbardt?" He stood and began to pace, hands linked behind him. When he spoke again, his tone had changed from friendly, to a cold, inquisitive nature Rosalie had never heard from him before.

"No one has ever caused you to suffer a temporary lapse of greed, have they, Miss Hackbardt? No one, that is, until Detective O'Shea, a few moments ago, when he convinced you to produce that double eagle. It *is* the one Miss Foxe paid you for her aunt and uncle's mortgage last June the twenty-ninth, *isn't it?*" He paused to stare at her.

Pinned beneath his cold, condemning gaze, Clarissa lowered her head, then faced him again with renewed conviction. "The ledger book in Lazarus's office proves that payment was never made!"

"That's a *false* ledger book! One you made up to omit record of payment!"

A flicker of astonishment crossed her features. Then she stood, her nose inches from Kenton's. "You're a despicable liar, Mr. McCune! There *is* no false book!"

In the next instant, the door to Kenton's room burst open and Police Chief Rennie strode into the room, ledger books in hand. "*You're* the despicable liar, Miss Hackbardt! And these prove it!" He held them inches from her face.

Clarissa gasped. Her face pale as cream, she took a faltering step back, dropping onto the sofa.

Rennie passed the ledger books to Kenton, then firmly took hold of Clarissa's elbow, raising her to her feet. "Come with me, Miss Hackbardt. I'm taking you in for defrauding the Marshalls."

Suddenly energized, she twisted hard, attempting to free herself from his grip. "You can't arrest me! You promised!"

The police chief held tight, shaking his head. "Detective O'Shea and Mr. Lyons promised you immunity from prosecution for making use of embezzled money in the case with New York Central in return for your help. Defrauding the Marshalls—that's another case entirely. Now that you've produced the coin—"

"It was all Lazarus's idea to foreclose on the mortgage! Hiding the coin, falsifying the record book—"

Rennie's mouth curved in amusement. "Somehow, I knew you'd say that! Come along. You're headed for the calaboose!"

Rosalie couldn't prevent a broad smile as she followed them into the foyer, closing the front door behind them. When she returned to the parlor, the others were on their feet, congratulations and handshakes being exchanged all around.

O'Shea was beaming. "A more cunning pair I've never seen than Ambrose and Hackbardt. Mr. Ambrose was quite the actor in civic theater back in Roch'ster, ya know."

Lyons said, "Small wonder he was so convincing in his new role here in Michigan."

Lottie said, "What a pity his talent went to such corrupt

273

purposes."

Rosalie added, "And Clarissa's. I wonder if either of them will ever be redeemed?"

O'Shea said, "They'll have plenty o' time to contemplate the evil o' their ways while they're in the clink."

Ben peeled off his glasses, wiping them with his handkerchief. "In the Bible, Jesus had a friend named Lazarus." Replacing his spectacles, he said, "Ambrose would see things different if he'd make Jesus *his* friend, too."

Lottie nodded. "I pray it may be so."

An idea coming to her, Rosalie turned to Kenton. "Mr. McCune, I *must* go to jail tomorrow." Following the chuckles at her inept statement, she explained. "Will you take me there, please, so I can deliver Bibles to Miss Hackbardt and Mr. Ambrose?"

"I'll take you first thing," he promised, admiration shining from his hazel eyes.

Several days later, however, Kenton was quite reluctant to deliver Rosalie to the depot on Park Street where she would board the train for her visit to North Carolina for Thanksgiving. The day was unusually warm and bright for November, but it didn't keep the chill from his heart when he thought about her leaving. She'd be away only six days, but they would be worrisome and lonely. While he worked in solitude at his office, he'd wonder if she was out riding with her sister and Willy Jo. While he ate Thanksgiving dinner with Ben, Lottie, and the Doyle sisters, he'd imagine Rosalie seated across from her longtime friend, steeped in reminiscences of their childhood.

Pulling to a halt in front of the depot, he tried to put away such thoughts and cherish these last few minutes with the young lady he was lifting from his surrey. Her brown braid hat trimmed with silk ribbons and velvet flowers, her matching cloak with its ruffled collar, seemed to accent the brown in her eyes and emphasize the pure ivory of her complexion. Her image would remain keen in his mind for a long time to come. He could only pray that she would return in a few days as she had promised, to help her aunt and uncle with their candy shop during the busy Christmas season.

Rosalie noticed that Kenton's hands remained at her waist a few moments longer than necessary when setting her on the boardwalk in front of the depot, and that a certain doubtful look was clouding his hazel eyes with grey. She forced a smile.

"I'm looking forward to returning north for the winter. You'd better have cold weather and snow waiting for me when I come back!"

He managed a twitch of a smile. "I'll order some up for you."

Arranging transfer for the larger of her two bags, he picked up her small valise, offering his free arm to escort her to the platform where she would board. Curious as she was to see Tanglewood again, she truly hated leaving Kenton behind. As her train approached and its destinations were announced, she turned to Kenton.

"Come to North Carolina for Thanksgiving!" she said on a whim, knowing full well the implications of a gentleman friend paying such a visit to her family home.

"I . . ."

"Go home, pack your bags, and take the next train south. Mama would welcome you with open arms, and you know it!"

"Rosalie, please," he said without conviction.
"Don't you want to spend Thanksgiving with me?"
"You know I do."
"Then come!"

CHAPTER

24

North Carolina

Rosalie's heart fluttered as she opened the door to welcome the Winthrops to their traditional day-after-Thanksgiving potluck buffet. After a holiday filled with Foxe family aunts, uncles, and cousins, and a feast that produced leftovers too abundant and delicious to be fed to the hogs, the neighborly get-together had become a yearly, less formal luncheon she had cherished from childhood.

But this year, it held special meaning. It would be the first time she'd seen Willy Jo since she'd left for Michigan at the start of the summer. How much easier the reunion would have been with Kenton at her side, but he had remained in Traverse City after all. Now, she watched closely as Willy Jo came up the walk behind Bobby Dan and his mother. Jabe's hand rested lightly on his elder son's shoulder, then he leaned close, saying something meant only for Willy Jo's ear that brought a smile to both their faces. She couldn't recall when she'd seen the two of them so at ease with one another.

Then Willy Jo's gaze met hers. She offered a tentative smile. He returned an equally uncertain one. The awkward moment passed when his mother entered the foyer.

Virginia took Rosalie's hand in hers. "Welcome home, honey! It's so good to see you. You look wonderful!" She brushed a kiss against Rosalie's cheek, bringing an aura of rose perfume with it.

Rosalie returned the affection. "And you, Mrs. Winthrop!"

Bobby Dan followed his mother inside. His impish grin firmly in place, he reached into his jacket. "I've brought you a little present!" Out popped a huge bouquet of silk flowers.

Rosalie laughed. "I can see you're as tricky as you ever were, Bobby Dan."

Jabe entered on his younger son's heels. "Trickier, if that's possible. Hello, Rosalie. You're lookin' well."

"Likewise, Mr. Winthrop."

He passed through the foyer, leaving her alone to face Willy Jo. He gazed into her eyes, his familiar blue ones reflecting the nervous anticipation she felt within. Undercurrents of conversation drifted from the parlor as Vanda Mae and her folks welcomed Willy Jo's family, but for the moment, Rosalie stood tongue-tied.

On past holidays, long separations at school had prompted prolific conversation. But not today. They were students no longer, and the distance between them was beginning to resemble the Yadkin, wide and silent.

But even the Yadkin was bridgeable, and when Rosalie finally found the right words, they erupted in spurts, nearly colliding with Willy Jo's.

"You're looking well."

"You're looking fine."

"It's nice to be home." She nibbled the inside of her lip knowing her sentiment was only true in part.

"Good to have you back." He shifted his weight, and she wondered if his regard for her had shifted as well.

Feeling as if an eternity has lapsed in only a few awkward moments, she gestured toward the parlor. "Let's join the others. The buffet will be ready soon."

In the parlor, though Willy Jo took the chair beside hers, his focus turned to the young lady on the couch next to his brother. While Bobby Dan performed a card trick, eliciting amazement from Vanda Mae and lively applause from everyone else, Willy Jo remained subdued.

Later, at the dining table, he was equally restrained when Vanda Mae drew stories from Bobby Dan about his experiences as an itinerant performer. But when Jabe took up the subject of hog farming, Willy Jo shared his opinion willingly and confidently. And from the attentive way his daddy listened, Rosalie perceived that a new, healthy respect had been flourishing between them since their reconciliation.

As the meal neared an end, the topic turned to horses. Rosalie's mother set down her fork and laid aside her napkin, making an observation. "I know of at least four horses in the meadow that would love some exercise on the trail through the woods, and I think you young folks ought to take it upon yourselves to grant their wish."

Vanda Mae was the first to respond. "I can't think of a better way to spend the afternoon! If I may be excused—"

Minnie waved her off. "Go! All of you! And leave us older folks to our parlor games."

Willy Jo helped Gaspar and Bobby Dan bring the horses into the stable and saddle them while Rosalie and Vanda Mae changed into suitable riding attire. So many years had passed since he'd seen Rosalie on horseback that he was unable to imagine it now, but he prepared Fergus's most docile standard-bred mare—a pretty, wide-backed sorrel—with care to ensure that the bit and bridle were properly adjusted and the sidesaddle wouldn't slip. He was tightening the saddle on Hurricane, and Bobby Dan was doing the same for Topaz when Rosalie and Vanda Mae joined them.

Rosalie suggested the route. "Let's ride down by the river. It's been nearly half a year since I've seen it."

Bobby Dan chuckled. "Same for me. We ought to check and see if it's still there."

Vanda Mae laughed. "If not, you ought to add that to your repertoire of magic tricks—making a river change its course!"

He pulled a wry smile. "Come on, Miss Champion of Forsyth County, I'll give you a hand up."

They were on their horses and gone in an instant, leaving Willy Jo eager to dash after them. He ignored the urge, patiently helping Rosalie mount the sorrel, which she accomplished with much greater ease, grace, and expediency than he had anticipated, considering her cumbersome riding habit and crippled right arm.

He found nothing cumbersome in her riding style, however. Trotting beside him, she crossed the meadow with a confidence and form that betrayed no evidence of her long held fear of horses. When they came to the gate at the opposite side, he dismounted to open it for her.

She quickly passed through, telling him, "You take the lead, Willy Jo. You know the river paths far better than I."

As he walked Tassie into the woods, he couldn't help recalling the times he'd been there with Vanda Mae, nor wishing she were the one riding behind him now. Glancing back at Rosalie, he suffered a sharp pang of guilt. After all their years of cherished friendship, after all the time she'd just spent up North, he should be thrilled to have her near. Instead, he could hardly think of a thing to say. And although she was making small talk about her aunt and uncle in Michigan, he could barely concentrate on her words, instead hearing Bobby Dan and Vanda Mae ahead of them on the path, their laughter drifting to him on the cool, gusty breeze that stirred new fallen leaves beneath naked trees.

Rosalie recognized Willy Jo's distraction and its cause. Minutes later, when they entered an opening on the bank of the Yadkin, she said, "Willy Jo, I'd like to stop for awhile by the river."

Though he longed to continue down the path toward Bobby Dan and her sister, he nodded, and without a word, dismounted and helped her down.

She watched the water laze its way downstream, tasted the sweet tanginess of a muscadine that had dried on its vine, and listened to the echoing voices of Vanda Mae and Bobby Dan as they shouted nonsense across the water. With a silent prayer that the Lord would give her the right words to say to Willy Jo, she turned to face him.

Despite his solemn expression, she made an attempt at a smile. "Things surely are different than I remember."

Looking past her to the watery scene, he shrugged. "The river seems the same to me . . . except maybe the reflection of the trees now that fall's come."

She drew a breath and spoke quietly. "I wasn't referring to the river, Willy Jo, I was referring to us." Her words capturing his full attention, she continued. "We were the same for so many years, the best of friends." Looking deep into his eyes, she added, "Though neither of us ever admitted it, we had assumptions about the future, that we'd always be together."

She hadn't meant to sound quite so melancholy. Her words were having a visible effect, causing an uneasy twitch beneath his left eye.

He drew a tight breath as if to speak, but remained silent.

She continued, adjusting her tone to sound lighter. "Like I said, things are different now. We've gone in separate directions. Other people and places have become important, where they weren't before." Though she stood only inches from Willy Jo, and was still gazing into his eyes, it was Kenton's face she longed to see, and Kenton's touch she longed to feel when the young man she'd known from childhood reached for her hand.

Willy Jo struggled with conflicting feelings. Though he'd known for months that Rosalie had struck up a friendship with a lawyer in Michigan, and he was pleased for her, he couldn't squelch the recurring guilt that her very own sister was stealing his heart.

Reading the apprehension in his countenance, Rosalie said, "In the time we've been apart, I can see you've grown fond of Vanda Mae. I can't think of anyone I'd rather have sweet on my sister than you, Willy Jo."

His brow lifted. "You knew?"

She smiled, giving his hand an affectionate squeeze. "It's more obvious than you think."

Breaking off contact, he propped his foot on a stump and leaned his elbow on his knee. Chin in hand, he regarded her thoughtfully. "You're sweet on a gentleman up North."

Though she'd contemplated this moment for days, she

was bereft of a reply.

Seeing her momentary discomfort, he said quickly, "Michigan agrees with you. When are you going back?" Suddenly flustered over his inept question, he stammered. "I . . . I didn't mean that the way it sounded."

She chuckled. "Sending me packing already, are you?"

Warmth flooded his face. He hung his head. The touch of her cool, gloved finger beneath his chin stemmed his embarrassment. When he met her gaze now, he found joy and anticipation glimmering in her brown eyes.

"I'm leaving the day after tomorrow. I'll be spending Christmas there." The thought, *and maybe the rest of my life*, came to mind, but she left the sentiment unspoken. Hearing Vanda Mae and Bobby Dan approaching on the trail, she said, "It's time you and I swap riding partners. You ride back with Vanda Mae. I'll go with your brother."

Two days later, Vanda Mae couldn't hold back the tears as she bid Rosalie good-bye at the train depot. "Christmas just won't be the same without you!"

Though her sister's cheeks were also damp, a glimmer of happiness shone in her brown eyes. "It won't be the same, but it will be wonderful, and it will be here before you know it! Now promise you'll be happy when you think of me!"

Reluctantly, Vanda Mae nodded, secretly doubting her sister's predictions, and her own ability to keep her pledge.

Nevertheless, the weeks following Thanksgiving passed quickly at Salem Academy. When the twenty-fourth of December arrived, Vanda Mae could hardly believe she was now riding to the Christmas Eve service at Home Church, now a century old, with her mama and daddy,

Aunt Ophelia, Uncle George, and her cousin Lida Jean with whom they were staying in Winston for the holiday. Though Vanda Mae looked forward to the Moravian religious celebration with fond anticipation, she couldn't deny some melancholy over Rosalie's absence. Her sister hadn't been there to enjoy the special foods such as her aunt's thin ginger Christmas cakes cut into shapes of reindeer, rabbits, and birds, and the beautiful and intricate putz, or Christmas scene set up every year in the Academy parlor.

And they'd never missed a Christmas Eve together, but now, her sister was hundreds of miles away in a climate so cold and snowy, it made Salem's forty-degree temperatures and gusty breezes sound warm and mild. Pulling her scarf tighter about her neck, Vanda Mae couldn't imagine why Rosalie actually liked winter up North with the snowdrifts and sleighs that she described in her letter. How odd, Vanda Mae mused, for someone who had lived all her life in the South to find happiness and romance in Michigan, especially after so many years of assuming her sister and Willy Jo would one day wed.

Willy Jo. As her uncle rounded the corner of Church Street and continued toward the lighted church spire, the sound of brass issued from the belfry. She pondered the fact that her neighbor had changed considerably since the difficult days when he'd lived at Tanglewood and worked in Winston for her daddy. On the few occasions she'd been near him this fall, she'd noticed his frown had disappeared, a smooth brow replacing the ever-present furrow of summer days.

On the Sunday after the fair, when he'd driven her back to the city, they'd talked incessantly about horses while their mothers, riding in the back seat, carried on a conversation of their own. But on the Friday after Thanksgiving, he'd seemed quiet, almost miffed when they'd ridden back to the stable together. Afterward, Rosalie had claimed that he was sweet on her, that there was no denying his jealousy when she'd been paying attention to Bobby Dan. But Vanda Mae wasn't convinced, especially not after this past weekend. Her mother had said that while Vanda Mae had been staying in town with her cousins, Willy Jo had showed up at Tanglewood delivering a gift of a ham he'd smoked himself. Though her folks had repeatedly invited him to join them at the church service tonight, he'd consistently declined. If Rosalie was right, wouldn't he have accepted in an instant?

She pushed puzzling thoughts of Willy Jo aside as her uncle paused at the curb in front of the church to let her and the others out. Beautiful strains of trombones in the belfry could be heard, beckoning worshipers forth, and she turned her thoughts to the celebration of the Christ child in the manger as her father held the door for her. Settling into the pew beside her cousin, her gaze was drawn to the illumination of Coreggio's nativity in the front of the sanctuary, the same decoration set on display year after year, framed by deep green laurel and spruce. It was lit from behind by candlelight. The gently flickering flame seemed to bring the manger scene to life, touching her heart with the uplifting knowledge of her savior's birth.

She marveled at the fact that the church tonight would be filled with Christians of many different denominations just as Salem Academy itself was, and that for more than two centuries, the Moravians had built a reputation of making all the faithful welcome to their special love feast. The air was already tinged with the delicious aroma of the special coffee they would serve, and she could almost taste the fresh, yeasty buns that would accompany the warm beverage.

As notes from the Tannenberg organ joined those of the trombones filling the sanctuary with glorious strains, she rose with her cousin, Lida Jean, preparing to share her Bible opened to Luke, from which the Bishop would read the Christmas story. It was then that she noticed a shuffling and shifting at the end of their pew. The next thing she knew, Lida Jean had stepped away and Willy Jo had taken the place beside her, his almost-smile providing unexpected comfort on this first Christmas Eve without her sister.

The Bishop's voice brought solace, too, as she concentrated on his words.

"And it came to pass in those days, that there went out a decree from Caesar Augustus, that all the world should be taxed . . . "

The story of Jesus' humble birth in the manger, of the angel of the Lord speaking to the shepherds who sought him there, brought warmth to her heart and a tear of joy to her eye. Willy Jo was evidently touched too, for his blue eyes were glistening in a way she'd never seen before. Later, when the lovefeast buns and coffee had been passed, and the congregation sang *Blest be the tie that binds,* Willy Jo's voice blended perfectly with hers, its timbre hushed and warm.

When the beeswax candles were passed throughout the congregation for the traditional candlelight and hymn ceremony that followed, Vanda Mae sensed stronger than ever the wonder of Christ's love moving in and around her, bringing a peacefulness and delight visible even in the shadowy face of the young man beside her. After the

Bishop had led the singing of Doxology and dismissed the congregation, Willy Jo escorted her out into the still night.

His hand at her elbow, he paused to peer into her eyes. "May I speak with you alone, Vannie-Mae?"

With a word to the others that she would join them in a minute, she allowed him to escort her to a more private place in front of the ivy-clad Main Hall. Across the street, moonlight poured down on Academy Square tracing bare elms and sycamores in black against the starry sky and glistening off the white dormers of the neighboring Inspector's House. In the hush of the night, she recalled again the brass voice of trombones and the clear message of the Bishop's story, fading now with the audible words of Willy Jo as he reached inside his coat and produced a small rectangular box which he pressed into her hand.

"I wanted you to have this before tomorrow."

In the gaslight, she could just make out the gold embossing against the black cover, *Wm. T. Vogler, Jeweler*. And in Willy Jo's eyes, his keen look of anticipation transcended the narrow distance between them, silencing the admonition on the tip of her tongue that he shouldn't have done it.

"Open it, Vannie-Mae," he quietly urged.

"But I have nothing for you," she argued feebly.

"Open it."

She impatiently worked the tight-fitting cover free. There, nestled in cotton, lay a miniature silver horse with shimmering gemstone eyes. With a tiny gasp, she carefully lifted it from its bed.

"The eyes are topaz chips," he informed her.

She could see the glimmer of satisfaction in his own eyes when she focused on him again. "Willy Jo, I hardly know what to say."

He shifted his weight. "Next summer . . . when the Academy lets out . . . maybe we can take some rides by the river again."

His halting words were so filled with hopefulness, they cantered straight into her heart. "I'll look forward to it. Thank you, for the invitation *and* the gift. Merry Christmas, Willy Jo!"

A smile crept across his face. "Merry Christmas, Vannie-Mae!"

As he ushered her back to the company of her relatives, then slipped away in the silent darkness, the wisdom of Rosalie's words replayed in Vanda Mae's mind, bringing an unsettling thrill she hadn't known before. *He's sweet on you, Vanda Mae! There's no denying it!*

CHAPTER

25

Michigan

The jangle of sleigh bells, the muted thuds of Judge's hooves against the snow-covered street, the frosting overhanging the rooftop and tapering to long, narrow fingers of ice at the corners made Rosalie's world full of wonder as Kenton turned into the driveway following the midnight Christmas Eve service at St. Francis Church.

In the front parlor window, the spruce tree they had decorated hours earlier now stood as a dark sentinel, its candles snuffed. Lottie and Ben had retired some time ago, exhausted from their efforts to keep up with demand for Christmas candy so popular they were still shaking their heads over their own success. Rosalie, too, felt the fatigue of long hours in the confectionery during the weeks since Thanksgiving.

Using unique molds her aunt and uncle had recently purchased, she had helped them turn out scores of red and yellow hard candy novelties in a vast array of shapes. Santa in a sleigh pulled by reindeer, a frog on a bicycle, a woman riding a horse sidesaddle, a dog begging, a fox holding a goose and an eagle, a large ship, a multi-car train, and dozens of smaller candy figures the likes of angels and snowmen had disappeared from the shelves almost as quickly as they had cooled. Twelve-, fourteen-, even six-teen-hour days had been commonly spent cooking, pouring, and trimming the delectable treats. The efforts had taken their toll, but the thrill of Rosalie's first winter in the North coupled with the excitement of the long-awaited holiday now arriving, kept drowsiness at bay.

Kenton parked by the side door, folded back the bear-skin robe that had been keeping them warm, and helped her down, promising, "I'll be in as soon as I unhitch Judge."

"I'll put on some hot chocolate," she told him, hurrying inside. Though the warmth of the kitchen offered relief from the nippy temperatures, she wasn't at all put off by the frigid Northern Michigan winter as some had predicted. Measuring cocoa, sugar, and milk into a pan and lighting the gas burner, she chuckled to herself recalling the dire predictions of the well-meaning Doyle sisters who had prophesied her hasty retreat to North Carolina after the first snowstorm of the season, and the equally daunting recollections sent through the mail by her very own mother who had once called Michigan her home.

But curiously, the colder the weather turned, the deeper the snow piled up, the better Rosalie liked the North. She enjoyed sleigh rides along country roads with fields so deep in white only the tops of their fenceposts showed. She loved ice skating on the Reddicks' pond with Kenton's arm tight about her to keep her upright. She even loved build-ing snowmen and tossing snowballs. Afterward, she espe-cially appreciated the crackling fire Kenton would build in the fireplace to warm her numb fingers, ruddy cheeks, and red nose. In fact, the longer she stayed in Michigan, the longer she *wanted* to stay.

She secretly admitted that a good part of liking this

place was the presence of Kenton McCune. She couldn't imagine anything that could interfere with the respect and kind regard building between them—sentiments that seemed to increase with each passing day. Kenton's affections had grown, too. She'd noticed it in the way he would squeeze her hand or kiss her cheek for the most trivial of reasons —moments she treasured in her heart.

He'd been especially considerate of her with Christmas approaching, asking time and again if she was sure she wanted to remain in Traverse City rather than returning to North Carolina for the holiday celebration with her kin. Though she'd suffered mild longings to visit Home Church with her family for the Moravian Christmas Eve service, those desires quickly died away when plans arose to attend the midnight celebration at St. Francis.

At the sound of Kenton stamping the snow off his boots on the porch, she took mugs down from the shelf and poured the cocoa. She was rummaging in the cupboard for the tin of marshmallows Aunt Lottie had made last night when he stepped up behind her, his hands encircling her narrow waist.

He turned her toward him, a subtle smile tugging his carefully trimmed mustache and goatee upward, softening the strong angles that defined his cheeks and jaw.

"Merry Christmas, Miss Foxe." When he bent to kiss her cheek, the essence of her peach toilet water temporarily displaced the aroma of hot chocolate. And when her brown eyes met his, their warmth hinted at the unspoken kinship between them.

"Merry Christmas, Mr. McCune." Her words, ex-pressed in a disappearing southern drawl, were quiet and breathy, making him wish more than ever that this time, she would return his kiss with one of her own, but he knew better than to expect it, even though this *was* Christmas.

Quelling the temptation to kiss her on the lips, he said, "I see you have the chocolate ready."

"All but the marshmallows. They're here somewhere." She released herself to continue her search.

"I'll rekindle the fire while you look for them."

In the parlor fireplace, the logs he'd started earlier for Ben and Lottie had died to a few red coals. Nurturing them to flame with the help of crumpled newspaper and kindling, he laid on a maple log and began moving the furniture. Customarily, he and Rosalie sat facing each other in the winged chairs on either side of the fireplace, the low mahogany table centered between them. Tonight, he had a new arrangement in mind. Moving chairs and table aside, he set the love seat in front of the fireplace and confiscated the knitted throw from the back of the sofa. He was checking his jacket pocket for the tiny box he'd stashed there earlier when Rosalie entered the room carrying a tray of cocoa and Christmas cookies.

She paused, studying the new arrangement. Though her pulse quaked at the prospect of sharing the love seat with Kenton, the coziness it offered made her reluctant to sit so near him. Each time he was close, she could barely control her responses, wanting to squeeze his hand whenever their fingers touched, or kiss his cheek in return for the kisses he pressed against hers. With their feelings for one another undeclared, she had been keeping a strict check on herself, unwilling to commit affections until Kenton's true intentions were known.

He must have sensed her reluctance. Taking the tray from her, he set it on the table, then led her to the center of the love seat, draping her with the throw and serving her a mug and cookie before settling on the floor at her feet.

The crackling of the fire seemed to suffice for conversation while they sipped their hot cocoa. Munching one of Rosalie's angel-shaped sugar cookies, Kenton privately reviewed the words he wanted to say.

A few days after Rosalie's return from North Carolina last month he had decided that tonight was the night he'd ask for her hand in marriage, but now that the time had come, the significance of the occasion seemed to grow more daunting with each passing minute. Doubts that had seemed of little moment, now loomed large.

Perhaps she was too young. More than ten years separated them in age. Though she seemed to genuinely enjoy his company, and a wonderful companionship had flourished between them in the past several months, perhaps she wasn't ready for a lifetime commitment.

His fear of rejection heightened at the thought that, despite claims of no future plans with Willy Jo, the lad had been her neighbor and close friend for as long as she could remember. The possibility existed that they would find their way back to each other if only Kenton wouldn't come between.

No sooner had he discarded that notion, than another one popped up to take its place. He'd never met Rosalie's father. Maybe he should wait until he'd seen the man in person. Though he'd secretly written her folks three weeks ago asking permission for their daughter's hand in marriage, and their blessings had been given posthaste, Rosalie might prefer that he visit her childhood home himself before agreeing to take him as her partner for life.

He wondered, too, if the novelty of snow and cold

weather would wear thin once the excitement of the holidays had passed. She appeared to be enjoying herself immensely on their wintertime outings, but the cold season had only begun. She could very well tire of it and go packing for a warmer climate before spring came knocking on Michigan's door.

The very thought brought another dreaded possibility to mind. He recalled the day Ben and Lottie learned their mortgage was in default and he had gone to the train depot to intervene with Rosalie on their behalf. If they were married, would she run home to Tanglewood at the first sign of trouble?

He couldn't possibly know the answer. Nor could he be absolutely certain that, despite all outward signs, she cared enough for him to accept a proposal of marriage, but he was more than certain of this—over time, he'd grown to love this Southern belle. She was on his mind morning, noon, night, and in his dreams. She'd given new meaning to his work and his leisure. He'd begun including her in every thought, every plan, every decision. And he'd begun to realize he couldn't imagine his future without her. For his own sake, for his own peace of mind, he must discover whether her sentiments for him ran as deeply as his for her.

He had eaten his way through two more of Rosalie's angel cookies when he set his mug aside and turned to face her on one knee. Her features, bathed in the soft glow of firelight, alluded to a peace and happiness within, but her lovely countenance couldn't completely quell the apprehension he felt inside.

Rosalie perceived a slight tremor in Kenton's hands when he enfolded hers between them. His expression was solemn, too. And the way he was kneeling at her side could mean only one thing.

She had sensed this moment building. She had dreamed, wished—even prayed for it to come. And she had hoped that it might arrive this very evening.

Now that it appeared her dreams and wishes were about to come true, her blood rushed. The notion of a lifetime with one man was almost too much to comprehend. Maybe she wouldn't be a good wife. Maybe someone better suited to Kenton, someone from the North, would come along if she would only go back to her Carolina home.

But how could she? Beyond any measure of emotion she'd experienced in her life, she had grown to love Kenton McCune. Being with him made her happy. Being parted from him made her miserable.

Her ponderings faded away as he began to speak.

"Miss Foxe," he paused to look directly into her eyes, ready to plead his best case, ready to point out that over time, they'd formed a good partnership in work and play, and now he wanted a lifelong union with her as husband and wife. But he abandoned his logic for the emotion he was feeling as he gazed at her upswept hair the shade of rich chocolate, her eyes soft as brown velvet, her oval face so full of expectation. Determined to start over, he cleared his throat.

"Miss Foxe—"

Keenly aware that Kenton was struggling within, Rosalie chose words intended to ease his tension.

"Mr. McCune, I'd be honored if you'd call me by my Christian name."

Encouraged by her suggestion, he began for the third time. "Rosalie . . . "

The sound of her name, caressed by Kenton's tongue,

was more captivating than any her ear had heard.

Borrowing images from poets he'd often read, he continued in a low, quiet voice. "I know we've run in separate channels for most of our lives. But of late, God has granted us the grace to draw nearer and nearer. And now . . . " He paused, his mouth tilting upward. "Now, my life is completely, divinely, gloriously lost in yours, and I can think of only one remedy for it." Squeezing her hands, he continued, barely exceeding a whisper.

"Rosalie, will you be my wife?"

Her heart stopped, then fluttered wildly. She flung her arms about his neck and pressed her cheek tight against his.

"Yes, Kenton! Yes! A hundred times, yes!"

On the way to Reddicks' for New Year's Eve a week later, Rosalie kept her hands snug inside her new rabbit fur muff, mindful of the soreness in her throat and the occasional chill running up her spine that portended the onset of a cold. She suffered a pang of guilt knowing she might infect others, but the Reddicks had a tradition of bringing in the New Year with Kenton, and Susan's heart was set on making this night a special celebration of his betrothal as well. So Rosalie kept her discomfort a secret, privately promising herself she'd rest once the holiday was over.

Inside her muff, she couldn't keep her hands still, twisting her new ring around her left, fourth finger. Putting worries of illness out of mind, she turned her thoughts to the large center stone and each of the smaller ones on either side, and mentally pictured the custom design Kenton had requested from the jeweler, J.N. Martinek—white diamonds banded in platinum, their mounts surrounded by a delicate filigree of yellow gold. Though she'd worn it for a week, she was still fascinated by the feel of it. And joy gladdened her heart each time she pondered the fact that in the months to come, on a date not yet determined, she would take Kenton McCune's name for her own.

Kenton stole a glance at his betrothed and smiled to himself. He couldn't remember a time when he'd felt as lighthearted and full of joy as he had this past week, knowing Rosalie's affections for him were as ardent as his for her.

A minute later, he turned down Reddicks' drive. Puddles of water stood on the hard pack of snow and ice, testimony to the unseasonably warm temperatures that had blown in on gusty breezes two days ago, melting most of the snow. He eased Judge ahead, cautious of the slick conditions made slipperier by the standing water. In the distance, he heard a faint rumble.

Rosalie asked, "Is that thunder?"

He nodded.

"Do you think it will actually rain?"

"It might."

Indignantly, she said, " I suppose the last of my beautiful snow is going to melt away, and the ice on the skating pond will go soft."

He chuckled. "Don't fret. Winter's just begun. You'll see plenty more snow and ice before the spring thaw." Pulling to a halt by Reddicks' front door, he helped her down from the buggy, wrapping his arm tightly about her waist to guide her along the wet walkway to the front porch.

The wreathed door opened within moments of his knock. He'd last seen John and Susan at church on Christmas Eve, and had been mighty surprised they'd come, knowing John hadn't darkened the door of a church since the death of his wife. Now, both father and daughter welcomed their guests with smiles, and Kenton couldn't remember ever seeing such peacefulness in John's countenance.

Their exchange of New Year's greetings in the foyer was interrupted by the patter of rain against the tin roof.

Helping Rosalie off with her coat, Kenton said, "I'd better put my rig in the stable before it gets soaked."

To Susan, John said, "Why don't you and Miss Foxe set the fixin's out on the buffet. We'll be right in."

Alone with John in the stable, Kenton commented as he wrapped Judge's reins about a post. "There's something different about you, John. You're looking better than you have in a long time—more rested." Privately, he wondered if the change had anything to do with John's recent visit to church.

John winked, a new light shining from his blue eyes. "I *feel* better. I'll explain sometime. Right now, our ladies are waitin'." He put a feed bag on Judge and headed for the door.

Inside, Rosalie had accepted Susan's profuse compliments on her ring, exchanged excited hugs over her betrothal, and had helped her set the buffet with a wassail bowl, cups, and a tray of holiday sweets by the time the men returned. After much prodding from Susan, she let Kenton catch her under mistletoe the young girl had hung especially for their benefit in the doorway between parlor and dining room, although she worried that he, too, would soon suffer from a sore throat. Afterward, while sitting beside him on the love seat, more chills plagued her, despite the warmth of conversation being shared. And in spite of the delectable flavor of the young girl's gingerbread cookies, miniature taffy tarts, and wassail, she would have preferred a cup of hot chicken bullion to soothe her worsening throat and ease her recurring chills.

At least the game they played to occupy the hours till midnight required little talking. While the pitter-patter of rain gave way to the silence of a winter eve's snowfall, she took turns with the others acting out various words and phrases in a contest of charades. At the stroke of twelve, when John lit into a lively chorus of *Auld Lang Syne*, she was thankful the others didn't notice she was barely singing.

Pulling on his coat, Kenton told Rosalie, "I'll bring the buggy around. We'd better go before the snow gets any thicker."

While Kenton headed to the stable with John, Rosalie and Susan cleared the buffet and washed dirty cups and plates. Kenton was escorting her down the wet walkway turned to snow-covered ice when a chilling wind whipped against her, plastering her with huge, wet snowflakes coming so thick and fast, even John, standing by the carriage only a few feet away, was momentarily obscured from view.

He held Judge steady as Kenton helped her aboard. "The weather's turnin' bad in a hurry. Why don't the two of you stay the night?"

Kenton shook his head. "We'd better get home while we can. Thanks, anyway."

He climbed aboard and urged Judge ahead. At the gelding's reluctance to move, he slapped the reins gently against his back. "Get along, Judge! We're going home!"

With uncertain steps, he started down the driveway.

Low spots that had been overflowing with water from rain and melting snow, were now beginning to crust over with ice. Kenton had to scold Judge many times to get him through the crunchy puddles. Several minutes later, he finally turned onto the main roadway.

The flickering flames of the buggy's brass lanterns revealed little of the country road on such a black night, but Rosalie could see from reflections against the fresh blanket of white that the deep drainage ditch had filled with runoff, and several patches of ice lay exposed by drifting snow. She was wondering how Kenton could see far enough ahead to know the way when a cottontail rabbit scampered across the road only few feet in front of Judge.

The gelding shied, then slipped.

The carriage jostled and jerked.

"Easy, boy! Easy!" Kenton commanded.

Veering left, then right, Judge danced sideways, slipped again, and went down on his chest and belly. Frantic, he overturned the buggy on its right side and slid helplessly off the road dragging the rig with him into the flooded ditch.

Kenton's weight crushed against Rosalie, pinning her inside. She screamed, the sound ripping from her sore throat amidst the horrifying shrieks of a horse in intense pain, and Kenton's futile commands.

The icy waters of the ditch quickly seeped into the rig, soaking the lap robe and her woolen overcoat. Somehow, Kenton managed to climb out and pull her out the left side. Standing thigh-deep in frigid water, she clutched tightly to Kenton's hand as he began climbing out of the ditch to the road. Losing her foothold on the icy incline, then her grip, she fell backward into the ditch with a splash.

"Rosalie!" Kenton cried, tromping into the water to pick her up.

On her feet again, teeth chattering, she told him, "I'm not hurt . . . just cold and wet."

Kenton clasped her tightly to his side, half-dragging her up the incline to the snowy road. Giant, wet snowflakes were falling in waves so thick, she could barely see Judge still struggling a few feet away, but she could clearly hear his wailing neighs.

Once on level ground, though quaking with a severe chill, she told Kenton, "You've got to . . . help Judge!"

"Stay here. I'll be right back!"

As she stood shivering, the wind howled, plastering thick snow against her dark wrap, giving her an overcoat of white. As she shook off the frosty adornment, she could hear Kenton splashing into the flooded ditch again, then talking to Judge, telling him he'd come back soon and get him out.

Returning to her side moments later, he wrapped his arm tight about her and started up the road toward Reddicks'.

"I've got to get you inside where you can warm up and dry off. Then I've got to get back here with a rifle as quick as I can. Judge's leg is broken."

She replied between uncontrollable spasms of chattering teeth. "I'm so . . . sorry."

Pausing to gaze at her, he kissed her wet cheek and hugged her to him. "Thank God you're only wet, not hurt." Clutching her against his side, he started toward Reddick's again, berating himself as he went.

"I should have listened to John! I shouldn't have forced Judge!"

"You did what you . . . thought was best," Rosalie argued sympathetically.

"And look where it got us!" he replied with disgust. Realizing he couldn't change the past, he drew up a plan for dealing with the crisis. "When we get back to the house, I want you to get out of those wet clothes, change into something dry, and stay by the fire while John and I see to Judge."

"But . . . you're wet, too!" she argued.

"I'll be all right."

Realizing further discussion was futile, and with her chattering teeth and sore throat, nigh unto impossible, Rosalie kept her silence and concentrated on the challenge of keeping her feet beneath her on the trek up the long, slippery driveway.

The Reddick home was dark as a tomb when Kenton reached the front door. Finding it unlocked, he helped Rosalie inside, announcing their presence. Soon, both John and Susan, donned in long flannel gowns and sleeping caps, came hurrying down the stairs by the light of an oil lamp. Within minutes, Susan had the kitchen stove roaring with fire, the tea kettle filled, and Kenton had gone with John to see about Judge after phoning Ben and Lottie.

As Rosalie divested herself of her waterlogged clothing, Susan hung it near the stove to dry, then wrapped her in a thick, woolen blanket and set her in a rocking chair close to the stove. "You stay right there and warm up while I find a gown for you," said the young girl, disappearing upstairs.

While she was gone, Rosalie continued to shudder with chills. In addition to the soreness in her throat, she seemed to be developing a headache, and pain in her legs and back which she attributed to the accident.

The clock in the parlor was striking half past one when Susan returned with a pink flannel gown. "This used to be Mama's, but you can use it," she explained, holding it near the stove to warm it before handing it to Rosalie.

"Are you sure?" Rosalie asked, hardly recognizing her own voice, so altered was it now by increasing pain, and a general feeling of weakness that was coming over her.

"You sound terrible!" Susan concluded.

"I'm coming down with a cold. Better keep your distance. I don't want you to catch it," Rosalie managed.

"I'll make you some tea and honey. It ought to soothe your throat."

Susan took a china teapot from the shelf, warmed it with a small amount of boiling water from the kettle on the stove, then added several spoonfuls of tea leaves before filling it to the top and covering it with a cozy.

By the time the clock struck two, Rosalie had sipped a full cup of strong tea sweetened with a generous portion of honey, but was feeling no improvement. Aside from her own discomfort, she worried about Kenton, fearing he'd taken a bad chill and would be seriously ill.

Susan, determined to serve as Rosalie's nursemaid, had pulled a second rocker near the stove, and was now sound asleep beneath a blanket, unmindful that her fire was beginning to die out.

Suffering constant chills, Rosalie hated to stir from her own woolen cocoon to add wood, but neither was she about to needlessly waken the girl. Reluctantly unwrapping herself, she opened the fire box, tossed in two sticks of hardwood, and latched the door as quietly as possible.

Susan stirred and yawned, but didn't wake. Rosalie envied her the ability to sleep, being too beset by her own discomforts to stay in slumber land for more than an hour at a stretch. When she awoke at three, she felt feverish, and knew *this* cold was going to be worse than others she'd had. She stoked the fire and settled down in her rocker again, increasingly concerned for the welfare of Kenton and John.

An hour later, Rosalie awoke with a tightness in her chest. She again added wood to the stove, then scraped frost from the window overlooking the stable and peered out. Light spilled onto white drifts of snow creeping higher and higher by the stable door, but neither Kenton nor John were in view.

She retreated to her rocker, waking at five with a hacking cough and feeling as though someone had slipped a band of steel about her lungs, making every breath painful. She retrieved her handkerchief from the pocket of her dress, still drying by the stove, so she could stifle her coughing fits, then snuggled into her rocker again. Her misery continued, as well as her worry for the men, until they finally came through the kitchen door a half hour later.

Kenton knew the moment he heard Rosalie's cough and saw the blue tinge to her skin that, despite the smile with which she greeted him, she was suffering from more than a cold. And when he pressed his lips to her forehead, he worried about her high fever, as well.

Kenton's kiss, though warm with affection, felt cool and comforting against Rosalie's flesh. Though she was relieved that he had finally come inside to warm himself by the kitchen fire, she couldn't resist mildly scolding him.

"I've worried every minute that you'd catch your death out there!"

No sooner had she delivered her admonition in a voice

weak with infection, than she lapsed into a fit of coughing. Touching the back of his cool hand to her burning cheek, Kenton replied, "I'll be just fine. Don't try to talk anymore, okay?"

She nodded, wanting to take his hand in both of hers, but he returned to the side entry to hang up his coat.

John kissed Susan's cheek. She stirred, mumbled acknowledgment of his presence, and fell asleep again even before her father had removed his jacket, hat, and gloves. Emerging from the side entry with Kenton, Rosalie heard John tell him, "If you come upstairs a minute, I'll find you a change of clothes. They'll hang a little loose on you, but it's better than stayin' in wet ones."

Kenton must had agreed, for she heard two sets of footsteps ascending the stairs.

Thankful for John's offer, Kenton followed his friend into the second floor bedroom. Removing his sodden pants, shirt, and underthings, he said, "I'm worried about Rosalie. She's running a high fever, and that cough is no simple cold. I'd like to set up a cot by the kitchen stove and ring up Dr. Sawyer."

"We can do better than that. We'll haul down the bed in the spare room." His brows narrowing, John added, "I don't think the doc will be able to make it out here from town, though, the way the road's driftin', but maybe he can tell us what to do."

Within minutes, they had erected a single bed in the kitchen, and with Susan's help, made it up with fresh sheets, layered it with woolen blankets, and tucked Rosalie snugly in. Whether Dr. Sawyer could make a house call or not was of little matter, for when Kenton picked up the phone to ring him, the line was dead. Placing the instrument on its hook with a firm click, he was wondering what to do next when Susan supplied an answer.

"Mama kept a medical book upstairs. I'll go fetch it."

Though Kenton didn't speak of it in front of Rosalie, he suspected she had contracted pneumonia, and when he sat down to the kitchen table with a lamp and read the symptoms described in the medical book, he discovered his fears well-founded. Studying the treatments for such a case, he took John aside, speaking confidentially. "I'm fairly certain Rosalie has pneumonia. Quinine is recommended, and a mustard poultice. Do you—"

Even before he could finish asking, John had gone to retrieve a bottle of quinine from the top shelf of a kitchen cupboard, and ground mustard from the pantry. While Kenton administered a full dose of the tonic, Susan fetched several old pieces of cotton from a rag bag and set about mixing the mustard with the beaten white of an egg and a small amount of flour. Spreading the paste on one of the cloths, she folded it over and layered other cloths on top of it to prevent soiling her mother's nightgown.

While Susan applied the poultice to Rosalie's chest, Kenton and John retreated to the dining room. Too preoccupied to sit at the table with his friend, Kenton leaned against the sideboard and stared idly down at the turned-up cuffs of the overly long pants John had loaned him. The sound of Rosalie's tight, frequent cough worried Kenton too much to care that the flannel pant legs didn't quite match in length. A heavy gust of wind battered the clapboard siding, making it creak, drawing John out of his chair and eliciting comment.

"This storm's gonna blow awhile, from the sounds of it."

His words only heightened Kenton's frustration. "Let it blow. When daylight comes, I'm going after a doctor. You'll loan me Penny, won't you?"

John shook his head.

"Then I'll go on foot! I've got to get Rosalie proper medical attention!"

John lay his hand on Kenton's shoulder. "It was bad enough out there draggin' Judge back to the barnyard and towin' your buggy to the stable. We nearly froze our faces off before we got the job done, and it's a lot worse now!"

His jaw taut, Kenton said, "It's my fault Rosalie's sick. I won't be to blame for her not getting proper care."

John's hand tightened, sending pain into Kenton's shoulder. "And I won't be to blame for lettin' my best friend commit suicide. You're stayin' inside this house if I have to strap you to a kitchen chair with ten yards of barbed wire!"

Kenton made no reply. A moment later, evidently interpreting silence as acquiescence, John released him, but inside, Kenton was seething. He sat in the empty rocker beside Susan, realizing he couldn't possibly stay there the whole day long listening to Rosalie's labored breathing and watching the young woman he loved get worse with each passing hour. If John wouldn't loan him Penny, he'd head out to the privy, sneak to the stable, then take the mare and go for help.

But by daybreak, snow had drifted so thickly against the side door, Kenton and John together could barely get it open, and before John could shovel a path to the outhouse and stable, he had to attach a length of rope to his waist to make certain he could find the house again, for the air was too thick with snow to see the outbuildings.

307

With a heavy heart, Kenton returned to the rocker beside Rosalie's bed. Susan dozed in the chair next to his, then went upstairs to her own bed, telling him to call her if Rosalie needed her. He rested his head against the chair back, drifting into fitful naps that alternated between moments of wakefulness and worry over Rosalie's coughing, and awareness of John tossing wood into the kitchen stove and warming himself there before returning to the cold outdoors.

By mid-morning, with Susan still upstairs asleep and John outdoors, he was too fidgety to remain still. He filled a wash basin with cool water, dipped a clean rag in it, and sat on the edge of Rosalie's bed, sponging off her face and neck, pushing up the sleeves of her nightgown to wipe down her arms, meeting no resistance even when he ministered to her crippled right one. As he worked over her, he noticed certain changes from hours earlier. She was perspiring now, her forehead felt cooler to the touch, and her cough, though not eliminated, was less severe—reactions detailed in the medical text that could result from a full dose of quinine, and could mean the disease had been aborted in its early stages. He silently thanked God that the attack of pneumonia had been so quickly thwarted.

Setting wash basin aside, he took Rosalie's hand in his. "Would you like some tea or broth? You should try to take something."

"Broth," she answered, suppressing the urge to cough.

"Crackers?"

She nodded.

Kenton searched the kitchen cupboards, ice box, and pantry, coming up with turkey broth left from the Christmas bird, a pan to heat it in, a tin of soda crackers, and even a small tray to serve it on. He poured a mug of the broth for himself as well, and sat in the rocker sipping the soothing liquid as Rosalie drank hers. They were finishing their last swallows when John came inside, his cheeks and nose bright red.

Divesting himself of jacket, cap, and gloves, he stood between Rosalie's bed and the stove, warming his hands as he cast a backward glance at the patient. "You're feelin' better, I see."

"I am," Rosalie replied, gaining quick control over the cough triggered by even those two tiny words.

As Kenton set their dirty dishes in the wash basin, he stated cheerfully, "She'll be good as new in a couple of days."

John made no reply. Done warming his hands, he stoked the stove, set coffee on to boil, then opened the ice box and hauled out a bowl of eggs, slab of bacon, and pitcher of milk. "Anyone for scrambled eggs and bacon?"

Rosalie shook her head, mouthing the words, "No, thank you."

Feeling relieved at her turn for the better, Kenton said, "Eggs and bacon would hit the spot with me. Can I help?"

While tending the stove, John talked Kenton through instructions for setting the table. The aroma of fried bacon must have aroused Susan's appetite. Soon, she was downstairs adding a place setting to the dining table and a bowl of the oranges she'd found in her stocking on Christmas morning.

When Kenton had helped himself to a portion of the fluffy eggs and three strips of crisp bacon, he told Susan and John, "If only the weather would improve as quickly as Rosalie, we could go home."

His voice low, John replied, "Her turn for the better could be a temporary thing."

Irked, Kenton stated quietly but confidently, "She'll be on her feet in no time. Mark my words."

With lines of doubt cutting deep into his forehead, John said, "I hope you're right."

The day passed in two more cycles of hopefulness followed by worry. Each dose of quinine produced improvements. When Rosalie was feeling relief, Kenton would venture from the house to help John with the shoveling, and the chores in the stable.

When the medicine was wearing off and Rosalie was beset by a return of the coughing, fever, and labored breathing, Kenton would remain by her side, laden with guilt over the accident that had brought on her illness. He asked himself time and again why he hadn't listened to John and agreed to stay overnight in the first place. Pangs of guilt set off prayers for her recovery, and prayers, too, that this first day of 1901 was no indication that a year of troubles would follow.

He sat with Rosalie throughout the night, half-awake most of the time. The second day of the New Year passed much the same as the first. Rosalie's condition seemed no worse, but no better, and neither did the weather. Again, Kenton stayed with her through the night, praying that God would bring her lasting relief with every wheezing breath she took, and asking himself just as often how he could live with himself if she should fail to recover.

The relief God granted on the third day of January, however, concerned neither Rosalie, nor his worry and guilt, but the world outside the Reddick home, described succinctly by John at six in the morning when he opened the door to go to the stable.

Holding his lantern high, he reported, "No wind. It's stopped snowing. I'm goin' to clear the driveway soon as I tend the horses." He closed the door with a thud, leaving the kitchen in darkness again.

Rosalie stirred, mumbled something, then coughed several times into her handkerchief.

Kenton lit an oil lamp to administer her morning medicine, immediately alarmed by the revelations of the flickering flame. The beauty of Rosalie's oval face was masked by anxiety and distress that hadn't been there the day before. Her white handkerchief was badly stained by rusty sputa from her coughing spells. Touching the back of his hand to her forehead, he realized she was burning up though she showed no sign of perspiration.

She pushed his hand away with a feeble effort and a frail plea. "Willy Jo . . . find Shani. I need Shani."

Kenton set down the lamp, kneeling at her bedside to take both of her hands in his. "Rosalie, my love, Shani isn't here, but I'll take care of you, I promise." He kissed her hands, afraid that he couldn't keep his word, terrified of losing her, and hating himself for letting her get this way.

She started to cough and reached for her soiled handkerchief. Kenton quickly tossed it aside, substituting his own, clean one. Then he fetched the quinine, pouring the tonic into a spoon. She swallowed it with difficulty, struggling to catch her breath afterward.

He left her side long enough to pump fresh, cool water into a basin. Taking up a wet rag, he wiped her face and neck, then consulted the medical book again, searching pantry cupboards and shelves for the remedies listed for this stage of the disease. Having little success, he was about to arouse Susan when he heard her coming down the stairs. She'd no sooner stepped foot past the kitchen door when he fired off his list of requests.

"I need carbonate of ammonia, camphor liniment, a flaxseed poultice, and lemonade with cream of tartar. Can you help me?"

"I'll try."

Listening to Rosalie suffer during the few minutes that passed while Susan gathered supplies from various parts of the house felt like a lifetime. Each labored breath, every racking cough, layered new feelings of utter helpless on Kenton. He wondered if any manmade decoctions could actually change the course of the disease. Realizing prayer and home remedies were his only hope, he asked God to continue guiding him in helping the woman he desperately wanted for his wife. His hopes lifted when Susan presented him with carbonate of ammonia and camphor liniment from the kitchen cabinet, flaxseed and cream of tartar from the pantry, and all the oranges from the fruit bowl on the dining table—her substitute for lemons to make a cooling drink.

While the young girl created a syrup for the carbonate of ammonia and a poultice from the flaxseed, Kenton squeezed the oranges. Mixing in the cream of tartar, he held the glass for Rosalie to drink, administered the carbonate of ammonia, then excused himself from the room while Susan rubbed camphor liniment on Rosalie's chest, replaced her mustard poultice with the flaxseed one, and helped her to relieve herself in the chamber pot.

When Susan called him back into the room, Kenton began donning coat and boots. "If you'll stay by Rosalie awhile, I'll empty the chamber pot. Then I need to talk to your father."

"Of course," Susan replied, taking up the wet cloth to sponge off Rosalie's face.

Outdoors, the chamber pot yielded what Kenton had feared from descriptions in the medical book—scanty, high-colored urine. When he had discarded it and relieved himself in the privy, he headed to the stable, mucking out Penny's stall as he talked with John.

"Rosalie's delirious with fever. I've got to get to town and bring back the doctor."

John paused to lean on his pitchfork. "You'll never make it."

Kenton's gaze met John's. "Penny can get me there."

John heaved a sigh of frustration. "There are drifts out there as high as my shoulder. The two of you will get stuck, then what are you gonna do?"

"We won't get stuck. We'll go around them. I'll take a shovel." He began untying Penny.

"Leave her be!" John warned.

Paying no heed, Kenton began backing Penny out of her stall.

John blocked his exit, shoulders back, feet apart, pitchfork erect. "We've been through this before. I won't let you risk life, limb, and *my* horse."

Kenton turned away from John's unyielding gaze. Settling his focus on Penny, he masked his anger with calm logic. "The storm's over. Rosalie's burning up. She'll die if I don't get help."

"I'll go."

Astonished by the offer, Kenton was silently asking a half-dozen questions when John began supplying answers.

"I'll clear the drive, then I'll start for town. But I won't let you leave Rosalie now. She needs you here."

313

Relief surged through Kenton. "I don't know how to thank you."

"Save your thanks. I might not make it. But at least I'm levelheaded enough to know when to turn back."

John put his pitchfork away and the two of them worked for an hour clearing a narrow path down the drive. Though the road was in bad shape, someone had already made tracks toward town which John could follow. In the stable once more, John went for Penny's bridle, Kenton seeing to her saddle blanket and saddle, still puzzled over John's willingness to make the difficult journey.

"I don't understand yet why you're doing this, John. What made you change your mind about going for the doctor?"

John adjusted a stirrup, then paused to answer, his expression melancholy, his words solemn. "My biggest regret is not bein' with the woman I loved when she needed me most. That's a mistake I'll live with for the rest of my life—a mistake I won't let you make."

Kenton meditated on the answer, saying, "I'll pray you get through."

John almost smiled. "I'm countin' on it—the prayers, that is. There's only so much a man can do."

Surprised by this new attitude in John, Kenton was curious to ask about the changes that had come over him, but his questions would have to wait until another time, for his friend was mounting up, heading for the stable door.

"Godspeed, John."

"Keep prayin'!" he reminded Kenton.

In the house, Kenton took up his vigil at Rosalie's bedside once more. The remainder of the day passed in worry, prayer, and constant attendance to Rosalie's needs.

He sponged her face and forehead frequently, administered carbonate of ammonia in syrup every two hours, and encouraged her to sip as much orange juice as possible. When she dozed off in a fitful sleep, he tried to nap also, but he felt as if he were sleeping with one eye open, waking each time she stirred, anxious whenever she muttered Willy Jo's name in her delirium.

As day gave way to night, so did his hopes that John would return before the morrow. Darkness settled over the countryside and in his heart, as well. He barely acknowledged Susan when she served him a hearty bowl of soup for supper. It grew cold before he'd finished more than a few spoonfuls, his appetite nonexistent, and he paid little heed when she took the remains away.

He vaguely noticed when she pulled on her coat and went outdoors, assuming she'd gone to the privy. When she returned with a heavy load of firewood, he silently berated himself for neglecting chores of necessity, making an apology.

"I'm sorry, Susan. I should have done that for you. I didn't notice the wood was getting low."

She mumbled an acceptance and blew her nose. He assumed the cold air had made it run, but when she bent to stoke the stove, he caught a glimpse of her moist eyes and cheeks and realized something more serious was amiss.

"Susan, what's troubling you?"

She closed the stove door with a clank and hurried from the room.

Though reluctant to leave Rosalie's side, he could see that she was napping and tore himself away to go in search of Susan. He found her curled in a ball on the parlor sofa, quietly crying.

He lay a hand on her shoulder. "Susan, what's the matter? Tell me, please?"

She responded with racking sobs that made her entire body tremble. Looking up at him, she blubbered through her tears. "Papa's not coming back . . . he's going to die . . . Miss Rosalie's going to die . . . like Mama did!" She scrambled off the sofa and hurried toward the staircase, her uneven footsteps playing syncopation on the steps.

Kenton followed her to the bottom of the stairs. "Susan, come back! Please!"

She disappeared into the darkness of the second floor.

Drawn in two directions at once, Kenton returned to check on Rosalie. She was awake, coughing up blood, and in need of another dose of syrup. When he had administered the carbonate of ammonia and settled her down, he wondered if he should go to Susan. Anguishing over the impossibility of administering to two women at the same time, he prayed for guidance.

As if in answer to his prayer, Susan quietly slipped into the kitchen, settling on the chair beside his. Though her eyes were red, they were also dry. She wore a contrite look when she spoke. "I'm sorry I got upset. I—"

"You have every right to be," Kenton sympathized. "But one thing you can count on. Your father, wherever he is tonight, is safe and warm."

"I know. 'God is our refuge and strength, a very present help in trouble.'" She quoted the first verse of the forty-sixth Psalm. "God can keep Papa safe, and He can heal Miss Rosalie, too. I just needed to ask Him, and believe."

For a moment, Kenton envied Susan's faith and the peacefulness now evident in her serene smile. He'd never seen such tranquility in the young girl, and was about to make mention of it when Rosalie stirred, mumbled his name, and coughed.

"I'm right here, my love." He rang out the washcloth and began mopping her forehead, offering words of assurance. "You're going to get over this, Rosalie. Your fever will break, and you'll feel much better."

His words were only lip service for Rosalie's benefit. In his heart, he feared she wouldn't even make it through the night, let alone the next five days described in the medical book for this stage of the disease.

When she had quieted down again, Susan told Kenton, "I'm going to make hot chocolate. Would you like some?"

He shook his head. "What I could really use is coffee. It's going to be another long night."

"I'll set some to boiling."

Later, when they had finished their hot beverages, Susan said, "I'm going up to bed. Call me if you need me."

Kenton nodded, but had no intention of interrupting the young girl's sleep. He alone was to blame for Rosalie's suffering, and he alone would tend her through the night, an endless routine of administering medicine, laying a cool, damp cloth against her forehead, and holding the small juice glass to her lips, a pattern interrupted only by moments in the privy to empty her chamber pot and relieve himself of the coffee he'd been drinking.

The following day differed little, except in mounting disappointment that John hadn't returned, and increased concern that Rosalie was growing weaker. Susan held up well, despite her father's absence, performing his chores in the stables as well as her own in the kitchen.

On the third evening of John's absence, the phone rang.

In a weak voice, John explained that though telephone service had been restored and the road was now open, both he and the doctor were suffering from a severe outbreak of influenza and incapable of travel.

Kenton immediately rang up Ben and Lottie to tell them of Rosalie's condition, learning they and several of their employees had contracted the virus and the candy factory and shop were both temporarily closed.

With a heavy heart, he returned to Rosalie's side. Somehow, she survived the next two days and nights, but the fever had sapped almost all her strength. In addition, the medicine was nearly gone. He rang the pharmacy to ask them to send out new supplies, but was told that would be impossible. Some of their own employees were sick, leaving them shorthanded, and the others were too busy with remedies and prescriptions for the sick in the city. As dusk turned to darkness on the fifth night of John's absence, Kenton stared at the tiny portion of cough suppressant that still remained and was convinced Rosalie couldn't make it through one more night.

When Susan had retired, he sat by Rosalie's side, his worry and hopelessness increasing with each passing minute. The night was measured by the rapid, shallow breaths she took and his fear that each one could be her last. At four in the morning, he administered the final dose of cough syrup. When she had settled her head against the pillow, he quietly left the kitchen. Helpless, terrified, and angry that God could let the object of his love and affection suffer so, he wandered into the parlor and slumped onto the sofa, fists tight, eyes heavenward.

"God, how can you do this?" he demanded through clenched teeth. "How can you make that innocent young woman suffer and die because of me?" Overwhelmed with grief at the thought of losing Rosalie, he cried out, "God, I hate you!"

Momentarily relieved of frustration, he forced himself to return to Rosalie and his deathwatch. Shortly after, Susan spoke to him from the dining room doorway.

"Is everything all right?"

When he turned to look at her, the gentle flickering of her candle softly illuminating her fair complexion, flowing, blond hair, and snow white robe, gave the brief impression of an angel.

He caught his breath, blinked, and looked again, this time aware of the deep concern in her eyes as she moved to the empty rocker beside his.

In a half-whisper, she spoke again. "I heard something. I thought I'd better come down and check." Her focus now on Rosalie, she reached past him to touch the back of her hand to the patient's forehead. "She's still burning up, isn't she?"

Kenton could only nod, his hope gone that Rosalie would survive more than an hour or two.

Quietly, Susan continued. "God says the prayers of faith shall save the sick."

"It's a lie," Kenton claimed in quiet anger. "I've been praying for Rosalie since she first took sick, and what good has it done?" He turned his focus on his frail beloved.

A minute passed, then Susan spoke again. "God won't forsake you. In his word, he makes that promise."

"Don't talk to me of God!" Kenton ground out. Though his gaze never left Rosalie, from the corner of his eye he could see Susan flinch. Nevertheless, he continued to vent his frustration. "The woman I love lies here struggling for every breath, and yet God stands by and watches her being strangled by disease."

"Anger won't make things better," Susan advised.

"How do you know? You're just a child!" he snapped.

Seconds later, Susan replied with cool confidence. "I may be young, but I'm wise enough to listen to my elders. Papa told me a little while ago how sorry he is that he wasted the last couple of years being angry with God. Instead of pushing God away, he should have been seeking Him, like he is now."

Refusing to reply, Kenton busied himself sponging off Rosalie's face and neck. When he'd tossed the rag into the basin of water, Susan's hand sought his.

"'Be strong and of good courage, fear not, nor be afraid . . . for the Lord . . . will not fail thee, nor forsake thee.' Deuteronomy 31:6. Father in heaven, I claim your promises for my friends. Heal Miss Foxe of her physical ailments, and Mr. McCune of his spiritual ones. In Jesus' name, Amen."

With a squeeze of his hand, she rose. He listened to the rocking of her empty chair and the scuffing of her slippers as she parted, her prayer echoing in his mind. Beside him, Rosalie had settled into a fitful nap. He leaned his head back and closed his eyes. Horrid, nightmarish visions of Rosalie's form, lifeless and cold, barred him from sleep. He stared up at the ceiling and watched the flickering of the oil lamp play shadows against the bumps and indentations of the tin pattern. Hollow and hopeless, his mind went blank, too tired for cogent thought.

His next awareness was of a small voice.

"Kenton . . . are you awake?"

Suddenly realizing he'd fallen asleep, he sat erect, startled to discover Rosalie raised up on one elbow, staring at him.

He reached for her hand, squeezing it in his. "My darling, what is it? What can I get you?" Seeing that she was damp with perspiration, he touched the back of his hand to her forehead. She was definitely cooler than she had been a few hours earlier. Clearly, she had passed to the next stage of the disease described in the medical book as the stage of resolution. She had survived!

"I'd like a drink," she informed him. Though her voice was still weak, it was stronger than it had been in days, and even in the dim light of the oil lamp, he could see new vitality in her brown eyes.

He reached for her glass, still half full of juice, and held it to her lips. She placed her hand over his, tipping the tumbler until it was empty, then she lay back on the bed.

He set the glass aside and took up the damp rag, sponging away the beads of moisture on her forehead. The clock in the parlor chimed six.

"That feels good," she told him. "I'm better today."

Though she started coughing, the spasm was neither as severe nor prolonged as before. When she asked for the chamber pot, Kenton stepped into the parlor. Taking advantage of these private moments, he dropped to his knees beside the sofa. "Forgive me Lord. I never should have doubted you. Thank you for Rosalie's improvements, for this new day, and for every day to come, whatever happens! In Jesus' name, Amen."

In a moment of doubt, he recalled from the medical book that pneumonia could progress from one part of the lung to another, or to the other lung. Fear seized him, then lost its grip as renewed faith in God planted seeds in his heart and mind in the form of three words.

She is healed!

With solid confidence, he returned to Rosalie's side, silently praising the Lord for answering prayers, and for the wisdom and faith Susan had offered in his darkest hour.

CHAPTER

26

North Carolina
June 1901

Dressed in a white morning suit, Kenton stood ramrod straight in the rose-adorned gazebo specially designed by Mr. Foxe for Rosalie's garden wedding, thankful that she had insisted on a modest affair with close friends and relatives rather than giving in to the extravagant celebration Mrs. Foxe had proposed. The scent of the pink, white, and yellow blossoms enhanced by the warmth of the moist southern breeze wafted about him, accompanied by the strains of Bach's *Jesus, Joy of Man's Desiring* being played by the violin orchestra. Too nervous to look out across the rows of chairs where the last of the fifty-or-so wedding guests were being seated, he gazed past the clematis-covered fence to the meadow and frolicking horses beyond, his focus on the filly named Jewel.

The yearling, a wedding gift from Vanda Mae that had pleased both him and Rosalie in equal measure, had come with a promise from his future sister-in-law. "When she's old enough, I'll train her and deliver her to Traverse City." To Susan, who had traveled south with him and Rosalie to serve as a bridesmaid in the wedding party, Vanda Mae had said, "When you go home, you tell your daddy to save a stall for her!"

Those thoughts faded when the notes of the string ensemble gave way to the opening chords of Beethoven's *Ode to Joy* which Ben and Lottie had helped choose as the wedding march. Kenton's only regret was that they were not there to hear it. Ownership and management of both the candy factory and shop—now permanent with the recent conviction of Lazarus Ambrose—had prevented them from traveling south.

Putting regrets aside, Kenton redirected his thoughts and his attention to the processional, admiring Susan as she started down the aisle. Her limp was barely noticeable beneath the pink organdy dress that flowed about her, its modest train brushing the white runner that had been rolled out across the grass. Behind her followed Vanda Mae in a mist of yellow silk as subtle as a southern sky on a summer's morn.

Then, just as Rosalie was about to start down the aisle on the arm of her father, a carriage came racing along the driveway to rattle to a halt on the lawn at the rear of the seated guests. Anger rose within Kenton that the commotion caused by the unthinking, insensitive driver had interrupted the most poignant moment of the processional. The music stopped, guests turned to stare, and Kenton bit his tongue to keep his annoyance in check. But indignation gave way to elation the instant the newcomers emerged from the buggy.

Ben and Lottie had come after all!

With hugs for the bride, they were quickly ushered to second row seats where their beaming smiles chased away Kenton's last remnants of apprehension and anxiety.

Striking up the processional anew, violins sent stirring notes of Beethoven through the air as Rosalie approached the gazebo in a sheath of creamy satin overlaid by sheer organdy, her fair complexion veiled by a film of the same. Kenton couldn't suppress a proud grin the moment he saw her, his heart joyful when her brown eyes met his and her pretty lips parted in a beautiful smile. Then he noticed the touch of pink circling the high collar of her dress—the crimped satin bow she so frequently wore, and he had as frequently admired from the first days of their acquaintance. How thoughtful that she would include it on this most special of days, and how perfectly the style of her entire wedding ensemble matched her personality. Neither frivolous nor severe, it symbolized her inner strength and her delicate beauty, qualities he most admired in the woman he had come to love more than life itself. Silently, he thanked God for rescuing her from the brink of death six months earlier and nursing her through a near-miraculous recovery that had actually made her stronger both physically and emotionally than before her illness.

As she advanced toward him to the stately rhythm of the processional, apprehension took flight, replaced by a God-given confidence that this union he was about to enter would be both fulfilling and satisfying, regardless of life's challenges.

Willy Jo was watching Vanda Mae intently from his usher's post at the rear of the small congregation in the rose garden. Though Rosalie and the lawyer from Traverse City were exchanging vows this day, he envisioned a time about two years off when he and Vanda Mae would be the ones in the gazebo pledging promises of a lifetime. She'd be finished at the Academy then. It would give him just enough time to get established as a full partner in his daddy's hog farming business and put up a pretty house for his bride. His daddy had already given him the plat next to his folks' place to build on, and Fergus had offered to provide lumber and labor at cost as soon as he was ready to break ground. Reflecting on the days when Vanda Mae and Bobby Dan had been best of friends and both families had assumed he himself would one day marry Rosalie, Willy Jo marveled at God's infinite wisdom and power in guiding and blessing those who truly seek and love Him.

Strains of the recessional sang out as Rosalie walked back down the aisle on her new husband's arm, the final words of the ceremony, "I now present to you Mr. and Mrs. Kenton McCune," ringing joyfully in her head.

At the rear of the rose garden, Kenton paused to press his lips to hers. When his sweet kiss ended, she opened her eyes to discover Hurricane looking on from behind the pasture fence a few feet away. The flick of his ears and bob of his head seemed to offer tacit approval.

Taking Kenton by the hand, she stepped up to the grey gelding she'd feared for years and patted his cheek. Turning to her husband, she said, "With you by my side, I believe I could even find the confidence to ride Hurricane again."

Brushing her fingertips with a kiss, Kenton smiled. "I'm sure you could, but not today. Our guests are waiting to wish us well."

Later that evening in Winston, Rosalie watched with pleasure as her husband scribed the names "Mr. and Mrs.

Kenton McCune" in the register of Hotel Quincy. Tomorrow morning, they would board a train for Asheville and their honeymoon stay in the mountains, but for now, she was simply thrilled to know that the hustle and bustle of pre-wedding days had passed and within minutes she and Kenton would share none but each other's company.

Following the bell boy to their second floor accommodations, they paused in the hall while he placed their bags inside the door. Kenton dismissed him with a generous tip, then turned to her, his gaze full of love and fondness as he swept her into his arms. His sentiments were a mere whisper in her ear as he stood just outside the bridal suite.

"Mrs. Kenton McCune, all of Grand Traverse Bay couldn't hold the love I feel for you!"

With soft words of her own, she replied, "My dear and precious husband, all of the Blue Ridge Mountains couldn't hold the love I feel for you!"

His lips covering hers, he carried her across the threshold and lay her on the sumptuous mattress beneath an arched canopy dripping with white silk lace.

ABOUT DONNA WINTERS

Donna adopted Michigan as her home state in 1971 when she moved there from a small town outside of Rochester, New York. She began penning novels in 1982 while working full time for an electronics company in Grand Rapids.

She resigned in 1984 following a contract offer for her first book. Since then, she has written several romance novels for various publishers, including Thomas Nelson Publishers, Zondervan Publishing House, and Guideposts.

Her husband, Fred, an American History teacher, shares her enthusiasm for history. Together, they visit historical sites, restored villages, museums, and lake ports, purchasing books and reference materials for use in Donna's research and Fred's classroom. A trip to the Con Foster Museum in Traverse City provided valuable insights regarding turn-of-the-century Grand Traverse Bay and its resorts.

Donna has lived all of her life in states bordering on the Great Lakes. Her familiarity and fascination with these remarkable inland waters and her residence in the heart of Great Lakes Country make her the perfect candidate for writing *Great Lakes Romances*®. (Photo by Renee Werni.)

HISTORICAL NOTES

Descriptions (but not always the exact dates) of many events in this novel were drawn from actual newspaper accounts and advertisements of 1900, including the Independence Day parade and carnival ball, Wallace Circus, and Boston Store sale in Traverse City, and the Fall Fair in Winston-Salem.

Regarding settings, Tanglewood has grown considerably from the 400-acre turn-of-the-century estate described in this novel. In 1921, William and Kate B. Reynolds purchased the estate and additional acreage where they maintained a home, fields, orchards, flower beds, and stables for many years. In 1954, they opened the estate to the public as a park which was purchased by Forsyth County twenty-three years later. Today, the 1200 acres of scenic rolling hills include overnight accommodations, golf, tennis, camping, extensive gardens, nature trails, horseback riding, and more.

Articles of note from **The Morning Record**

Friday, July 27, 1900—EVENTS IN SOCIETY

A delightful watermelon party was enjoyed on the shore of the river in front of residence of Frank Friedrich last evening. One of the watermelons had the misfortune to fall from the basket, and it rolled into the river and was drowned, but the other served the party most pleasantly. A jolly time was enjoyed by all.

Thursday, July 19, 1900
CONDENSED NEWS OF MICHIGAN

It is announced that 15 couples from Stark County, Indiana will go to St. Joseph in a body to be married the first Sunday in August. They are members of a matrimonial club and by paying monthly assessments, sufficient funds have been collected to pay all the necessary expenses. Several hundred relatives and friends will join in the unique pilgrimage.

Sunday, July 22, 1900
DRUNKEN SQUAW.
Called Out the Fire Department This Morning.

The entire fire department was hustled out of bed this morning at 3 o'clock by the ring of the telephone. Chief Rennie went to 210 South Division Street at the call of a lady who said that a crazy woman had been sitting on the porch almost all night.

Rennie found a drunken squaw with a papoose. The squaw said, "My man gone Pashabatown with one more squaw."

She was placed in the coop, and will probably make it hot for "her man" later.

Wednesday, July 25, 1900
THE POWER OF HOME
Its Relation to Society and
Its Influence In the Church

The unit of society is the home. Enrollment that assumes to be thorough is not a registration by individuals, but by families. If we were to say that the structure of society is cellular, we should have to say that it is the family that constitutes each separate cell. No man, however entire, is a cell. No woman, however complete, is a cell. There is no finished cell except in the grouping of several individuals bound by the ties of domesticity. A bachelor is a dislocated fragment. His female counterpart is in the same category. It may not be their fault. It may lie in the necessity of their case. Still, all in all, it is a condition foreign to divine intention.

It is to the family, therefore, that we shall have to look as being the prime point of concern in all that relates to the weal of our times and our kind. The strength and health of society are to be measured by the amount of affectionate emphasis that is laid on the home idea, and the wholesomeness of society is simply the sanctity of the home writ large. Homes are each of them the separate roots that carry their several contributions to the organized structure of the general life.

All of this holds whether society be considered in its religious relations, which we know as the church, or in its secular ones, known as the state. The home is the first church, and the home is the first state. There is nothing in either of the two that is not initially present in a small way inside the home circle. As regards the former there is a very important idea conserved in so arranging our church auditoriums as to combine the congregation without sacrificing the identity of its families. The pew system of worship is the deft way that our church architecture takes to teach the doctrine that each home is a little religious organism. This is one of those interesting cases where a sense of fitness, even without being distinctly conscious of it, nevertheless asserts itself and creates a very substantial expression of itself. and there is no preacher— at least there is no pastor—who does not carry distinctly in his head, and particularly in his heart, this cellular structure of his congregation and does not feel that the significance of his congregation depends not on the number of its individuals, but on the number of its families.

Rev. C.H. Parkhurst in Ladies' Home Journal.

More *Great Lakes Romances* ®

For prices and availability, contact:

Bigwater Publishing, P.O. Box 177, Caledonia, MI 49316

Mackinac

by

Donna Winters

First in the series of *Great Lakes Romances*

(Set at Grand Hotel, Mackinac Island, 1895)

Her name bespeaks the age in which she lives . . .but **Victoria Whitmore** is no shy, retiring Victorian miss. She finds herself aboard the *Algomah*, traveling from staid Grand Rapids to Michigan's fashionable Mackinac Island resort. Her journey is not one of pleasure; a restful holiday does not await her. Mackinac's Grand Hotel owes the Whitmores money—enough to save the furniture manufactory from certain financial ruin. It becomes Victoria's mission to venture to the island to collect the payment. At Mackinac, however, her task is anything but easy, and she finds more than she bargained for.

Rand Bartlett, the hotel manager, is part of that bargain. Accustomed to challenges and bent on making the struggling Grand a success, he has not counted on the challenge of Victoria—and he certainly has not counted on losing his heart to her.

The Captain and the Widow
by
Donna Winters
Second in the series of *Great Lakes Romances*
(Set in Chicago, South Haven, and
Mackinac Island, 1897)

Lily Atwood Haynes is beautiful, intelligent, and ahead of her time . . . but even her grit and determination have not prepared her for the cruel event on Lake Michigan that leaves her widowed at age twenty. It is the lake--with its fathomless depths and unpredictable forces—that has provided her livelihood. Now it is the lake that challenges her newfound happiness.

When **Captain Hoyt Curtiss**, her husband's best friend, steps in to offer assistance in navigating the choppy waters of Lily's widowhood, she can only guess at the dark secret that shrouds his past and chokes his speech. What kind of miracle will it take to forge a new beginning for *The Captain and the Widow? Note:* The Captain and the Widow *is a spin-off from* Mackinac.

Sweethearts of Sleeping Bear Bay
by
Donna Winters
Third in the series of *Great Lakes Romances*
(Set in the Sleeping Bear Dune region of
northern Michigan, 1898)

Mary Ellen Jenkins is a woman of rare courage and experience . . . One of only four females licensed as navigators and steamboat masters on the Western Rivers, she is accustomed to finding her way through dense fog on the Mississippi. But when she travels North for the first time in her twenty-nine years, she discovers herself unprepared for the havoc caused by a vaporous shroud off Sleeping Bear Point. And navigating the misty shoals of her own uncertain future poses an even greater threat to her peace of mind.

Self-confident, skilled, and devoted to his duties as Second Mate aboard the Lake Michigan sidewheeler, *Lily Belle,* **Thad Grant** regrets his promise to play escort to the petticoat navigator the instant he lays eyes on her plain face. Then his career runs aground. Can he trust this woman to guide him to safe harbor, or will the Lady Reb ever be able to overcome the great gulf between them? *Note:* Sweethearts of Sleeping Bear Bay *is a spin-off from* The Captain and the Widow.

Charlotte of South Manitou Island
by
Donna Winters
Fourth in the series of *Great Lakes Romances*
(Set on South Manitou Island,
Michigan, 1891-1898)

Charlotte Richards' carefree world turns upside down on her eleventh birthday . . . the day her beloved papa dies in a spring storm on Lake Michigan. Without the persistence of fifteen-year-old **Seth Trevelyn**, son of South Manitou Island's lightkeeper, she might never have smiled again. He shows her that life goes on, and so does true friendship.

When Charlotte's teacher invites her to the World's Columbian Exposition of 1893, Seth signs as crewman on the *Martha G.*, carrying them to Chicago. Together, Seth and Charlotte sail the waters of the Great Lake to the very portal of the Fair, and an adventure they will never forget. While there, Seth saves Charlotte from a near fatal accident. Now, seventeen and a man, he realizes his friendship has become something more. Will his feelings be returned when Charlotte grows to womanhood?

Aurora of North Manitou Island
by
Donna Winters
Fifth in the series of *Great Lakes Romances*
(Set on North Manitou Island,
Michigan, 1898-1899)

Aurora's wedding Day was far from the glorious event she had anticipated when she put the final stitches in her white satin gown, not with her new husband lying helpless after an accident on stormy Lake Michigan. And when Serilda Anders appeared out of Harrison's past to tend the light and nurse him back to health, Aurora was certain her marriage was doomed before it had ever been properly launched.

Maybe Cad Blackburn was the answer—Cad of the ready wit and the silver tongue. But it wasn't right to accept the safe harbor *he* was offering.

Where was the light that would guide her through these troubled waters?

Bridget of Cat's Head Point
by
Donna Winters
Sixth in the series of *Great Lakes Romances*
(Set in Traverse City and the Leelanau Peninsula
of Michigan, 1899-1900)

When Bridget Richards leaves South Manitou Island to take up residence on Michigan's mainland, she suffers no lack of ardent suitors. Only days after the loss of his first wife, Nat Trevelyn, Bridget's closest friend and the father of a two-year-old son, wants desperately to make her his bride. Kenton McCune, a handsome, wealthy lawyer in Traverse City, showers her with kindness the likes of which she's never known before. And Erik Olson, the son of her employer in Omena, shows her not only the incomparable beauty and romance of a Leelanau summer, but a bravery and affection beyond expectation.

Who will succeed in winning her heart? Or will tragedy swiftly intervene to steal away the promise of lasting happiness and true love?

(Note: The fourth, fifth, and sixth books in the series constitute a trilogy about three sisters in a lightkeeping family in northern Michigan.)

Jenny of L'Anse Bay
by
Donna Winters
Special Edition in the series of
Great Lakes Romances
(Set in the Keweenaw Peninsula of
Upper Michigan in 1867)

A raging fire destroys more than Jennifer Crawford's new home . . . it also burns a black hole into her future. To soothe Jennifer's resentful spirit, her parents send her on a trip with their pastor and his wife to the Indian mission at L'Anse Bay. In the wilderness of Michigan's Upper Peninsula, Jennifer soon moves from tourist to teacher, taking over the education of the Ojibway children. Without knowing their language, she must teach them English, learn their customs, and live in harmony with them.

Hawk, son of the Ojibway chief, teaches Jennifer the ways of his tribe. Often discouraged by seemingly insurmountable cultural barriers, Jennifer must also battle danger, death, and the fears that threaten to come between her and the man she loves.

Elizabeth of Saginaw Bay
by
Donna Winters
Pioneer Edition in the series of
Great Lakes Romances
(Set in the Saginaw Valley of Michigan, 1837)

The taste of wedding cake is still sweet in her mouth when Elizabeth Morgan sets out from York State for the new State of Michigan. Her handsome bridegroom, Jacob, has bought land in the frontier town of Riverton in the Saginaw Valley, and Elizabeth dreams of building a home and raising her family in a pleasant community like the one where she grew up. But she hasn't counted on the problems that arise the moment she sets foot on the untamed shore of the Saginaw River.

Riverton is almost non-existent. Her temporary lodgings are crude and infested with insects. And a dangerous disease breaks out among the neighboring Indians, threatening the white folk, as well. Desperately, she seeks a way out of the forest that holds her captive, but God seems to have cut off all possible exits. Surely, He can't mean for her to stay in this raw wilderness?

Sweet Clover: A Romance of the White City
Centennial Edition in the series of
Great Lakes Romances

The World's Columbian Exposition of 1893 brought unmatched excitement and wonder to Chicago, thus inspiring this innocent tale by Clara Louise Burnham, first published in 1894.

A Chicago resident from age nine, Burnham penned her novels in an apartment overlooking Lake Michigan. Her romance books contain plots imbued with the customs and morals of a bygone era—stories that garnered a sizable, loyal readership in their day.

In *Sweet Clover*, a destitute heroine of twenty enters a marriage of convenience to ensure the security and well-being of her fatherless family. Widowed soon after, Clover Bryant Van Tassel strives to rebuild a lifelong friendship with her late husband's son. Jack Van Tassel had been her childhood playmate, and might well have become her suitor. Believing himself betrayed by both his father and the girl he once admired, Jack moves far away from his native city. Then the World's Columbian Exposition opens, luring him once again to his old family home.

Hearts warmed by friendship blossom with

affection—in some most surprising ways. Will true love come to all who seek it in the Fair's fabulous White City? The author will keep you guessing till the very end!

Also by Bigwater Publishing

*Bigwater Classics*_{tm}
A series devoted to reprinting literature of the Great Lakes that is currently unavailable to most readers.

Thirty-Three Years Among the Indians
The Story of Mary Sagatoo
Edited by Donna Winters

Volume 1 in the series of *Bigwater Classics*_{tm}

In 1863, a young woman in Massachusetts promised to marry a Chippewa Indian from the Saginaw Valley of Michigan. He was a minister whose mission was to bring Christianity to his people in the tiny Indian village of Saganing. Though he later became afflicted with consumption and learned he hadn't long to live, his betrothed would not release him from his promise of marriage. Soon after the newlyweds arrived in

Michigan, this Chippewa Indian extracted a deathbed promise from his new wife.

"Mary . . . will you stay with my people, take my place among them, and try to do for them what I would have done if God had spared my life?" Joseph asked, caressing her hand.

"Oh, Joseph, don't leave me," she begged, "it is so lonesome here!"

"Please make the promise and I shall die happier. Jesus will help you keep it," he said with shortened breath.

Seeing the look of earnestness in Joseph's dark eyes, Mary replied, "I will do as you wish."

Thus began a remarkable woman's thirty-three years among a people about which she knew nothing—years of struggle, hardship, humor, and joy.

READER SURVEY—*Rosalie of Grand Traverse Bay*

Your opinion counts! Please fill out and mail this form to:
Reader Survey
Bigwater Publishing
P.O. Box 177
Caledonia, MI 49316

Your
Name:_____

Street:_____

City,State,Zip:_____

In return for your completed survey, we will send you a bookmark and the latest issue of our *Great Lakes Romances Newsletter*. If your name is not currently on our mailing list, we will also include four note papers and envelopes of an historic Great Lakes scene (while supplies last).

1. Please rate the following elements from A (excellent) to E (poor).

_____Heroine   _____Hero   _____Setting   _____Plot

Comments:_____

_____

2. What setting (time and place) would you like to see in a future book?

_____

(Survey questions continue on next page.)

3. Where did you purchase this book? (If you borrowed it from a library, please give the name of the library.)

_____

4. What influenced your decision to read this book?

_____Front Cover _____First Page _____Back Cover Copy

_____Title _____Friends

_____Publicity (Please describe)_____

_____

5. Please indicate your age range:

_____Under 18 _____25-34 _____46-55

_____18-24 _____35-45 _____Over 55

If desired, include additional comments below.